D0286752

Lynda La Plante wa[...] trained for the stage [...] and work with the National Theatre and RSC led to a career as a television actress. She turned to writing – and made her breakthrough with the phenomenally successful TV series *Widows*. Her four subsequent novels, *The Legacy, Bella Mafia, Entwined* and *Cold Shoulder*, were all international bestsellers, and her original script for the much acclaimed *Prime Suspect* won a BAFTA award, British Broadcasting award, Royal Television Society Writers award and the 1993 Edgar Allan Poe Writers award. Lynda La Plante also received the Contribution to the Media award by Women in Films, and most recently, a BAFTA award and an Emmy for the drama serial *Prime Suspect 3*.

SHE'S OUT

LYNDA LA PLANTE

PAN BOOKS

First published 1995 by Pan Books

an imprint of Macmillan General Books
Cavaye Place London SW10 9PG
and Basingstoke

Associated companies throughout the world

ISBN 0 330 34013 1

1 3 5 7 9 8 6 4 2

A CIP catalogue record for this book is available from
the British Library

Typeset by CentraCet Limited, Cambridge
Printed and bound in Great Britain
by Cox & Wyman Ltd, Reading, Berkshire

For Ann Mitchell
'Dolly Rawlins'

The book *She's Out* is also dedicated to six very special women. They are the actresses who brought the characters of Gloria, Julia, Ester, Connie, Kathleen and Angela to life. I will always value their talent and friendship, and wish them the greatest success and accolade they each deserve.

ACKNOWLEDGEMENTS

My thanks to Verity Lambert, Jonathan Powell, to my script editor Betina Soto Acebal, and my executive assistant Liz Thorburn and Alice Asquith, my research assistant, from La Plante Productions.

Thanks also to Suzanne Baboneau and Hazel Orme at Macmillan, and my appreciation as always to Jackie Malton, Chris Tchaikowsky and to all the staff at Holloway and Brixton prisons.

I would also like to take this opportunity to thank all the crew of the film, the stunt girls, make-up and wardrobe, and all the production staff. A very special thanks to Colin Munn and Annie Fielden.

Last, but by no means least, my sincere thanks to the director of *She's Out*, Ian Toynton, who also directed my first television series *Widows*. Ian's inspiration and talent make us all fortunate to have worked with him; his patience with each and every one of us was, as he was, inexhaustible.

CHAPTER 1

THE DATE was ringed with a fine red biro circle, 15 March 1994. It was the only mark on the cheap calendar pinned to the wall in her cell. There were no photographs, no memorabilia, not even a picture cut out of a magazine. She had always been in a cell by herself. The prison authorities had discussed the possibility of her sharing with another inmate but it had been decided it was preferable to leave Dorothy Rawlins as she had requested – alone.

Rawlins had been a model prisoner from the day she had arrived. She seemed to settle into a solitary existence immediately. At first she spoke little and was always polite to both prisoners and prison officers. She rarely smiled, she never wrote letters, but read for hours on end alone in her cell, and ate alone. After six months she began to work in the prison library; a year later she became a trusty. Gradually the women began to refer to Rawlins during recreational periods, asking her opinion on their marriages, their love lives. They trusted her opinions and her advice but she made no one a close friend. She wrote their letters, she taught some of the inmates to read and write, she was always patient, always calm and, above all, she would always listen. If you had a problem, Dolly Rawlins would sort it out for you. Over the following years she became a very dominant and respected figure within the prison hierarchy.

The women would often whisper about her to the new inmates, embroidering her past, which made her even more

1

of a queenlike figurehead. Dorothy Rawlins was in Holloway for murder. She had shot her husband, the infamous Harry Rawlins, shot him at point-blank range. The murder took on a macabre feeling as throughout the years the often repeated story was embellished, but no one ever discussed the murder to her face. It was as if she had an invisible barrier around her own emotions. Kindly towards anyone who needed comfort, she seemed never to need anything herself.

So the rumours continued: stories passed from one inmate to another, that Rawlins had also been a part of a big diamond raid. Although she had never been charged and no evidence had ever been brought forward at her trial to implicate her in it, the hints that she had instigated the raid, and got away with it, accentuated her mystique. More important was the rumour that she had also got away with the diamonds. The diamonds, some said, were valued at one million, then two million. The robbery had been a terrifying, brutal raid and a young, beautiful girl called Shirley Miller had been shot and killed.

Four years into her sentence, Rawlins began to write letters to request a better baby wing at Holloway. She began to work with the young mothers and children. The result was that she became even more of a 'Mama' figure. There was nothing she would not do for these young women, and it was on Rawlins's shoulders that they sobbed their hearts out when their babies were taken from them. Rawlins seemed to have an intuitive understanding, talking for hour upon hour with these distressed girls. She also had the same quiet patience with the drug offenders.

Five years into her sentence, Dolly Rawlins proved an invaluable inmate. She kept a photo album of the prisoners who had left, their letters to her, and especially the photographs of their children. But only the calendar was pinned to the identical chipboard in every inmate's cell. Nothing ever took precedence over the years of waiting.

She would always receive letters when the girls left Holloway. It was as if they needed her strength on the outside, but usually the letters came only for a couple of weeks then stopped. She was never hurt by the sudden silence, the lack of continued contact, because there were always the new inmates who needed her. She was a heroine, and the whispers about her criminal past continued. Sometimes she would smile as if enjoying the notoriety, encouraging the stories with little hints that maybe, just maybe, she knew more about the diamond raid than she would ever admit. She was also aware by now that the mystery surrounding her past enhanced her position within the prison pecking order. She wanted to remain top dog and she accomplished it without fighting or arguments.

After seven years, Rawlins was the 'Big Mama' – and it was always Dolly who broke up the fights, Dolly who was called on to settle arguments, Dolly who received the small gift tokens, the extra cigarettes. The prison officers referred to her as a model prisoner, and she was given a lot of freedom by the authorities. She organized and instigated further education, drug-rehabilitation sessions and, with a year to go before she was released, Holloway opened an entire new mother-and-baby wing, with a bright, toy-filled nursery. This was where she spent most of her time. She was able to help the staff considerably and enjoyed caring for the children. They became a focus for Dolly, who had no visitors, no one on the outside to care for or about her. And the caring for the babies began to shape a future dream for when she would finally be free.

Dolly Rawlins did have those diamonds waiting and, if they had been worth two million when she was sentenced, now she calculated they had to be worth three, possibly

3

four million. Alone in her cell she would dream about just what she was going to use the money for. She calculated that fencing them would bring the value down to around one million. She would have to give a cut to Audrey, Shirley Miller's mother, and a cut to Jimmy Donaldson, the man holding them for her. She would then have enough to open a home, buy a small terraced house, maybe in Islington or an area close to the prison, so she could come and visit the girls she knew would still need her. She even contemplated opening the home specifically for the pregnant prisoners who, she knew, would have their babies taken. Then they could know they were in good care as many of the girls were single parents and their babies might otherwise be put up for adoption.

The daydreaming occupied Dolly for hours on end. She kept it to herself, afraid that if she mentioned it to anyone they would know for sure she had to have considerable finances. She did have several thousand pounds in a bank account arranged for her by her lawyer and she calculated that with that, a government grant and the money from the gems, the home would be up and running within a year of her release. She even thought about possibly offering a sanctuary for some of the drug addicts who needed a secure place to stay when they were released. And, a number of the women inside were battered wives: perhaps she could allocate a couple of rooms for them. The daydreaming relieved any tension that she felt. It was like a comforter, a warm secret that enveloped her and helped her sleep. The dream would soon be a reality as the months disappeared into weeks, and then days. As the ringed date was drawing closer and closer, she could hardly contain herself: this would give the rest of her life a meaning – she would have a reason to live. Never having had a child of her own it had touched her deeply to have been so close to newly born babies: their fragility, their total dependency opened the terrible, secret pain of her own childlessness. Soon she would have a houseful of children who needed her. Then she could truly call herself 'Mama'.

They all knew she would soon be leaving. They whispered in corners as they made cards and small gifts. Even the prison officers were sad that they would lose such a valuable inmate, not that any single one of them had ever had much interaction with her on a personal level. She rarely, if ever, made conversation with them unless it was necessary, and one officer hated her because, at times, it seemed she had more power over the inmates than the officers. A few years back, Rawlins had struck a prison officer, slapped her face, and warned her to stay away from a certain prisoner. She had been given extra days and had been locked up in her cell. The result had been that Rawlins was fêted when she was eventually unlocked and the officer, a thickset, dark-haired woman called Barbara Hunter, never spoke or looked at Rawlins again. The animosity between Hunter and Rawlins remained throughout the years. Hunter had tried on numerous occasions to needle Dolly, as if to prove to the Governor that the model prisoner 45688 was in reality an evil manipulator. But Dolly never rose to the bait, just stared with her hard, ice-cold eyes, and it was that blank-eyed stare that, Hunter suspected, concealed a deep hatred, not just of herself, but of all the prison officers.

Finally the day came, and Dolly carefully packed her few possessions from her cell. She waited for the call to the probation room for the usual chat with the Governor before she would finally be free. The suit she had worn the day she arrived hung on her like a rag, as she had lost a considerable

5

amount of weight. The years she had spent banged up had made her face sallow and drawn; her hair was grey and cut short in an unflattering style.

On 15 March, she gave away all her personal effects: a radio, some tapes, skin cream, books, and packets of cigarettes. Then she sat, hands folded on her lap, until they called her to go into the first meeting. She appeared as calm as always but her heart was beating rapidly. She would soon be out. Soon be free. It would soon be over.

The old Victorian Grange Manor House was in a sorry state of disrepair, although at a distance it still looked impressive. The once splendid grounds, orchards and stables were all in need of attention. The grass was overgrown and weeds sprouted up through the gravel driveway. A swimming pool with a torn tarpaulin was filled with stagnant water, and even the old sign 'Grange Health Farm' was broken and peeling like the paint on all the woodwork of the house. The once stained-glass double-fronted door had boards covering the broken panes, many of the windows had cracks and some of the tiles from the roof lay shattered on the ground below. The double chimney-breasts were toppling and dangerous. The house seemed fit only for demolition. The once vast acreage that had belonged to the manor had been sold off years before to local farmers, and the dense, dark wood that fringed the lawns had begun to encroach with brambles and twisted trees.

A motorway had been built close to the edge of the lane leading to the manor, cutting off the house from the main road. Now the only access was down a small slip road that had been left, like the house, to rot, with deep pot-holes that made any journey hazardous. The rusted, wrought-iron gates were hanging off their hinges, and the chain threaded through them with the big padlock hung limply as if no one would want to enter.

The Range Rover bumped and banged along the lane, dipping into one deep rut after another as it made its slow journey towards the house. The grass verges were spreading on to the lane, the hedges either side hiding the fields and grazing cows.

Ester Freeman swore as the Range Rover dipped badly; it was even worse than the last time she'd been there. She was a handsome woman in her late forties, but the dark hair scraped back from her chiselled features made her look hard, and as she drove she clenched her teeth with fury. She was five feet six, slender and always looked good in clothes. A smart dresser, who wore good designer labels, there was an elegance to her that belied and covered a toughness that even her well-modulated voice sometimes couldn't disguise. She continued to swear as the Range Rover splashed through yet another water-filled pot-hole. The muddy puddles splashed water over the wheels and sides of the vehicle as it lurched down the lane.

Sitting beside Ester, Julia Lawson stared non-committally, at the lane. She was much younger than Ester and taller, almost six feet, with a strong, rangy body accentuated by her jeans and leather jacket. She wore beat-up old cowboy boots and a mannish denim shirt, and there was an arrogance to her face that was at times attractive, at other times plain. Unlike Ester, Julia had a deep, melodic, cultured voice. She, too, swore as they bounced along. 'Jesus Christ, Ester, slow down. You're chucking everything over the back of the car!'

Ester paid no attention as she heaved on the handbrake. Julia watched as she slammed out and crossed to the old wrought-iron gates. She didn't even need a key to open the padlock – she just wrenched it loose and pushed back the old gates.

As they drove up the Manor House driveway, Julia laughed. 'My God, I think it needs a demolition crew.'

'Oh, shut up,' Ester snapped, as they veered round a hole.

'You know, I don't think they'll find it.'

'They'll find it, I gave them each a map. Don't be so negative. She's out today, Julia. Come on, move it!'

Julia followed Ester slowly out of the car and looked around, shaking her head. She stepped back as a front doorstep crumbled beneath her boot. 'You know, it looks unsafe.'

'It's been standing for over a hundred years so it's not likely to fall down now. Get the bags out.'

Julia looked back to the piles of suitcases and bulging black binliners in the back of the Range Rover and ignored her request, following Ester into the manor.

The hallway was dark and forbidding: the William Morris wallpaper hung in damp speckled flaps from the carved cornices and there were stacks of old newspapers and broken bottles everywhere. The old wooden reception desk was dusty, the key-rack behind it devoid of keys and hanging almost off the wall. Even the chandelier above their heads looked as if it was ready to crash down.

Their feet echoed in the marble hall as Ester opened one door after another. The smell of must and mildew hung in the air, chilling them immediately.

'You'll never get it ready in time, Ester.'

Ester marched into the drawing room, shouting over her shoulder, 'Yes, I will, and there's enough of us to help me out.'

Julia picked up the dust-covered telephone. She looked surprised. 'The phone's connected,' she called to Ester.

Ester stood looking around the drawing room: old-fashioned sofas and wing-backed chairs, threadbare carpet and china cabinets. The massive open stone fireplace was still filled with cinders. 'I had it connected,' she snapped as she began to draw back the draped velvet curtains. They hung half off their rings and she turned her face away as dust spiralled down – four years of it, maybe more. Even when Ester had occupied the place no one was ever that interested in dusting.

The Grange Health Farm had been defunct when Ester bought the manor with all its contents, but she had no ideas about refurbishing the old house as it was a perfect cover for her real profession. All Ester had done was spread a few floral displays around the main rooms and brought in fourteen girls, a chef, a domestic and two muscle-bound blokes in the event of trouble. The Grange Health Farm reopened, and for men who wanted a massage, Ester would provide that with a sauna, but her clients mostly wanted a lot more physical contact – and Ester provided that too . . . at a price.

'We should have started weeks ago,' Julia said, as she lolled in the doorway, looking around with undisguised distaste.

'Well, I didn't, so we're gonna have to work like the clappers,' Ester snapped again, then looked up to the chandelier, trying the light switch. Two of the eighteen bulbs flickered on.

'Bravo, the electricity's on as well,' laughed Julia.

Ester glared around the room. 'We'll clean this room, the dining room and a few bedrooms. Then that's it, we won't need to do any more.'

'Really.' Julia smiled.

Ester pushed past her, wiping her dusty hands, and Julia followed her back into the hall, watching as she banged open shutters. One almost fell on top of her and she kicked out at it.

The dining room was in the same condition but with empty bottles and glasses smashed on the floor and littered on the table. Ester was flicking on lights, dragging back curtains, cursing all the time. But she seemed to deflate when she saw the wrecked kitchen, broken crockery and more smashed bottles. 'Shit! I'd forgotten how bad it was.'

'I hadn't. I told you this was a crazy idea from the start.'

Ester crossed to the back door. She unlocked it, pushing it open to get the stench of old wine and rotten food out of the kitchen.

'Must have been some party,' Julia mused.

'It was,' Ester said, as she looked at the big black rubbish bags bursting at the seams.

'Surprised the rats haven't been in here.'

'They have,' Ester said, as she looked at the droppings.

Julia pulled a disgusted face. Ester became even more irate, pushing past her into the hallway.

'Don't just bloody stand there, help me.' Ester stood in the darkened, musty-smelling hall – even the oak panels had lost all lustre from the damp that crept from every corner. She hadn't realized just how bad the place was. When she and Julia had visited a few weeks earlier, there had been no electricity and they had arrived at dusk. Ester sighed: it had been some party, all right. There used to be one every night but she had not been able to see the last one through to the end. She had been arrested along with her girls. She reckoned most of the damage had been done by the few who were left behind or who had even returned when they knew she had been sentenced, come back to grab whatever they could. A lot of the rooms looked as if they been stripped of anything of value.

She had not bothered to come to see the damage before; she knew the bank held the deeds as collateral for her debts. She had dismissed the place from her mind until she got the news that Dolly Rawlins was going to be released. Then she had begun thinking – and thinking fast: just how could she use the old Grange Manor House to her benefit? Now she began to doubt she could ever get it ready in time.

Julia strolled to the back door and looked out into the stable-yard. The old doors were hanging off their hinges and even more rubbish and rubble were piled up.

Ester began banging open one bedroom door after another. Every room stank of mildew, and some of the beds were still as the occupant had rolled out of them. In a few rooms clothes and dirty underwear lay discarded on the floor.

Julia walked up the old wide staircase, where there was more peeling wallpaper; her hands were black from the dust when she had rested them on the rail. On the previous visit they'd used candles to have a quick look over the place. Now, in daylight, it was even worse than Julia remembered.

Ester appeared at the top of the stairs. 'Go and get the cases.'

'You're not serious, are you, Ester? We'll never get it ready in time. This is madness.'

'No, it isn't. I've already laid out cash for a bloody Roller and a chauffeur so we just get down to it, and the others will be here to give us a hand. There's caterers, florists . . . I'm not losing cash I've laid out, so we just get started.'

Julia sat on the stairs and began to roll a cigarette. 'So, you gonna tell me who you've invited for this celebration?'

Ester looked down at her. Sometimes she wanted to slap her – she could be so laid-back.

'You don't know them all. There's Connie Stevens, Kathleen O'Reilly, and I've asked that little black girl, Angela, to act as a maid.'

Julia laughed. 'She's gonna be wearing a pinny and hat, is she?'

Ester pursed her lips. 'Don't start with the sarcasm. We need them, and they all knew Dolly.'

Julia looked up at her. 'They all inside with her like us?'

'Not Angela, but the others. And I don't want you to start yelling but Gloria Radford's coming.'

Julia stood up. 'You joking?'

'No, I'm not.'

'Well, count me out. I can't stand that demented cow. I spent two years in a cell with her and I'm not going to spend time outside with her. What the hell did you rope her into it for?'

'Because we might need her, and she knows Dolly.'

Julia began to walk down the stairs in a fury. 'She reads aloud from the newspapers, she drove me crazy, I nearly killed her. I'm out of here.'

'Fine, you go. I don't give a shit if you do, but it's a long walk to the station.'

Julia looked up. 'Gloria Radford on board and this is a fiasco before we even start. She's cheap, she's coarse, she's got the mental age of a ten-year-old.'

'So, are you so special, Doctor? We needed as many of us as I could get, Julia, and I needed ones that were as desperate as us. Now, are you staying or are you going?'

Julia lit her roll-up and shrugged. 'I'm leaving.'

Ester moved down the stairs. 'Fine, you fuck off, then, and don't think you'll get a cut of anything I get. You walk out now, I'll never see you again. I mean it, we're through.'

Julia hesitated, looked back to Ester, standing at the top of the stairs. Her wonderful face, her dark eyes, now blazing with anger, made her heart jump. She knew she'd be staying. She couldn't stand the thought of never seeing or touching Ester. She was in love with her.

'I'll get the cases but don't ask me to be nice to that midget.'

Ester smiled, and headed back to the bedroom. 'The only person you've got to be nice to is Dolly Rawlins.'

Julia got to the front door. 'What if she doesn't come, Ester? *Ester?*'

Ester reappeared, leaning on the banister rail. 'Oh, she'll come, Julia, I know it. She'll be here. She's got nobody else.'

Julia gave a small nod and walked out to the car. She began to collect all the cases and boxes, then paused a moment as she looked over the grounds. There was a sweet peacefulness to the place. She was suddenly reminded of her childhood, of the garden at her old family home. She had been given her own pony and suddenly she remembered cantering across the fields. She had been happy then . . . It seemed a lifetime ago.

The bedroom Ester chose for Dolly was spacious, with a double bed and white dressing table. Even though the carpet was stained, the curtains didn't look too bad, and with a good polish and hoover, a few bowls of flowers, it would be good enough. After all, she had spent the last eight years in a cell. This would be like a palace in comparison.

Julia appeared at the door. 'You know, we could call the local job centre if they've got one here, get a bunch of kids to start helping us. What do you think?'

Ester was dragging off the dirty bed-linen. 'Go and call

them. We'll have to pay them, though. How are you off for cash?'

'I've got a few quid.'

Ester suddenly gave a wondrous smile. 'We'll be rich soon, Julia. We'll never have to scrabble around for another cent.'

'You hope.'

'Why are you always such a downer? I know she's got those diamonds, I know it . . .'

'Maybe she has, maybe she hasn't. And maybe, just maybe, she won't want us to have a cut of them.'

Ester gathered the dirty sheets in her arms. 'There'll be no maybes. I've worked over more people than you've had hot dinners, and I'll work her over. I promise you, we'll get to those diamonds, two million quid's worth, Julia. Just thinking about it gives me an orgasm.'

Julia laughed. 'I'll go call a job centre. This our bedroom, is it?'

'No, this one's for Dolly.'

Ester patted the bed, then sat down and smiled. Just thinking of how rich she was going to be made her feel good, safer.

Mike Withey looked over the newspaper cuttings. They were yellow with age, some torn from constantly being unfolded, and one had a picture of Shirley Miller, Mike's sister. It was a photograph from some job she had done as a model, posed and air-brushed. The same photograph was in a big silver frame on the sideboard, this time in colour. Blonde hair, wide blue eyes that always appeared to follow you around the room, as if she was trying to tell you something. She had been twenty-one years of age when she had been shot, and even to this day Mike was still unable to believe that his little blue-eyed sweetheart sister had been involved in a robbery. He had been stationed in Germany when he received the hysterical call from his mother, Audrey. It had been hard to make out what she was saying, as she alternated between sobs and rantings, but there was one name he would never forget, one sentence. 'It was Dolly Rawlins, it was her, it was all her fault.'

The following year Mike married Susan, the daughter of a sergeant-major. His mother was not invited to the wedding. Their first son was born before he left Germany and his second child was on the way when he was given a posting to Ireland. By this stage he was a sergeant; Audrey wasn't even told about his promotion. He had sent her a few postcards, wedding pictures and baby photographs. Susan was worried about him being stationed in Ireland and, being heavily pregnant with a toddler to look after and hardly knowing a soul because all her friends were in Germany, she persuaded Mike to quit the army. He was reluctant at first, having signed up at seventeen: it was the only life he knew. It had been his salvation, it had educated him and, most important, given him a direction and discipline lacking in his own home.

Mike's second son was born on the day he found out that he had been accepted by the Metropolitan Police. He never felt he had traded one uniform for another; he had ambitions and with the excellent recommendations from his CO, it was felt that Mike Withey was a recruit worth keeping an eye on. He proved them right: he was intelligent, hard-working, intuitive and well liked. Mike became a 'high flyer', an officer a lot of the guys joked about because he never missed an opportunity of furthering his career prospects. No sooner was a new course pinned up on the board than he would be the first to apply. It was the many courses, the weekends away at special training colleges, that made Susan, now coping with two toddlers, suggest that Mike should contact his mother again, not just for company but because she hoped Audrey could give her a hand or even baby-sit. Mike's refusal resulted in a big argument. Susie felt his boys had a right to know their grandmother as her own parents were still in Germany.

Mike took a few more weeks to mull it over. He might have been honest with Susan about his younger brother Gregg, who had been in trouble with the law, but he had not disclosed to her that his sister was Shirley Ann Miller, killed in an abortive robbery. It had been easy for him to cover it because they all had different fathers, different surnames. He was unsure if his mother had ever divorced or married each one, they had never discussed it, and his father had left when he was as young as his eldest boy was now.

Audrey was working on the fruit and veg stall when Mike turned up as a customer, asking for a pound of Granny Smith apples. She was just as he remembered her, all wrapped up, fur-lined boots, head-scarf, woollen mittens with their fingers cut off.

'Well, hello, stranger. You want three or four? If it's four it'll be over the pound.' She took each apple, dropping it into the open brown-paper bag, trying not to cry, not to show Mike how pleased she was to see him. She wanted to shout out to the other stall-holders, 'This is my son. I told yer he'd come back, didn't I?' She had always been a tough one, never showed her feelings. It had taken years of practice – get kicked hard enough and in the end it comes naturally. She didn't even touch his hand, just twisted the paper bag at the corners. 'There you go, love. Fancy a cuppa, do you?'

He had not expected to feel so much, not expected to hurt inside so much as she pushed him into the same council flat in which he had been brought up. No recrimi-nations, no questions, talking nineteen to the dozen about people she thought he might remember, who had died on the market stalls, who had got married, who had been banged up. She never stopped talking as she chucked off her coat, kicked off the boots and busied herself making tea.

She still chattered on, shouting to him from the kitchen, as he saw all his postcards, the photo of his wedding, his boys, laid out on top of the mantelshelf, pinned into the sides of the fake gilt mirror. There had been a few changes: new furniture, curtains, wallpaper and some awful pictures from one of the stalls.

'Gregg's doin' a stint on one of the oil rigs,' Audrey shouted. 'He's trying to go on the straight an' narrow, there's a postcard from him on the mantel.'

Mike picked up the card of two kittens in a basket and turned it over. His brother's childish scrawl said he was having a great time and earning a fortune, saving up for a motorbike. The postmark was dated more than eight months ago. He replaced the card and stared at himself in the mirror. It was then that he saw her. The thick silver frame, placed in the centre of the sideboard, a small posy of flowers in a tiny vase in front of it. She was even more beautiful than he remembered. It was one of the pictures taken when she was trying to be a model, very glamorous. Shirley smiled into his heart.

'It's her birthday tomorrow,' said Audrey, 'and you've not seen her grave.'

'I'm on duty tomorrow, Mum.'

She held on to his hand. 'We can go now.'

*

Audrey hung on to his arm. It was dusk, the graveyard empty. Shirley was buried alongside her husband Terry Miller. The white stone was plain and simple, the ornate flowers in a green vase were still fresh. 'Tomorrow she'll have a bouquet. They do it up for me on the flower stall, never charge me neither.' Her voice was soft and she no longer held his arm, staring at the headstone. 'She came to me two days after it happened.'

'I'm sorry, what did you say?'

She remained focused on her daughter's name. 'That bitch – that bitch Dolly Rawlins came to see me and I've never forgiven myself for letting her take me in her arms.'

'We should go, Mum.'

She turned on him, hands clenched at her sides. 'She was behind that robbery, she organized the whole thing. They never got the diamonds . . .'

Mike stepped forward, not wanting to hear any more, but there was no stopping her. 'No, you listen. That bitch held me in her arms and I let her, let her use me just like she used my Shirley. She had them, she had the bloody things.'

'What?'

'The diamonds! She had them – got me to – she got me to give 'em to a fence, said she would see I was looked after, see I'd never want for anythin'.'

Mike's heart began to thud, unable to comprehend what he was hearing, as Audrey's voice became twisted with bitterness. 'I *did it*, I bloody did it. She got me so I couldn't say nothin', couldn't do anything, and then . . . she fuckin' shot her husband.'

Mike took her to a pub, gave her a brandy, watched as she chainsmoked one cigarette after another. 'No mention of the diamonds at her trial – they never got anythin' on

18

her for that robbery, they never had any evidence that put her in the frame. She got done for manslaughter.'

Mike was sweating. 'You ever tell anybody what you did?'

'What you think?' she snapped back at him. 'She got me involved, didn't she? I could have been done for fencin' them, helpin' her. No, I never told anybody.'

'Did you get paid?'

She stubbed out her cigarette. 'No. Pay day is when the bitch comes out. Bitch thinks she's gonna walk out to a fortune.'

Mike gripped Audrey's hand. 'Listen to me! *Look at me!* You know what I am. You know what it means for you to tell me all this?'

Audrey lit another cigarette. 'What you gonna do, Mike, arrest your own mother?'

He ran his fingers through his hair; he could feel the sweat trickling down from his armpits. 'You got to promise me you will never, *never* tell a soul about those diamonds. You got to swear on my kids' lives. You don't touch them – don't even think about them.'

'She'll be out one day. Then what?'

Mike licked his lips.

'She as good as killed Shirley, I had to identify her, they pulled the sheet down from her face.'

'*Stop it!* Look, I promise you I'll take care of you. You don't need any dough – but I'm asking you, Mum, don't screw it up for me, please.'

She stared at him, then leaned forward and touched his blond hair, same texture, same colour as Shirley's. 'I'll make a deal with you, love. If you make that bitch pay for what she done to my baby, you get her locked up—'

'Mum, she *is* away, she's in the nick right now.'

Audrey prodded his hand with her finger. 'But one day

19

she'll be *out*, and I keep a calendar. She'll be out, rich and free. I don't care about the money, all I want is . . .'

Audrey never said the word revenge but it was blatantly obvious, and Mike made a promise. It sounded hollow to him but he had no option. He promised that when Dolly Rawlins came out of Holloway, he would get her back for her part in the diamond robbery. Five years later, the promise was to haunt him, because his mother never forgot it. She called him and asked him to come round. As if unconcerned, she suddenly suggested he look in the left-hand drawer of the side table. Audrey was tut-tutting over some character's downfall on the TV. Every single news-paper article about the diamond robbery was stacked in the drawer. Calendars, one year, two years, three years, scrawled in thick red-tipped pen. He eased aside the news-clippings and there was an old black and white photograph, taken at some West End night club. He had never seen Dolly Rawlins, wouldn't know her if he was to come face to face with her in the street, but he knew which one she was: she had to be the blonde, hard-faced woman sitting at the centre of the large round table. She had a champagne glass in her hand, a half-smile on her face, but there was something about her eyes: unsmiling, hard, cold eyes . . . The handsome man seated next to her had almost an angry expression, as if annoyed by the intrusion of the photogra-pher. Mike recognized his brother-in-law, dead before Shirley. Terry Miller always looked like he never had a care in the world: his wide smile was relaxed and he exuded an open sexuality, unafraid of any photo, one arm resting along the cushioned booth seat as if protecting or guarding his pretty, innocent, child-like wife. Shirley Miller.

The TV was turned off and Audrey turned to Mike. 'You read them, have you?' She pointed to the black and white picture of Dorothy Rawlins. She was crying, clutching a sodden tissue in her hand. 'You never seen her, have you, love?'

The big headlines screamed out her name and beneath her picture was a smaller one of her husband: 'Gangland Boss Murdered by his Wife'. Harry Rawlins had been a notorious criminal: a handsome, elegant, cruel-faced man, yet his picture made him look like a movie star. In comparison, the hard gaze of his wife made them appear an incompatible couple but they had been married twenty years. Harry Rawlins was one of the biggest gangsters in London, a man who had never been caught, never spent a day behind bars, and yet had been questioned by the police so many times his name was known by most of the Met officers. He had always been too clever to get arrested. He had lived a charmed life until his wife shot him. The newspaper article stated that Dorothy Rawlins had killed her husband when she had discovered his betrayal, that he had a mistress and a child. There was no mention that he had instigated a robbery where Shirley Miller's husband had been burned to death, and the news coverage only talked about the shooting. They had nicknamed Dolly the 'Black Widow' because throughout her trial she had always been dressed in black.

Audrey prodded Dolly's face in the paper. 'Eight years. Eight years. Well, she's out, any day now,' she said, wiping her eyes.

What Audrey had never told Mike about that last visit from Dolly was that she had been pregnant and had lost the baby she was expecting. She blamed that on Dolly Rawlins as well, and she could see her, as clearly as if it were yesterday. Audrey even remembered the coat – stylish. Funny, she could recall the coat but little of what was said apart from the promise. Dolly had not sat down but stood in the small hallway, her head slightly bowed, her voice a low whisper. 'I'm sorry about Shirley. I am deeply sorry for Shirley.'

Audrey had been unable to reply, she was in such a state. 'Nothing will make up to you for her loss, I know that.'

Still Audrey had been unable to reply. Then Dolly had lifted her head, her pale washed-out eyes brimming with tears. 'You'll get a cut of the diamonds, that I promise you. Just hand them over to Jimmy Donaldson. Jimmy'll keep them safe. When this is all over, I'll see you're taken care of, Audrey.'

Then it went blank. Audrey couldn't recall anything else they had said or not said but Dolly had eventually walked out. She wiped her eyes and blew her nose loudly. Mike looked over the cuttings and she wondered if she should tell him but she was scared. Everything had changed after she had read in the paper that a small-time fence called Jimmy Donaldson had been arrested for dealing in stolen property. Audrey had then done something she would have believed herself incapable of. She had done it all by herself and, having done it, she had been terrified. But the weeks passed and gradually she grew more and more confident that what she had done was right. She deserved it. But now she was scared, really scared, because Dolly Rawlins was coming out and she didn't know if she should tell Mike or not. But she knew one thing: Dolly would come out looking for her, she was sure of that.

Mike was feeling depressed and uneasy. It was back again, that constant undercurrent of guilt whenever he was with his mother. He had made that promise, but what could he do? He held on to his temper. 'Mum, there is nothing I can do—'

'You're a ruddy police officer, aren't you? Re-arrest her. She did that robbery, Mike – I know it, you know it. She as good as killed our Shirley, never mind her bloody husband.'

The tears started again. He was due at his station in half an hour; he wished he'd never called in. 'Look, Mum, the main problem will be if it implicates you – and it could.'

Audrey clung to him. 'I've got an offer. Friend's got a villa in Spain, I can stay as long as I like. That way I can't be involved.'

'Look, I'll see what I can do but I can't promise anything.'

Audrey kissed him. 'Let her sleep in peace, let my little girl sleep in peace.'

Mike sighed and turned on the ignition of the car but the last thing he felt like doing was going into the station. He checked his watch again and then drove to Thornton Avenue in Chiswick. He knew that he was making a mistake, that this was a stupid move, but he needed to get his head straightened out. He parked the car and walked up the scruffy path. He was about to ring the front doorbell when he heard someone calling his name.

Angela was running up the road, waving. Her face was brimming with a big wide smile. 'Mike, Mike . . .'

Mike turned as she threw herself into his arms. He held her tightly as she kissed his neck.

'I knew you'd come and see me again, I just knew it.'

He walked hand in hand with her to his car, already wanting to kick himself for coming to her place.

'I've missed you,' she said, hanging on to his arm.

Mike released his hand. 'Look, I shouldn't have come, Angela. It was just . . . I'm sorry.'

'Oh, please stay, please. Me mum's down at the centre, there's no one in the house, and, please, I got something to tell you, please . . .'

Mike locked the car and followed Angela into her mother's ground-floor flat. It was dark and scruffy and kids' push-chairs and toys littered every inch of the floor. Angela guided him towards the small back bedroom, and all the time he kept on saying to himself that he was dumb, he was stupid to start this up again. Angela began to undress as soon as she shut the door but he shook his head. 'No, I can't stay, Angela, I'm on duty in an hour. I just . . .'

She slumped on to the bed. 'I been waitin' for you to call for weeks. You know the way I feel about you. Why did you come here, then?'

He shook his head. He was feeling even worse. 'I dunno, I was over at my mum's place and she starts doing my head in over my sister, and I just . . .' She wrapped her arms around him, kissing his face. 'No, don't, Angela, I shouldn't have come.'

She broke away. 'Well, get out, I don't care, I'm goin' away anyway.'

'Where you goin'?'

'Friend's place, just a few days, bit of work.'

Mike looked at her, shaking his head. 'What kind of work?'

Angela plucked at her short skirt, her face puckered.

'You're not going back on the game, are you?'

'*No, I am not*,' she shrieked.

Mike sat on the bed and rested his head against the wall. He closed his eyes.

'I was never on the game and you know it. You of all people should know it. I just worked as her maid, Mike, I swear I did.'

'This Ester Freeman, is it?' he asked.

Angela crawled on to the bed to sit next to him. Mike had been on the Vice Squad when Ester Freeman had been busted for running a brothel. Angela was one of the girls who had been arrested along with twelve other women but they had all, including Ester, insisted that little Angela was not on the game, just serving drinks. Mike and Angela, who was then only fifteen, had begun an affair, a stupid, on-off scene that he constantly tried to break. He never saw her regularly, once a month, sometimes twice, over the years, but he was very fond of her. He even gave her money sometimes but he had no intention of ever leaving his wife. She had been a useful relaxation and he didn't really believe she was in love. If it hadn't been for Mike, she might have been sent to an approved school, and whatever excuses he made regarding his friendship with Angela were just excuses. The sex was good and he simply refused to admit that that was what he used Angela for.

'Ester called yesterday. I'm to go to her old manor house.'

'Oh, yeah? She back running another brothel?'

'No way. She's holding some kind of party, for a woman called . . .'

Angela frowned as she tried to remember, and then grinned. 'Oh, I dunno, but she was in Holloway wiv her, shot her old man, you know. She was famous. He was a big-time villain. Anyway, she's comin' out of the nick and Ester is arranging a group of old friends to sort of welcome her, you know, give a party, and she wants me to act as a waitress.'

Mike fingered the knot in his tie. His mouth felt rancid. It couldn't be – couldn't be who he thought it was, could it? 'Dolly Rawlins? Is that who it is?'

'Yeah, she was in Holloway with Ester.'

Mike leaned against Angela, undoing the buttons of her shirt. 'Who else is going?'

'I dunno, but it'll be some kind of scam, you can bet on it. I got to wear a black dress an' apron. Ester never did nothin' for nobody without there being something in it for her. She's a hard cow but I need the cash. Said she'll pay me fifty quid.'

Mike eased back Angela's shirt, slipping his finger under her lace bra. 'She say anything else about Dolly Rawlins?'

Two young prisoners peeked into Dolly Rawlins's cell, looking at the small neatly packed brown suitcase, a coat placed alongside it. Apart from these two items the cell was empty.

Footsteps could be heard on the stone-flagged floor. The two girls scuttled back down the corridor as Rawlins, with a prison officer, headed towards her cell. Whatever they were expecting to see, they were disappointed. The infamous Dolly Rawlins seemed pale and worn, like a schoolmistress. They didn't get a look at her face, it was just her manner, the way she was walking, and her short, grey hair. The officer hid the rest of her as she stood outside the cell waiting for prisoner 45688 to get her case and coat.

The corridors were strangely silent, with faint whispers. Nearly all of the women were waiting, hiding, whispering.

The Tannoy repeated a message that Rawlins, prisoner 45688, was to go to landing B. They all knew that was the check-out landing. She was almost out.

The coat was too large since she had lost so much weight but it was good quality: she had always liked the best. She did up each button slowly and then reached for her case. She refused to admit to herself or show that she was sad: none of the girls had spoken to her or said goodbye. She looked to the officer and gave a brief nod. She was ready.

As Dolly headed towards landing B, the singing began, low at first, then rising to a bellow as every woman began to sing.

'Goodbye, Dolly!'

They bellowed and stamped their feet, they called out her name and clapped their hands. 'Goodbye, Dolly, you must leave us . . .' They screeched out their thank yous for the cigarettes, for her radio, her cassettes, for every item she had passed around. Some of the girls were sobbing, openly showing how much they would miss 'Big Mama'. One old prisoner shouted at the top of her voice, 'Don't turn back, Dolly, don't look back, keep on walking out, gel . . .'

She could feel the tears welling up, her mouth trembling, but she held on, waving like the Queen as they walked on to the landings. They continued to sing, their voices echoing as she was ushered along the corridor towards the Governor's office. She was almost out. It wouldn't be long now.

Mike thumbed through the files and then sat, drumming his fingers on the mug-shot of Dorothy Rawlins. He had read so much on Dolly Rawlins and her husband that he knew that if the diamonds existed she would go after them. He thought about Angela on her way to Ester Freeman. He wondered about a lot of things, trying to think if there was any possibility of doing something for his sister, for his mother – if he could get Dolly Rawlins back inside.

Mike checked the files over and over again, then went through Harry Rawlins's files. Then he received a phone call, nothing to do with Dolly Rawlins, nothing to do with his mother or his sister. It was from Brixton Prison: a boy called Francis Lloyd wanted to give some information.

A lot of police officers have their private snitches in the prisons, someone wanting to do a bit of a trade. Lloyd was a youngster Mike had arrested on a burglary eighteen months ago. He had been sentenced to two years because of a previous conviction. He was a likeable kid, and Mike had even got to know his mum and dad, so he returned the call – and for the second time in one day he heard the name Dolly Rawlins. Francis had some information but he didn't want to talk about it over the phone.

Governor Ellis rose to her feet from behind the desk as Dolly Rawlins was ushered into her bright, friendly office. She offered tea, a usual ritual when a long-serving prisoner was leaving. Mrs Ellis was an exceptionally good governor and well liked by the inmates for her fairness and, in many instances, her kindness and understanding. Rawlins, however, seemed never to have needed her on any level and as she passed the floral china cup to her, Mrs Ellis couldn't help but detect an open antagonism that she had never sensed before.

She eased the conversation round, discussing openings and contacts should Dolly feel in need of assistance outside, making sure she was fully aware that she would, because of the nature of her crime, be on parole for the rest of her life. When she asked if Dolly had any plans for the future she received only a hushed, 'Yes, I have plans, thank you.'

'Well, I am always here if ever you need to talk to me, or ask my opinion. You must feel there is a network of people who will give you every assistance to readjust to being outside. Eight years is a long time, and you will find many changes.'

'I'm sure I will,' Dolly replied, returning the half-empty cup to the tray.

Barbara Hunter remained with her back to the door, staring at Rawlins whose calm composure annoyed the hell out of her. She listened as Mrs Ellis passed over leaflets and numbers should Rawlins require them. She kept her eyes on Rawlins's face, wanting to see some kind of reaction, but Dolly remained impassive.

'You have been of invaluable help with many of the young offenders and especially with the mothers' and children's ward. I really appreciate all your hard work and I wish you every success in the future.'

Dolly leaned forward and asked, bluntly, if she could leave.

'Why, of course you can, Dorothy.' Mrs Ellis smiled.

'Anything I say now, it can't change that, can it?' Dolly seemed tense, her body arched.

'No, Dorothy, you are free to go.'

'Good. Well, there is something I would like to say. That woman . . .' Dolly turned an icy stare to Barbara Hunter who straightened quickly. 'You know what she is, we all know it, and I've got no quarrel with anyone's sexual preferences so don't get me wrong, Mrs Ellis. But that woman should not be allowed near the young girls comin' in. She shouldn't be allowed to get her dirty hands on any single kid in this place, but she does, and you all know it. She messes with the most vulnerable, especially when they've just had their babies taken from them. You got any decency inside you, Mrs Ellis, you should get rid of her.'

Mrs Ellis stood up, flushing, as Dolly sprang to her feet, adding, 'I know where she lives.'

Mrs Ellis snapped, 'Are you making threats, Mrs Rawlins?'

'No, just stating a fact. I'll be sending her a postcard. Can I go now?'

Mrs Ellis was infuriated. She pursed her lips and gave a nod as Hunter opened the office door. Dolly walked out, past Hunter, and never looked back. Two more officers were waiting outside for her as the door closed.

Mrs Ellis sat down and drew prisoner 45688, Dorothy Rawlins's file towards her. She opened it and stared at the police file photographs, then slapped the file closed. 'I think we'll be seeing Dorothy Rawlins again.'

Hunter agreed. 'I've never liked her or trusted her. She's devious, and a liar.'

Mrs Ellis stared at Hunter. 'Is she?' she said softly.

'Jimmy Donaldson was in the canteen two nights ago and I was next to him, I couldn't help but hear.' Francis Lloyd looked right and left, lowering his voice. 'He said that he was holding diamonds for Rawlins, that you lot copped him for peanuts compared to what he'd got stashed at his place. Diamonds . . .'

Mike leaned back in the chair. 'You sure about this, Francis?'

'Yes, on my life. Diamonds, he was braggin' about them, honest. Said he'd held on to them for eight years, diamond robbery, I swear that's what he said.'

Mike leaned forward and pushed two packs of Silk Cut cigarettes forward. They'd been opened and there was a ten quid note in each.

'Thanks, thanks a lot.'

On his way back to the station, Mike went over everything he had picked up and started to knit it together. Coincidences always needled him, and with Angela first and then Francis, it was certainly food for thought. By the time he'd parked his car in the underground car-park at the station he was feeling very positive, and even thinking that maybe, just maybe, he would be able to get Dolly Rawlins put back inside. He couldn't wait to see his mother's face when he told her, but first he had to go by the book and run it by his governor.

Detective Chief Inspector Ronald Craigh was a flash good-looker, well-liked and hungry. He was a high flyer and a sharp officer, with a good team around him. His other side-kick was Detective Inspector John Palmer, steady, cool-headed and a good personal friend. The pair of them often joked about Mike being over-eager but that was not a stroke against him – far from it. Craigh listened attentively as Mike discussed the information he had received that day.

'I have a good reliable informant who told me Rawlins is going to a big manor house. There's a bunch of ex-cons waiting for her. I then get a tip-off from my informant in Brixton nick.'

Craigh leaned forwards. 'Hang about, son, informant this or that . . . are they on record? They in my file?'

'Yes, it's Francis Lloyd – he's in Brixton.' Mike made no mention of Angela. She was not on the governor's inform-ant list but he skipped over that. He was excited as he presented the old files on the diamond robbery, explaining how he believed that Dorothy Rawlins would be out any minute and would, he estimated, go for them.

'Well, that'll be tough, won't it?' Craigh smiled. 'If Jimmy Donaldson is holdin' them for her and he's banged up, how's she gonna get to them?'

Mike paced up and down. 'What if we were to bring him out, talk it over with him, see what he has to say? I mean, we might be able to have a word with his probation officer or the Governor at Brixton, see if we couldn't get him shipped to a cushy open prison.'

'No way,' Craigh said.

Palmer held up his hand. 'We might be able to swing something that'll make him play with us.'

Craigh shook his head again. 'Come on, you know we got no pull to move any friggin' prisoner anywhere – and if we get him out, then what?'

'We get the diamonds,' Mike said, and grinned like a Cheshire cat. 'One, there's still a whopper of a reward out for them, two, we clean up that robbery – nobody was pulled in for it. What if it was Rawlins all along the way? We'll find out if she contacts Donaldson. It'll be proof she knows about the diamonds.'

Craigh was still iffy about it. 'According to the old files, it was suspected that Harry Rawlins was behind it.'

'She shot him,' Mike interrupted.

'I know she did. What I am saying is there was never any evidence to connect her to that blag.'

'There is if she goes for those diamonds.'

Craigh sucked on his teeth and then picked up all the old files. 'Okay, I'll run it by the Super, see what he's got to say about it.'

Mike followed him to the door. 'She's out today, Gov.'

Craigh opened his office door. 'I know that, son, just don't start jumping over hurdles until we know what the fuck we're gonna do.'

Mike looked glumly at Palmer as Craigh slammed the door. 'It's just that she's out, and she might call Donaldson, find out he's in the nick and . . .'

'Maybe she knows already,' Palmer said, doodling on a note-pad.

'Maybe she doesn't,' snapped Mike, eager to put the cavalry on to it, eager to get cracking.

But Palmer yawned. 'Just sit tight. If the Super gives the go-ahead, we'll see what they decide. In the mean-time . . .'

Mike sighed. He knew that he had a load of reports he had to complete so he took himself off to the incident room. As he reached his desk, his phone rang. It was Craigh. They were going out to talk to Donaldson, if he wanted to come along. Mike grinned; it was going down faster than he'd thought.

Ester ordered the six boys from the job centre to collect every bottle and piece of broken glass and clear the place before they started to hoover and dust. A florist's van had arrived with two massive floral displays that were propped up in the hall. Julia was using a stiff brush to sweep the front steps when she saw the taxi at the open manor gates. 'Someone's coming now,' she called out.

The taxi drove slowly down the drive, skirted the deep hole in the gravel and stopped by the front steps. Kathleen O'Reilly peered from the back seat. She had boxes and cases and numerous plastic bags. 'Hi. You moving in or on the move, Kathleen?' asked Julia.

Kathleen opened the car door. 'They're all me worldly possessions. I had to do a bit of a moonlight but Ester said I could doss down here for a few days. Will you give the driver a fiver? I'm flat broke.'

Kathleen: overweight, wearing a dreadful assortment of ill-matched clothes – a cotton skirt with two hand-knitted sweaters on top of a bright yellow blouse. She had dyed red hair spilling over a wide moon face and big wide blue eyes. Her false teeth needed bleaching as they were yellow with tobacco stains but she had a marvellous, generous feel to her, an open Irish nature. Julia delved into her pocket to pay off the driver as Kathleen hauled out her belongings. 'They said this was closed down,' she bellowed as she staggered into the hallway. Kathleen dumped her bags in the hall and looked around. 'Holy Mother of God, what a dump! Is that chandelier safe, Julia?'

33

Julia dropped one of Kathleen's cases. 'Ask Ester – she's running the show.'

At that moment Ester moved down the stairs. 'Hi, there. You made it here, then?'

'Well, of course I did.' Kathleen embraced her. 'I was glad you called, darlin'. I was in shit up to me armpits, I can tell you, with not a roof over my head. So . . . is she here, then?'

Julia turned, listening.

'Not yet, and I hope she won't be for a few hours. We've got to get the place ready in time.'

Kathleen plodded to the stairs. 'Well, let me unpack me gear, darlin', and I'll give you a hand.'

Ester instructed Kathleen to use one of the second-landing bedrooms and passed into the kitchen, squeezing past the boys as they scrubbed the floor. Julia picked up the broom again, trying to remember what Kathleen had been in prison for, but she couldn't recall and her attention was diverted by yet another car making its slow process down the driveway.

Connie Stevens sat next to the railway-station attendant, a nice man who, seeing Connie outside the small local station waiting for a taxi, had offered her a lift. Men did that kind of thing for Connie: she had such a helpless Marilyn Monroe quality to her, they went weak at the knees. She even had a soft breathy voice, blonde hair dyed to match her heroine's, and recent plastic surgery gave a dimple to her chin, tightened her jaw and removed the lines from her baby eyes. She worked hard to retain her curvaceous figure as she was already in her mid-thirties, not that she ever admitted it to anyone – she had been twenty-five for the past ten years.

Julia watched as the flushing man lifted an enormous case on wheels from the boot of his car.

'Thank you, I really appreciate this so much,' Connie cooed. The station attendant returned to his car, offering her a lift any time she needed it, but seeing Julia's amusement made him even more embarrassed so he drove out as fast as he could, hitting the pot-hole as he left and all but killing his suspension.

Ester leaned out of an upstairs window. 'Hi, Connie, come on in. Kathleen's already arrived.'

Connie dragged her case towards the steps. Julia tossed away the broom and took her case by the handle. 'Here, lemme help, Princess.'

Connie gave a breathy 'aweee' as she looked at the hall. 'It's changed so much since I was last here.'

Ester jumped down the stairs and embraced Connie warmly, then held her at arm's length to admire her new face. 'You look good – *really* good. Just drag your case upstairs and get into some old gear. We've got to clear the place up and make it ready for Dolly.'

'How many more are coming?' asked Kathleen. 'I mean, are we gonna cut it between us all?'

'I don't know. Like I keep saying, Ester's in charge, ask her. She hasn't told me what she plans on doing.'

Kathleen moved closer. 'They're worth millions, the diamonds, everyone used to talk about them. Are you certain she'll be coming?'

Julia picked up the broom and started sweeping the steps again. 'Ester seems to think so, that's why she's got us all here.'

Kathleen returned to hoovering with a venom. She certainly hoped this wasn't all a waste of time. She needed money, a lot, and fast. She was in deep trouble: the thought of a cut of all those millions had been like a raft to a drowning woman . . . Kathleen was drowning and her three kids had been taken into care. Dolly Rawlins's diamonds would be her only way out of the mess she had got herself into.

Way down the lane, Gloria Radford threw up her hands in fury. She'd been down one dead end after another, up on to the motorway three times, and still not found the manor house. She slammed out of her dilapidated Mini Traveller and headed towards a man on a tractor in the middle of a field. 'Oi, mate, can you direct me to the Grange Manor House?'

The old farmhand turned in surprise as Gloria, small, plump and wearing spike heeled shoes over skin-tight black pants, waved from the field gates. Her make-up was plastered on thick: lipgloss-smudged teeth, mascara-clogged lashes with bright blue eye-shadow on the lids, like someone stuck in a time-warp of the late sixties. Gloria Radford was a real hard-nosed character and was in a fury as she wafted the hand-drawn map Ester had sent her. The old boy wheeled his tractor towards her.

'Down there.' He pointed.

'I been down there and I been back up there and I keep gettin' back on the bleedin' motorway.'

'Ay, yes, they cut off the access road. Just keep on this slip road and you'll get to it. The manor's off to the right.'

Gloria stepped over the clods of earth and headed back to her Mini. He remained watching as she reversed straight into a pot-hole and let rip with a stream of expletives. He was gobsmacked.

Ester was now checking the cutlery. Some of it was quite good but it all needed cleaning, as did every plate and cup and saucer. Kathleen was now on duty in the dining room, dusting the chairs, when the crate of wine was delivered. She was ready for a drink and about to open a bottle when they all heard the tooting of a car horn and the sound of Gloria Radford arriving, towed in by a tractor.

They all stood on the doorstep, watching the spectacle. Julia turned to Ester. 'Subtle as ever. I suppose you wanted the entire village to know we were here.'

'Me bleedin' back end's fucked!' yelled Gloria, as she heaved out a case.

Julia winced as Gloria made some financial deal with the old man on his tractor to tow the car to the nearest garage. She was so loud and brassy that she was almost comical: her fake-fur leopard coat slung round her shoulders, her too-tight, puce, wrap-around shirt. 'Er, Ester, you got a few quid I can bung 'im?'

Julia saw Ester purse her lips and join Gloria at the tractor.

'Is she 'ere yet, then?' screeched Gloria.

Ester paid ten quid to the tractor driver and directed him to the nearest garage that would be able to repair the Mini.

Gloria banged into the hallway. 'Cor blimey, this is the old doss-house, is it? Hey, Kathleen, how are you doin', kid?' Kathleen said she was doing fine, then Gloria pointed at Connie. 'I know you, do I?'

Connie shook her head. 'I don't think so, I'm Connie.'

'You one of Ester's tarts, then, are you?'

Connie's jaw dropped. 'No, I am not.'

Gloria seemed unaware of how furious Connie was. She turned to Julia. 'I didn't know you was on this caper, Doc.'

'I didn't know you were,' said Julia sarcastically.

'You sure you got Dolly comin'? I mean, I come a hell of a long way to get here, you know. This is all on the level, isn't it? She is coming, isn't she?' Julia had to turn away because she wanted to laugh out loud.

Ester clenched her fists: Gloria had only been there two minutes and she was under her skin like a rash. 'She'll be here, Gloria. Just get some old gear on and start helping us, we've got a lot to do.'

'Right, you tell me what you want done, sweet face. I'm ready, I'm willin' and nobody ever said Gloria Radford wasn't able.'

Ester looked at her watch. She thought she should have received a call from Dolly by now but she said nothing, just hoped to God she had played her cards right, that Dolly would, as she had anticipated, arrive. She had laid out a lot of cash already and if wily old Dolly Rawlins copped out, she was in trouble. Like the women she had chosen, Ester was in deep financial trouble. They were all desperate but Ester more than any of them.

Dolly was out. She had walked out a free woman two hours ago. The fear crept up unexpectedly. Suddenly she felt alone. She stood on the pavement, as her heart began to beat rapidly and her mouth went bone dry. She was out – and there was no one to meet her, no one to wrap their arms around her, no place to go. She saw the white Rolls Corniche; it was hard to miss, parked outside the prison gates. She stepped back, afraid for a moment, when a uniformed chauffeur stepped out and looked towards her.

'Excuse me, are you Mrs Rawlins, Mrs Dolly Rawlins?'

Dolly frowned, gave a small nod, and he smiled warmly, walking towards her. 'Your car, Mrs Rawlins.'

'I never ordered it.'

He touched her elbow gently. 'Well, my docket says you did, Mrs Rawlins, so, where would you like to go?'

Nonplussed, she allowed herself to be manoeuvred to

38

the Rolls. He opened the door with a flourish. 'Anywhere you want. It's hired for the entire day, Mrs Rawlins.'

'Who by?' she asked suspiciously.

'You, and it's paid for, so why not? Get in, Mrs Rawlins.' Dolly looked at the prison, then back to the car in which there was a small bouquet of roses, a bottle of champagne, and an invitation. 'I don't understand, who did this?'

The chauffeur eased her in and shut the door. Dolly opened the invitation.

Dear Dolly,
Some of your friends have arranged a 'SHE'S OUT' party. Take a drive around London and then call us. Here's to your successful future, and hoping you will join us for a slap up dinner and a knees-up,

Ester

Dolly read and reread the invitation. She knew Ester Freeman but she'd not been that friendly with her.

'Where would you like to go, Mrs Rawlins?'

She leaned back, still nonplussed. 'Oh, just drive around, will you? See the sights.'

'Right you are.'

She saw the portable phone positioned by his seat. She leaned forwards and picked up the phone.

'Call any place you want, Mrs Rawlins.'

She turned the phone over in her hand, never having seen one before, and then she smiled softly. 'My husband would have loved one of these,' she whispered.

CHAPTER 2

J AMES 'JIMMY' Donaldson was a small, sandy-haired
man. He looked younger than his fifty-five years
because he was so compact and his hair was thick with
a deep widow's peak at the temple. He was exceedingly
nervous, having been brought from a woodwork class to be
confronted by DCI Craigh and DS Mike Withey. The
prison officers left the three men alone, which seemed to
unnerve Donaldson even more, and his eyes darted back
and forth from one man to the other.

Craigh asked quietly if he knew a woman called Dorothy
Rawlins. Donaldson shook his head, then shifted his but-
tocks on the chair to sit on his hands, as if afraid they would
give him away because they were shaking.

'You sure about that, Jimmy?'

He nodded, blinking rapidly, as Craigh, still speaking
softly, asked him about the diamonds.

'I don't know anything about them,' he stuttered.

'She's out today, Jimmy. Dolly Rawlins is out.' Craigh
began to wander around the small, cold room, suggesting
that if Donaldson could assist them, then perhaps they
could make things much easier for him, maybe even get the
authorities to move him a nice, cushy open prison.

Two hours later, Donaldson was taken from Brixton
Prison to their local nick. It was done fast and Craigh made
sure that it was put out that Donaldson required a small
operation, just in case the word spread they had got him,

so that when and if they sent him back he wouldn't be subjected to threats for grassing. All he had admitted so far was that he might know about the diamonds but he refused to say anything more unless he was taken out of the jail.

On the journey he brightened up at the prospect of being moved, even going home to visit his wife. Craigh had laughed. 'Don't get too excited, Jimmy, because we'll need to know more – a lot more. You're doing time for fencing hot gear right now and we've not got much sway with the prison authorities. All we do is catch 'em, the rest is not down to us unless you have some very good information.'

It was almost six thirty by the time Donaldson was taken into the station, and he was given some dinner before they really began to pressure him. He admitted that he knew Dolly Rawlins but he had known her husband better, and had held the stones for her as a favour. When asked if Rawlins instigated the diamond raid, he swore he didn't know and he was certain that Mrs Rawlins couldn't have done it because she was a woman. He knew she had killed her husband but word was he'd been fooling around with a young bit of fluff who'd had a kid by him. At the time of the shooting, there were many rumours around as to what had happened, but the truth had always been shrouded by mystery – and fear, because Harry Rawlins was a formidable and exceptionally dangerous man, nicknamed the 'Octopus' because he seemed to have so many arms in so many different businesses. No one was ever sure how much power he had but a lot of men known to have crossed him had disappeared.

Harry Rawlins had instigated a raid on an armoured truck: the plan had been to ram it inside the Strand underpass but the raid had gone disastrously wrong. The explosives used by his team had blown their own truck to smithereens; four men inside had died, their charred bodies unrecognizable. Dolly Rawlins had been given a watch, a gold Rolex from the blackened wrist of one of the dead men. She had buried his remains, the funeral an ornate affair, with wreaths from every main criminal in England. In many instances they were sent not out of sympathy, but relief.

Dolly Rawlins had been in deep shock. The husband she had worshipped for twenty years was gone, and the void in her life could not be filled, made worse by the pressure from villains trying to take over her husband's manor. Her grief had turned to anger when they approached her at his graveside, but then to icy fury. When she found Harry's detailed plans for the abortive robbery, Dolly Rawlins drew together the widows of the men who had died alongside him in the truck. She manipulated and cajoled them into repeating the raid that had taken their men. Always a strong-minded woman, Dolly grew more confident and arrogant each day. Her belief that they could handle it quelled their fears, and her constant encouragement and furious determination ensured that they not only succeeded in pulling off one of the most daring armed robberies ever, but she also made sure they got away with it. She had been doing it for Harry, using his carefully laid plans. Never for one moment had she believed or even contemplated his betrayal.

Harry Rawlins was alive. He had been the only one to escape from the nightmare raid that killed his men. Rawlins had arranged that when the raid was over, he would never return to his wife, would leave Dolly for his mistress, a twenty-five-year-old girl. To his stunned amazement, Harry Rawlins had watched as Dolly went ahead with the raid, and laughed because he knew that if she succeeded he would take the money. Her audacity amused him. Safe in his girlfriend's apartment, he had watched and waited, had played with his baby girl, the child Dolly had craved to give him. But Harry Rawlins had underestimated his wife.

Dolly succeeded in the raid and she also found out the terrible truth. She never confronted him – it would have been too dangerous, not for herself but for the other women concerned. Instead she planned their escape from England, leaving him penniless and desperate.

For a while the widows had lived high but the bulk of the money became a monster they could not control. Dolly returned to England where she knew Harry would come after her. And she waited, while planning another robbery: the diamond raid. She used the same women, the widows, but this time not everything had gone according to plan. One of them, Linda Pirellie, was killed in an automobile accident; a second, the young, beautiful Shirley Miller, was shot during the robbery. Dolly got away with the diamonds but the police net was drawing in. Yet again she reacted as her husband would have. She knew Jimmy Donaldson could be trusted; small-time he might be but he had done a lot of work for Harry in the past and had never been charged so she used that as a lever to ensure that he would keep the diamonds safe. She could have got away with it but something was more important than the diamonds: her guilt about little Shirley had pushed her to Audrey, Shirley's mother, because she felt she owed her a debt. She was the only other person she felt she could trust, because Dolly had used Audrey in the first raid when they had escaped from England. Audrey would be unlikely to go to the police and she was broke, so the promise of a cut of the diamonds would atone for the shock and grief of Shirley's death. All Dolly had asked Audrey to do was wait and in time she would get her share. She had not said how long the wait would be as she didn't know herself. Because even though she might just get away with murder, in truth she hadn't cared. All she had wanted, more than any millions, had been to get revenge. So Audrey had wept but had agreed to take the diamonds to Jimmy and had delivered them that same night, as Dolly had instructed. The agreement had been that they would have no further contact until Dolly gave the word. Neither Jimmy nor Audrey knew that, as they met, Dolly was waiting for Harry with a .22.

Harry had been relieved, the hiding-out over. He had known as soon as she saw him that he would be able to talk her round, make her believe that he'd had to lie low because he would have been arrested. He had had to allow her to go through the charade of a funeral because if he hadn't, the filth would have known he was still alive. So he had waited, confident he could manipulate her. Never had he considered the pain he had caused her, the terrible grief he had put her through, the wife who had stood by him for twenty years.

Harry had smiled when Dolly approached and had taken a few steps towards her. He had still been smiling when she fired at point-blank range into his heart.

Dolly Rawlins was arrested and charged with man-slaughter, a nine-year sentence to be served at Holloway Prison. She had never stopped loving him and the pain never did go away, but the years eased it. In prison she embraced the hurt inside her, like the child she was never able to conceive.

Jimmy Donaldson hadn't found out the truth – nobody had – but his fear of Harry Rawlins remained. He hid the diamonds and stuck to his story throughout the lengthy question-and-answer session following his removal from prison by DCI Craigh. He never mentioned Audrey's name. All he admitted to was having received a package from Dolly Rawlins. Even after his subsequent arrest for fencing, he remained silent about the diamonds. In reality, he had been too scared to fence them or mention them to anyone else. Now he began to talk.

'She's a tough bitch, you know, hard as nails. Everyone knew how much her old man depended on her – gave him more alibis than you had hot dinners, mate.'

Donaldson became quite cocky as he told them how Dolly had promised he'd get a nice reward for keeping her property safe.

'So where are they, Jimmy?' asked Craigh.

Donaldson pursed his lips. 'Well, that would be telling. I mean, you gonna let me see my wife?'

Craigh became tougher, prodding him with his finger. 'We make the deals, Jimmy, not you. You're lucky we're not gonna slap more years on for not coming out with this at your trial.'

'Fuckin' hell, you bastards, you just been stringing me along. Well, no more, no way, I retract everythin' I said, I dunno anythin'.'

The truth was that Craigh was in no position to offer a deal until he had spoken to the prison authorities and to Donaldson's parole officer to see if they could get him moved. Mike was eager for them to make any promise and he was the one who asked Donaldson if Dolly Rawlins had contacted him since she had been in Holloway.

'No, never – she's not stupid. But a few times I sort of felt a finger on the back of the neck, so to speak.'

Donaldson never divulged that Dolly Rawlins had quite a hold over him because of all the other times he had fenced stolen gear for her husband. Donaldson would have been put away for a lot longer than five years. Dolly had known about his background and his work for Harry and she had virtually blackmailed him into holding on to the diamonds. Now he felt almost relief because they seemed to want to put her away again and it would mean he was free of her.

'How is she going to collect the diamonds?'

'Well, she'll call me. She was never arrested or charged for that gig, was she? I mean, nobody knows she's got them, do they?' Mike Withey was also relieved. At no point had Donaldson mentioned the part his own mother, Audrey, had played.

Still not knowing the location of the diamonds, Craigh and Palmer talked it over with the Super and decided to take Donaldson to his home and give it a few days to see if Rawlins made contact.

When Donaldson knew he was going home, would see his wife – even if a police officer was to be with him at all times – he told them where the stones were hidden. His wife still ran his junk and antique shop and the main wall had a four-brick hideaway; if they removed the bricks, they would find the gems.

Craigh and Palmer thumped each other; it had worked like a little jewel up to now and there was, or had been, a whopper of a reward out for the return of the stones. They congratulated Mike, who was well chuffed because if it did pan out, if Dolly Rawlins contacted Donaldson, if they got the diamonds and had Donaldson hand them over to her, they could arrest her and and have her sent right back to prison. Rest in peace, Shirley Miller.

Dolly stood outside her old house in Totteridge. She stared at the new curtains, the fresh paint. It no longer was or had any part in her life but for the twenty years of her marriage that was where she lived. She had always been house proud, and it had been a show palace. Harry entertained regularly and she had always set a nice table with good, home-cooked food. She had thought she was happy, had believed he was, too, but nothing had prepared her for his betrayal and, as she stood there, she clenched her hands, not wanting to break down, refusing to after all these years. He had forced her into a grief-driven fury – she had even buried him when all the time he had been alive. Alive and cheating on her. It was so bizarre, so insane what she had done, what she had become. She had confronted him, and even when he faced her, knowing that she knew everything, he had still been so sure of her love for him that he had opened his arms and said, 'I love you, Doll.'

She had pulled the trigger then, almost nine years ago, and she had served the sentence for his murder. She was free now. She walked back to the waiting chauffeur and he opened the car door for her.

'That was my home,' she said softly.

He helped her inside the car.

'Now it's someone else's.' She seemed so sad and lost he felt sorry for her, but she suddenly gave him a sweet smile.

'Can I use this portable phone, then?'

Ester grabbed the phone after two rings, knew it had to be Dolly. Only she knew the new number: she'd got it when the phone had been reconnected. She was right. Dolly was on her way. Ester sighed with relief and then hurried into the dining room.

The table was almost ready but Gloria and Kathleen were having a go at each other. 'She's drinking, Ester. I keep telling her not to get pissed.'

Ester snatched up one of the bottles as Kathleen shouted that all she was doing was getting them ready for the decanters, recorked the bottle and banged it on to the table. 'She's on her way, and as soon as those lads are finished we'd all better have a talk, get us all sorted. She's not stupid so we got to make this look good. Where's Connie?'

'I'm here. I've been repairing my nails. I've chipped two already – they're not supposed to be in too much water, you know.'

Gloria raised her eyes to heaven as Connie showed off her false-tipped nails. Ester told her to start bringing up extra chairs from the cellar. She had to show her the way and as they walked down the hall, Connie pulled her to one side. 'What were they in prison for?'

Ester told her that Gloria had been in for a long stretch for fencing stolen guns and Kathleen was in for forgery and kiting.

'And what about Julia? What was she in for?'

Gloria appeared, overhearing. 'The doc was in for sellin' prescriptions. She was a junkie.'

Connie flushed with embarrassment.

'I heard you, Ester. I wasn't done for the guns, that was a total frame-up. I was stitched up.'

Ester sighed, already sick and tired of Gloria. She ushered Connie along to the cellar door, which led down to saunas, steam rooms and the old laundry. There was also a gymnasium, showers and changing cubicles, all from the days when the manor had been a health farm.

Connie went down to inspect the chairs as most of the ones in the dining room were broken. Confronted by banks of mirrors, she couldn't resist looking at herself and pouting, and jumped with nerves when the droll voice of Julia asked what she was doing. Connie squinted in the semi-darkness, looking over the stack of chairs. 'I love to work out, I do it whenever I can – it's like a fix.' She put her hand to her mouth. 'Oh, I'm sorry, I didn't mean that the way it came out. I meant, you know, not *fix* fix but like . . . er . . .'

'I know what you mean. You worked for Ester, right? What were you, then?'

'I'm a model. I don't do any of that kind of thing now, not any more.'

Julia smiled. 'Well, I don't use drugs, you're not selling that lovely body, so we both seem to have improved our lives, don't we?'

Julia banged out and Connie sighed. She hated it when anyone insinuated she was or had been a prostitute. But that was what she had been, like it or not. Then when Lennie, who she had trusted – believed had loved her – had tried to make her go back on the game it had hurt because she had dreamed of being a model, a proper one, one that kept her clothes on. She had written to agents and now, with all the work done on her face, she reckoned she might even get a TV commercial. She had big plans for herself: she would have a big-time photographer do a good contact sheet, send out a portfolio. She was sure she could have a chance. Lennie had laughed and told her she was too old, told her that was the reason he had paid for her surgery, so she could make money on her back, but she had refused. Connie sat down on one of the dusty chairs and started to cry. He didn't touch her face, at least he didn't ruin that, but her body was still covered in bruises and she had said she would do whatever he wanted, just for him to leave her alone. The following morning Ester had called, not to ask her to go on the game as she had first thought, but to give her a chance of cashing in on a lot of money. Connie had grabbed the chance, thrown a few things into a case and done a runner. She knew Lennie would be going crazy, knew he would be out looking for her: he'd want his money back for the surgery at the very least, but Ester had said that she'd have more money than she would know what to do with so she had packed up and run for it. Now she wasn't so sure about all this big money. She'd never really met Dolly Rawlins.

'What the hell are you doin' down here?' yelled Gloria.

Connie picked up the chair and walked out, past her.

'You see any big trays around here? Ester said we need one.'

Connie hadn't, so Gloria began to burrow around the odd bits and pieces of furniture in the gym. She was filthy and she sighed when she caught her reflection. Then she inspected the black roots of her hair. She needed a tint badly, had to have it done before she went to see Eddie.

Eddie Radford was serving eighteen years for arms dealing and armed robbery. He was going to be away for so long that sometimes Gloria wondered if it was worth going back and forth to the prisons. He'd spent most of their marriage in one or another. They were two bad pennies, as she had been in and out for this and that since she was a teenager. Eddie was trouble – she'd known it when she first met him. He was even worse than her first husband. Now he'd got a stash of weapons hidden at their old house with two of his bastard friends trying to get them. She had no money and Eddie kept telling her he'd arrange a deal, that she just had to sit tight and wait until he'd made the contact. Gloria was behind in the rent, and the council had told her to leave. It seemed like everyone was always telling her what to do and it always ended up a mess. She was scared of handling such a big stash of guns, scared of his so-called contacts and she was sick to death of always being on the move, always looking over her shoulder in case one of Eddie's bastards tracked her down. When Ester called, it was like a breath of fresh air. The thought of getting away from that pressure, away from Eddie's bloody heavies, was like a God-given present. And with the promise of big money tied in with it, who could refuse? Not Gloria Radford.

*

Ester checked the table. It was looking good. As it grew darker it was harder to see the dilapidation, and she had bought boxes of candles and incense sticks, plus room sprays, so gradually the stench of mildew was disappearing. Gloria said it smelt like someone had farted in a pine forest but it wasn't that bad.

The food had been delivered on big oval throw-away platters, and all they had to do was heat it up. The Aga was on, the boiler was working and fires were lit in the dining room and drawing room. Julia had cut logs and carried them in, and slowly the firelight and the candlelight gave warmth to the old house. The kids from the job centre had gone and only the women remained. Ester shouted for them all to meet up and have a confab as Dolly would be arriving in a couple of hours.

The doorbell rang and Ester swore, looking at her watch. It couldn't be her yet ... Then she remembered Angela.

'You took your bloody time getting here. I said this afternoon. It's almost six,' she snapped.

Angela dumped her overnight bag. 'I had to bleedin' walk all the way from the station, it took hours. And I missed the train so I had to wait ...' She looked at the bank of candles. 'Eh, this looks great, I thought it was wrecked.'

'It was, it is, we've done a good bandage job.'

Angela hadn't seen the old house for years, not since it was busted, so she was impressed by the big floral displays in the hall, the banisters gleaming from the hours Kathleen had spent polishing.

Gloria walked out from the dining room and glared at Angela. 'Who's this? What're you doing?'

Ester said that Angela was a friend who had come to serve the dinner.

'Oh yes, we cut this any more ways and there's not gonna be much to go round, you know.'

Ester pushed Gloria against the wall. 'She doesn't know anything, she doesn't know Dolly and she's not in for a cut. She gets fifty quid to wait on us at dinner. Now will you get the others in the dining room so we can have a talk?'

Angela went into the kitchen. Ester pointed to the food, what needed heating, what was to be served cold and showed her the low oven of the Aga for the plates to be heated. Angela looked around, nodding, and trailed after Ester to the dining room.

'There's a room ready for you. Dump your bag. Did you bring a black dress and an apron?'

'Yes, ma'am,' said Angela.

'Okay, all of you read these.' Ester handed round old newspaper clippings she had xeroxed. They were clippings about the diamond raid: there were photographs of Dolly Rawlins after the shooting of her husband and several of Shirley Miller.

'Holy shit, you read this?' said Gloria. '"Diamonds worth more than two million were last night stolen in a daring raid."'

Julia grabbed the clippings. 'Gloria, we can read it for ourselves, okay? There is no need for you to read it aloud.'

Gloria picked up another. 'Fuckin' hell, says here, head-line, "Criminal murdered by his wife". Oh, listen to this, "Harry Rawlins was last night shot at point-blank range by his wife. His body was discovered in an ornate pond in . . ."'

Julia snatched it from her. 'Shut up, just shut up.'

They read in silence, one clipping after another. Kathleen

looked at Ester. 'This was some raid. Did she set it up? Dolly?'

'She was never shopped for it if she did.'

Gloria frowned. 'This was no doodle at Woolworth's. Look at the gear they got away with, and guns. See this?' She held up a cutting. '"Shirley Miller, aged twenty-one, was shot and killed during a terrifying armed raid that took place at a fashion show last night. The models were wearing *over two million pounds' worth of diamonds . . ."'*

Julia glanced at Ester in exasperation. She couldn't stand Gloria reading aloud. She had put up with it when they shared the same prison cell and she was about to intervene for the third time when Ester held her back.

'If they were worth two million nearly nine years ago, you can double the value now.'

Kathleen let out her breath in awe. Gloria's face was puckered in concentration. 'I mean, I know there were rumours, Ester, but, like, she might have started them. How can you be sure she's really got these diamonds?'

'Because nobody ever found them after the raid.'

'That don't mean she got 'em,' said Gloria.

'She said she had, she's hinted enough times that she had.'

Julia sighed. 'Let's take it that she does have them.'

'Okay, she's got them, and now she's out and she's coming here tonight.'

'Right. She's coming here, to friends, and that's what we are going to be for her, old dear friends.'

'You must be joking. She don't know the meaning of the word. She was like edgy, very edgy, Ester.'

'Gloria, will you keep it shut for ten minutes and *fucking listen to me?*'

Ester ran her hands through her hair. 'I know she has no one, had no visitors. She's going to be very lonely, even frightened, so we make her welcome, we make her have a great night . . .'

Gloria nodded. 'Yeah, well, I'm with you so far, darlin'. Then what? When do we get our hands on the stones?'

'None of you, not one of you, mentions diamonds. We just want her to feel like we're her friends, that she can trust us. She might need a good fence – Kathleen knows enough. She might have trouble getting the stones – Gloria's got contacts. She will need us, do you understand? Above all, we make her trust us. When she tells us about the diamonds, we go for them, we take them if we feel like it, and we share them between us.'

'The five of us?' asked Gloria.

'Yes, Gloria, the five of us, or six—'

'Who's the sixth, then? Not that little black chick you got in for the nosh?'

'No, Gloria, Angela is not the sixth, but I reckon Dolly might want a cut of her own gear.'

'Well, if I was her I'd just say piss off. I mean, why give us a cut?'

'Maybe she won't want to give us anything, Gloria. If that's the case, we just take it, you understand? We only need to know where the bloody things are stashed.'

Ester sighed, beginning to think the entire idea was a fiasco, when Connie suddenly giggled. 'Two million . . . Oh, yes.'

They all started to laugh and then Ester broke it up and told them to start getting changed: Dolly was already on her way and would be there within the hour. Like kids they trooped out.

Julia began to rub Ester's neck, feeling the tension. 'I hope to God this works, Julia, and works fast because I don't think I could stand more than a few hours with that bloody demented gerbil, Gloria Radford.'

Julia cupped Ester's face in her hands and kissed her lips. 'Don't say I didn't warn you. You'll pull it off – if anyone can, you can. I just hope there really are diamonds. It could all be a fantasy, you know that, don't you, darling?'

Ester gripped her wrists. 'No. There's diamonds, believe me, I know it. And I know that hard bitch has got them somewhere . . . and we'll get them away from her and then . . .'

Julia stepped back. 'Then?' she said softly.

'I'm free, Julia. I'll be free. No bastard trying to slit my throat. I'll even airmail their wretched tape back to them. With all those millions I won't need to grovel or beg from anyone. I don't reckon in all honesty I've ever been free but this time I will be.'

'I hope for your sake you'll get them. I love you, Ester.'

Ester was already walking out of the room. She didn't hear or if she did she pretended not to. Alone, Julia looked round the old, ornate, once magnificent room. Maybe Dolly would be taken in if she didn't look too carefully, if she didn't see the cracks, if she believed Ester was her friend, that all of them were her friends. Julia sighed. In some ways she felt sorry for Dolly Rawlins because she was walking into a snake pit and she was ashamed to be a part of it.

The candles threw shadows on the wall and she raised her hand to make a silhouette of a bird flying, flapping its wings. Dolly Rawlins's first day of freedom in eight years. Julia watched the shadow bird flutter and then broke the shadow as she moved her hands away from the candle. Ester had planned this evening carefully, each one of them chosen because they were desperate, herself included. She was desperate not to lose Ester, desperate to safeguard the lies she had told her ailing elderly mother, lies she had spun round her arrest and prison sentence. Julia's mother never knew her daughter the doctor was an ex-drug addict, that she had been struck off and that for the last four years she had been in prison. She had arranged an elaborate charade via friends who passed Julia's letters written in Holloway to look as if they were sent from around the world. Julia's mother never suspected, never knew her daughter's double life, just as she had no notion that her daughter could or would be deeply in love with another woman. It was beyond her comprehension, and Julia was determined her mother would never know. Keeping up the pretence had taken money, and still took every penny she could lay hands on, as she paid all her mother's bills. Julia, too, although she hated to admit it, needed those diamonds but, unlike the others, she was ashamed to acknowledge the awful con they were all about to begin on Dolly Rawlins.

CHAPTER 3

JIMMY DONALDSON'S wife had been informed that her husband was returning home on a 'special leave' from prison. She was asked not to mention the visit to anyone and to remain in the house until he was brought home. When he did arrive, in the company of two plain-clothes officers, they had only one or two moments alone before he was taken into their sitting room. One officer placed a tape-recorder and bugging device on their telephone in the hope that Dolly Rawlins would make contact.

The small antique shop was already being searched. DCI Craigh arranged for a rota of officers to remain in the house and to keep an eye on Jimmy. Mike Withey was to take the following morning shift: he couldn't wait to see his mother and tell her of the developments that had moved faster than he could have anticipated.

At the same time Dolly Rawlins was about to arrive at Grange Manor House. The women had all changed into cocktail dresses. Ester had laid out one of her own dresses for Dolly to change into and as she saw the head-lamps of the Corniche turning into the driveway, she gave hurried orders for the women to remain in the dining room and stay silent. Next she briefed Angela that when the doorbell rang she was to open the front door and welcome Dolly into the house. Ester would then make her appearance.

Dolly stepped out of the car. She looked around in confusion and felt unsure, even more so than she'd been when driving down the dark, pot-holed lane leading to the house. The massive manor looked daunting but in the shadows it was difficult to detect its run-down, neglected grounds. The chauffeur guided her towards the front steps. She stopped.

'Are you staying?'

'If you would like me to, Mrs Rawlins. It's entirely up to you.' He rang the bell. Some of the stained glass was broken in the panels but the steps had been swept and Dolly wasn't paying much attention; she was feeling edgy.

Angela opened the door, wearing a neat black dress and white apron.

'Good evening, Mrs Rawlins. Welcome to the Grange.'

Dolly hesitated and then saw the elegant Ester standing with her arms wide. 'Dolly. Come on in.'

She walked into the hall.

'What's going on?'

'It's a welcome-out party for you.'

'Is he going?' She was almost prepared to walk after the chauffeur.

'Oh, he'll be back, and we've all got our cars round the back.'

'All?'

'Your old mates, Dolly, from Holloway.'

She watched as Angela closed the door, taking Dolly's small case from the chauffeur, and then Ester embraced her warmly, kissing her on both cheeks.

'Come, let me show you around. You'll want a bath, won't you?'

Dolly looked at the banks of flickering candles, still nonplussed as Ester guided her up the stairs. She stopped. 'Why are you doing this?'

Ester continued up the stairs. 'We've come out to nothing and no one, Dolly. We all know what it feels like. We wanted to make sure you got a special party, to sort of kick you off in the right direction.'

Dolly followed Ester up the stairs, impressed by the house, then the clean room with the black lace dress laid out on the bed. There were stockings and clean underwear, even a couple of pairs of high-heeled shoes.

'You did all this for me?' Dolly said, still nonplussed.

'It's not a new dress but it is a Valentino. Would you like me to run a bath for you? Wash your hair?'

Angela slipped in with Dolly's suitcase and placed it by the bed. She was out again before Dolly could say a word. 'Who's that?'

'Oh, she's just a kid that used to work for me.'

'A tart, is she?'

'No, she's just here to serve us so we don't have to do anything but enjoy ourselves.'

Dolly wandered around the room. 'Who else is here?'

Ester turned on the taps, felt the hot water – it wasn't what you'd call *hot* hot – and poured in bath salts.

'Kathleen O'Reilly, you remember her?' Ester listed the other names.

Dolly sat on the bed. 'Well, I wouldn't call any of them friends, Ester. They all here, are they?'

'Yes, well, I tried to get as many women as I thought you knew so it'd be a bit of a knees-up.'

'I'm not sure what to say.'

Ester smiled. 'Just have a nice bath. I'll go and tell them you'll be down soon, okay?'

Dolly slowly took off her coat, and then smiled. 'Yeah, why not? I could do with a drink.'

*

They all looked towards the double doors as Ester came into the dining room. 'She's getting ready, won't be long.'

'I hope not, I'm starving,' Gloria muttered.

Julia lolled in her chair. 'She knows who's down here?'

'Yes, she does, and don't drink any more, Kathleen. We've got to work her over and if you get pissed you'll open that yapping mouth. That goes for you too, Gloria.'

She glanced over the table and then went to the kitchen. Angela had her feet up, reading a magazine. 'We'll have the first course, then I'll ring for you.'

'Yeah, you told me that before.'

'When she's ready to come down, I want you to bring her in. Go up to her room when I tell you. I don't want her wandering around.'

'You told me that as well.'

'Fine, I'm just making sure everything's ready.'

Ester walked out. Angela waited a moment, then followed. As soon as she saw her heading up the stairs she crept to the phone, eased it off the hook, and dialled. She waited, eyes to the dark, candle-lit hallway.

Mike answered the phone. Susan was dishing up dinner. He spoke softly and then replaced the receiver. He was smiling like he'd just been given good news.

'Who was that?'

'Mum. I said I'd go over later after dinner.'

'Oh, I'd like to have come with you. Why didn't you tell me? I could ask the girl next door to baby-sit.'

'I'm only going for a few minutes.'

Mike sat down as Susan passed him a plate of stew. She was a pretty girl, with long blonde hair, similar to Mike's sister Shirley. She was almost as pretty. Both their sons had already been put to bed and she'd half hoped they could have an evening together.

'Is your mum still planning to go to Spain?'

Mike nodded, his mouth full. 'Yeah, that's why I said I'd drop in, see if she needed me to do anything.'

'Funny time to go, isn't it, winter?'

Mike shrugged, forking in another mouthful. 'Got some friend there with a villa, be good for her, she needs to get away.'

'Don't we all. It's been ages since we had a holiday – be nice to get away.'

'We will,' he said, eyes to the clock, wondering if they'd found the diamonds.

Susan watched him: he'd been very distracted of late, moody and snapping at the kids. 'Everything all right at work, is it?'

'Yep.' He pushed the plate aside, only half finished, and wiped his mouth with a napkin. 'I'll shove off. Sooner I see her, sooner I'll be home.'

She picked up her knife and fork and he reached over and kissed her forehead.

'There's nobody else, is there, Mike?'

'What?'

'It's just I hardly have time to talk to you, you're always out, and most weekends you've been on duty. If there is somebody else . . .'

He sat down again. 'There isn't anyone else, Sue, okay? It's been a bit heavy lately, I've got a lot on and—'

'Yes?'

'Well, it's to do with Shirley. The woman Mum blames for her being killed, Dolly Rawlins, got released today, so Mum's been a bit hysterical, you know the way she always harps on about it.'

61

'Well, you can't blame her. If one of our boys was killed I'd feel the same.'

'I won't be long, I promise, okay?'

Mike left and Susan carried on eating but she wasn't hungry. She was sure Mike was seeing someone else – she'd even searched his suit pockets, looking for evidence. She hadn't found anything but, then, he was a detective so he wouldn't be stupid enough to leave anything incriminating. But he *was* different – colder and impatient towards her and the boys. She told herself to stop it: it was just as he said, overwork, he was tired and she was reading more into his moods than she should. She swiped at the table, muttering to herself. What about *her* moods? Nobody ever seemed concerned about her or the way she felt.

Ester cocked her head to one side, sprayed lacquer over Dolly's hair and stepped back. 'That's much nicer, softer round your face with a bit of a wave. So, we all set to go down?' Dolly stood up and admired herself in the wardrobe mirror. 'This is a lovely frock.'

Ester opened the bedroom door. 'It was a lovely price a few years back, Dolly. Come on, they're all starving down there.'

They walked down the stairs together, Angela waiting at the bottom.

'No men invited, then?' Dolly asked.

Ester laughed. 'Well, we could always get the chauffeur back.'

'Couldn't you get the Chippendales? They're all the rage in the nick – girls have got their posters on the walls. Good-looking lads, they dance for women.'

'I know who they are, Dolly, but they're a bit *passé* now.

62

That's always the problem in the nick. Years behind what's going down.'

Angela opened the dining-room doors wider and Ester stepped back to allow Dolly to walk in ahead of her.

The women all rose to their feet and began to sing. 'Good luck, God bless you . . .'

The banks of candles, their dresses and the beautifully laid table made Dolly gasp: it seemed almost magical. The room with its carved ornate ceiling, the huge stone fireplace with a log-fire blazing, the women all lifting their glasses in a toast.

'To Dolly Rawlins. She's out.'

Dolly slowly moved from one woman to the next. Like a princess, she touched their shoulders or kissed their cheeks.

Ester drew out the carved chair at the head of the table. 'Sit down, Dolly. This is your night, one we won't let you forget.'

Dolly sat down, near to tears. Nothing had prepared her for this. She accepted a glass of champagne and lifted it. 'God bless us all.'

In the soft firelight with the flickering candles, they looked almost surreal: five women enjoying a celebration dinner. No one caught the strange glint behind the star guest's eyes because she was smiling, seemingly enjoying every precious moment. In reality she was waiting, knowing they wanted something, and she had a pretty good idea what it was. But she could wait. She was used to waiting.

The officers found it difficult to search the dark, poky little antique shop. There was a lot of junk and clutter to be moved aside and Donaldson had said the diamonds were hidden in a wall recess, but by ten o'clock they still had not been found. The men decided to call it quits for the night and to start again early the following morning.

Audrey was in her dressing gown when she opened the door to Mike. He beamed as he hugged her. 'Have I got news for you.'

She shut the door and waited impatiently.

'She's out, Mum, and, I know exactly where she is, and—'

Audrey sat on the settee as Mike gave her all the details about what had gone down that day, ending by clapping his hands together and laughing. 'Right now we got blokes searching for the diamonds, right? When they find them, we'll have Jimmy Donaldson wired up. If she calls, and she will, she'll go straight for them. We'll be ready and waiting. She's going to go right back inside, Mum, just what you wanted.'

Audrey had gone pale. 'You should have warned me, told me what you were doing.'

'How could I? It all happened today. It was such a bloody coincidence I couldn't believe it. First Angela—'

'You're not still messing around with that little tart, are you?'

'For chrissakes, Mum, she's very useful. Right now I know where Dolly Rawlins is, I know she can give us her every move. Then I got a tip-off about Jimmy Donaldson. It was beautiful, just beautiful, I got my governor jumping around. You know there was a reward for those stones and—'

'You got to stop this, Mike,' Audrey interrupted.

'Why? It's what you've been bleatin' on about for the past eight years, isn't it? Well, I'm going to have Dolly

Rawlins put back inside for that robbery. She's going to be copped for those diamonds.'

'No, she isn't, love.'

'What are you talking about?'

'The diamonds.'

'Yeah, we got blokes stripping Donaldson's place for them.'

'They won't find them.'

'Why not?'

'Because they're not there.'

'How do you know?'

'Because I took them.'

Mike's jaw dropped. He couldn't take it in.

Audrey started to cry. 'When I read about Jimmy being arrested, I . . . You see, he knew about them, so did I – she always said I'd get a cut.'

'Jesus Christ, I don't believe this.'

'So when I read he'd been picked up, I went round to his shop. I've known his wife for years and, well, she asked if I wanted a coffee, then she went round to a café to bring it back and I knew where he'd stashed them, so I took them.'

'You've got them?'

'No, I had them.'

'What the fuck have you done with them?'

'Sold them.'

Mike stood up. He was shaking. 'You sold them?'

Audrey took out a tissue and blew her nose. 'Yes. God help me, I didn't know what to do with them once I'd got them here and I was scared. I mean, they just sat there and I got more and more scared having that much stuff in the flat.'

Mike slumped into a chair, his head in his hands. 'Holy shit, you've really landed me in it. Who's got them now?'

Audrey twisted the tissue. 'Well, I couldn't really shop

around, could I? I knew this dealer, Frank Richmond, he's dodgy but I took them to him and he said he'd get what he could for them. But you know, they weren't easy because they were still hot. Well, that's what he said.'

'He paid you for them?'

'He give me four hundred and fifty grand.'

Mike leaned back, his eyes closed.

'They were worth millions, I knew it, but I wasn't gonna start pushing for more money, was I? I was desperate – I knew she'd be out, knew she'd go to Jimmy and then come here.'

Mike snapped to his feet. 'You've bullshitted me, haven't you? All that crap about Shirley, you've lied to me.'

'*No, I haven't!*'

'Yes, you bloody have. This wasn't for Shirley. It was for you, *you*, and now you got me caught up in it.'

Audrey sobbed as he paced up and down the room.

'Where's the money?'

'Well, some of it's in my bank, some's in a building society and the bulk of it's in Spain.'

'*Spain?*'

Audrey waited, and Mike wanted to shake or slap her, he didn't know which. 'Is that why you're going there?'

She sniffed. 'Yes. Wally Simmonds bought a villa for me.'

Mike gaped. 'A villa?'

She nodded. 'It was ever such a good buy and we did a cash deal. I'm leaving for good. I was gonna tell you when I'd sorted myself out.'

Mike swallowed. It was getting worse by the second. He could feel the floor shifting under his feet.

'What am I going to do, Mike?'

'I don't know.'

'Do you want a cup of tea?'

66

He turned on her in a fury. *'No, I bloody don't.* Just shut up and let me think this one out.'

She sat snuffling as he remained with his head in his hands. Eventually he asked flatly, 'Do you know anyone who could make us up some dud stones that'd look like the real things?'

Audrey licked her lips, hesitating, trying to think.

Mike continued, 'I could stash them at Donaldson's. It could still work but we'd only have a few hours, a day maybe, to get the stuff ready. Do you know anyone?'

'I'm sorry I've done this to you, love. Will you get into trouble?'

He stared at his mother. 'I could lose my fucking job – that good enough for you? Now, do you know anyone?'

Audrey chewed her lips then took out a worn address book from her handbag. 'There's Tommy Malin – he's probably the best – and if we said we'd pay cash for it he might do us a favour.'

'Us now, is it?'

'Well, I'll just do whatever you tell me to.' Her brain was a jumbled mess of her own screeching questions. Why, why had she been so stupid? Why had she done it? Was it because she just wanted to get back at Dolly? Was that it? As dumb as Audrey sounded, there was another element: greed. She wanted money. She had always wanted it but it had always been out of her reach. When she read about Jimmy's arrest, she had believed all the waiting was for nothing and it was her fury at being cheated that pushed her into getting the diamonds. She had not contemplated how deeply she would bring her son into it all. Somehow she had thought he'd just arrest the bitch and put her away, or out of reach, because Audrey was scared. She had always been scared of Dolly Rawlins.

'I'm so scared of her, Mike. I know she'll come after me.

She won't understand – like, the fear I had with them stones in the flat and then—'

She started to cry again, and Mike sighed. 'Mum, you're in it, whatever excuses you make. Gimme the address book. I'll call this fence bloke but I can only do so much. Then I gotta walk away from it – from you if necessary.'

They had all had a considerable amount to drink: champagne, white and red wine. The booze had eased the tension and now they all talked freely. Kathleen, well away, was going into an elaborate story about how she found her ex-husband in bed with a lodger and how she'd locked him in a coal-hole. Connie was drawing the details of her plastic surgery operations on a paper napkin. Gloria was having a heated argument with Julia about body fat. Their voices were like music to Dolly. She didn't listen to whatever anyone was saying: it was the freedom, the roaring laughs, and the relaxed atmosphere. Ester did not drink as much as the others but watched Dolly throughout, noting how often her glass was refilled, biding her time to choose the right moment to open up the conversation about Dolly's future arrangements.

Angela carried in a tray and said that coffee and liqueurs were now served in the drawing room.

Ester saw Dolly stumble slightly as she pushed back her chair. She was obviously enjoying herself and even took hold of Gloria's hand as they wove their way into the drawing room, where there were more candles and another big blazing fire, the perfumed incense disguising the damp smell, the gentle light hiding the darkened patches on the wallpaper and the holed curtains half off their rails. The room was comfortable and friendly, the glasses of port and brandy handed round liberally.

Julia whispered to Ester to keep her eye on Kathleen as she was well pissed and now thumping out a song on the piano, having a ball, almost forgetting why she was there. Julia passed out the drinks, as Gloria picked up the box of After Eight mints. 'Here you go, Dolly love. Have a mint and tell us what you're gonna be up to now you're out?'

Ester edged closer, wanting Gloria to shut up. Not the most subtle of women, Gloria now plunged right in. 'So you got yourself a nice nest egg, have you, Dolly?'

Dolly laughed as she sipped her brandy. 'I might have.'

'Eh, I bet that old man left you a few quid, didn't he?' Gloria continued, and then shut up as Ester stood firmly on her foot.

'He left me comfortable,' Dolly said, and moved towards the mantelpiece. Then she turned to face them all as Kathleen staggered away from the piano stool to slump into a big winged chair. 'So, why don't you all come clean? What you all after?' Dolly said it softly but there was an edge to her voice.

Ester played it beautifully. 'After? What's that supposed to mean?'

'Well, this is all very nice but none of us were what you would call friends. So I just wondered what you wanted.'

Ester stood up, a furious look on her face. 'Oh, thanks a lot, Dolly. We all worked our butts off today to get this place ready for you. You think we did it for what? What you got that any of us would want? We did it, I arranged it, because in the nick you belted that cow Barbara Hunter. I admired that, we all admired that, but if you think we've all come here for some ulterior motive, then screw you. We only wanted you to come out to friends, to have one night to find your feet.' She marched angrily towards the door as if about to make an exit.

'I'm sorry,' Dolly said quietly.

69

'So you bloody should be. I know it's hard to trust people inside but we're not inside. We're all out. All we wanted was to give you a bit of a party.'

'I said I'm sorry. Come on, sit down.'

Ester gave a tiny wink to Julia as she grudgingly sat on the arm of the easy chair, close to Gloria so she could control her.

Dolly turned towards the fire. 'Truth is, I do have a few quid put by.'

A low murmur from them all, and sly glances flicked between them.

'Well, that's good to know,' said Connie. 'I hope you have a good and successful future.'

They all raised their glasses and toasted Dolly yet again.

'So how much you got, then?' asked Gloria, and got a dig in the ribs from Ester.

'It's not a fortune but . . . I'm all right, comfortable.'

They waited with bated breath as Dolly drained her glass and replaced it on the tray. 'I'm going to tell you something.'

They leaned forward slightly, listening attentively, hoping she was now about to say 'diamonds'.

'For eight years, I've been sort of planning it, in my head. It's my dream, my future.'

A row of faces waited.

'I want to put back something into society, might sound crazy, but I really want to make something of the rest of my life.'

No one spoke. They felt a trifle uneasy, though – she was coming on like something from *The Sound of Music*.

Dolly took a deep breath. 'I want to buy a house and I want to open it up as a home, a foster home for kids, battered wives, a home run by me, for all those less fortunate than me.'

None of them could speak. They looked at Dolly as if she had two heads. She had taken the carpet from beneath every one of them.

Tommy Malin agreed that he could make up a bag of fake stones, using some real settings and some fake ones. He could do it for two grand cash and have it ready by the following afternoon. Mike tried to push him to have them done by the following morning but he refused, saying if they wanted the stuff to look good, really good, he would need that time. He'd have to shop around for some good cut-glass fakes, maybe throw in a couple of zircons, but he needed that much time. Mike agreed and said Audrey would collect them as soon as he called to say they were ready.

By the time Mike got home he was worn to a frazzle and it was after twelve. Susan heard the front door shut and turned over to her side of the bed, not wanting to speak to him or confront him. She was sure he had another woman and it was breaking her heart.

Mike cleaned his teeth. His eyes were red-rimmed, his face chalk white; he was in it up to his neck and he just hoped he would be able to get away with what he was doing. He had to find some way of stashing the fakes in Jimmy Donaldson's place. He splashed cold water over his face, patting it dry, half hoping that Dolly Rawlins would never make contact about the bloody diamonds.

Susan heard him undressing and then he got into bed beside her, turning his back towards her. Neither said a word, Susan because she was sure he was cheating on her,

Mike hearing his own heart thudding as he went over the mess he had got himself caught up in. Whatever excuses he tried to make for Audrey, or she had made to him, didn't alter the fact she had trapped him into the world he had tried so hard to walk away from all his life. Shirley had been well caught up in it and he knew it, together with her husband and the subsequent robbery, but nothing he could have thought up or dreamed in his worst nightmares would measure up to the reality that Shirley had been shot. He found himself, like his mother, making excuses and eventually laying the blame on Dolly Rawlins. If he could get her put away, it would, he told himself, get them all out of trouble. And he was even able to tell himself that she deserved everything she got or anything he could have her framed and done for.

Ester had a mink coat slung round her shoulders and Dolly wore Gloria's fluffy wrap as they walked towards the stables. 'I mean, look at this place, Dolly. You could have ten, twelve kids here, get a horse even. And there's a swimming pool, needs a bit of work, the whole house does, but it's crying out for kids. It'd be a perfect place.'

Dolly looked back at the vast house. 'I dunno, Ester. I was sort of thinking about a small terraced job, near Holloway.'

'No. This is much better. Country air, grounds, and it'd be cheaper than any terraced house. I'll even throw in all the linen, crockery and furniture. You can have the lot for two hundred grand. I've even got surveyors' reports. It's on the market right now but if it's out of your league then . . .'

Dolly considered. It wasn't out of her league – in fact it was smack in it: she'd got about two hundred and fifty grand to be exact but after shelling out here and there it'd be around the two hundred mark.

They walked on round the stables to the front of the house, Ester pointing over towards the swimming pool. 'There's an orchard, vegetable patch. You could grow your own veg, be self-sufficient. It's a dream place for kids, Dolly.'

Dolly sighed. 'I dunno, Ester, it's an awfully big house.'

'All the better. And we can all give you a hand, stay on and work it up for you, get the place shipshape. Hell, none of us have got anythin' better going for us. We'd be your helpers, it's a brilliant idea.'

The women watched from the slit in the curtains. Kathleen turned away. 'Home for battered wives! She's out of her mind. I've been one most of me life and I'm not about to start livin' with a bunch of them. She's got a screw loose.'

Gloria kicked at the dying embers of the fire. 'Well, I'm pissed off. I think this was all Ester was after from the start. She wanted us to break our backs cleaning the fuckin' place up so she can flog it to Dolly. That's what she got us here for – she's used the lot of us to sell this bleedin' place.'

Julia poured another brandy and swirled it in her glass. 'No, she hasn't, she's being clever.'

'You can say that again. We all done it up and she's the only one that's gonna make any dough out of it.'

Connie joined in. 'I didn't even know she was selling this place, she never told me. I mean, is this why she's got us here?'

'You really are dumb, all of you, aren't you?' Julia shook her head. 'You heard Dolly say she's got two hundred grand. Well, this place will swallow that right away so where's she going to get the money to get this place up and running as a kids' home?' She drained her glass. 'She'll have to go for those diamonds. Ester knows it. Can't you see what she's doing? She's creaming her, you stupid cows.'

Gloria frowned. 'So when she's laid out the cash for this dump, you think she's going to go for those diamonds?'

'What do you think she'll go for?'

They looked at each other and then Kathleen yawned. 'Well, in that case I'm staying on.'

They all agreed to stay on and wait – wait for Dolly to go for the diamonds.

Ester showed Dolly all the estate agents', valuers' and solicitors' letters, all the old surveys of the manor house. It had been on the market for over two hundred and fifty thousand. She offered it to Dolly for two hundred.

'That wipes me out, Ester.'

Ester felt her belly tighten: she'd guessed right. It tickled her that she could always suss out people's cash-flow. It came with dealing for the girls, pushing the punters to the limit. She gave a wide smile. 'But you'll get big grants for the kids.'

Dolly looked over the documents again. 'I dunno, Ester. What if the others won't stay on? I can't run this place on my own.'

'All the better. And listen, none of them have got a place to go. They'll stay on, believe you me. And then we got Julia, she's a doctor, you got a strong group behind you.'

Dolly was still unsure.

'Look don't do anything right away, think about it, take your time. If you're not interested, fine, I'll sell it to someone else. No skin off my back, think about it . . .'

74

Dolly suddenly took out her cheque book. 'You're on. Here, I'll give you a cheque right now.'

'Now don't do anything you're going to be sorry for. Maybe you should sleep on it. I don't want you thinking I bamboozled you into this. It's your choice. The only thing that might be a problem is the other offer that I got but it can wait at least until tomorrow.'

Dolly wrote out the cheque there and then, still heady from the wine. She insisted Ester take it and she did, fast, and pocketed it.

'You got a telephone here?'

'Course. You called in, remember?' smiled Ester.

Ester slipped out of the kitchen, leaving Dolly looking over the papers. The women had all gone up to bed, the fires were dead, the candles burnt out. She went upstairs, to her bedroom, closed the door silently and crept to the bed. She leaned over Julia and showed her the cheque. 'I'll put this in the bank first thing tomorrow before the old cow changes her mind.'

Julia took the cheque from Ester to look at it for herself.

'Bet you any money she'll go for those diamonds. She's got to when she sees how much this place needs pouring into it. She'll be desperate.'

Julia leaned back. 'She might change her mind.'

Ester shook her head. 'No, she won't, because we're going to work that woman over, every one of us. We make her believe we love this place, want the home to be up and running. We all egg her on and keep it going until she . . .'

'Goes for the diamonds.'

Ester smiled. 'Right, and then . . .' She made a plucking motion with her fingers. 'We take them, and then, Julia, we're free, we're rich.'

Julia stared at the cheque for two hundred thousand pounds. 'You could do okay on this.'

Ester sighed. 'Yeah, but do you think I could cash it? I got debts that'd eat up more than two hundred grand.'

'What if she doesn't want to share with you, with any of us?'

'Like I said, we take them. I don't give a shit about the others, we're using them as well. All I care about are those diamonds, two, three million quid's worth, Julia, and I'm going to have them.'

'I love you when you're like this,' Julia whispered.

'Like what?'

'Cruel. Come to bed.'

Ester gave a soft sexy laugh as she crawled towards Julia and then froze, slithered from the bed to listen at the door.

Dolly stood in the marbled hall, the phone in her hand. 'Jimmy, is that you?'

Jimmy Donaldson was in his pyjamas, his hand shaking, as DI Palmer gestured for him to keep talking.

'Yes, this is Jimmy Donaldson. Who's this? You know what time it is?'

'Oh, I'm sorry to ring so late. It's Dolly, Dolly Rawlins.'

Palmer leaned forward, hardly able to contain himself. It was going down even faster than any one of them had thought. Mike Withey had been right. Dolly Rawlins was going for the diamonds. Again he gestured for Donaldson to keep talking.

'I need to see you,' Dolly said softly. 'Tomorrow. I'm out, Jimmy. Have you got my things for me?'

'Yes, yes, I've got them.'

'Well, what say we meet up tomorrow, about noon?'

Jimmy looked to Palmer. They still didn't have the stones but he reckoned they would by the following day. He wrote on a note-pad. Jimmy nodded. 'Can you make it later – like late afternoon?'

'They are safe, aren't they, Jimmy?'

'Yes, of course.'

'Fine, I'll call you tomorrow, then.'

Dolly hung up.

Donaldson looked at Palmer. 'She's gonna call me tomorrow. She hung up before I could say anythin' different.'

Frowning, Palmer drummed his fingers on the telephone table. 'We better find those diamonds, Jimmy. You sure they're where you said they are?'

'If they're not some bastard's nicked them.'

Palmer jerked his head for Donaldson to return to his bed. He checked the time and replayed the message. Dolly Rawlins had carefully not said the word diamonds but she certainly hadn't wasted much time. She'd only been released that afternoon. She was out all right.

CHAPTER 4

DOLLY WOKE with a start, unable for a moment to orientate herself, and it scared her. Her heart thudded, she started to pant, then to talk herself down. It was the sound of birds, ravens cawing from the woods, an alien sound, one she had not heard for a long, long time.

The curtain was drawn and the fast recall of the evening made her feel good until she looked out of her window. 'Holy shit.' Now she took in the derelict gardens, the dank, dark pool-side. 'Oh, my God, what have you got yourself into, gel?'

She was used to rising at six and she listened at her door, could hear no sound of movement so she went out on to the landing. In the cold light of morning, she moved silently round the old manor, peeking into each unoccupied room, from the attic to the ground floor, her heart sinking at every level as the realization dawned of what she had let herself in for. The place was a monster, not only in proportion but the run-down state of the house was obvious, from the peeling wallpaper to the cracked ceilings and crumbling woodwork. The banister rail was fine, thick mahogany, but many of the pegs were missing and the carpets worn and dangerous on the old wide stairs. The smell of mould, damp and mildew made her nostrils flare but she kept on moving from room to room until she entered the old kitchen, easing back the bolts from the back door to walk outside into the stable-yard.

She had inspected the pool, the woods and the run-down orchard, the vegetable garden that was a wild, overgrown mess of brambles and throttling weeds. She had muddied her shoes, her legs were scratched from the brambles, the hem of her coat sodden, before she eventually returned to the kitchen. No one was up so she put on the kettle, working out how to use the big lidded Aga, fetching a mug and making a cup of tea, her mind working overtime.

The house was a dog, she knew that – any fool could feel it – but she couldn't help liking it. Was she really prepared to take it on? She knew she'd given Ester a cheque but that could always be stopped. Dolly sat with her hands cupping the chipped mug. The place could certainly accommodate at least ten, fifteen kids with ease; there were enough rooms and she hadn't even been down to the basement. She went over all the old deeds and survey reports, all a few years out of date. She started to calculate on the back of an envelope just how much money it would take to get a place this size back into order. All her cash would go with the one cheque to Ester so it would mean she was dependent on the sale of the diamonds. If they had been valued at two million all those years ago, she reckoned they'd be worth maybe three and a half to four now. If she fenced them, she'd probably clear maybe one and a half million cash. The house would need a hell of a lot of money spent on it but just how much she would have to check into. From the plumbing to the decoration, she began to list all the blatantly obvious requirements. The project was much bigger than she had dreamed of but if it was fate, then maybe it was meant for her to take on such a giant enterprise. She could use ex-prisoners to help her, perhaps even the women from last night.

Dolly spent over an hour making notes and working out costs and then went down to the basement. There were saunas, steam cabinets, an old gym and a large laundry room. None of the machines appeared to be in working order and the stench of damp was even worse down there. She looked over the old boilers and knew they'd all have to be replaced. She began to doubt seriously that she would take on the project because the more she calculated, the more money she knew she would have to raise.

By the time she returned to the kitchen, Gloria was up and Ester and Julia were washing dishes in the big stone sink. Angela was clearing the debris in the dining room and passed Dolly carrying a tray filled with dirty glasses. 'Good morning, you're up bright and early, Mrs Rawlins.'

Dolly gave a brittle smile. 'Yes. Is everyone else up yet?'

'No, not yet. Do you want breakfast?'

'Yes.'

'Eggs and bacon coming up.'

Dolly opened the front door to look down the big wide drive.

'Good morning, Dolly.' Connie beamed, wrapping a silk kimono round herself.

Dolly turned round as Kathleen appeared. 'My God, I've got a hell of a headache. How about you, Dolly?'

The relaxed atmosphere of the women coming and going made Dolly feel good – or better. 'Get some coffee down you,' she said to Kathleen, and then walked behind the old reception desk to look for a telephone directory. The shelves were dusty and old circulars had been stuffed beneath the desk so she rummaged around.

Ester appeared at the kitchen door. 'Hi, good morning. You looking for something?'

'Directories.'

Ester wandered to the desk. 'Be out of date, get the operator. Who are you calling?'

Dolly sighed. 'Well, I should have a word with the local social services, just to see about the possibilities of opening this place up as a home.'

'You don't waste much time, do you?'

'Nor do you, Ester. You certainly hustled me into this place.'

'What? Look, it was up to you, love. I mean, I'm not forcing you into anything you don't want to do.'

Dolly raised an eyebrow. 'Fine, just don't bank the cheque yet. I'm not too sure about this.'

Ester moved into action, instructing the women to get the breakfast on the table and to look as if they loved the place. By the time Dolly joined them, the kitchen was filled with the smell of sizzling bacon and eggs, hot toast and coffee, all laid out ready and waiting. Their smiling faces greeted Dolly warmly as she sat down.

'I been all round the grounds. Place is in a terrible state.'

'Get a few locals to clear the gardens. It used to be beautiful, in the summer especially.' Ester continued to sell the manor, hinting time and again what a wonderful place it would be for children.

Angela gave Dolly the number for the social services but it was almost nine thirty when Dolly put in a call and arranged for a meeting at the town hall. She was still unsure and not giving much away. She had only the few things she had brought with her so she would need to do some shopping. Good opportunity to see what the local village was like.

The other women looked at Ester to know what they should or shouldn't do, exchanging furtive glances and nudges. As soon as Dolly was out of earshot, they whispered questions to each other: Was Dolly serious? How long was she going to keep them all waiting? When would she go for the diamonds? Ester hissed at them to keep their mouths shut, no one was to mention diamonds.

'Yeah, well, that's why we're all here, Ester, and so far she's not said a dickie about them. All that's gone down is you're two hundred grand up. What if they don't exist?' Gloria was irritable.

'They exist,' snapped Ester. She crossed the kitchen and looked out into the hallway, drawing the door shut. 'Make her think we're all behind the project, right? Offer to stay and help out, start clearing the place up. She's gonna need hard cash to get this place up and rolling so we watch her like a hawk and—'

Dolly called from the stairs, asking if the boiler was working as she wanted to have a bath before she left. Ester opened the door and shouted that the water was on and hot. She waited until she could hear the thud of the old pipes before she went to give the women more instructions. She then paid off Angela and said that when they went into the village she could catch the next train home.

'I got to go and see Eddie,' Gloria said tetchily.

'Fine, you go,' said Ester.

'I need my gear.' Connie pouted.

Ester sighed. 'Look, all do what you have to but, whatever you do, keep your mouths shut about being here. You don't say a word to anyone about us being holed up here and especially not about the diamonds. Is that clear?'

By eleven they were all waiting for Dolly, Ester out in the yard in her Range Rover. Julia was looking into the stables. 'You know, this place must have been something,' she said.

'It was. What the hell is she doing in there?'

Ester paced up and down, impatient to go into the village to bank the cheque.

Julia came close. 'You going to be okay?'

Ester nodded. 'Yeah. Nobody knows I'm here and besides, I got to bank the cheque to get her the deeds of the house.'

Julia cocked her head to one side. 'Well, you take care.'

Gloria teetered out with Connie behind her. 'I'm off, see Eddie. I'm givin' Connie a lift in. Can you take us to the garage see if me car's ready?'

Connie put her bag into the back of the Range Rover. 'I won't even see Lennie. He always leaves by twelve so I'll just get my stuff and come straight back.'

Kathleen wandered out. 'Where you all going?'

Ester sighed. 'Into the village. Where's Dolly?'

'She's on the phone, the social services again, asking what they want her to bring in. I dunno.'

'Are you stopping, then?' Ester demanded.

'Yeah, I got nowhere else to go, have I?' muttered Kathleen.

Angela joined them, followed by Dolly, so they all squashed into the Range Rover and departed, leaving Kathleen alone.

'I'll need builders' estimates, see how much the place will cost to get into order,' Dolly said, as they bounced down the lane. 'Get these pot-holes filled in,' she said, staring out of the window. She looked back at the house. 'I don't know about this, Ester, I mean . . .'

Ester pulled on the brake. 'Dolly, look at the place. Take a good look. It's crying out for kids, isn't it?'

A dull chorus of, 'Oh, yes, kids'll love it here.'

Gloria's car wasn't ready so Connie and Angela were dropped off at the local railway station. Ester took Dolly on to the Aylesbury town hall. 'I'll wait here for you.' She smiled.

Dolly nodded but seemed ill at ease. 'I'll just see what they say. I shouldn't be too long, then I'll need to do a bit of shopping, tights and stuff like that.'

As soon as she walked into the town hall, Ester drove straight to the bank. She kept a good look-out for anyone following her and hurried inside.

Dolly waited in the anteroom and eventually a pleasant-faced woman called Deirdre Bull asked if she would come into her office. Dolly was offered a seat and coffee, as Deirdre sat down behind her cluttered desk. The walls were lined with posters for foster carers and adoption societies.

'Now, it's Mrs Rawlins, isn't it?'

'Yes, Dorothy Rawlins. I've come to ask you about opening a foster home. I've done a bit of research with a probation officer but I thought I'd just run a few things by you.'

Deirdre nodded and began opening drawers. 'First there are some forms you'll need to look over and fill in. Have you ever been a foster carer before?'

'No, I haven't, but I'm buying a big house and I could accommodate up to ten or twelve kids easily.'

Deirdre was so relaxed and friendly that Dolly began to

ease up, as Deirdre patiently passed her one form after another to look over.

'Are you married?'

'I'm a widow.'

Deirdre nodded, not really listening, just passing leaflets across the desk.

'Do you have children?'

'No, but I have worked with a lot of babies recently, and I have some letters from . . .'

Ester handed the cheque to the cashier. Impatient, her eyes on the clock, she'd had to stand in a queue for ten minutes. The cashier's pace was slow, steady, which Ester found infuriating. He looked first at the cheque, then at Ester's paying-in slip.

'There's nothing wrong, is there?' Ester asked sharply, leaning closer into the counter. 'I'm in rather a hurry and I have someone waiting.'

The cashier peered at Ester. 'It's Miss Freeman, isn't it? Could you wait one moment?'

'Why? All I want are the documents I've listed. Can't you just get them for me? I'm in a hurry.'

'The manager will need to speak to you, Miss Freeman,' the cashier said pleasantly.

'But there's nothing wrong with the cheque, is there?'

'No, not that I can see, but he will need to talk to you. Your account has been frozen.'

'I know that,' Ester retorted. It was hard for her not to know just what her financial situation was. She was in debt up to her eyeballs, tax inspectors breathing down her neck, and the only asset she had was the manor – and that was frozen like her accounts. Ester had no way of getting any cash without Dolly, and it hurt to hand over the cheque.

She tried a different approach. 'I just want the deeds to Grange Manor House.' She gave a soft smile. 'I have a cash buyer and surely it's worth considering that part of the overdraft could be paid off. If the bank tried to sell the house, they'd not get as good a price. And I'm sure I'll be able to cover any further outstanding debts within a few weeks.'

It sounded good. She just hoped the little prick would see it made sense and she knew he had when he looked up and gave her a tight nod: he was going to release the deeds of the house. He excused himself and left Ester waiting. She checked her watch again, willing him to move his arse because she didn't want to miss Dolly.

Deirdre looked at Dolly's neat handwriting on the forms, and showed not a flicker when she read that she had only just been released from prison.

'The house is well situated, with gardens and a swimming pool. It will need a lot of work and I don't know how I apply for grants and allowances – or if I am acceptable as a foster carer.'

Deirdre nodded. 'Well, you'll have to go before a board of committee members – I can't say whether or not you'll be acceptable, Mrs Rawlins. All this takes considerable time and your property will have to be reviewed and assessed by the committee.'

'But you don't think it's out of the question?'

'I can't say. If you like, I can ask Mrs Tilly, who is my superior, to come and talk to you.'

Dolly leaned closer. 'I would be grateful if you would. I don't want to go ahead with the house if I don't stand a chance with my application – if my background goes against me, you understand?'

Deirdre smiled warmly. 'Mrs Rawlins, there are so many children in need. Obviously your background will be taken into consideration but, that said, there are so many ways we can approach the board. If you can give me ten minutes I'll go up and have a word with Mrs Tilly, see if she can tell you the best way to approach it. But I would think positively if you have a substantial property and the means to open a home.'

'I'll wait,' Dolly said, becoming more confident by the second. She had finances, she would be able to make the manor house look like a palace. As soon as the door closed behind Deirdre, Dolly inched round the desk and drew the telephone closer. She looked to the door a moment before she dialled.

Jimmy Donaldson was sitting with a mug of tea. It was almost twelve and there had not been any further contact from Rawlins. DI Palmer was sitting reading the morning paper. He also had a tea and chocolate biscuits. In the hall another officer sat on duty and had even opened the door earlier for Mrs Donaldson to cook breakfast. She was confused as to what was going on, especially as she had had little time alone with her husband. Even when they slept, an officer sat outside their bedroom. Jimmy was nervous and twitchy, and had said that whatever was going down meant that he'd be home for good sooner than they had anticipated. She was asked to speak to no one, to remain at home and continue her housework as if they weren't there, so she was preparing lunch in the kitchen.

The phone rang and she turned from the sink. The door was closed, the officer in the hallway giving her a pleasant smile. Palmer on the other hand gave a brisk nod for

Donaldson to pick up the phone as he slipped on his headphones to listen to the call.

'Jimmy? It's Dolly.'

He looked nervously at Palmer who gestured for him to continue the call.

'Hello, Dolly. How are you?'

'I'm fine. I'd like to collect.'

Palmer nodded and Donaldson hesitated. 'Okay. When do you want to come over?'

'I won't come to your place, you bring them to me. You know Thorpe Park?'

'What?'

'It's a big amusement park. About four o'clock this afternoon. I'll see you there.'

She hung up before Donaldson could reply. He sat looking at the receiver in his hand. Palmer swore, told him to hang up and then put a trace on the call.

'Have they found them yet?' Donaldson asked.

Palmer said nothing as he waited for the trace to give the location of where Dolly had called from. DCI Craigh came in as Palmer was jotting something down. He passed it to Craigh. 'She made contact from Aylesbury town hall, social services.' Craigh took the memo. 'She's asked for a meet. You want to hear the call?'

Craigh nodded, his face uptight. 'She's moving fast, isn't she? What the hell is she doing at the town hall?' When he heard where Dolly wanted to meet Donaldson, he swore and gestured for Palmer to come out for a private chat. 'We've still not traced the stones, they're ripping his entire shop apart.'

'Shit.'

'Yeah, well, we'll just have to stall her, or Jimmy will.'

Palmer looked back to the closed door. 'You think he's

spinnin' yarns? If we've not found the ruddy diamonds maybe they're not there and he's playin' silly buggers.'

Craigh sighed. This wasn't working out the way he'd hoped. Now they'd have to drag Donaldson out to Thorpe Park, which would mean even more officers assigned to the case and his super had only given the go-ahead because, as Craigh had said, it would be fast. As soon as she contacted them, they thought they'd have her. Well, she'd contacted faster than they'd anticipated and now they were screwed if they didn't find the stones by four o'clock.

'Look, see if you can get his wife shipped out – to a relative. I don't like her being around. And meanwhile I'll go and see what I can work up for the four o'clock meet. Why Thorpe Park?'

Palmer shrugged. 'I dunno. She said it, then hung up.'

Tommy Malin worked until late the previous night and went straight back to it in the morning. He reset the stones one by one and he was a true professional: they looked good. He used a lot of settings from a previous little job he'd done, only then they had contained some beautiful emeralds and diamonds. Usually he melted down settings, anything that could cause aggravation. He had never, that he could remember, been asked to make up a whole bag of glass but far be it from him not to earn an easy two grand cash. He had some business to attend to at lunch-time. Audrey called to ask if they were ready and he said they'd be finished later on in the afternoon.

'They're not ready yet,' Audrey said to her son, as he paced up and down the living room. 'Has she called? Do you know if she's talked to Jimmy yet?'

'No, I'm going over there now. I'll come back later and pick them up. And for chrissakes don't tell anyone about this.'

'Who'd I tell?'

Mike stared at her, his anger at what she had got him involved with still close to the surface. 'Just get the stones, Mum, and as soon as you've got them, call me on my bleeper.'

Mike slammed out of the flat and hurried to his patrol car as his bleeper went. By the time he'd called in, he was instructed to meet DCI Craigh at the station and not, as he had previously been told, at Donaldson's house.

Mrs Tilly looked over Dolly's forms. She then stacked them in a neat pile. 'Well, I think you stand a good chance but you'll have to be interviewed by the board and have your details assessed. Until such time, I wouldn't do too much structural work on the house because we will have to view the property to make sure it meets our requirements. It will take time for us to give you a positive answer and you'll obviously require grants, which is another area you'll need to be instructed in as there are so many different sections and application forms.'

Dolly was feeling good, her dream already shaping into reality and so fast it took her breath away. Mrs Tilly frowned as she re-read the top form.

'Grange Manor House? It had a bad reputation, you know.'

Dolly looked confused. 'I'm sorry? I don't understand. It was a health farm, wasn't it?'

'It used to belong to an Ester Freeman. Oh, I'm going back maybe three or four years. It's been closed – I thought it had been demolished, to tell you the truth, not just because the motorway was built across the main access, but because it was such a scandal—'

'I'm sorry, I don't know what you're referring to,' Dolly interrupted.

'Grange Manor House was run as a brothel. The police raided it and arrested, oh, fourteen women, I think. It was run by Ester Freeman. I think she went to prison.' Suddenly Mrs Tilly flushed. 'Did you buy it from Miss Freeman?'

'No I did not,' Dolly lied, her hands clenched tightly. 'Thank you for all your help.' She managed to keep a smile on her face but she was so angry she could have screamed. This was all she needed. Trying to open a foster home as an ex-prisoner was one hurdle to get over, but now she knew that the place had been run as a brothel any association with Ester would obviously go against her.

Dolly stormed out of the town hall. Ester was not waiting as she had promised. She forced herself to remain calm. She'd get out of this, and fast. She'd do a bit of shopping, get the next train to London, collect the diamonds and do just as she had planned to do: buy a small terraced house near Holloway and screw that bitch Ester Freeman.

Ester faced the bank manager, a small, dapper little man with a faint blond moustache. He shuffled Ester's thick file of documents. The cheque from Mrs Rawlins, he assured Ester, was or would be cleared as he had already contacted Mrs Rawlins's bank, but this still left Ester three hundred thousand pounds in debt. She would be declared bankrupt unless she had means to cover the outstanding balance.

'But I've just paid in a cheque for two hundred thousand.'

The manager nodded, over-patient. 'Yes, I know, Miss Freeman, but the bank are holding the house as collateral for the outstanding monies. I cannot release the property deeds.'

'Fine. Then I have to take that cheque out. The money is for the sale of the manor and you know that it won't get that price on the market. You sell it and the bank'll lose out. This way, at least I've paid off some of it and I give you my word you'll get the rest within a few weeks.'

He sighed. What she was saying made sense. 'So, Miss Freeman, is this cheque from Mrs Rawlins for the sale of the property?'

'Yes. That's why I got to have the deeds returned to me. If you refuse, there will be no sale. You then have to put it on the market and—'

He interrupted, drawing back his chair, 'I will, however, have to wait for the cheque to be cleared, Miss Freeman.'

She swore under her breath and asked if he could at least give her copies so she could pass them on to the buyer, then as soon as the cheque was cleared, the originals could be sent to the new owner, Mrs Rawlins.

'That still leaves your balance over three hundred thousand pounds in the red, Miss Freeman, and unless this situation is rectified then we have no alternative but to begin proceedings against you.'

She leaned on his desk. 'Give me just one more month – you'll get the money. I am waiting to be paid a considerable amount, more than enough to cover my overdraft.'

Ester would have liked to scream at him 'Try three million quid's worth of diamonds, you fuckin' little prat', but instead she smiled sweetly as he sighed and flipped through her bank statements.

'Well, we'll give it three weeks, Miss Freeman, but then—'

'You'll get me the deeds? Yes?'

He nodded. 'Yes. I'm prepared to trust you, Miss Freeman.'

'You won't regret it,' she said softly, having no intention whatsoever of paying in another penny, not from the diamonds, not from anything. She was going to skip the country and fast, just as soon as she laid her hands on Dolly Rawlins's diamonds.

Mike met up with DCI Craigh in the station corridor. 'She only called from the Aylesbury social services and you won't believe where she's asked Donaldson to meet her.'

'Oh, they find the diamonds?' Mike asked innocently, knowing it was an impossibility.

Craigh shook his head. 'I'm gonna need extra men, sort this out at the bloody theme park, and we'll get Donaldson wired up. He'll just have to stall her or get her to implicate herself. I'm beginning to wish we'd never started it in the first place.'

Craigh had no idea just how much Mike wished he had never mentioned Dolly Rawlins's name, let alone the diamonds.

Gloria eased her way round the visitor tables, crowded with the wives and mothers, girlfriends, kids. It never ceased to amaze her how many women were always there every visiting day. Never as many men as women – they were all banged up like her old man.

Eddie Radford was staring at his folded hands, a glum expression on his Elvis Presley features. Eight years younger than Gloria, he'd never even bought an Elvis record but she had. She'd been a great fan and the first time she'd set eyes on Eddie she'd seen the similarity, with his thick black hair. If he'd had sideburns he'd have looked even more like Elvis.

'You're bleedin' late,' he muttered angrily.

'Well, the back end of the van went, then I hadda get a train, missed the tube, waited fifteen minutes.'

'Oh shuddup. Every time you come I got to listen to a bleedin' travelogue of how you got here. You get me some fags?'

'Yes.'

'Books? Any cash?'

'Yeah, in me left sleeve, can you feel it?'

Eddie leaned over and kissed her as he slipped his hand up her sleeve and palmed the money. 'How much?'

'Sixty quid, and that's cleaned me out. I got to pick up me giro.'

'Where've you been? I called the house three times.' Eddie opened the cigarettes and lit one, looking around the room at the men and their visitors. The racket was mind-blowing.

'The council have given me marching orders for non-payment of rent.'

'Oh, great! What you let them do that for?'

'Could be because I've not got any cash and that Mrs Rheece downstairs is a bloody zombie. She let them in, found that bloke kipping down and so they said I was sublettin'.'

'What bloke?'

'You know, him with the squint, friend of your brother's. I asked him to leave an' all but he still stayed on. Pain in the arse, he is.'

'So where've you been stayin'?'

'I'm in Aylesbury, with some friends. You don't know them, Eddie. I wish you wouldn't grill me every time I come, it gets on my nerves.'

'Who you staying with in Aylesbury then?'

She sighed. 'Ester Freeman, you don't know her. She did time with me. Julia Lawson, she was also in Holloway, Kathleen O'Reilly, a stupid cow called Connie and—'

'Ester Freeman? They all tarts then, are they?'

'No, they're not. Dolly Rawlins, she's there.'

'Oh yeah, Dolly Rawlins, yeah, I remember Harry. So what you all there for?'

'For God's sake, I needed a place to doss down, all right? So we're all sort of helping Dolly out until—'

'Until what?'

Gloria flushed. 'I always get a headache in here. They should keep the kids to another section.'

Eddie reached out and gripped her wrist. 'I said, *what are you doing there*?'

She wrenched her wrist free and rubbed it. 'Word is, she's got some diamonds stashed and we're, well, we're waiting for her to get them.'

'And then what?'

She smiled. 'Well, we want a cut and if she doesn't like it, we're gonna take it. But you keep your mouth shut about it.'

'Who would I tell?' he said bitterly.

She touched his hand. 'You'll have some nice things, I'll get you anything you want, Eddie.'

He eased his hand away. 'Who's looking after my guns?'

Gloria looked round nervously, then leaned close to whisper, 'They're still out in the coal hut, I ain't touched them.'

Eddie closed his eyes. 'Brilliant! You're not even at the fuckin' house, that idiot bloke is hanging around and I got thirty grand's worth of gear stashed out back. You fuckin' out of your mind, Gloria?'

'I don't want anythin' to do with them. I get picked up

95

again and that's me for ten years, Eddie. I told you I don't want to know about them, it's too dangerous.'

Eddie stared at her, shaking his head slowly. 'I don't believe you, Gloria, I don't.'

She sat back. 'Ah, Eddie, it's too dangerous, you know it is.'

'You listen to me, slag, you move them out of that place. I'll get you a decent contact, you'll flog them when I say so, understand me? You move them, you do that, Gloria. Get the gear, stash it where you're staying with all the tarts, then I'll get my friends to contact you. Gimme the number there.'

'I can't, the phone's not connected, Eddie, on my mother's life.'

Her mother had been dead since she was twelve but Eddie seemed to believe her, even though he also knew her old lady was six feet under. He swore and then the bell rang for the first section of visitors to move out. He gripped her hand tightly. 'Get them. Then next time you come I'll arrange for you to meet someone. You do it, Gloria, they're all I got left in the world, them and you, so I'm depending on you, understand me? I depend on you, Gloria.'

She nodded and he drew her towards him and they kissed. She always felt like crying when he did that but this afternoon she was all on edge and she'd gone and told him about Dolly Rawlins. For a second she'd hoped he'd forgotten but he suddenly smiled. 'And if that cow don't want to part with her diamonds, you got the gear to make her, haven't you? Use them, sweetheart. You get me some dough and we'll go abroad, nice holiday when I get out.'

He was already being monitored by the officers, pointing for him to return to the corridor outside and be returned to his cell.

'I love you, Eddie,' she said softly.

'I hope so, Gloria. Tarra, see you next week.'

He seemed quite cheerful as he walked after the prison officer, even offering him a cigarette. He'd got eighteen years and there he was talking about when they would go on a bloody holiday together. She'd be on a zimmer frame by the time he got out.

Dolly paid off the taxi and carried her purchases inside the front entrance of the manor. Ester's Range Rover was nowhere to be seen. She went straight to her bedroom and sorted out what she would wear for the afternoon, then started to pack her few things. She was leaving and would leave without a goodbye. She would get the cheque stopped. She swore at herself: she should have done that as soon as she came home. Dolly headed down the stairs as Ester breezed in, wafting a big brown envelope.

'Hi! They said you'd left when I went to the town hall so I did a grocery shop. Here you go, Dolly, the lease all signed, and now the place is really all yours.'

'Oh, is it? Well, you can take it and stuff it. I don't want this place, I don't want anything to do with you and I'm gonna stop that cheque.'

'What?'

Dolly glared at Ester. 'I said, I'm stopping that cheque. You really did me in, didn't you? Never thought to mention this place was a brothel.'

Ester tossed the envelope down. 'You knew what I was.'

'I didn't know you ran a whore house from here, though, did I?'

'All you had to do was ask.'

'They all know about this place, they told me at the social services.'

'So what?'

97

'This place has got such a bad reputation that, along with my record, you think they'll give us the go-ahead?'

Ester looked to the ceiling. 'Why should they even know I'm here, for one? This is bloody stupid, Dolly. For chrissakes, look at the place.'

'That's just what I have been doing and I'm out.'

Dolly was about to walk back up the stairs when Ester yelled, 'You tell me where you'll find a better place for kids. There's a swimming pool, stables, you can bloody have twenty kids here. They'll be more likely to give you the go-ahead on a place like this that's crying out for kids than any terraced place in fucking Islington or Holloway or wherever you planned to buy it – and they cost, Dolly. You've been away a long time, any house in that area's gonna cost you at least a hundred and fifty grand. Here you got beds, furniture, linen, all thrown in, but if you don't want it, then that's up to you . . .'

Julia walked out and leaned on the kitchen door. 'She's right, you know, Dolly. This is a fabulous place for kids.'

Dolly hesitated. Julia's soft voice seemed to calm her. 'The orchard and the gardens, the pool doesn't need much doing to it, then you can even get a horse for the stables . . . You list all those to the services and . . .'

Ester winked at Julia. 'She's right, Dolly. I mean, you'd get grants, wouldn't you? Each kid'd bring in about two hundred a week. I'm right, aren't I, Julia?'

'Yep, and then you'd get grants to rebuild and convert . . .'

Dolly sat down on the stairs, more confused than ever. Ester glanced at her watch. All she needed was a few more hours for the cheque to go into the system then Dolly couldn't stop it as it would have gone through.

'Look, why don't we make an inventory, list all the gear?

98

There's all the crockery, glasses, tableware – that'd cost if you started from scratch.'

Dolly frowned. 'I got to go to London, let me think about it.'

'You want a lift, do you? To the station?'

Dolly nodded, got up and went to her room.

'By tomorrow the cheque will have gone through,' Ester said quietly to Julia. 'Where do you think she's going?'

'I don't know, do I?'

Ester pulled her into the kitchen. 'What if she's going for the diamonds?'

Julia chewed at a fingernail. 'If she's got millions of quid's worth of diamonds, how come she's getting so hot under the collar about laying out cash for this place?'

'Because she's a tight-fisted old bag, that's why!'

'Yeah, you may be right, but if she's tight-fisted now, how do you think she'll feel if we were to take the diamonds off her?'

'I don't give a shit how she feels. If she gets them, then so do we. You make some excuse, say you got to go to London as well, see where she goes and who she talks to.'

'Oh, for chrissakes, Ester, that's ridiculous. You mean follow her around?'

'What the hell do you think I mean?'

By the time Dolly came back downstairs, Julia was already sitting in the Range Rover.

'Julia's got to go and see her mother so she'll catch the train with you.'

'What's the matter with her mother?' Dolly asked as she followed Ester out.

'She's old and being kept in the lap of luxury by her beloved daughter. She has no idea Julia was even picked up and put in the slammer, never mind that she was a junkie.

Julia's been paying for her for years, she's in a wheelchair or somethin', so that's housekeepers and cleaners and . . . you name it. That's why Julia's broke.'

Julia knew Ester was talking about her and she turned to stare across the stable-yard. Sometimes she hated Ester. As soon as Dolly got into the car, she started asking her about her mother. 'She's very old, Dolly. I don't see why she should be upset or for that matter know what a mess I've made of my life.'

'Where does she think you are, then?' Dolly asked.

'Well, when I was in Holloway I got friends to send postcards from Malta. She thought I was working over there with the Red Cross.'

'And now?' Dolly asked.

'Well, since my release, I told her I've been looking for a new practice. She doesn't know I was struck off – she doesn't know anything about me, really.'

Dolly nodded and looked at her watch: she was going to be late for the meeting with Jimmy Donaldson. She didn't know how she was going to get all the way over to the theme park on time. Well, if he left, he left. She'd just have to rearrange the meeting.

Connie had asked the cab driver to wait. She had then hurried into the mansion block of flats. Lennie always left just before lunch, did the rounds of his girls, then checked his club for the previous night's takings. He would then come home, change and have something to eat. Connie had usually cooked him a light meal before running his bath. He would change and leave the flat between eight and eight thirty in the evening, rarely returning until early morning. Lennie was a well-organized man – frighteningly well-organized. His girls, his club, his Porsche and his well-furnished flat came before any love or relationship. Connie knew that now. She hadn't, not for a long time. She had truly believed Lennie cared for her. She had been with him for three years, cooking, cleaning, keeping his flat spotless. Occasionally she went to the club and they dined out frequently, but then he had started knocking her around and a few times told her to be 'very nice' to friends of his. When they became a regular weekly session, she knew it was all over between them, that she was no longer his 'special'. He was getting ready for a change, as if she was part of the fixtures and fittings. He had beaten her up so badly one night, broken her nose, that he had arranged for her to have facial surgery. She had her eyes done, her nose remodelled, a cheek implant and a breast implant. She had felt wonderful. He had visited her in the clinic and been kind to her when she came home in the bandages. She had believed he'd changed, that perhaps he really did care for her, but when the bandages came off and she admired herself, preening in front of him as he lay in bed, he had said, lighting a cigarette, 'Well, now, girl, you can make up the money, seven grand you owe. I reckon you've a few more years in you now so you're going to share with Carol and Leslie.'

Connie couldn't believe it. They were two of his girls and he was moving her out and in with them, as if there had been nothing between them. 'But, Lennie, I want to try going straight. You know, get a proper agent and do some modelling.'

He had laughed. 'No way. You can earn more for me than doing any bleedin' cereal advert . . .'

She hadn't said anything, not argued back, afraid he'd maybe whack her. She had simply waited for him to leave at his usual time, called Ester Freeman and said she would be free to come to the manor. She had packed fast and run off. Now Connie was back she let herself in and went straight to the kitchen. She began unplugging all the movable equipment she could lay her hands on. She then went into the bedroom and cleared out her side of the wardrobe. At least she was alone; he hadn't moved anyone else in yet.

Lennie's portable phone was on the stand, recharging. She was so busy filling the suitcase that she didn't notice it. Lennie never went anywhere without his portable. Right now he was swearing as he realized he'd forgotten to put it in his pocket, right now doing a U-turn and heading back to the flat to pick it up.

The cab driver noticed the metallic blue Porsche park, watched the dapper West Indian straighten his draped suit as he headed back towards the mansion block. He returned to reading the *Sun*, giving a quick look at the meter. It was ticking away and he wondered how long the girl would be; she'd said about ten minutes but she'd already been gone that. He swore, wondering if she'd just done a Marquess of Blandford on him and wouldn't be coming out, but he saw she had left a bag on the back seat so continued to read his paper.

Connie had filled two cases when he walked back in. She heard the front door slam and backed in terror. He kicked open the door and looked at her.

'Hello, Lennie, I was just packing me gear.'

'I can see that. You missed anything? Like the light fittings?'

'I've not taken anything that wasn't mine, Lennie.'

'I gave you the cash for everything you're standing up in, sweetheart. Now what the fuck do you think you're doing and where've you been dossing down?'

She was terrified of him, blurting out she was staying in Aylesbury with some friends. He came closer and closer. 'Don't hurt me, please don't.'

He laughed. 'Aylesbury? You kiddin'? Who you staying there with?'

'Dolly Rawlins, you don't know her, but listen, Lennie, I might be on to a good thing. She's got diamonds, a lot of diamonds and—' Connie panicked, trying anything to stop him coming closer. His fists were clenched and she backed away, repeating what she had said, but he did not believe her and she pressed herself against the wardrobe, bracing herself for what she knew was coming. She tried to protect herself, pleading for him not to hit her in the face.

The cab driver saw the smart alec sweep out and get back into his Porsche; it roared off. He got out of his cab and opened the passenger door to peer inside. He picked up the bag Connie had left. It was full of vitamins. He tossed it on to the back seat, getting more and more pissed off, when he saw her coming out. She carried a suitcase and was wearing dark glasses and a headscarf. He took the case from her. 'You all right, love?'

'Take me to Marylebone station, please.' She got into the back seat as he stashed her case up front, then he started up the engine.

'Right, station . . .' He could see her in the mirror. She had a handkerchief pressed to her face and it was covered in blood. 'You sure you're okay, love?'

'Yes, yes, I'm fine, thank you.' She could feel the swelling coming up under her eyes. Her nose was bleeding, but she didn't think he'd broken it, her neck covered in dark red bruises. She had pretended to be unconscious so he had walked out, saying he would see her when he got back. She was never going back. She would kill him if he laid a finger on her again.

'Kathleen? *Kathleen?*' Ester shouted. Kathleen was on her bed. She'd had a few drinks and was sleeping it off. Ester barged into the room. 'Didn't you hear me calling you?'

'What do you want?'

Ester shut the door. 'I think she might be going for the diamonds today. Who do you know that we could trust to fence them?'

Kathleen lifted her head and then flopped back. 'Well, it depends, doesn't it? I mean, they're still hot but I've got a few people I'd trust.'

Ester was pacing up and down. 'If they were valued at two million when they were nicked almost nine years ago, what do you reckon they're worth now?'

'Could be double, it all depends on the quality. Soon as I see them I'll be able to tell you the best man. Are we going to see them, Ester?'

'I think she's maybe doing something about them this afternoon.'

Kathleen sat up, rubbing her head. 'Well, shouldn't you or one of us be with her?'

'Julia's on her, I hope.'

'Have you mentioned to Dolly that you know about them?'

Ester shook her head. 'No, and we don't. Let's just take it stage by stage.'

'Fine by me, but she's such a wily old cow she might pick them up and that's the last we see her.'

'No, she'll be back. All her gear's still in her room.'

104

'Ah, she might be back. I'm not that interested in her, darlin', but will she be bringin' back the diamonds?'

'I bloody hope so.'

Ester walked out as Kathleen slowly got off the bed. She heard Ester tell her to stop nicking booze as she ran the cold water in her washbasin, splashed her face with cold water and patted it dry. The photographs of her three daughters were placed on the dressing-table, positioned so she could see them from her bed. They were the last thing she saw at night and the first in the morning: the nine-year-old twins, Kathy and Mary, and five-year-old Sheena. They were in care, a convent home, but how long they would remain together Kathleen couldn't be sure. All she knew was that when she got the cut of the diamonds, they were going home, all of them, going back to Dublin. She'd be safe, the cops wouldn't find her there. She hoped they wouldn't find her here either. 'You get the diamonds, Dolly, love,' she whispered to herself. 'Pray God you get them before the cops trace me.'

Kathleen, like every one of them apart from Dolly, was in trouble. But Kathleen's problem was not some bloke out to make her a punch-bag: a warrant was out for her arrest on two charges of cheque-card fraud. She had simply not turned up for the hearing. Ester's invitation to come to the manor not only gave her hope for a lot of cash, but also a safe place to hide.

Dolly trailed from one station to another until she eventually got a taxi for the last stage of the journey to Thorpe Park. Julia was right on her heels, train to train, and lastly the taxi. She didn't have to say, 'Follow that cab,' but she did say, 'You see that woman with the short haircut, the blue coat? Will you follow the taxi she's in?'

As they arrived at the theme park Julia began to doubt that Dolly was collecting the diamonds. In fact she started to curse at the stupidity of trailing Dolly around like she, Julia, was Sherlock Holmes but, follow her she did, keeping her distance until Dolly headed towards the funfair section.

Meanwhile, positioned at each exit and entrance, were plain patrol cars and plain-clothes officers. Sitting in another plain patrol car was a moody Jimmy Donaldson. They had arrived at three fifteen and he'd been in the car for over an hour and a half. They were all almost giving up when they got the contact. 'Suspect has entered gate C, over.'

Donaldson was wired up, instructed to move slowly, and told not to approach any of the officers. He would be monitored at all times. He was still angry they had not found the diamonds because it meant that some other bugger had, and he spent his time trying to think who could have shifted them. Only Audrey and Dolly knew where they were, and maybe his wife. Could she have moved them? Did she know? Had she found them? It was possible, and they had now shifted his poor wife to stay with her sister in Brighton, so the 'you'll be at home, Jimmy' was all a cock-up. He wished he'd never agreed to it but then he thought that if they could swing it for him to be in a nice, cushy, open prison, why not? What did he care? Well, he knew Dolly Rawlins was a hard-nosed cow but without her old man, just how hard could she be? It was Harry who had had enough on him to put him behind bars for years. Now he was dead. Then he got to thinking that as Dolly had shot Harry she might just whack him one, so Jimmy Donaldson was not a happy man, and getting more and more pissed off by the minute.

DCI Craigh beckoned him out of the car, pressing his earpiece into his ear, listening. 'Okay, Jimmy. She moved to the hoop-la stand or something, so you start walking in by gate B, the one closest to us. Just act nice and casual, and don't keep looking round. Off you go.'

Donaldson shook his head. 'You know this won't work. She's not gonna like it me not having them with me, you know. She won't like it.'

Craigh sighed. None of them liked it one little bit but they couldn't do anything about it. 'Just do the business. Tell her to meet you back at your place, that it was unsafe to bring them here – tell her anything.'

'This is entrapment, you know,' Donaldson whined.

'You fuckin' do the business, Jimmy, or you'll be trapped and for longer than you got in the first place.'

He moved off on his own, walking through entrance B and heading, as he had been told, to the hoop-la stand. When he got there he couldn't see Dolly so he went over to the shooting arcade and paid over two quid for three shots. 'Let her find me,' he said to himself as he took aim. 'Let her bloody find me.'

Dolly walked casually around, enjoying the stands, looking at the amazing rides. It was all beyond anything she had ever come across when she was a kid, and it all cost a hell of a lot more. She fingered the hoops, fifty pence a throw. In her day as a kid it had been threepence but she paid over her money and took aim with the wooden hoop.

'Rawlins is at the hoop-la stand. She's throwing hoops now.' Palmer wandered past, not even looking at Dolly as she threw her third hoop and was presented with a goldfish in a plastic bag. As she reached for the fish, she caught sight of Julia, hovering at another stand. She did a double-take and stared.

Julia sighed. She was hopeless at it and she was so tall she stuck out like a sore thumb. As Dolly walked towards her, she smiled weakly. 'I was following you,' she said lamely.

'Well, you just won yourself a prize. Here, take it back to the manor.' As Julia took the goldfish bag, Dolly looked up at her, 'Why you following me?'

'Ester told me to.'

'Oh, I see, and what she tells you to do, you do, is that right?'

'Yeah. Well, now you've caught me at it, I'll push off.'

'You do that, love. I'm only here for the entertainment.'

Julia couldn't help but smile but Dolly remained poker-faced, watching the tall woman as she threaded her way out of the area. Dolly was piecing it all together: they were, as she had suspected, after her diamonds. Well, they were going to be in for a shock. They wouldn't get anything out of her. As soon as she had them, she would be on her way and they could all rot in hell as far as she was concerned. Apart from Angela: she liked that little kid.

Dolly wondered if she'd missed Jimmy Donaldson – maybe he'd got tired of waiting.

'She's looking around now, handed a fish to a woman who's walked out. Should be coming through exit E, check her out.'

Julia made her way to the courtesy bus stop and waited, unaware she was being monitored. She had decided she would go and see her mother. It had been a long time since she had seen her.

Dolly saw Donaldson and walked off in the opposite direction towards a Ferris wheel.

'I think she saw him but she's walked off, straight past him. Now at the Ferris wheel. She's talking to the boy on the ticket box.'

Dolly smiled at the spotty young kid and slipped him a tenner. 'I'll be back for a ride in a bit and you'll get another if you make sure I get a nice view from the top of the

108

wheel. Say about five minutes' worth of view, all right, love?'

He grinned. It was not unusual, he often had requests, and for twenty quid, why not? He watched as she strolled back into the crowds of kids and families. It was not a busy day – mid-week and not during school holidays it was often quiet, apart from the shooting arcade that was a constant battle with the ear-drums.

Donaldson had another three shots. On his last he got a bull's-eye and the stall owner begrudgingly handed over a stuffed white rabbit. He turned to see Dolly standing directly in front of him.

'Okay, they're together. He's just won a white rabbit so we can't miss them. He's walking off with her to the other stands.'

She didn't speak for a while and he chatted on. 'You're looking well, long time no see.'

'I am well, Jimmy, very well. How's your wife?'

'Oh, she's her usual. Gone to see her sister in Brighton.'

'That's nice for her. Would you like a ride?'

He looked at the Ferris wheel. 'No. Can't stand those things.'

'Oh, come on, it'll be fun. I'm here to enjoy myself. Reason I chose here is because I saw an article. Princess Diana brings the princes here, did you know?'

He nodded. 'That's the big theme rides over the other side. This is another part, a fairground. It's not part of the main park.'

'I fancied that water ride, down a chute. I saw them in the paper. Never mind, we'll make do with this now we're here.'

Dolly winked at the spotty boy and paid for the ride, slipping him another tenner. He unbuckled the seat bar and helped her sit down.

'Dolly, I've not got a head for heights.'

'Oh, get in, Jimmy, I want to see the view.'

Donaldson was ushered into the seat and locked into his safety harness; below, the static interference was breaking up on the radios. Jimmy's and Dolly's voices were coming and going with a crackle and a buzz.

'They're on the Ferris wheel,' a droll-voiced officer said into his radio.

'We can see that,' DCI Craigh muttered back. They could see them, hear them just about, and so far not one word about the diamonds. Mike was in the car, listening on the radio, clocking the time, wondering if his mother had picked up the fakes yet, getting more and more agitated. He hadn't even seen Rawlins yet; he didn't know how he'd deal with it if he did.

'They're on the ride,' crackled his radio.

Mike pushed his earpiece further into his ear, wincing as the static caused by the steel girders on the Ferris wheel deafened him.

Donaldson clung to the safety bar as the wheel turned slowly. 'There's nobody else getting on,' he panted.

'Oh, there will be,' she said, smiling.

'Why are they doing it so slowly?' he gasped, as they inched higher.

'They got to allow for the punters to get on. So, have you got them for me?'

She said it so casually, he felt even sicker. 'Er, not with me, it's too dangerous.'

She stared ahead, and the wheel turned higher until they were almost at the top.

'You've not got them, is that right?'

'Yes – no – I've got them but not on me. You crazy? I couldn't carry them around . . . Oh, oh, holy shit, is this bleedin' thing safe?'

They remained poised at the top of the wheel and Dolly

110

leaned forward, looking down, around and out to the views ahead. 'Oh, isn't it lovely? Isn't it lovely, Jimmy?'

'No, I'm gonna be sick.'

She faced him, her eyes like those of a small angry ferret. 'You will be sick, Jimmy, if you're trying it on. Are you trying it on with me, Jimmy?'

'No, no, I swear. Listen, is there an alarm? I'm feeling sick, really I am. I hate swings, I hate heights, I'm dying, Dolly.'

She pushed at the seat with her feet. It swung backwards and forwards. 'Where are they?'

'*At home! I got them at home!*' He was shaking in terror, his knuckles white from gripping the safety bar.

She looked down, waving cheerfully to the boy, and the wheel began to move down. 'I'll come for them tomorrow. I'll call you.'

'All right, all right, anythin' you say . . .'

She nodded, and then leaned closer. 'Life is too short to mess around, isn't it? You won't mess with me, will you, Jimmy? You see, I've been waiting eight years.'

'Yeah, well, I got to get a good fence. I'm nowhere near big enough. I mean, you're talking millions so you'll need the very best.'

'No, love, you won't get anything but what belongs to me. I'll do the rest and you'll get your cut.'

DCI Craigh was ripping out his hair. They still had not mentioned the word 'diamonds'. 'Jesus Christ, say it, woman, *say* it.'

She never did. She left a white-faced Jimmy Donaldson leaning against the fence, throwing up, as she went out of the exit, carrying the white rabbit. They couldn't lose her, couldn't miss her, but she had not said the word diamonds, and neither had the stupid bastard Jimmy Donaldson.

*

Julia arrived at the station and put in a call to Ester, who when she was told that Dolly had spotted Julia, went into a screaming fit. Julia yelled back, saying that if she wanted to follow Dolly then she should have done it herself. 'I'm going to see my mother, okay?' Then she slammed down the phone, picked up the goldfish Dolly had given her and walked on to the platform to wait for the train. She wished she'd never agreed to the Dolly Rawlins business. She wished she didn't know Ester, she wished she had not fucked herself up so badly, she wished she could start her life over again. She was such an idiot, such a stupid bitch to have got herself into such a mess.

It was after eight by the time Gloria arrived at her old place, which looked even more run-down in the dark. Just as she got out, Mrs Rheece came out of the front door. Gloria ran up the path. 'Mrs Rheece, it's me, Gloria Radford. I just come to pick up my stuff. Is that okay?'

'You can do what you like, no business of mine. I don't give a shit what anyone does. The council have been round askin' after you and that bloke was here last night again, the one with the squint. I said to him you wasn't here and he was fuckin' abusive.'

'Oh, I'm sorry. You tell him to sod off the next time.'

'There won't be a next time, Mrs Radford, 'cos I'll call the law on him.'

The old woman went off with her shopping trolley down the road, still muttering to herself about the council, as Gloria slipped round the back of the house to the old coal hut. It had been used as a bike shed, and rubbish bins were stacked up inside and out. She shone a torch round and began to move aside all the junk, ripping her tights and swearing. She was filthy as she squeezed her way into the back of the hut and then eased away old wooden boards. She was scared of being disturbed so she switched off the torch and fumbled around in the inky darkness. Then she felt the big canvas bag and began to heave with all her might. It was very heavy, but she managed to drag it out. She went back three times for two more bags before she shut the coal-hut door. She dragged each bag out to the Mini Traveller and hauled them inside, terrified that someone would see her, but no one even passed her in the street. Then she went up into her old flat, washed her hands and face, and collected a suitcase full of clothes before she left. She drove slowly, frightened of every passing police car. She knew that if she was stopped and the car was searched, she'd be arrested. Eddie's stash, Eddie's retirement money, was all in the back of the Mini: thirty thousand pounds' worth of weapons.

She headed on to the motorway towards Aylesbury, her hands gripping the steering wheel, her whole body tense. 'Please God, nobody stop me, please God, don't break down, please God, let me get to the manor safely.'

Ester heard the front door slam and looked over the banisters. Connie, still wearing her dark glasses and head-scarf, was dragging in her case.

'Where the hell have you been all day?'

'I need a fiver for the taxi, Ester.'

Ester thudded down the stairs. 'I'm not a bloody charity, you know. I paid for everyone's taxi yesterday.' Ester stopped in her tracks as she saw Connie's face. 'What the hell happened to you?'

113

Connie burst into tears and ran past her, up the stairs, so Ester had to go out and pay off the taxi driver.

Audrey was in a right state. She had twice paged Mike on his mobile and he'd not returned her call. She now had the fake diamonds from Tommy and just having them in the flat made her freak. She kept on opening the pouch bag and looking at them, closing it up again, then standing over the telephone. 'Ring, come on, ring me. I've got them, I've got them.'

Mike didn't call until after ten. He was just coming off duty and he'd come round to collect them. As he put the phone down, Angela paged him. He arranged to meet her outside Edgware Road tube station, then called his wife to tell her he would be late. He had just replaced the phone when DCI Craigh wandered to his desk.

'We've got Donaldson back at his place. He says that maybe we should take him over to his shop, maybe they've not been looking in the right place. I said to him, "You drew the map, Jimmy, we're looking just where you told us to look."'

Mike could feel the sweat trickle under his armpits. 'You want me to go over there and see who we've got searching the shop? They may have missed them, you know.'

Craigh rubbed his nose. 'Yeah, okay, I'm taking myself off home. We've been over all the tapes from the fairground. Useless. They could have been talking about anything. He's a smart-arsed prick, you know, Donaldson.'

Mike nodded in agreement. 'Yeah, well, we know what she meant though, don't we?'

'Yeah, we know, but it wouldn't stand up in court. Still, we'll see what we get tomorrow – she's calling him again then. Goodnight.'

Mike dragged on his coat. It was another hour, sitting in traffic, before he picked up Angela. As far as she knew, she told him, the women were all still together at the manor; Dolly had bought it from Ester, paid her by cheque. She had not heard any mention of diamonds but they were all edgy, especially Ester.

Mike paid her a tenner. She wanted him to take her out for a hamburger, but he refused. 'When will I see you again, then?'

Mike cleared his throat. She was too close to Rawlins and tied in even closer to him. It made him nervous but he didn't want her to get suspicious of anything he was doing so he grinned. 'Soon as I get some free time. It's getting a bit heavy with Susan right now – she's asking a lot of questions about where I am. We just have to cool it for a bit.'

She started to sniffle and he hugged her. 'Come on, now, don't start. I've got to be on duty in half an hour otherwise I could see you, but right now it's too difficult.'

'You just used me.'

He turned away from her. 'I'm sorry if it looks or feels that way but I didn't, and you knew I was married right from the start, Angela, I got kids.'

She sniffed again and opened the car door. 'All the same, you used me, Mike. I give you all that information and you can't spare ten minutes for me. How do you think that makes me feel?'

'Look, let me get this Rawlins business sorted. I'm doing this for my sister, Angela. Let me do what I have to do and then I promise I'll call you, okay?'

He reached over and squeezed her hand. She gave a sweet smile and closed the door, watching as he drove off. She felt cheated and slightly guilty. Mrs Rawlins had seemed quite nice, not like the others. She hunched her shoulders and went back into the tube station to head for her mother's place.

Audrey showed Mike the fake diamonds. 'Two grand I paid. They're very good, Tommy's a professional. What do you think?'

Mike was tired out. He stuffed the bag into his pocket. 'Okay. Now you should get packed and out of here as soon as you can. I'll stash these tonight.'

'Did she meet up with Jimmy, then, today?'

'Yeah, but they played games.'

'She's clever, Mike. Watch out for her, don't trust her.'

He looked at his mother. 'You mean like I trusted you?'

'How can you say that? You know why I did it! You *know* why!'

He pursed his lips. 'You did it for the money so don't give me the sob story about Shirley because it won't wash any more. I'm doing this tonight and then that is it, you hear me? I want you out of here, out of my life.'

'You don't mean that, do you?'

'Yes, I do.'

'But the villa! You and the kids can come for holidays.'

'No, Mum, I don't want to know about the fucking villa. You got it, you stay in it. Now pack your bags, like I said, get your ticket sorted and leave.'

Audrey burst into tears and started talking about Shirley but Mike walked out. She followed him. 'I had a right to them. *I had every right. She killed Shirley!* You know she did. She should have gone down for life, that's what she should have got.'

He ran down the stone steps, hearing his mother's grating, screeching voice, and he hated her. At this moment, he even hated his sister. If he was caught replacing the

116

stones at Jimmy Donaldson's antique shop he'd be arrested and it would all be whose fault? Dolly Rawlins's!

By the time he got back into his car, he hated Dolly Rawlins as much as his mother did. Crashing the gears, he sped off down the road. The pouch bag of fake diamonds felt like a red-hot coal in his jacket pocket.

CHAPTER 5

JULIA KISSED her mother's soft powdery cheek and then stepped back, holding up the goldfish. 'I got you a present.'

Mrs Lawson smiled and gently stroked Bates the cat. 'Well, I'll have my time cut out watching Bates doesn't eat it.'

'We used to have a fish bowl somewhere, didn't we? I remember it.' Julia searched in the kitchen and eventually found it, filled it with water and tipped in the fish. Then she carried it into the drawing room. Her mother was still stroking Bates, sitting in her wheelchair, a cashmere shawl wrapped round her knees. The room was oppressively hot, the gas-fire turned on full.

'So, how are you?' Julia said as she sat down, peeling off her sweater.

'Oh, Mrs Dowey takes good care of me and her husband still looks after the garden.'

Julia could think of nothing to say so she got up and looked over a stack of bills placed in a wooden tea-caddy on the sideboard. 'Are these for me?'

'Yes, dear. I was going to send them to your accountant as usual but as you're here . . .'

They were the usual telephone, gas and electricity bills, Mrs Dowey's and her husband's wages, and bills for repairs and maintenance to the house. Julia even paid for the groceries.

'You know, dear, if this is too much for you . . .'

Julia turned the wheelchair round to face her. 'If it was I'd say so. Besides, who else have I got to look after?'

'I always hope you'll meet someone nice, marry and settle down. It would be nice to have a grandchild before I die.'

Julia smiled, touching her mother's wrinkled hand. 'I am trying, Mother, but you know my job – it's always taken precedence over my personal life.'

'You look very well, dear.' Changing the subject deftly, Mrs Lawson smiled sweetly. 'Will you be staying tonight?'

'No, sadly I can't. I've got surgery this evening.'

'Ah, yes, of course. Perhaps a cup of tea?'

Julia nodded and stood up. She was so tall that the low ceiling felt as if it was pressing on her head. 'I'll put the kettle on.'

'That would be nice, dear, thank you.'

Julia stood at the window and wanted to cry. Everything was exactly as she remembered it, as she had always remembered it. Nothing had changed for years. Only her mother had got older and more frail, softer, her voice light and quavery. Nothing else had changed. It always seemed so strange that her mother never noticed how different she was. Didn't it show? Couldn't she tell? 'I'll make the tea.' Julia left the room and Mrs Lawson turned to stare at the solitary goldfish swimming round and round in the empty glass bowl.

'We should get some green things for the fish, shouldn't we, Bates? He seems very lonely.'

Bates dozed, Mrs Lawson continued to stare as if hypnotized while the fish went round and round. 'Poor little soul,' she whispered.

*

119

Angela let herself in, hating the smell that always hung in the air – babies' vomit and urine. 'I'm back, Mum,' she yelled as she dropped her bag.

Mrs Dunn was making a half-hearted attempt to iron, feed the two kids and cook all at once. She was a tired-looking woman: everything about her was tired – her face, her hair, her clothes and, worst of all, her eyes. They seemed devoid of any expression.

'Where've you been?' It came out as a single sigh, the iron thudding over the drip-dry shirt that always creased.

'Working.'

Mrs Dunn thumped the iron back on its stand. She pulled more semi-damp clothes from the wooden rail, tossed them into an already laden basket, switched off a steaming kettle and took an empty Mars Bar paper out of her youngest son's mouth, all in one slow, tired swing.

'Here's a tenner for you.'

'Put it in the tin on the sideboard. Eric's going crazy – you don't pay any rent or anything towards the food, we don't know where you are, when you're coming in, you treat this place like it was a hotel, you use the phone. There's been call after call for you.'

'Who from?'

'I don't know, that girl Sherry, John at the ice rink. I'm not your social secretary. Where've you been?'

Angela sat down, kicking her heels against the table leg. 'Ester Freeman gimme a job for a night – *just* waitressin'.'

Mrs Dunn moved slowly back to the ironing. 'I've told you not to mix with her, she's no good, she'll have you on the game next. Eric said he wouldn't be surprised if you're not on it anyway.'

'Eric would know, wouldn't he? He's a pest, a dirty-minded, two-faced shit. This is your house and he has no right to ask me to pay rent in it.'

'He does if he's paying the bills, love, and he is. And don't speak about him like that.'

'He's not my dad.'

'No, he isn't, thank Christ, or we'd have no roof over our heads. Eric's taken you on.'

Angela snorted, looking around the dank kitchen. 'Yeah, I'm sure. This is a dump, it always was, and it's got worse over the years. You should complain to the council – you got every right, you know. There's empty flats either side, they're moving everyone else round here. You'd be up for a new place, five kids, no husband.'

Mrs Dunn banged the iron. 'Now, don't start. I know you always start like this. Just because you've got nothing in your life you got to have a go at me! Well, just stop it or you're out on your ear.'

Angela sighed. She hated being home – hated everything about it – even more since Eric had taken over as 'man of the house'. He was half her mother's age and constantly made moves on Angela, but her mother refused to believe or take any notice of it, fearful that if Eric was confronted he would walk out on her.

'So, where have you been?'

'I just told you. You don't listen to what I say. I went to Aylesbury.'

'Oh, yes, Ester Freeman.' Mrs Dunn suddenly sagged into a chair. 'Don't go back to working for her, Angela, she's no good. I just don't know what to do about you, I really don't.'

Angela got up and slipped her arms around her mother. 'Mum, I've got a boyfriend, I was sort of working for him in a way. He's asked me to go and live with him. He's got a nice house and—'

121

'Oh, just stop it, Angela, you make up stories all the time. What man is this now? That copper? It was all in your head and she's got you back at it, hasn't she?'

Angela shrieked, 'No. Why do you always think I'm on the game? I'm not, and I never was. I just used to clean for her!'

Mrs Dunn put her head in her hands. 'I don't know what to do with you. You won't got back to school, you got no qualifications. How you gonna get a job with no qualifications? You tell me that.'

Angela stuck out her lower lip. Since she'd been picked up after the bust at Ester's, she'd had a string of part-time jobs. Nothing kept her interested for more than a few weeks and the pay was bad in all of them. She'd been a waitress, a barmaid, a clerk, a trainee at two hair salons, part-time sales girl in numerous boutiques and she'd even helped out a few market-stall owners at Camden Lock. But in reality she was just drifting around and she knew it. She didn't know how to stop it and in a way she had hoped Mike would guide her – but he just fucked her, like everyone else.

'I dunno what to do, Mum. Nothin' seems to work out for me.'

Mrs Dunn kissed her daughter. She was such a pretty girl: her thick hair hung in a marvellous Afro spiral cascade and she was a pale tawny colour with big, wide, amber brown eyes. 'I want you to go and talk to your old teachers, see what they say, maybe get on some government training course. You can't just live your life wanderin' from one part-time job to another, you got to have a purpose.'

'You mean like you?' Angela said sarcastically, and saw the pain flash across her mother's face.

'No, what I don't want is for you to have a life like mine, I wouldn't want it for my worst enemy.'

Angela started to cry. She just felt so screwed up, with nothing in the future. She knew Mike didn't want to see her any more – he hadn't for a while now. 'I'll go and see them tomorrow, okay?'

Mrs Dunn smiled and suddenly all the tiredness evaporated. 'Just stay away from Ester, that woman's a bad influence.'

Angela nodded and went upstairs. She packed her bag, stuffing anything that came to hand into it. She'd had enough, she was leaving. She heard Eric come in so she never even said goodbye to her mother – she could hear him shouting and yelling at her in the kitchen.

She had no place to go. She called Mike at home but his wife answered so she put the phone down. She had no place to go but back to the Grange. She knew she shouldn't have told Mike about the women but she hadn't thought about the repercussions. She just wanted somewhere to stay until she sorted herself out. Maybe when she told Mike he would help her, find a job for her. Then she'd come back to London.

By the time Dolly returned it was after nine and she was still carrying the white rabbit. Ester was waiting in the hall as she had seen Dolly's arrival from the bedroom window.

'Did you have a nice day?'

'Didn't you ask Julia? Here, she got the fish, you get the rabbit.' Dolly threw it at her and walked slowly up the stairs as Connie wandered out of the kitchen.

'I got some stew on.'

Dolly looked at her. She had cotton wool stuffed up her nose, which was swollen and puffy, both eyes were black and she was crying. 'What the hell happened to you?'

Connie snivelled and went back into the kitchen just as

Kathleen was coming down the stairs. 'Boyfriend, if you can call him that, whacked her one.'

Kathleen passed Dolly, raising an eyebrow at Ester. 'Well, who gave you the bunny?'

Dolly washed her face and hands. She heard Julia returning and went downstairs, when the doorbell rang. Ester came hurrying out from the kitchen. 'I'll get it. You go on in and sit down and have your dinner, Dolly.' She swung open the front door to see Angela huddled on the doorstep.

'What do you want?' Ester snapped.

'Oh, please, Ester, I've had to leave Mum's house. It was terrible and I had no other place to go.'

'Well, you can't stay here, you can sod off.'

Dolly walked further down into the hall. 'What's this?'

'It's Angela, she's come back. I said we don't want her here.'

'Well, she can't go back at this hour. Let her in, we've got enough rooms.'

Ester stepped aside and Angela said, 'Thank you very much, Mrs Rawlins,' giving Ester a snooty look.

'There's some stew on so put your bag in a room and come into the kitchen,' Dolly said, smiling. She headed into the kitchen.

Ester gave a half smile. There was no way that Dolly could get the two hundred grand back now: it would have gone through from her bank into Ester's overdrawn account.

Julia was already sitting at the table, helping a still tearful Connie serve up the stew. They heard Gloria returning and she banged in from the back yard. She was filthy, and went straight to the sink and ran the taps over her hands. 'I brought me gear from the house.'

They all concentrated on the food, and the scraping of their knives and forks was accentuated by the silence.

Dolly cleared her throat. 'Right. Things have changed since last night. I'm not taking on this house. I'm sorry, but I've had time to think and I reckon it'll be too expensive to do up and as it had such a bad reputation I think I'll go back to my original plan and open up a smaller place back in town.' She placed her knife and fork together.

'You should have told me this morning, Dolly,' Ester said.

'I'm telling you now. I want my money back, Ester.'

'Well, if you'd told me this morning that might have been possible but you're too late now. I put it in the bank.'

'You can take it out again, can't you?'

'No. I'm bankrupt and they gave me the deeds of the house. They were holding them as collateral. I've still got about three hundred grand to pay off, but they won't cash a cheque for a tenner right now.' Ester looked dutifully crestfallen and her voice took on an apologetic whine. 'I'm really sorry, Dolly. Like I said, you should have told me this morning.'

Dolly's face tightened. 'If you'd told me you were bankrupt I'd never have walked out without getting my money.'

'But you did and now there's nothing I can do about it. The house is yours, Dolly, lock, stock and barrel.'

Dolly pursed her lips. 'You really stitched me up, didn't you, Ester? I should have known there'd be some hitch. I really walked into this one, didn't I?'

'With your eyes open, Dolly, I never pushed you. I told you to think about it, if you recall. Now there's nothing I can do. But we're all here, we can all lend a hand, get this place up and rolling.'

Dolly clenched her hands. 'You any idea how much this will cost to get fixed up?'

'No, but we can start getting estimates in tomorrow. Local builders are cheaper than up in London.'

'And how do I pay them?' Dolly said quietly.

Ester flicked a look at Julia, shrugging her shoulders. 'Well, they give you grants, don't they? Unless you've got more dough stashed away.'

Dolly got up and fetched a glass. 'Any wine left from last night?'

Ester sent Angela to get a bottle from the dining room. All the women were looking at Ester, then back to Dolly as if at a tennis match.

Dolly followed Angela out, and went into the drawing room, where Angela was at the desk, reading a stack of newspaper cuttings. When she saw Dolly, she tried to stuff them back into the drawer. 'I couldn't find any wine, Mrs Rawlins.'

'It wouldn't be in a drawer, would it, love?' She pushed past Angela and opened the drawer as Angela backed away from her. She flicked through the cuttings, headlines about the murder of her husband, headlines about the shooting of Shirley Miller – and the diamond raid, then folded them and picked up her handbag.

'What you staring at me like that for?' she demanded.

Angela stuttered, 'I'm not, I just – just didn't know about all that.'

'What? That I'd been in prison? You knew, they all know. Now go and get the bottle. Try the dining room, dear.'

Angela scuttled out, and Dolly, taking a deep breath, walked back into the kitchen. The room fell silent.

Angela uncorked the wine as Dolly sat waiting, her hands clenched over her handbag. As soon as the wine was poured, Ester lifted her glass. 'Well, here's to the Grange Foster Home.' Echoing her, they sipped the wine. Dolly took only a small mouthful before she replaced the glass.

'Isn't it about time you all cut the pretence and came clean?'

'About what, Dolly?' Ester asked innocently.

'Why you're all here,' Dolly replied calmly.

Again they looked at Ester to take the lead. She smiled sweetly. 'You know why. We were all at a bit of a loose end and thought it would be nice, you know, to have a little welcome-out party, that's all. As it turned out, you got this place.'

'Off your hands,' said Dolly.

'Well, if you want to put it that way.'

Dolly opened her bag slowly. 'Well, maybe I will be able to open up but that isn't what you all bargained for.'

'I don't know what you mean, Dolly,' Gloria said.

'Don't you?' Dolly threw the newspaper cuttings on to the table. 'Not too clever leaving them lying around, was it? That's why you're all here. That's what you're all after, isn't it?'

'The diamonds?' Connie asked, and received a kick under the table from Ester.

'Yes. The bloody diamonds.' Dolly rarely, if ever, swore.

Mike drew up outside Jimmy Donaldson's run-down antique shop. The lights were on and a patrol car was parked outside. He patted his pocket, felt the pouch bag, and then walked into the shop.

Arc-lights were turned on and three uniformed officers were strip-searching the place. It was a tough job as furniture, junk and bric-à-brac were crowded into every inch of the shop space. An officer looked up at Mike as he entered. 'There's another floor even more stuffed than down here, plus a backyard crammed full, and an outside lav.'

'You not found them, then?' Mike asked innocently.

'No. According to Donaldson, they were hidden behind a wall. Well, we've nearly had the place come down on us, we've chipped away at so many bricks, but we've come to the conclusion he's playing silly buggers.'

Mike eased his way round a Victorian washstand. 'Well, carry on. I was just passing so I'll give you a hand for an hour or so.'

The officer nodded. 'You want a cup of tea? We're about to brew up out back.'

'Yeah, milk, one sugar.'

Left alone, Mike looked round the shop. He could see the wall where they had been removing bricks and he inched towards it. He had to be fast as the men were within yards of him. He pulled back two bricks and stuffed in the pouch, then rammed the bricks back into place. When the officer returned with two mugs of tea, Mike was standing by the opposite wall. He was inspecting the brickwork. 'Go over every inch of all the walls again. Donaldson is still insisting it's behind the brickwork.'

Mike stayed for another half-hour, helping move furniture around but keeping well away from where he had stashed the pouch, concentrating on the opposite wall. As he left, he suggested they stay at it.

He got home after eleven. His wife was already in bed and when he got in beside her, she didn't move.

'You awake?'

'Yes.'

'Sorry I'm so late. It's this bloke we brought out of the nick, taking up a lot of extra time.'

'Phone call for you.'

'Oh yeah, who?'

'I don't know. She put the phone down.'

Susan turned to face him. He sighed. 'If whoever it was put the phone down, how do you know it was a she?'

'I can tell. And that's what I'm asking you to do, Mike. Tell me if there's somebody else, just tell me.'

'There isn't, Sue, honestly, there's no one. I'm not seeing anyone else, I swear to you, and this is starting to get on my nerves.'

She turned over again, and lay awake for about ten minutes, crying silently, until she couldn't stand it any longer and turned back to him, but he was fast asleep. She'd been through his pockets again and this time she'd found a crumpled half page torn from an old diary. There was a phone number and a name. Angela. She'd called the number, asked to speak to Angela, but a woman had said she no longer lived there, had no idea where she was, and slapped down the receiver. Susan realized she should have said that the girl on the phone had said her name was Angela, confronted him, but then he could have asked the real Angela if she'd called and spoken to his wife. She punched the pillow. Nothing in the world was worse than lying next to someone, hearing them sleep, when you couldn't. She lay on her back and stared at the ceiling. She wondered who Angela was, if it *was* her, if there was *any*body, or if it was her own paranoia, because she sensed, deep down – probably like every woman who suspects their lover or husband is seeing someone else constantly makes excuses, because she is afraid of the truth.

The bottle was empty. The women sat listening to Dolly as she twisted the wineglass round by the stem. 'There were the four of us, all widows, Linda Pirellie, Bella, Shirley Miller and me. They're all dead.'

Angela stared. She knew the name Shirley Miller, knew it very well because it was the name Mike was always saying. It was his sister's.

'Anyway, when it was over, I knew it would be just a matter of time before they picked me up so I sorted out the stones. I left them with a friend of mine, someone I knew I could trust.'

'You left them with someone for eight years?' Ester asked uneasily.

'Yes, but, like I said, I knew he wouldn't try anything because I got so much on him. Well, my husband did.'

'Harry,' Gloria said eagerly.

'You've read about him, have you?' Dolly looked at the old newspaper cuttings, the xerox copies. One had his face on the front page: 'Harry Rawlins Murdered', screamed the headline. 'I know what I did was wrong,' Dolly said softly. No one spoke, but they all watched and listened intently. 'I killed him. I paid the price. And probably I'm the only person who still mourns him, I always will. In some ways I tried to be him, before I knew what he'd done to me, before I knew he had a cheap little tart of a girlfriend, before I knew she'd got his kid. I tried to be him, as if keeping him alive inside me, but the laugh was on me because he was alive.'

The women began to inch towards them the old reportage of the robbery and the murder; hearing her speaking so softly about what she had done was unnerving.

'I'm serious about putting something back into society. He took it out for years and years, and I want to make up for it. I truly want to open a foster home. It's serious with me and I know I can do it. I can give a home for the unwanted, the kids with babies, the drug addicts . . . I want to have a purpose for the rest of my life.'

Ester nodded. 'Yeah, well, we all agree it's a great idea, and you may regret buying this place now but when you done it up, Dolly, think how many kids you can give a place to.'

Dolly sighed. 'Yeah, it's just the finances, isn't it? And

that's what I'm going to use the diamonds for. Now, if any of you have any thoughts about getting a cut, then you've not got a hope in hell. I'm not planning on sharing this with any one of you. They are mine, all mine, and I'll need every penny.'

'But we know that. All we're offering is to help you run this place,' Ester said warmly, and the other women muttered in agreement.

Julia leaned forward. 'Will you need any help in getting them from this guy? Any help fencing them? Surely we can help you there.'

'For what? A cut?' Dolly asked.

'Hell, no, just to show you how we all feel,' Ester said, beaming. She could almost feel the money in her hands, she was so close.

Dolly leaned back. 'Well, you can stay or go, up to you, but you'll have to earn your wages. I'm going to maybe need some help, I've been away a long time, and I'm not sure who to fence them to.'

Kathleen received a dig beneath the table. 'Eh, Dolly, leave that to me, I know the best. You get them and we'll soon have them sorted out, and cash in your hand. How much you reckon they're worth?'

Dolly paused before she answered. 'Maybe three and a half million . . . I doubt if I'll see more than one, maybe one and a quarter back.'

There was a lot of murmuring and quiet sneaky looks as they each suddenly felt rich, their good mood lifting them into suggesting ways of fencing. Then Dolly stood up. 'I'm collecting them tomorrow so we'll soon see what the value is. Now I'm off to bed, maybe just have a walk around. Goodnight.'

They all chorused goodnight, as Dolly fetched her coat, refusing everyone's offer to join her.

As soon as the door closed behind her, Ester put out her hand. 'Put it there. What did I tell you?'

A few slapped Ester's hand, but Julia rocked in her chair. 'She doesn't seem eager to give us a cut, Ester. Maybe you're starting to celebrate a bit too early.'

Ester gazed at her. 'She brings them here and we don't get a cut, we don't wait for her to fence them, we simply take them! Agreed?'

They all nodded. They seemed to have forgotten Angela who had not said a word throughout. Ester suddenly realized she was there and reached out to prod her. 'You just got lucky, darlin', but open your mouth to her about this and you'll be sorry, very sorry.'

Angela hunched her shoulders. 'I won't say anything to anyone.' But her mind was buzzing. This was a way to get Mike on the phone. At least he'd talk to her if she told him about the diamonds.

Ester twitched back her bedroom curtain, the room in darkness. 'She's still out there, Julia, looking up at the house, as if she's checking us out.'

'Try just checking out what you lumbered her with,' Julia drawled, lying in the bed.

Ester jumped on the bed, crawling towards Julia who opened her arms to her.

'Can I ask you something?' Julia said as Ester nuzzled her neck. 'Would you kill her for them?'

Ester lay back against the pillows. 'No. Let me ask *you* something. If she caught us taking them, do you think Dolly would kill?'

Julia thought for a moment and then said, very softly, 'I'm sure of it.'

*

Dolly paced round the garden. She was cold, the night chilling her, but she didn't want to go inside. It was talking about him, it brought it all back. She walked slowly towards the swimming pool: the dank, dark water made her remember even more clearly. The way he smiled at her, waiting there by the big ornate lake. He never expected her to kill him, not for a second, and she would never forget the look of total surprise on his face when she brought out the gun and fired: a half mocking smile, then that moment of fear. And then he was dead, his body falling backwards into the water.

She rubbed her arms, turning back to the house. She was going to make this work, with or without that bunch of slags. She knew that she would need help, though, and she toyed with giving them a few hundred each, but the bulk was going to be put into bricks and mortar, into making Grange Manor House her dream come true, on a bigger scale than she had ever hoped for. And it had been her dreams that had kept her going for all those long, empty years in prison.

CHAPTER 6

DOLLY WAS up at six. She went through the *Yellow Pages* and earmarked the local building companies. She couldn't wait to get started. At nine, she had Angela sitting at the reception desk, calling all the companies and asking for them to come and give estimates. She had been making out copious lists of all the contents of the manor, giving the women orders to list what they felt needed to be done in different parts of the house. They all went about the delegated duties with a zest and energy that sparkled like the diamonds they all expected to get a slice of.

By ten o'clock, the drive was filled with an odd assortment of trucks as builders arrived. They eyed each other and had hushed private conversations with the new owner, Mrs Dorothy Rawlins. They walked around the grounds, studied the pool, the stables, all of them trying hard to win the race. Mrs Rawlins wanted an immediate verbal estimate. She wanted the work to start immediately, that afternoon if possible.

Dolly felt more alive than she had for years. She drove into the village in Gloria's Mini and bought provisions, wellington boots, sweaters and jeans. If the women were genuine, she'd soon find out. She then went into the town hall to speak to Mrs Tilly again, more confident than the last time, and she asked if there was any possibility of being

134

interviewed by the board before she gave the go-ahead for structural work to begin on the house. Mrs Tilly promised she would do what she could but she doubted the board could see her straight away. It would be more like five to six weeks so that they had time to assess her details.

Mrs Tilly liked Dolly, her forthrightness, her eagerness and, above all, her genuineness. When she went to see the chairman of the board, she asked if there was any possibility of moving Mrs Rawlins's application forward. He looked over his diary and mused that the earliest would be in three weeks' time.

Dolly handed out the wellington boots and jeans and asked for the groceries to be unloaded. She had ordered a giant deep freeze, plus a new fridge. The women looked on as trucks delivered wheelbarrows, spades, brooms and cleaning equipment. It was still only twelve o'clock when the builders began to ask to speak to Dolly about their estimates, and she sat in the dining room listening to each man. She eventually chose John Maynard, Builder and Carpenter. He was a one-man business that hired in work-men. His yard was only a mile from the manor and his estimates were lower than any of the others. The reason she hired 'Big John' was not only because his estimates were low, but she reckoned that as he was a one-man show, she could make a cash deal and cut down on the VAT payments.

Like a royal princess, she began the tour with Big John, working from the top of the house down to the cellars. He pointed out what structural work was required; mainly the roof needed to be replaced and the chimneys were danger-ous. Every window sash had to be renewed; ceilings and all décor must be refurbished, and all the plumbing in every bathroom, the boilers. In other words, the manor needed to be stripped back to the bare boards and rebuilt. He said it would cost at least between sixty and seventy thousand pounds, and that excluded fitments and fittings; with those it would come to at least a hundred and fifty thousand.

Dolly was unfazed as Big John pointed out the dry rot, wet rot, failing damp courses, and he had not even taken into consideration the gardens, stables, swimming pool and orchard. Work on them would mean extra cost but his charges were still way under any of the larger firms.

'How long will it all take?' Dolly asked.

'Six months at least.'

She frowned: she would have to have that meeting at the town hall to find out what grants she would be entitled to because it was now obvious that Ester's big deal about all the furnishing being part of the sale meant nothing. Everything needed to be replaced – cutlery, linen, beds, mattresses, carpets. She knew she was looking at around half a million to get the manor back into shape – and that was for only the bare necessities because she would also have to install fire alarms and child safety equipment, but she was almost jubilant. She felt she was able to finance the place and still come out with money in the bank for emergencies, perhaps schooling and further education for the kids, home helps, nannies. She embraced everything in one huge confident sweep. Big John agreed to cut out the VAT for cash payment and departed a happy man to begin hiring workmen, plumbers, carpenters, brickies. Mrs Rawlins had agreed to pay him in fifteen-thousand-pound instalments as and when necessary, throughout the months of work. Big John ordered scaffolding, as the first payment from Mrs Rawlins would be on the first day of work commencing. The start date was virtually that afternoon and Big John was almost as ebullient as his new employer.

The women, in wellington boots, jeans and old sweaters,

began to 'look busy', with a lot of comings and goings, but none were doing much or over-exerting themselves. They were more intent on keeping an eye on Dolly, but monitoring her phone calls was difficult as Angela was constantly on the phone making calls for her.

Ester passed Angela twice. 'You're not still on the phone, are you, Angela? Maybe Dolly wants to call somebody.'

'I'm calling people for her. She's given me a list.'

Angela was telephoning the social services, trying to find out what the building requirements and stipulations were, and if there was any information that could be sent, but she kept on being switched from one department to another.

Out in the stables, the women were half-heartedly clearing away years of rubbish, old wine crates and bottles. Rotting bags of garden debris mixed up with old garbage bags made it a hard physical job that none of them were trying too hard at.

Ester marched out. 'That bloody Angela is *still* on the phone. It's crazy, she's been on it all morning.'

'I thought Dolly was gonna call about the diamonds,' bellowed Gloria.

'Can you say that any louder, Gloria? Maybe the station attendant didn't pick it up!'

Kathleen hurled a crate from the loft. 'Well, get her off the bloody phone.' She climbed down the ladder as Ester paced up and down. 'If she's paying cash to that builder, she's either got to have more than she let on or she's going for them later today.'

Kathleen began to load the wheelbarrow and yelled that somebody else should also look as if they were working apart from her. Ester climbed up the ladder and began to kick down crates as Gloria dragged out an old table with three legs.

'Gloria, come up here. *Gloria!*'

'*What do you want?*' she yelled back, and then looked up at Ester as she peered down from the loft.

'You come up here, Gloria!' Gloria sighed and went up the ladder. As her nose appeared at the top, Ester pointed to some old straw covering suspicious-looking bags. 'Are these yours?'

Gloria shrugged. 'Maybe. What's your problem?'

Ester knelt down and dragged forward one of the open bags. 'They're full of guns, Gloria.'

'So bleedin' what? What's that got to do with you?'

'A lot. There's gonna be builders coming back this afternoon, and they'll be swarming all over the place. If they find them, they'll think the bloody IRA have taken up residence. Move them.'

'Where to, for chrissakes?'

'Somewhere out of sight, not left up here for anyone to find.'

'I'll move 'em but I'll need you to help. They weigh a ton.'

Dolly was reading the leaflets from the social services when she heard a yell from below. She crossed to the window to see Gloria staggering towards the house with Ester, carrying what looked like a body in a bag.

They stumbled through the kitchen, all the guns wrapped in an old piece of carpet. As they went into the hall, they found Angela on the phone.

'Well, I have to see you, it's important.'

'Get off the phone,' Ester snapped.

Angela whipped round. 'I'm still calling for Dolly,' she lied, and began to redial.

The two women continued on towards the cellar and

down into the sauna. Dolly watched from the landing, wondering what they were taking down there. She moved slowly down the stairs as Angela hurriedly dialled again. 'Keep getting put into different departments, Mrs Rawlins.'

Dolly pressed her finger over the button and then lifted it up. She asked Angela to dial a number for her and to ask for Jimmy. Angela did as she was told. Dolly leaned forward, listening. 'Ask him if he has got them,' she whispered, as Angela held her hand over the phone.

'Got what?'

Dolly gave her one of her strange, sweet smiles. 'I'll maybe tell you about it but just do as I say, love.'

Angela hesitated and then spoke into the phone. 'Have you got them?' she stammered.

Donaldson looked at Palmer. They had still not found the stones but Palmer nodded for him to say that he had them, and to stall for time. 'Yes, I've got them, but not here.'

Dolly wrote on a note-pad and passed it to Angela. She read it and then said into the phone, 'I'll collect them at two o'clock tomorrow afternoon.'

Dolly pressed on the cradle to cut off the call, and as Ester and Gloria came up from the cellar told Angela to carry on contacting the social services. 'Still clearing the junk from the stable, Dolly.'

'Good, keep at it. We'll have some skips delivered soon so a lot of it can be chucked into them. I'm going to London tomorrow afternoon.'

They smiled, and went out to report that it looked like Dolly was going to pick up the diamonds the following afternoon. They started clearing the rubbish with renewed vigour.

Dolly waited until Angela had started telephoning again before she slipped down into the cellar and looked around for what she had seen Gloria and Ester carrying. She went into the old sauna locker room. Some of the cupboards were dented and hanging open but a row of three was locked, dusty fingerprints showing they had been opened and used recently. Dolly looked around and found an old screw-driver left on a bench. She prised open a locker and found herself looking at a thick canvas bag. She swore, and then sighed, leaning against the old locker. 'Stupid, stupid, stupid . . .'

The women were all worn out from their efforts. The scaffolding was being erected around the house and the men worked hard until seven when they left. The women sat watching TV, all of them knackered, apart from Dolly who remained at the kitchen table making notes and copious lists.

When they had gone to bed, Ester suddenly sat bolt upright, nudging Julia. 'Somebody's downstairs, can you hear?'

Julia listened, and then crept to the doorway. She could hear nothing. Ester looked out of the window and whispered, 'She's out there again, look, up by the woods. What is she doing?'

Dolly was standing, staring at the manor, looking from one window to the next. She wore wellington boots and a raincoat she had found in a closet, a man's raincoat, stained and torn.

'What's she doing out there?'

'I dunno. Maybe reviewing her property. Come back to bed.' Julia yawned.

'I don't trust her one bit,' Ester said, but she returned to bed. Hours later she woke again as she heard someone on the stairs. She listened and then heard Dolly's bedroom door opening and closing.

'I don't trust her,' she murmured, but fell back into a dreamless sleep.

The workmen arrived at six. They were still putting up the scaffolding, but they had also begun to clear out old carpets and broken furniture, laid down planks for easy access by wheelbarrows into the hallway, and bags of cement had been delivered and left by the open front door. Dolly was up and having breakfast when Big John tapped and entered. 'Scaffolding should be up by this afternoon and we'll start clearing out anything you don't want, get ready for the roof. Er, I've hired eight men so . . .'

'You'll get the first payment end of the week, if that's okay, just a couple of days.'

'Oh, fine. It's just I'm laying out cash for all the tiles and the men'll want wages come Friday.'

'I know, love, but I have to go to London to get the cash. You'll have it, don't worry.'

'Okay, Mrs Rawlins.'

'Thank you, John.' She sat a moment, tapping her teeth with a pencil, as one by one the women drifted down for breakfast.

'Will you all start clearing the vegetable patch? I got bags and bags of seeds we can start planting,' Dolly said, as they started frying bacon and eggs.

Julia walked in, face flushed. 'You know, those old stables are in quite good nick – be nice to get a horse. I used to have one when I was a kid. They're not that expensive to keep, or to buy, you'd be surprised.'

Dolly paid no attention but concentrated on her notes.

'Did you hear what I said, Dolly?' Julia said, as she threw off her jacket.

'Last thing we need right now, love, is a horse. Let's get the garden in order first. We can start that while the house is being done over, no need to fork out for gardeners, most of it's just rubbish that's got to be shifted.'

The women looked at one another, having no desire to 'shift' anything but the eggs and bacon.

'I'm going up to London this afternoon. I'll take Angela with me.' Dolly left the kitchen and went to the yard.

Ester closed the door behind her. 'Told you, she's going for them this afternoon. Get Angela in here, go on.'

Gloria caught Angela dialling. She crooked her finger. 'Who you callin'?'

'My mum, let her know where I am.'

'Well, do it later. Come in here, we want to talk to you.'

Dolly walked up to the woods. It was a beautiful clear day but she stopped as she heard the sound of a train from the small local station. She watched the level-crossing gates open and close, and saw a square-faced boy sitting on a stool, a train-spotter. He was making copious notes in a black school-book, checking his watch, face set in lines of concentration. Dolly strolled down from the woods on to the small narrow lane by the crossing.

'Good morning,' she said cheerfully.

The boy looked up: his face was even squarer close to and his thick black hair stuck up in spikes. 'Good morning. My name is Raymond Dewey,' he said loudly. 'I'm here every day, checking on the trains. I'm the time-keeper. That was the nine o'clock express, on time, always on time.'

'Really? You have an important job then, don't you? Raymond, is it?'

142

'That is correct, Raymond Dewey of fourteen Cottage Lane. Who are you?'

'Well, Raymond, I'm Dolly, Dolly Rawlins.'

'Hello, Dolly, very nice to meet you.'

She smiled at his over-serious face. Bright button eyes glinted back as he licked his pencil tip and returned to his work.

'Well,' Dolly said then, 'I won't disturb you. Bye-bye.'

He stuck out his stubby-fingered hand and she shook it. His grasp was strong, almost pulling her off her feet. Close to, he was much older than she had first thought but she thought no more of him as she wandered back towards the manor, going via the small narrow road, then cutting back up to the woods.

Mrs Tilly replaced the receiver and checked her watch. She thought it was probably best to discuss it with Mrs Rawlins personally, so she left her office.

The women were grouped around the vegetable patch. Connie was peering at seed packets as Julia dug the soil, turning it over. Two wheelbarrows were filled with weeds and rubbish.

'Should these be goin' in now?' Gloria asked, as she opened another packet.

Julia began to stick in rods. 'Bit late, but if the weather keeps fine it'll be okay.'

Gloria sprayed out the packet.

'*Not there!* Over here, what do you think I'm putting the rods in for?' Julia shouted.

'Well, I didn't know. What you got in your packet, Connie?'

143

Connie pulled at the top to open it and the seeds all fell out.

'Pick them up,' said Julia, bad-tempered.

'What, all of them?' asked Connie. 'There's hundreds!'

Gloria laughed and kicked at the seeds. 'Who gives a bugger? Just push them over there.'

They saw a Mini Metro pull up by the front path. 'Who's that?' Julia asked.

'I dunno, she's driving this way now.'

It was Mrs Tilly. 'I'm looking for Mrs Rawlins.'

'Try the back door,' said Gloria. 'Drive round the back, past the stables. She was in the kitchen.'

Mrs Tilly smiled her thanks and pulled away.

'Who's that?' Gloria asked.

'Why didn't you ask her?' said Julia, impatiently.

Connie, on her hands and knees, was picking up one seed at a time. 'Ugh, the soil's gettin' under my nails. It feels all gritty and horrid.'

'Take them off, then,' said Gloria as she kicked more soil over a mound of seeds.

'No, I won't – they cost a lot of money.'

Gloria peered down at her. 'Come this afternoon, sweet-face, you'll have a lot too, so come on, let's go and see what the Metro wanted.'

Mrs Tilly tooted the horn and stepped out of the car as Dolly hurried out from the kitchen.

'Mrs Tilly, good morning.'

'Good morning, Mrs Rawlins. I can't stop but I wanted to tell you personally. We had a cancellation for this afternoon so the board are reviewing your case and, if you're available, can see you this afternoon at four thirty.

144

I'm sorry it's such short notice but as they're all gathered, it seemed a shame not to jump the queue, so to speak.'

Dolly beamed. 'Is there any advice you can give me, anything I should take with me?'

Mrs Tilly smiled, then said earnestly, 'My advice to everyone applying for foster caring is always tell the truth because everything is always checked and double-checked.'

'Thank you very much, Mrs Tilly. Are you sure you won't come in for a cup of tea?'

'No, I shouldn't have really left the office unattended.'

'I'll see you later then.'

Angela had overheard. She came to the kitchen door. 'Mrs Rawlins, about this afternoon—'

Dolly turned and frowned at Angela to shut her up, then turned back to Mrs Tilly. 'Four thirty, then, Mrs Tilly. Should I wear a suit, do you think?'

'Wear anything you feel comfortable in. You'll be asked a lot of questions, some very personal, so whatever you feel most confident and relaxed in. Goodbye.'

Dolly waved. She felt like skipping – everything was coming together so fast and they were obviously taking her proposals seriously. She waited until Mrs Tilly's car had disappeared before she clapped her hands. 'Did you hear, Angela? I've got a meeting before the social services board. This is positive, isn't it? I'm going to make this work.'

Angela wrinkled her nose. 'But what about that Jimmy bloke? You said you'd see him this afternoon. I phoned him yesterday, remember? You can't go to London for two and be back by four thirty. It's after eleven now.'

Dolly folded her arms. She'd forgotten – unbelievable but she had. It was the excitement. She'd not felt like this since she was a kid. She hugged her arms tightly around herself. 'Get the others in. Tell them we need to talk.'

Angela shaded her eyes as the women slowly trooped into the yard. 'They're coming in now.'

Dolly whipped round. 'I hope that Mrs Tilly didn't cop sight of Ester. Is she with them?'

'No, I'm here, Dolly,' Ester called from the kitchen.

Dolly went into the house. She didn't say a word to Ester but hurried up to her room to sort out what she would wear for the afternoon's meeting.

They all looked at Angela, then Ester. 'Don't ask me what went down, Angela was here. What did that woman want?'

Angela told them about the board meeting and they shrugged, not interested, until Angela said, 'She was taking me to London this afternoon. Well, now she can't go.'

Dolly was brushing her hair, talking to herself, trying to sort out exactly what she should do. She had intended making a few calls, just to check out some of Harry's old fences, preferring to use people she knew rather than trust Kathleen's contacts. Now she sat on the dressing-table stool. Could she trust them? she asked herself. Sure she couldn't, but she reckoned little Angela was on the level. She made up her mind. She didn't like leaving Jimmy Donaldson holding the stones for too long. He could get itchy fingers and she'd kind of given him an ultimatum. She didn't like going back on that as it made her look weak, as if she didn't mean business. Harry had something on Donaldson but without him, Donaldson might just try it on.

They were sitting at the table in the big kitchen, obviously waiting. As soon as she walked in, she could feel the tension. 'Okay, this is how we work it. One of you will have to collect the stones for me. I can't risk losing this opportunity with the board members. They're doing me a big favour as it is. Someone dropped out and I'm being upped to meet them, so . . .'

Ester looked at Julia. 'What do you want to do?'

Dolly sat down. 'Jimmy's waiting for me to come at two o'clock. I said I'd be there, to collect at two this afternoon as I'm not too keen on leaving them with him. He'll have them by now so one of you'll have to go and do it for me.'

There was a unanimous 'I'll do it' but Dolly shook her head.

'What, don't you trust us?'

'No, if you want my honest opinion, but if I say I'll give you each a cut, then whoever picks them up will do every one of you in. So that's a bit of an incentive to come back, isn't it?' Dolly's mind was racing. She never said how much of a cut but it was only to be a few hundred quid each. They could fight that out later, when she'd fenced the diamonds.

She looked them all over: Ester was Julia's partner, so they wouldn't do together; Kathleen she wouldn't trust with a loaf of bread, or Gloria, so she went for Ester, the least trustworthy – but with Julia at home Dolly reckoned she'd return. 'Okay, Ester, you go.'

Ester couldn't hide her smile.

'You sure, Dolly? I mean, what do you think, Ester?' Julia said, and Ester could have smacked her.

'I'll do it. Don't be stupid.'

Julia shrugged her shoulders. She knew that Ester had people after her but she said nothing. 'Okay, if you say so.'

'Take Angela with you, pair of you do it. Ester collects, you drive, Angela.' Dolly pointed at them in turn.

Angela seemed scared to speak, looking from one to the other.

'Why Angela?' Ester demanded.

Dolly gave an icy smile. 'I trust her.'

'And you don't trust me?'

'No, but I don't think you'd leave Julia in the lurch – leave us all in the lurch – would you?'

They glared at Ester, almost as if warning her that she'd better not try anything. Dolly felt good. Yeah, she'd made the right decision.

'So get yourselves together, take the Range Rover and get moving.'

Julia walked in as Ester was changing, and shut the door. 'You're coming back, aren't you?'

Ester snapped, 'Of course. She's not as dumb as you think. She knows I've got people after me. I'm not likely to fence the gear all by myself in one afternoon, am I?'

Julia sat on the bed. 'I dunno. Just seems odd she'd choose you, not me.'

'Why you?'

'Because she knows I'd come back if you were here, but I don't know if you would – that answer your question?'

Ester leaned over Julia. 'I'll be back, don't think I won't, and she's tied me to Miss Goody-Two-Shoes, so she'll be watching me like a hawk. I'll be back, Julia.'

'Then what?'

Ester straightened and clenched her fists. 'Well, you said it the other night. You reckoned Dolly would kill for those diamonds. Maybe, just maybe, I would too if she tried it on. You'll see which of us is tough. They're my ticket out, Julia, and I won't be content with some fucking measly little cut.'

'What about the others?'

'Fuck 'em. Now, how do I look?'

'Great, but then I'm biased.' Julia smiled: Ester always turned her on when she was hard like this. She liked her like this; she was so icy cold, so arrogant and, uppermost, so dangerous.

Angela stood in front of Dolly, who was close, her voice soft. 'You watch her all the time. You stay in the car, see her collect, then you put your foot down and come straight back here, okay? This is the address, twenty-one Ladbroke Grove Estate. You all right?'

'Yes, but I wish you'd ask one of the others.'

'No, love, I only trust you, maybe because you're the only one who hasn't been inside. You've still got some honesty about you, some integrity none of the others has. They'd have 'em and be away, I know it. You're my safety lever.'

Angela was in turmoil but couldn't see any way out of it. She was still shaking as Ester walked in, dangling the car keys. 'Okay, we're all set, sweetface, let's go and collect.'

Gloria looked at the clock. 'Well, you got plenty of time.'

'Maybe we'll stop off for lunch.'

'Yeah. Just as long as you don't stop off any place after you picked them up.'

Ester laughed, unaware that Dolly had already searched her room and pocketed her passport. She was, as they all said, not the pushover they had thought, and now she was sitting drumming her fingers on the side of the desk, wondering if she had made the right decision. She decided to make a few calls just to be sure.

Ester and Angela climbed into the Range Rover. Ester gave Julia a little wink. 'Right, might as well get on with it then. See you all later.'

Julia slammed the door as the engine fired. She banged on the side of the door. 'Take care, Ester, see you later.'

Gloria leaned on a rake. 'If she doesn't show, I'll shove this up her arse.' They watched the Range Rover drive out and Julia stared towards the vegetable patch. Gloria called after her. 'She will come back, won't she?'

Julia walked. 'Yeah. I'm the love of her life, aren't I? She'll come back. So get your spades, we have to dig a deep trench so the water drains.'

Wandering back to the vegetable garden, dragging a spade, Gloria said, 'How come you know so much about gardening? I thought you were a doctor.'

'Bit similar, actually.' Julia laughed. She had always loved the outdoors. In fact, she liked being at the manor. She just didn't have the guts to say so.

Dolly dialled and waited. She recognized Tommy's throaty, chesty breath immediately. 'Hello, Tommy, it's Dolly, Harry Rawlins's widow.'

'Good God, you're out then, are you, gel?'

'Yeah, I'm out, but I need a favour.'

'You know old Tommy, lovey, if he can do you one, he will.'

'Just so long as you get paid for it, right?' Dolly chuckled.

'On the nail. So what can I do you for?'

Dolly lowered her voice. 'I've got a few things I want to run by Jimmy Donaldson, then maybe bring to you.'

'Jimmy Donaldson?' Tommy wheezed.

'Yeah, you know him?'

'Course I do. Runs a gig over in Hackney, or he did. You know he's been away for a few years – still is as far as I know.'

'Away? Where?'

'Banged up. Got pinched for floggin' some Georgian silver. Didn't you know?'

'You sayin' he's still in the nick? You sure?'

'Yeah, reason is, a few days back someone was asking after him and . . . hello? Hello?'

Dolly felt cold, her hand still gripping the receiver. If Donaldson was nicked, how come he was answering his phone? It didn't make sense. She sat down and ran her hands through her hair, trying to remember everything he had said at the fairground. The more she thought about it, the more she began to think that maybe she was being set up.

The women turned as they heard Dolly calling for Ester. 'She's gone. Dolly?'

Dolly ran towards them. 'They've gone? But why, why didn't they talk to me? I never told them to go.'

'Well, they couldn't wait.' Gloria started to laugh, but seeing Dolly's expression straightened her face. 'What is it?'

'I'm being set up. Jimmy Donaldson's supposed to be in the nick.'

'*You!*' stormed Julia. 'They've *gone!*'

Gloria hurled aside her rake. 'Get me car, we can catch them up. Come *on!*'

Julia ran after Gloria, Dolly following. Kathleen looked at Connie, who was still half-heartedly digging the trench. 'What did you make of that?'

'I don't know. What do you think?'

Kathleen gazed down at the trench. She rammed in her spade. 'Keep digging. This looks like a grave. Maybe we'll be putting somebody in it . . .'

CHAPTER 7

ESTER MOVED on to the fast lane as soon as they hit the motorway.

'No need to go so quick, Ester, you'll get picked up for speeding.'

'Then keep your eyes peeled for cop cars – and stop biting your nails, it drives me nuts.'

The Mini backfired and Dolly hit the dashboard. 'Next turning there's a hire firm. Pull in and get a car with something under the bonnet.'

'Who's paying for it?'

Julia shouted that she would, and Gloria headed towards Rodway Motors, garage and rental. She drove on to the forecourt and asked who had their licence to hire the car, but as only she had hers with her it was she who went into the reception. The others waited impatiently on the roadside.

'They should have waited!' Dolly seethed. 'If they'd waited I'd have told them not to go.'

'Well, they didn't,' said Julia, looking at her watch, 'but we'll be there in plenty of time.'

Dolly was clenching and unclenching her hands. 'If I miss this board meeting, I'll – I'll—'

Julia glanced at Dolly, curiously. She seemed not to care about the diamonds, only that she had been set up. 'What about the diamonds, Dolly?' she said.

'If Jimmy has done me over, he'll regret it, he'll pay for it, and he'll cough up. His shop, his house, I'll clean the little shit out, then I'll have him taken out. I might even do it myself.'

Julia blinked, and then heard the *toot-toot* of a horn as Gloria drove up in a red Volvo. Dolly ordered her to move over as she wanted to drive, and they set off towards the motorway.

At twelve fifteen, one of the officers at long last returned to the wall they had first checked, but it wasn't until almost one o'clock that they found the pouch of diamonds. There was no time to record it, just to get it driven at top speed to Donaldson's house on the Ladbroke estate. It was handed over to DI Palmer, who snatched it with hardly a thank-you.

'I've not logged it yet, Gov.'

'I'll do it, thanks.'

Palmer looked up and down the street, afraid the exchange might have been seen, but there was no new vehicle parked so he hurried into Donaldson's house.

DCI Craigh was standing in the hall. 'They got them,' Palmer gasped.

Craigh relaxed. 'Talk about cutting it fine. Let's have a look at them.'

'They've not put it on record yet.'

'I'll do it when I go in,' Craigh said, as he eased open the velvet pouch. 'Holy shit, look at the size of some of those stones,' he said in awe, then pulled the drawstring tight. 'Look, we don't let these out of our sight – that's your job and yours only, you watch these babies, okay?'

Craigh walked in and held up the bag to Jimmy Donaldson. 'Saved by the bell, sonny Jim, we got them.'

Donaldon looked over with baleful eyes. 'Just so long as you get her. She plugged her old man and I don't want her loose and after me.'

Craigh smirked. 'That's the whole point of the exercise, Jimmy. We want her back inside for nicking these.'

Mike stared blankly from his position by the window. He'd just about given up on them finding the stones in time but he couldn't say anything, daren't risk going back to Donaldson's shop or it would look suspicious. All he hoped for now was that Rawlins would arrive, get nicked, and whatever happened about the diamonds could be laid at Donaldson's feet, or somebody else's. Anyone could have switched those stones over the past eight years and he and his bloody mother would be in the clear.

'What time is it?' he asked. Everyone looked at his watch, including Donaldson.

'We've almost an hour to wait until she collects.'

As expected, Angela and Ester were in London with time to spare. They were parked close to Ladbroke Grove tube station, eating hamburgers. Well, Ester was, Angela couldn't stomach anything. She was in a state of nerves, wondering if she would have to face Mike.

'I don't drive.'

Ester turned to her with her mouth full. 'What did you say?'

'I said I don't drive. Well, I do, but not very well. I never passed my driving test and now, with my nerves I – I just don't think I'll be able to drive.'

Ester tossed the half-eaten hamburger out of the window. 'Well, it's a fucking brilliant time to tell me.'

'I'm sorry.'

Ester sighed. 'Okay, we switch. You collect, I'll drive.'

Angela chewed at her nails. 'I don't think we should do this, Ester. I'm scared. What if we get arrested?'

'For what? For chrissakes, stop bleatin'. All we're doing is picking up some hot gear. Now shut up, it's one thirty, we can start to head up the road soon.'

'It's one thirty,' squawked Gloria.

'You tell me the time just once more . . .' snarled Julia, and then looked up ahead. 'Oh shit, look at the traffic! It's a bloody jam.'

Dolly slowed down, took a look at the clock on the dashboard. 'We can still make it. We get on to the flyover, it's only about fifteen minutes from there.'

'We're nowhere near the bloody flyover,' yelled Gloria, and Julia reached over and whacked her one. Gloria pressed back into the seat as they inched forward, a long line of cars up ahead, bumper to bumper. 'This is not what I call very professional. You should have made a better arrangement, Dolly. I mean, just saying you'd pick 'em up at two o'clock.' She yelped as Dolly pulled out and drove up alongside the rows of orange cones and signs depicting workmen on the road. 'Fuckin' hell, you'll get us arrested next,' she screeched. But they made it to the head of the traffic, nudged into the line of cars as an irate driver gave the V sign, then one finger and a flow of verbals. Gloria wound down her window. 'I got a pregnant woman here, you prick, *fuck off*.'

The man stared as Dolly pressed on, horn blasting, as she cleared the rest of the traffic and headed towards Edgware Road.

*

Ester checked her watch. It was ten minutes to two. She eased into first gear. 'Let's go for it. We wait any longer and you'll be chewed down to your knuckles. It's at the end of Ladbroke Grove and off to the right.'

They drove down Ladbroke Grove, passing the police station on the right-hand side. 'Police station,' Angela whispered.

'Thank you, I might not have noticed it,' Ester said, but she drove carefully, not wanting any aggro at this stage.

Heading from the opposite direction, racing off the Harrow Road, came Dolly. Now she asked for a time-keep every two minutes as they headed down the road.

'It's off to the right. If they keep to two o'clock, we'll just catch them.'

Craigh looked at the clock. It was nine minutes to two. Donaldson was sweating now and Craigh leaned towards him. 'When she rings the doorbell, you answer, bring her in here, bag is open, and all she's got to do is . . .'

Mike turned from the window. He pressed his radio earpiece closer. 'Nothing yet, road's still clear.'

The two officers outside waited, eyes to the front, eyes to their wing and rear-view mirrors. The road remained empty.

Then it happened. The Range Rover was coming towards them just as, screaming up from the opposite end of the road, was the red Volvo but they couldn't see it clearly because the Range Rover obstructed their view. They saw Angela get down and then all hell broke loose. The Volvo mounted the pavement, Gloria hanging out of the window. '*Get back, get out of here!*'

Angela was hauled into the Volvo, Julia legged it after the Range Rover and jumped aboard, and the two cars disappeared, the exchange taking no more than half a minute. The two officers got out. They turned this way and that, as DCI Craigh hurtled out of the house.

'What the fuck is going on?'

'We dunno. Woman ran from one car, driven off in another.'

Craigh started to swear. 'Was it her? *Was it Dolly Rawlins?*'

Mike was at the window, shouting, 'What the hell is going on? It was her – it was Dolly Rawlins, for chrissakes. Why aren't they going after the goddamned car?'

Palmer turned on Mike. 'What the fuck for? Drivin' too fast? We dunno if it was her or not. Just stop actin' crazy.'

Mike ran out of the house. It was a total cock-up and it was at this moment Jimmy Donaldson saw his chance. He saw the stones, he saw Palmer with his back to him, and he was alone. He picked up the heavy glass ashtray, whacked Palmer over the back of the head, picked up the bag of diamonds and he was out, closing the door. The kitchen door closed as he let himself out the back way, leapt over a fence and took off down the narrow alley running between the houses.

Craigh leaned into the patrol car. He couldn't believe what had happened. They had three digits of the index on the vehicle, but the two officers were just as confused as to what they'd seen.

'We saw a Range Rover, right? Cruised up behind us, I mean, it wasn't a blonde at the wheel, right? But a reddish-haired woman. We saw it stop, young kid gets out, sort of walks a few paces, next minute this fucking car screams up.'

157

Craigh rubbed his head. 'You see the driver at all?'

The officer pulled at his collar. 'Yeah, it looked like a friggin' car full of women, one was blonde.'

The second officer peered across to the sweating Craigh. 'No, two were blonde. There was one hanging out the window doin' all the screamin'. Two blondes.'

Craigh breathed in, told them to see if there was any police car within the vicinity.

'What you want, Gov?'

Craigh turned in a fury. 'Not this fuckin' mess for starters. Just see if we can get a full reg on the car.'

'Which one? One with the blondes or the Range Rover?'

The Range Rover was already moving out on to the Shepherd's Bush flyover, Julia panting with fear as Ester pressed her foot down. 'Not too fast, slow it down, keep in the near lane.'

'What the fuck happened?' Ester screamed.

Julia was white-faced with fear, eyes to the front, to the back as they could hear sirens. 'Dolly sussed she was being set up, that's all I know.'

Gloria screamed that Dolly was out of her mind. She had gone right round the Shepherd's Bush roundabout and was heading back the way they had come. 'You're crazy! You're driving us right back to Ladbroke Grove – you should have gone up on the motorway.'

Dolly said nothing. She turned left on to Ladbroke Grove again and began to move into the side-streets criss-crossing Ladbroke Grove.

'*What* are you *doing*?'

'What we supposed to have done, Gloria? If we get

stopped we was just up in London shopping, now shut up! Besides, if they're trying to find us, they won't be looking for us right on his bloody doorstep, will they? I'm going back on to the Harrow Road and then to the station. There's a train at three and I'm gonna be on it.' Dolly knew that if she was picked up, they must have Donaldson and he must have talked. She could be arrested.

Palmer was sitting with a damp cloth held to his neck. DCI Craigh was out in one of the cars searching for Donaldson. It was now bordering on utter farce and one they would all be in heavy trouble about.

Mike sat on the stairs, shaking his head in disbelief. His radio crackled. There was still no sighting of Jimmy Donaldson, who was at that moment running for his life with a bagful of fake diamonds. But only Mike knew they were fakes.

Jimmy Donaldson didn't know he'd risked everything for a bag of glass. He was running and dodging down the alleyways, hugging the pouch bag to his chest. He reached the end of Ladbroke Grove and he was still in the clear. He ducked and dived down Portobello Road, in and out of the stall-holders, catching his breath in antique shops. He was making his way towards a back link road that led on to Harrow Road, and he knew he'd be able to nick a motor easy. They were sometimes being worked on by blokes he knew so he reckoned if he made it there he'd be away.

Dolly forced Gloria into the back seat of the Volvo as she knew they'd be looking for a middle-aged blonde. Then she dragged Angela out of the car and shoved her into the driving seat. 'Get in and drive.'

Angela had never driven an automatic in her life. Dolly crouched in the back seat with Gloria. 'Just put the gear into "Drive", Angela, and take it nice and easy. Go up to the end and you take a right. There's a small slip road, we can ease through it onto the main Harrow Road.'

Dolly was calm, quiet until Angela took a left instead of a right, then she almost punched the back of Angela's head.

Donaldson was panting, sick with having run himself into the ground as he wove in and out of the parked cabs and trucks. He saw the car, saw the door open with the keys inside, and his heart lifted. He got another surge of adrenalin and was ready to make a charge for the parked car.

As he did the run, Angela careered down the alley, terrified, still shouting that she couldn't control the car, that she had never driven an automatic and hadn't even passed her test on an ordinary car. Dolly gritted her teeth with fury. She knew they'd only be looking for a middle-aged blonde woman.

'Stay fucking calm,' screamed Gloria. 'I dunno where we are. Where the hell are we? It's a dead end, Dolly.'

Dolly knew exactly where they were and told Angela to keep going straight ahead. Either side of the road were garages, some with their doors open, mechanics working on vehicles, but no one was paying them much attention. By now they were moving more slowly. As they turned at the top end of the narrow yard and Dolly told Angela to put her foot down on the accelerator, Jimmy Donaldson, scared he was being followed and looking back over his shoulder, didn't see the car and ran out straight into the Volvo.

His body took the full impact of the car side on. It threw

him up into the air, he rolled across the bonnet and slithered to the ground on the opposite side. Angela rammed on the brakes, both Gloria and Dolly lurching forward in their seats. 'What the bloody hell was that?'

'A bloke! You've gone an' hit a bloke, for chrissakes!' bellowed Gloria. She then screamed as Donaldson, still alive, tried to stand, his face pressed against the window, clawing at the door.

'Back up,' shouted Dolly, ramming the car into reverse. Angela slammed her foot down on the accelerator again and as the car lurched backwards, Donaldson's body disappeared.

'He's under the fucking car,' shrieked Gloria. She leaned over and pressed the car into 'Drive'. Angela was sobbing hysterically as the car bumped forward. They all felt the hideous bump and heard the sound beneath the wheels.

Donaldson's chest was crushed. He lay face down in the gutter and, as Dolly ran from the car, two mechanics from one of the nearby garages, hearing the women screaming, began to look over. They were too far away to see who was in the car or what had happened.

Dolly almost fainted when she turned the body over and recognized Jimmy Donaldson. As she felt his pulse, she saw the black velvet pouch containing the diamonds. It was half in, half out of his jacket. She didn't miss a beat. She snatched them, stuffed them into her pocket, and returned to the car. Neither Gloria nor Angela saw her do it. Both were in a state of shock.

'Get out of here and fast. *Move it, Angela!*'

Now the watching men were more interested in what was going on at the bottom of the yard. The Volvo's tyres screeched as it hurtled round the corner and disappeared. Not until they stood in the centre of the road did they see the body.

161

By the time the police arrived at the scene, Donaldson's body was covered and being lifted into a stretcher. No diamonds and, for DCI Craigh, useless witnesses who could not say for sure the exact make of the car or even give a description of the driver. All Craigh did know was that it had been a major cock-up. Jimmy Donaldson was dead and no one had seen Dolly Rawlins anywhere near his home. If she had been in the car that killed Jimmy, they had no evidence. They had, as he put it to DI Palmer, fuck all. What was worse, they could all get into very deep trouble over what had taken place, and they all knew it.

Dolly made it to the train just in time. She had to run along the platform and opened one of the doors as the train was moving. The guards shouted but she was on it and she hauled Angela after her. They sat in the compartment heaving for breath. Dolly felt the pouch bag in her pocket sticking into her stomach. She leaned back, closing her eyes.

'We made it.'

Angela was still panting, scared to death. 'That – that man I ran over.'

Dolly opened her eyes. 'Not your fault – you couldn't stop. Eh, this is where we both get arrested for not having tickets.'

She smiled, but Angela couldn't. All she could see was that grey object as it hit the windscreen, felt that hideous bump as she ran over him, not once but twice. She started to cry.

'Pull yourself together, Angela, we don't want anyone to . . . remember us. So I'll sit up front, away from you, all right, love?'

Dolly made her way up the train, slipped into the toilet

and held the bag of diamonds tightly to her chest. She'd got them and she'd still make the meeting.

Gloria took a steady, almost scenic, route back to the rental garage, first stopping at a car-wash and checking for any signs of damage or blood on the bumpers, but the car didn't even have a dent. The windscreen wasn't cracked either. She was impressed with the Volvo. It dawned on her that there were no diamonds, and she was depressed and fed up by the time she collected her Mini and drove back to the manor. She had Eddie's guns, though – they'd make a nice packet. Gloria decided she should have stuck with what she knew, not been drawn into the diamond scam by Ester Freeman and her big ideas – she'd get the hell away from that Dolly Rawlins. She reckoned she was unlucky anyway.

Dolly went into the washroom at the town hall and told Angela to see which room they should go to. When she returned, Dolly had carefully stashed the bag of diamonds on top of one of the old toilet cisterns. She reckoned she might have a visit later: if some bastard set her up, they wouldn't leave it as it was. Somebody was bound to come sniffing around at the manor.

She turned as Angela slipped in and whispered, 'I said we'd been here for fifteen minutes waiting down the hall. They said they're running a bit behind and for you to go into the waiting room outside the boardroom.'

Dolly examined her face in the mirror. She looked a bit ruffled but she put on some lipstick and only then did she realize she was shaking.

*

163

Angela was biting her nails as she sat next to Dolly in the waiting room. Ten minutes ticked by, during which two women came in and walked out, Dolly making a point each time of saying, 'Good afternoon.'

Angela suddenly started to cry again and Dolly squeezed her hand tightly. 'Don't. Just hold on.'

'I think he was dead, Dolly. I'm sure I killed him.'

'You did, love.' Angela gasped with shock but it calmed her, just as the boardroom doors opened and Mrs Tilly walked out.

'I'm so sorry to have kept you waiting, Mrs Rawlins, but please do come in.'

Dolly smiled and straightened her jacket. She noticed Mrs Tilly looking at her watch and she said quietly, 'We got here early. I didn't want to be late, this is too important for me.'

Mrs Tilly held open the door, allowing Dolly to walk into the boardroom ahead of her. As the door closed behind them, Angela sniffed and pressed her hand to her mouth. She'd killed that poor man, she'd killed him and she couldn't face it. She pressed her hands to her mouth, then got up and hurried out.

Mike's wife picked up the phone. She could hear someone sobbing on the other end. 'Look, whoever this is, don't keep calling here, do you hear me? Leave us alone.'

Angela sobbed out that she had to talk to Mike, it was urgent, and there was something in her terrified voice that made Susan not put down the receiver. She didn't know where Mike was, but she paused. 'What's your name? Do you have a number he can contact you on? Hello? *Hello*? Who is this?'

'It's Angela, it's—' Susan couldn't make out what else

was said because of the sobbing, and then the phone went dead. She called the office and they said he was out. She called her mother-in-law. Audrey answered.

'Is Mike there, Mum?'

'No, love, I'm waiting for him to call. Did he tell you? I'm going to Spain, I'm just waiting for my passport.'

Susan asked Audrey to get Mike to phone her straight away if he happened to call.

'Are you all right, Susan?' Audrey asked, concerned.

'No, Mum, I'm not. If I ask you something, will you be honest? I mean it, Audrey, I don't want you to lie to me.'

'I won't, love.' Audrey had never heard Susan so agitated.

'I think Mike is seeing someone else. I'm getting hysterical phone calls and then sometimes they just put the receiver down on me.'

'Oh, Mike wouldn't, love, it'll be somethin' to do with his work, he wouldn't carry on.'

Susan clutched the receiver tighter. 'You ever heard him mention a girl called Angela?'

Audrey sighed because she had. In fact, he'd called an Angela a couple of times from her flat. When she asked about her, he had said she was a kid he was trying to help out. Maybe he'd been doing a bit more than helping her out. 'I'll talk to him, don't you worry about it. I'll find out. But I think you've got it wrong – he wouldn't, not Mike. I've got to go now, love, don't you worry.'

Audrey could hear Susan crying and then the phone cut off. She replaced the receiver, feeling a bit guilty, but there were more important things on her mind. She looked at the clock: it was almost five. She crossed her fingers. Dolly Rawlins should have been arrested by now. She went back to her packing, half an ear listening for the phone, selecting her clothes for the trip to Spain. The face of her dead daughter stared back from the picture frame. Shirley Miller looked on with that sweet, vague smile.

The women were huddled in the kitchen as Gloria told her side of it, then Ester hers. Julia said nothing. Kathleen looked glum and Connie wanted to cry. She said, 'So, there's no diamonds?'

Ester gave a slow, burning stare. 'That's fucking bright of you to fathom out, Connie. What the hell do you think we've been talking about, Smarties?'

Mr Arthur Crow, the Chairman of the Board of Directors, looked over Dolly Rawlins's forms and listened intently to her answers. She seemed nervous but that was only to be expected. She described the manor and her intentions, how many staff she felt would be required to run it, how many children she could easily accommodate. That section was impressive: she was concise and to the point, saying the grounds were ample, there were stables and a swimming pool but truthfully that the house was in a poor state of repair. That was why she had pressed Mrs Tilly for an on-site visit as she wished to make the house suitable for children and therefore any structural work required by the social services she would carry out, but did not want to go to unnecessary expense. She had costed the rebuilding and was able to give estimates and overall costs of running the home. No one there could have queried her good common sense. They now turned to her criminal record and she made it clear what her crime was, how many years she had been sentenced to, and, as she had been sentenced for murder, that she would be on licence for the rest of her life. She said quietly that she had never been involved in any criminal activity before the shooting of her husband and that it had been at a time when she was emotionally unstable because she had at first been told he was dead, then had discovered he was alive and living with another woman who had his child. She spoke candidly about the therapy sessions she had been given at Holloway and that she had required no therapy for the past five and a half years.

'I found great solace in working with the young female offenders, especially in the maternity section of the prison. I developed an interest in working in the group-therapy sessions for the inmates and became a trusty, working with probation officers and therapists, not as a patient.'

Deirdre gave Dolly small encouraging nods and Mrs Tilly was a constant source of encouragement. The men were off-hand and cool, showing much more restraint.

'You have no children of your own, no near relative with young children?'

'No, I have not.' Dolly looked directly at a ruddy-faced man, who had made copious notes throughout.

'You have specifically requested young children.' It was the stern-faced Arthur Crow's turn; his thin wispy hair hung in a strand across his bald head.

'If that were possible, but I would hope for any child, or children, and having so much space and accommodation, if there were children that came from the same family and were to be separated, then I would accept any age, male or female.'

Dolly was asked further questions about whether she would be prepared to work with a foster carers and resident home advisory officers, and she agreed to be available and prepared to do anything the board suggested that would enable her to open the manor as a home.

'Mrs Rawlins, how are you at this present moment financing the running of the Grange?'

Dolly explained that she had a considerable private income that had enabled her to purchase the manor.

'Do you know the previous owner?' It was slipped in fast.

'No, I do not. I believe her name was Ester Freeman and the place had a very bad reputation. Perhaps that is why I think and my lawyers feel I paid a fair price for such a substantial property. At some time in the future I hope I can be self-sufficient as there is a large orchard and a considerable amount of good fertile soil for growing vegetables.'

Eventually, after over an hour and a half of questions and answers with Dolly maintaining her composure, she was asked if she would allow a visit within the next few days to assess the property. She agreed and stated that they were free to come at any time – in fact, the sooner the better. Mr Crow ended the meeting by saying that everything she had said would be assessed and obviously her past checked into in some detail. They thanked her for her honesty and wished her every success.

She walked out confidently, and was further gratified by Mrs Tilly's light touch on her arm as she left. 'Thank you so much for coming in to see us at such short notice, and we apologize for keeping you waiting.'

Dolly returned to the manor by taxi. At the level crossing they were held up for almost ten minutes. The cab driver shook his head and turned to the back seat. 'Sorry about this, it's the mail train. Holds us up for sometimes ten, twelve minutes. One night it was fifteen.' The gates opened, and they drove on down the narrow country lane back to the manor.

*

Dolly breezed in, all smiles, trailed by a downcast Angela. 'Well, it went very well. I feel positive and they're gonna assess everything then come and look over the house.' She shut the back door and tossed her handbag on to the table. 'I don't know about anyone else but I'm starving. Who's on the dinner tonight?'

Ester stared at her in disbelief. 'Is that all you've got to say? I'm glad everything went well for *you*!'

The police cars moved silently up the driveway, two officers from Thames Valley in front, followed by DCI Craigh, accompanied by DC Mike Withey and one uniformed driver. Craigh was first out. He walked up the manor steps, side-stepping the sacks of cement, and waited as the local police moved around to the back yard to enter from there. Then he radioed in that he was about to enter.

He gave one soft knock and murmured it was the police and that they had a warrant to search the premises. He then stepped back as the locals banged on the door. They didn't need much force as it was only on the latch, and they burst into the hallway, Craigh holding up the warrant.

'We have a warrant to search the premises. This is the police.'

Kathleen ran up the stairs, on to the first landing and legged it out on to a low roof at the back and stayed there. The other women ran this way and that, only Dolly remaining unflustered as she picked up the kettle to put it on the stove. Angela cringed back, crying, terrified that they had come to arrest her for the hit-and-run.

Seeing Angela in such a state was the only time Dolly worried. 'Angela, keep your mouth shut, you don't say one word. Just give them your name, nothing more, understand me?'

Gloria was clasping the back of the chair. She grabbed at Ester. 'What the fuck do we do?'

Ester shrugged her away. 'Nothing. There's nothing here.'

Gloria was almost passing out. 'Yes, there is. We put the bloody things in the cellar. *Eddie's guns are in the cellar.*'

Ester froze, but could say nothing as they were surrounded by police and herded into the drawing room.

Craigh looked at Dolly as she calmly opened a tea caddy. 'I am Detective Chief Inspector Craigh.'

Dolly smiled. 'Dorothy Rawlins.' She held out her hand for him to shake.

'Do you mind if I talk to you first? Do you want to see the warrant?'

'Of course. I'd also like to know what this is about.'

Craigh passed her the warrant and watched her study it. He looked into the hallway to Mike. 'I'll take Mrs Rawlins's statement first, then the others. Get their names, addresses, you know the deal.'

He looked back at Dolly. 'My men will begin searching the entire house and outbuildings.'

She nodded, seemingly still intent on reading the warrant. He waited patiently.

The women wandered around the drawing room; Gloria was now crying and Angela hadn't stopped, but it was Julia who asked in a furious whisper what the hell they were getting so upset about.

'There's an arsenal of weapons down in the sauna, Gloria's husband's guns, three bags full of them.'

Ester sat down, her face drawn in fury. Julia looked at Gloria, stunned. 'Are you serious?' But she knew she was because she had never seen Gloria so scared. Before she could say a word, Mike Withey walked in.

'I'll need all your names, dates of birth, present and past addresses.'

Behind Mike, the women could see the officers searching, moving up the stairs, some heading down to the cellar. They remained silent, all of them waiting with trepidation for the police to find the weapons.

CHAPTER 8

CRAIGH SAT with his notebook open as Dolly drank a cup of tea, never offering him one. She had agreed that she knew James 'Jimmy' Donaldson immediately, and seemed shocked when told he was dead.

'Dead? But he can't be. I only spoke to him yesterday. I met up with him a few days ago.' She sat sighing, asking how it had happened.

'Would you mind telling why you met Mr Donaldson?'

'Er, no, no, I don't mind. You see, he was keeping something for me. I've been in prison, you see, and, oh, this is a shock . . .'

Craigh tapped his pen on the table. 'What was he holding for you, Mrs Rawlins?'

'Well, they were nothing to look at, really. You wouldn't even think they were valuable, but they are, they're worth a lot of money.'

He leaned close. 'What exactly, Mrs Rawlins?'

'They used to be in my front garden at Totteridge, gnomes, two Victorian garden gnomes. Not the bright plastic things but old carved stone ones. Jimmy Donaldson was holding them for me until I got out. I called him about them, asked him if he still had them and told him I was going to collect them today, as a matter of fact.'

Craigh wrote down every word, gritting his teeth. 'Did you collect them from Mr Donaldson?'

'I couldn't get away because I had a very important meeting at the town hall.'

'What time?'

Dolly slowly repeated that she was at the town hall from three fifteen until after five – in fact up to shortly before they had arrived: she had been there for an assessment interview.

'Can anyone verify that, Mrs Rawlins?'

'Oh, yes.'

Craigh dug the pen in deeply as he wrote one name after the other. He had a terrible sinking feeling in the pit of his stomach that he had been well and truly stitched up.

The officers searched every room, lifted the floorboards, opened cupboards and cases. They went into the attic, they were out in the stables. Kathleen remained stuck on the roof, half hidden by the gables, and didn't move a muscle. They searched the grounds, the swimming pool and the cellars for eight hours, with fifteen men.

Kathleen inched back to the room from which she had escaped and fell asleep under the bed. The police were now concentrating on the sauna and steam room and the lockers. The women waited, expecting any moment the scream to go up but it never came. They smelt bacon being cooked and, to their amazement, Dolly walked in with a tray of bacon butties. Gloria was about to blurt out to Dolly that they were in trouble but Dolly shoved a sandwich into her hand. 'Eat it and say nothing.'

Gloria rammed the sandwich into her mouth and sat down.

Craigh was looking over the sauna when Mike joined him. 'They're searching the grounds now but so far nothing.'

Craigh felt knackered and, even worse, foolish. 'We've fuckin' been had, you know that, don't you? She's got about eight or nine names as alibis. She was at the ruddy social services.'

Mike didn't know whether this was good news or bad but he was as tired out as Craigh.

'This all stinks, you know that, don't you?' Craigh paced up and down, then jerked his head for Mike to come close. 'The Super's gonna have a seizure about the whole cock-up – Donaldson was in our custody.'

'I'm sorry,' Mike muttered.

'You're sorry. Jesus Christ, *sorry*? Have you any idea what a mess we're in? Donaldson dead, no sign of the diamonds . . .' Craigh hesitated and then licked his lips. 'Look, until we've sorted this, keep schtum about those stones. I never put it in the record sheets so maybe we can—'

'Fine by me,' Mike said quickly.

Craigh stared at him. 'Nothing's fine, Mike son. We have big problems and we've got to sort them.'

Mike nodded, his brain ticking away. He thanked God nothing had been found as it let him off the hook, but all he could do was look as glum as Craigh obviously felt.

Dolly watched the London mob, as she referred to Craigh and Withey, leaving, then let the curtain fall back into place. She yawned and said she was going to bed.

'Sleep? You can sleep, can you?' Ester said.

'Not easily, but I need to do a lot of thinking.'

Gloria was pulling at a piece of sodden tissue. 'Did you move them, Dolly? Did you?'

She turned her face, hard. 'What the hell do you think, you stupid idiot? Of course I bloody moved them – and thank God I did or we'd all have been arrested. I've been

174

waiting for you to talk about them. I saw you and Ester carrying them into the house.'

'I got nothing to do with them,' interrupted Ester.

'But you bloody knew they was in the house.'

Ester turned away. It was always the same: instead of being grateful to Dolly, she said nothing, whereas Gloria would have kissed her feet. But none of them was prepared for Dolly's next admission, dropping the line in quietly, with that smile of hers on her face. 'I also got the diamonds but I'm not talking about them yet. Like I said, I need to sleep, get my head straight.'

'You got them?' Ester said in wonder.

'Yes, Ester, I got them but they're not here. What is here smells, because someone had to tip them off. Somebody here's grassing on me – one of *you*. One of you hates me enough to get me put back inside and I'm going to find out which one of you it is.'

She walked out, slamming the door, and they stood there in mute silence, not believing what they had heard her say, hardly daring to believe they still had a chance of a cut of the diamonds. Then Gloria said, 'Grassin'? What she friggin' talkin' about? None of us'd do it, I mean, we want them diamonds as much as she does. She's nuts if she thinks it's one of us! None of us'd do it.'

Angela started to cry again and Julia looked at her angrily. 'Oh shut up howling, Angela. You're a pain in the arse.'

Angela ran out of the room, bumping into Kathleen, who was creeping down the stairs as the last of the Thames Valley police drove away. She walked into the drawing room and they all turned on her.

'Where the hell have you been?'

*

Dolly hunched the pillow up beneath her shoulders. She couldn't sleep. She stared at a stain on the wall, wondering. Who would hate her enough to want to put her back inside? Because that's what it came down to. If she'd been picked up with the diamonds, virtually holding Donaldson's hand, the cops would have got her. Even if they couldn't pin the old robbery on her, they'd have her for fencing the stolen diamonds. Either way, with her out on licence, she'd have been back in a cell and with no hope of bail. Was it just that dirty little con-man, Jimmy? If it was, then he'd got his just deserts but something inside her said there had to be more to it than that. Harry had taught her, 'Always remember, sweetheart, it takes two to tango. One leads, the other follows.' So who was in with that rat Jimmy Donaldson? If it was one of the women she would find out and God help them.

Dolly left the house and drove straight to the town hall. She hurried into the ladies' and found the pouch bag exactly where she had left it. She kissed it with relief. She then got down, straightened her skirt and slipped out, bumping into a surprised Mrs Tilly in the corridor.

'Mrs Rawlins?'

'I was just passing. I know there's no possibility of you having any answers for me yet but I just wanted to ask you how I did. Was I all right?'

'Yes, you were. I thought you handled yourself very well but it'll be some time before we have any definite news. I'll let you know as soon as I hear anything.'

'Thank you. I really appreciate all your help.'

Dolly hurried out and Mrs Tilly went in to speak to Mr Crow.

'You know, Mrs Rawlins is so keen, I think we should

push forward an on-site visit. I worry she may spend too much money without approval and I don't want her to waste her savings.'

He looked up from his diary. 'Well, we'll have to get some appraisals from her probation officer and the prison authorities. And we're nowhere near ready even to discuss the project yet.'

'Well, I would just like us to inspect the manor house. She was so enthusiastic.'

He smiled, flattening down his few strands of hair. 'I'll see what I can do. If we're visiting anyone near the location we can possibly have a look over the place as well. You like her, don't you?'

'Yes, I do. That said, far be it from me not to do everything through the correct channels.'

'As I said, I'll see what I can do but I was also impressed by her. I very much doubt if she will ever be allowed access to very young children, not enough experience, but she may be useful for the older children, the problem ones particularly. Leave it with me.'

Mrs Tilly smiled and left the office. She doubted if Mr Crow would show Dolly Rawlins any favours. He showed nobody any as he was a stickler for rules and regulations, but she knew he had been impressed by her. Everyone had.

Dolly stopped at a phone booth and called Tommy Malin. She asked if he was still in business, unlike Jimmy Donaldson. They had a few laughs, and she said she would be around later in the afternoon as she had something that might interest him. He agreed to meet her but she made no reference to what it was. She then returned to the manor. As she came in she saw Angela on the telephone. 'Who you calling, love?'

Angela spun round. 'Oh – my mum. I've not told her where I am.'

'Don't, and don't make private calls – that goes for all of you. Fewer people who know what's going on here the better.'

'Okay.'

'I'm going to London. You want to come with me?' Angela nodded. 'Good, in about an hour, then.'

The others, who had overheard the conversation in the kitchen, whispered and nudged each other, sure that Dolly was going to fence the stones. Ester gave them all a quiet talking-to: they were to show a lot more willing, they were to get out to that vegetable patch and look like they were working and loving every minute of it. They got to their feet, went out and trudged around with wheelbarrows, spades and rakes, and when Dolly and Angela left in the local taxi, they appeared to be too intent on their labour even to see them go.

As the cab passed them, Dolly laughed. 'Amazing what a bit of incentive can do, isn't it?'

'I don't understand,' Angela said, looking towards the women.

'Well, they all know I'm going to fence the diamonds this morning and they all want a slice so "Let's show Dolly how hard we're working!" Understand?'

'Oh, yes, I see what you mean.'

Mike had waited when Angela put down the receiver. He was hoping she would call back directly but after waiting half an hour he gave up. It had unnerved him to be told that Dolly Rawlins had the diamonds but he didn't know what the hell to do about it. He could tell Craigh but it was all getting like treacle and he felt his shoes sticking to it.

Susan walked in from the front door with a bag of groceries and looked at him. 'Hi, I didn't wake you when I went out, did I?'

'No, I'm up, had something to eat. I was just going to go actually.'

'Oh, were you? You stayed out all night. Surely they can't expect you to work today?'

He sighed. 'Yes, they can.'

'There was another call from your girlfriend yesterday – I tried to contact you, she seemed upset.'

'What?'

'Angela, she was crying, in a terrible state.' She stared at him, waiting. 'She said her name was Angela.'

'I heard you,' he snapped.

'What's going on with her, then?'

He took a deep breath. 'She's a tart, sweetheart, a young kid I helped out a while back when I was on Vice. Now sometimes she acts as an informant. There is nothing going on between us, it's business, all right? *Is that all right with you?*'

'I don't like tarts having your home phone number or ringing me up screaming and yelling. *Is that all right with you?*' Susan went into the kitchen. He dithered, knew he should talk to her, straighten it out, but instead he grabbed his car keys and left very quietly.

Dolly was feeling pleased with herself as she and Angela hailed a taxi heading for Tommy Malin's address. 'That Mrs Tilly is such a nice woman, I really like her. You know, Angela, if I get the manor opened as a kids' home it'll be my dream come true. It was all I used to think about when I was in Holloway.' She took the girl's hand. 'Don't worry about that hit-and-run. Gloria said there wasn't a mark on the car and if they'd got anything on you – on any of us – we'd have been copped last night.' Angela clutched Dolly's hand tightly. 'Will you want to stay on, help me?' She nodded. 'Good, I'll be able to pay you a decent wage and you can have cookery classes. Would you like that?'

'Yes, I would.'

She wanted to tell Dolly about Mike, about everything. She liked her so much, felt protected by her – but how *could* she tell her? And now, with that poor man she'd run over, it was all so complicated. She wanted to talk to Mike, needed to ask his advice.

The cab headed towards Elephant and Castle and then veered off down a small one-way road, stopping outside a paint-yard. Dolly got out, saying, 'You wait here, love, I shouldn't be too long.'

Angela watched as Dolly tapped on the door and disappeared inside the yard.

A young kid in filthy overalls pointed Dolly to the office and then rejoined his colleagues who were stripping down pine furniture.

'Dolly Rawlins,' wheezed Tommy Malin, leaning against the doorframe.

'Hello, Tommy.' She shook hands and he gestured for her to go in ahead of him. He waved at the workmen and closed the door.

'I'll put the kettle on.'

'That'd be nice,' she said, looking around, taking in the cheap desk, rows of bulging and dented filing cabinets and the massive cast-iron safe. Dolly eased herself on to a newspaper-filled chair. She looked over the equally cluttered desk: the scales, the rows of diamond cutters and pinchers, and rolls of velvet cloth, the only indication that perhaps

Mr Malin's paint and pine-stripping factory was used for other purposes. Tommy Malin would deal in literally anything he could turn round fast. He was famous for his high percentage and his 'no risk' attitude. He would deal in hot stuff but always insisted on a long chilling period. That was why he was so wealthy and had so far avoided arrest. He was very, very careful.

The women had done a half-day's work. Rods had been fixed up, more seeds sown, and the rubbish was now tipped into a skip left for them by the builder. Big John was getting a bit edgy; it was almost pay-day, he'd laid out all his savings to buy the materials, and still Mrs Rawlins hadn't given him the down payment. He'd seen all the women working out in the garden but Mrs Rawlins was not with them. He had even looked for her inside the house.

Connie was testing the sauna temperature when he asked if he could have a word with her. She turned and gave him a wonderful smile that made him flush.

'I'm sorry to bother you but is Mrs Rawlins around?'

'No, I'm sorry, she's gone into London. Can I help at all?'

He could feel his cheeks burning. 'Well, it was just we had an arrangement and Mrs Rawlins is a bit behind in the first instalment, you see, and I have to pay the men, pay for the materials and—'

'Oh, she's gone to get some money this afternoon.' Connie gave another wide smile. 'You couldn't have a look at the sauna for me, could you? I think I've got it working but I'm not sure.'

He nodded and she brushed against him as they went

into the small Swedish sauna hut. John checked the temperature dials and the coals. 'Do you like it hot?' he asked seriously.

'Oh, yes, as hot as you can give it to me.' He flushed again but she seemed to be concentrating on the temperature gauge. 'Do you work out?'

He stepped back – he couldn't deal with her closeness. She was the most glamorous woman he had ever seen or been this close to in his entire life. 'Yes, there's a good local gym, very well equipped.'

'Ah, I thought you did, I can always tell. You've got marvellous shoulders.'

Now the heat of the sauna was making him sweat but he didn't want to leave, didn't want to move away from her. He was automatically flexing everything, tightening his bum cheeks.

She leaned close, touching his biceps. 'What's your name?'

John breathed in gratefully as she opened the sauna door. He was getting dizzy. 'John Maynard.'

She started to swing her arms from side to side. 'Thanks for your help, John.'

When Connie joined the others, they were sweating and filthy. 'Sauna's working, it's really hot. Do any of you want to work out first?'

She received a barrage of abuse – as if after digging and wheeling the barrows they needed to work out! All they wanted was a cold drink and a long afternoon in the sauna.

Ester pushed Julia ahead of her. 'Don't worry about Dolly, she'll be gone ages. She'll only just have got there. We got hours.'

*

Tommy's wheezing breath and halitosis were overpowering. The drawn blinds, the bolted door and the hissing gas-fire made Dolly feel dizzy. She took off her coat. Tommy's thick stubby fingers began to unfurl the cord round the pouch bag. He pulled it open and laid it out flat.

'Is this some kind of joke?'

'No. Why?'

'I just made these up for somebody.'

'What?'

He turned his lamp out and pushed his eye-glass on to his forehead. 'You didn't pay a bundle for these, did you, sweetheart?'

'What are you talking about?'

'I made them up. They're glass, good settings . . . I mean, I did spend quite a few hours—'

'*You made these?*'

Tommy stared at Dolly, whose face was chalk white.

'Who for, Tommy?'

He wouldn't usually have said – clients are clients, and he was always a man to keep his mouth shut – but he knew she wasn't going to leave his office until he told her. He hedged as she leaned across the table, picking up a handful of the stones.

'I nearly went back inside for this crap, Tommy, so you tell me who ordered you to make them up.'

Mike knew something was up the moment the Tannoy rang out for him to go into DCI Craigh's office. Craigh looked up at him as he knocked sheepishly and entered. He pointed to the chair in front of his desk and told Mike to sit down. Mike could see a stack of files on his desk, one with Dolly Rawlins's name printed across it. 'Right, let's go from the top and don't bullshit me.'

'I don't follow.'

'I think you do. I am in it right up to my fucking ears over this Donaldson business. I've got the Super, the prison authorities, Donaldson's wife, his parole officer, all breathing fumes all over me so I'll kick it off, shall I? How did you know that Rawlins had bought the manor house?'

'My informant.'

'Oh, yeah? Which one?'

Mike flushed and explained about Angela, how he'd busted her along with Ester Freeman.

'You booked her, did you?'

'No, she was never charged. She wasn't on the game, she was just serving food at the house for the tarts and their punters.'

'So she told you all about Rawlins, her buying the manor?'

'Yes.'

'So who was the informant on the diamonds? Same source? You said it was a kid in Brixton with Donaldson. That's the only name I've got down as an informant.'

'Yes, that's true. When he told me, I contacted Angela and that's how I knew all the women were staying there.'

Craigh pushed his chair back and wandered around the office, hands stuffed in his pockets. 'Anything else? I mean, is there anything else you've not told me?' Mike licked his lips as Craigh came to stand close, leaning down so his face was almost touching Mike's. 'What about that diamond robbery, Mike? You want to tell me about that? Better still, tell me about Shirley Miller.' Mike closed his eyes. Craigh prodded him and he hunched away. 'This was personal, wasn't it?' Mike nodded. 'Your sister was killed on that diamond raid.'

'Yes.'

'Not on your original application form, Mike. There is no mention that you even had a fucking sister.'

Mike gave a half-smile. 'I didn't reckon it'd look good on my CV, Gov.'

'Don't you fucking joke with me, this isn't funny. Let's go from the top again. Your sister worked with Dolly Rawlins and—'

Mike interrupted, 'She used her, she manipulated her, she was only twenty-one, a beauty queen and . . .'

Craigh returned to his desk. Mike was close to breaking down, his voice faltering. 'I didn't have all that much to do with her. I was in the army, stationed in Germany when she was killed. Then when I joined up with the Met it was, like, all in the past, but my mum, er—' He was floundering, trying not to implicate Audrey. The sweat was pouring off him. 'I saw her grave, right? And I felt guilty that I'd never come home, never even sent flowers, and . . . my mum, always on and on about Dolly Rawlins. I'm sorry, I am really sorry . . .'

Mike sniffed, trying to hold on to his emotions because he wasn't acting any more. The more he tried to explain about Shirley, the more her face kept flashing across his mind and in the end he bowed his head. 'I loved her a lot. She was a lovely kid.' Craigh remained silent, staring at him. 'I know Rawlins instigated that robbery, I know it.'

'Eh, Mike son, Rawlins was sent down for murder, she killed her husband. It was never proved that she ever had anything to do with that diamond heist.'

'But she had.'

'You don't have any proof.' Craigh pursed his lips. 'Listen, to what I'm saying, Mike. Dolly Rawlins was *never* even charged with that heist. There was never a shred of evidence to link her to it. But your sister was no angel, her husband was a known villain, so don't give me all this whitewash Mother Teresa act. All I know is you used personal motives to instigate a full-scale operation, drawing in me, DI Palmer, the whole team on a mad caper that has landed us all in shit, making us all look like prize fucking idiots.'

'I know she was going for those diamonds,' Mike stuttered.

'*No, you don't.* You don't know anything. It's all been supposition because *you* had a private and personal motive against Rawlins.'

'She got away with murder.'

'She didn't, she served her sentence, and as far as being implicated in the Donaldson business she has an alibi, and a very strong one, that she wasn't even near Ladbroke Grove the day he was run over.'

'We had any joy tracing the car?'

'What car? How many red Rovers or red Volvos are there in London?'

Mike remained silent as Craigh jangled the change in his pockets, relenting slightly.

'We've got Traffic running around like blue-arsed flies – they always love a challenge. We got nothing from the road where Donaldson got hit, we've not got one decent eyewitness. In fact we've got bugger all. But we do have a nasty, dirty mess that I've got to clear up.'

'I'm sorry.'

'I hope to Christ you are. And from now on you stay clear of this Rawlins bitch or I'll have you back wearing a big hat, understand me?'

'Yes, sir.'

'Now piss off and I'll see if I can iron all this out.'

Craigh watched Mike walk out with his head bent.

Picking up Rawlins's file, he stared at her hard profile in the mug-shots and began to flick through her record sheet. He put in a call to the Aylesbury social services to double-check one more time that Rawlins was, as she had stated, being interviewed by the board members of the council.

Angela knew something was very wrong when Dolly walked stiffly back to the taxi. She opened the door and got in. 'Go back to the manor – get the train home.'

'Aren't you coming with me?'

'No. Just get on your way. I've got someone to see.'

'Well, don't you need a lift?'

'No, I want to be on my own for a while.'

Dolly passed over a ten-pound note and walked off down the road as Angela directed the cab driver to take her back to Marylebone station.

Mike let himself in and called Susan, but the house was silent. He checked the time and assumed she was collecting the kids. He sat down in the hall, knowing he'd had a narrow escape. The phone rang and he jumped.

Angela was at the station in a phone booth. She was relieved when Mike answered but taken aback when he yelled at her never to call his home again.

'Well, I needed to speak to you. I'm in London, I came here with Dolly. She got the diamonds, Mike, she had them with her.'

Mike stood up, trying to keep his voice calm. 'You sure? Where is she now?'

Angela told him where she had been, and then Mike said

he had to go, he couldn't talk any more. His head felt as if it was blowing apart. If Dolly Rawlins had the diamonds then she had to have run over Jimmy Donaldson. She had to have killed him. She had the diamonds, she killed Donaldson, she must know by now they were fakes. It seemed that any way he moved the shackles were on him, getting him in deeper and deeper. One thing, there wasn't a lot she could do about it. She wouldn't go to the law, but he knew one place she would go and his panic went into overdrive. He hoped to Christ his mother was out of the country. He grabbed the phone and dialled her number.

Angela sat on the station platform. She had tried to call Mike again but the number was engaged. She kept trying but it was constantly busy. She was near to tears, sure he'd taken it off the hook. There was also something else she had to tell him: she'd missed two periods.

Audrey picked up the phone and Mike started yelling before she'd even said hello. 'She knows about Tommy. She's been to see him about the diamonds this afternoon.'

'Who?'

'Who the hell do you think? Rawlins. She got the diamonds then went to Tommy Malin.'

Audrey's legs were like jelly.

'Have you got your passport yet?'

'Yes, it came today, and I've booked my ticket, leave tomorrow.'

Mike rubbed his chin. 'You'd better go tonight.'

'You think she'll come here?'

He closed his eyes. 'Look, the best thing you can do is go away, just clear out.'

Audrey burst into tears and he yelled at her to pull herself together. He said he'd see if he could come round later, and hung up.

She sat for a moment, still cradling the phone before shakily going back to her packing. Half an hour later the doorbell rang shrilly and Audrey dropped her case as she ran to the door. She thought it would be Mike but when she swung the door open she froze.

'Hello, Audrey. It's Dolly – Dolly Rawlins.'

Audrey forced a smile. 'Good heavens! So you're out then, are you?'

'Yes. You going to ask me in?'

Audrey swallowed and held the door wider.

Dolly walked past her, straight into the sitting room. The first thing she saw was the big eight-by-ten coloured photograph of Shirley. She reached out, touched it, and laid it face down on the sideboard. Then she spotted the passport and aeroplane tickets. 'Going away?'

Audrey could hardly breathe, she was so nervous. She gestured to the half-packed suitcases in her bedroom. 'Just to Brighton, see a friend for the weekend.'

'Taking a lot of gear for just a weekend, aren't you?' Audrey flushed as Dolly held up her passport. 'Won't be needing this then, will you?'

Audrey's eyes almost popped out of her head as Dolly slipped it into her pocket. 'Why did you do that?'

Dolly sat down on the settee, unbuttoning her coat. 'Because, Audrey, we've got to talk. Sit down.'

Audrey moved to a hard-backed chair and perched on the edge of the seat.

'How long have you been out?'

Dolly gave an icy cold smile. 'I bet you know the exact minute. Come on, Audrey, how much did you get for the diamonds?'

189

She knew it was pointless to deny she'd taken them. 'It's not the way it looks.'

'I'm all ears.'

Audrey gulped. 'Well, when I read that Jimmy Donaldson had been arrested—'

Dolly interrupted, 'You went round and collected. But you never thought to contact me, did you?'

'Well, it was too risky, wasn't it?'

'How much did you get?'

'Not a lot.' Audrey cleared her throat.

'How much?'

'Four hundred and fifty thousand.'

Dolly leaned back and gave a short barking laugh, without humour. 'Don't mess me around. *How much?*'

Audrey began to blubber, swearing on her life that was all she got, and said Dolly could even check it out with Frank Richmond.

'Frank Richmond? You fenced them through him, that cheap bastard? Why didn't you fence them with Tommy?'

'I didn't think, I was scared, I mean, they were here in the flat.'

Dolly leaned back and closed her eyes. 'Eight years I waited, Audrey, eight years . . .'

'Shirley's been dead eight years.' Audrey became even more scared as Dolly went rigid, her eyes shut tight, hands clenched. 'I only got a few thousand cash I can give you. I put the bulk of it in Spain.'

'Spain?'

'I bought a villa and . . . it was all done in such a hurry because I was terrified I'd be nicked.'

'I was, Audrey. I did almost nine years and right now I'd do ten for you. You get me my share and I want it by tomorrow.'

'But I haven't got it.'

'*Get it!* And when you have, call me. This is my number.' Dolly opened her bag and scrawled her phone number. She stood up to pass it to her, leaning in close, her face almost touching Audrey's. 'Until I get it, I'll hold your passport. You call me by tomorrow or, like I said, I'll shop you, go down for you and don't think for a second I don't mean it.'

Mike listened in stunned silence as Audrey told him about Dolly's visit. 'I got to get money, Mike, or she'll shop me.'

Mike could feel that treacle forming like cement round his ankles now. 'Does she know about me?'

'She thinks it was just me. I got to get money, Mike. She wants me to call her, I got until tomorrow.'

'What the fuck do you want me to do?'

'Can I come round and see you? I'll need the money I put in the kids' building society savings accounts.'

'*What?* Are you telling me some of that cash is in *my kids' accounts?*' Audrey sobbed. He couldn't make any sense of what she was saying. 'Mum, get in a cab and come round. Now.'

Mike slapped down the phone. He then ran up the stairs and began searching through drawers for his kids' account books.

Mr Crow looked out of the window as he drove up the manor-house driveway. Mrs Tilly sat in the back seat with Mr Simms, another member of the board.

'There's a lot of land, wonderful place for kids.'

They drove slowly up to the front door, where workmen's tools were lying around.

'Looks like a lot of work has started,' mused Mr Crow, looking up at the scaffolding.

191

They all got out and looked over the grounds again before heading towards the front door. Mrs Tilly had wanted to warn Dolly of their arrival. They had been to visit another foster family and decided to make an on-site visit to the manor afterwards.

As the door was open they all entered the house. Mrs Tilly called Dolly and, receiving no reply, peered into the lounge. 'It's huge. I had no idea it was such a big property,' she said, impressed.

'Hello? Anyone at home?' Mr Crow called, as he looked towards the kitchen. They all followed him and stood in the kitchen doorway, again impressed by the size of the vast old-fashioned kitchen. They were about to leave the leaflets and documents they had brought on the hall table when they heard the screams and laughter from the cellar.

Kathleen tried the first shower and could hear nothing but a low rumbling from the pipes. No water seemed to be connected to the showers and she banged the pipes with a shoe as Gloria came out of the sauna. 'Showers aren't working,' Kathleen said, grinning when she saw the hose-pipe. 'How about bein' hosed down, shall we try that?' Gloria pulled a face. 'Forget it. I'm gonna have a bath in me own room.'

Gloria hitched a towel round her and wandered out, heading up the cellar stairs. Mr Crow and his party were just coming out of the dining room when she appeared. She took one look, shrieked and dived back down to the cellar.

'Was that Mrs Rawlins?' Mr Crow asked.

Mrs Tilly shook her head on her way towards the cellar door. She called again for Dolly but could hear only shrieks from below.

Kathleen had turned on the hose-pipe. Connie, stark naked, had her hands up as Kathleen turned it on her full blast. Gloria yelled for her to switch it off but Kathleen pointed the hose at her just as the three visitors appeared in the doorway. They were sprayed with water as the women screamed and yelled like schoolgirls. There was a lot of fumbling for towels as Gloria shot out past them. But Connie, still naked, bent over to pick up her towel.

Mrs Tilly was red-faced with embarrassment as she opened the sauna door. She gasped and slammed it shut.

'I think we should leave.' She hurried out, appalled at what she had just seen: Ester and Julia in an embrace, both naked, locked in each other's arms.

Ester grabbed her towel and ran out after them as they disappeared up the cellar stairs. 'Just a minute! *Wait!* Wait a minute.'

But they couldn't get out fast enough even when Mr Crow suggested that perhaps they should apologize.

'Apologize? We should just leave. You didn't see what I did and this is the last place I would recommend a child be sent to. It's disgusting.'

Mr Crow turned as Ester, draped in a towel, followed. He stared and then hurried out. She looked down the stairs to Julia. 'I think they were from the social services. We'd better not mention this to Dolly.'

It was getting dark when Angela appeared. When they saw her alone the women downed tools and called to her. 'Where's Dolly?'

'I don't know, she sent me home.'

'Shit!' Ester marched over to Angela. 'Where did she go? She's coming back, isn't she?' she demanded, her heart sinking. Would Dolly just up, take the cash and leave them all here? She went into Dolly's room. All her belongings were there, including the deeds of the house, so she felt a little easier, reckoned she would be back.

By the time Dolly did come back, a few hours later, the women were all having supper. When she walked in, they started talking at once about how much work they had been doing, how they loved the house, but slowly their conversation petered out as Dolly chucked the pouch bag on to the table.

'Take a look. They're worthless, glass, all of them.'

They gaped, fingering the glittering stones, before looking at Dolly in confusion.

'There's no money, no cuts, nothing.'

Kathleen picked up one of the biggest stones, held it in her pudgy hand, then rested it against her cheek. It felt cold but it soon warmed up. She hurled it against the side of the Aga where it shattered into tiny fragments. 'Fucking glass, all right.'

Each one of them would have liked to smash something, anything, as their initial confusion turned to anger, their dreams smashed like the fake diamond. And the realization of the lengths to which they had gone to get the fakes made the atmosphere explosive. Eyes met eyes, hands clenched, hidden beneath the table, but no one voiced their innermost feelings. Gradually their anger subsided and left them almost bereft. Depression hung in the air. Dolly slowly sat down and picked up a piece of bread, picking bits off it as she looked from one crestfallen face to another. 'So, will you be staying on, Ester?'

'Well, I've got to admit it, Dolly, I've never been one for kids so I guess I'm out of here.'

'What about you, Julia?'

Julia shrugged her shoulders, then looked at Ester. 'I guess I'll leave with Ester. That's not to say I don't love this place because I do but—'

Dolly interrupted, looking at Connie. 'What about you?'

Connie flushed. 'Well, to be honest, I know I've got this problem with Lennie and I need a place to lie low for a while but as a long-term thing, I want to start off my career proper, you know, get an agent and . . .' She trailed off, head bent, not able to meet Dolly's eyes.

Kathleen coughed. 'I'll stay put with you, love. I need a place, I got nowhere else.'

Angela reached out and touched Dolly's hand. 'I'll stay too. We'll maybe be able to make it work – you'll apply for grants and things.'

Dolly held Angela's hand tightly, as Gloria pushed back her chair. 'I'll be here for a few weeks.' Dolly looked up at her, surprised. 'You got Eddie's gear some place and we'll have to sort something out about that.'

'I see,' Dolly said quietly. 'Well, at least I know where I stand. So, those that are going, pack up and leave. It'll save on food bills. Goodnight.'

They waited until they heard her footsteps going up the stairs before discussing it, each one examining the fake stones.

'That's it, then,' Ester said flatly. She poured a glass of wine. 'Well, I'm out of here.'

They knew they all were. None of them cared about the house or Dolly or her dreams, but they had all just lost theirs.

Dolly stared at her reflection in the dressing-table mirror. She calculated that with the money from Audrey she might still be able to pull off something. It might even be better that it had worked out this way – at least she knew who she could trust, now that she'd found out it was Audrey, poor Shirley Miller's mother, who'd grassed her.

CHAPTER 9

DOLLY HAD only just come down to breakfast when John asked to speak to her. He was obviously angry: the men wanted paying, he wanted paying. She had successfully put off the first instalment but now it was Friday and there was still no cash.

Dolly felt guilty and apologized: she said she was having problems releasing the cash but assured him that he would have it by the following morning.

John was hesitant but trapped. What could he do? He had no choice but to wait and believe she would pay him. His workers were really pissed off when he told them they'd have to wait until Monday. They put down their tools and walked off the site, saying they would come back when he paid up.

The house, with the scaffolding and debris surrounding the grounds, looked in an even more dilapidated condition than before. Loose tiles had been thrown from the roof, the chimneys were still at a dangerous angle, windows were out in some rooms, sections of the front of the house had no plaster, the rough old bricks exposed. It was a depressing sight and the only thing that kept Dolly's spirits up was that she had done well with the social services and that money was coming her way via Audrey.

*

Audrey, in a state of nerves matched only by her son's, gathered all the money she could lay hands on. The only plus was that Dolly still had no knowledge of Mike's part and, thankfully for him, neither did the police. However, they'd just heard that DCI Craigh's chief was pushing Traffic to trace the hit-and-run car that killed James Donaldson. Mike's part had been played down by Craigh and there was no mention that he had a personal motive for bringing in Dolly Rawlins. Nor was there mention that the police had succeeded in tracing the stolen gems at Donaldson's antique shop. That, too, was glossed over.

Traffic liked nothing better than a hopeless case – or one that seemed like one – and now, with the incentive to pull out all stops, they went to work. They had only a part index and a vague description of the vehicle, but they checked on paint colour co-ordination with both Rover and Volvo companies, their computers triggering off further developments as they began slowly to narrow down the make and year of the vehicle. The bonus was the section of the number plate and the massive, detailed, computerized cross-references moved into action. They were positive that they would be able to trace or narrow down the vehicle owner. All they required was time.

Although the women had agreed they would be leaving, none seemed eager to depart. Julia and Ester had argued: in reality Julia did not want to leave and felt guilty about the on-site visit from the social services. Ester eventually told her that if she wanted to stay she should. She, Ester, had better things to do with her life than sit buried in the country. Julia knew that she would be in deep trouble if she returned to London and tried to make her see sense. 'Maybe, I just got to sort it for myself, Julia, by myself. You do what the hell you like.'

Julia had flounced out in a bad temper and taken herself off to the local pub. She asked for a double Scotch on the rocks and leaned on the bar. Across the room, seated at one of the bay windows, was Norma Hastings. She had been riding and was wearing jodhpurs and a hacking jacket. She watched Julia, lowering her newspaper. Norma was an attractive woman, thick, red hair, a pleasant round face and obviously fit: her cheeks had that ruddy glow. In comparison, Julia seemed pale, her skinny frame mannish and her long, wiry brown hair like an unruly mop-head. Norma continued to watch her as she pretended to read the paper until she could not be bothered to hide her interest. She tossed it aside. She reckoned she was right about her – it was rare that she wasn't – but she didn't make a move. Instead, she enjoyed studying the woman at the bar. Just like a man would covet a woman he fancied, Norma's eyes roamed over the unaware Julia. Norma liked her hands, the way she leaned on her elbow; she liked her mane of hair, her hawk-nosed features. And yet she knew something must be wrong because she was ordering one double Scotch after another, knocking them back in one gulp, then staring at the polished wood counter. Norma noticed how she dug into her pockets to count out the cash to pay the barman. Her trousers were skin-tight and she had a perfect, tight arse.

As Julia's boots were mud-spattered, Norma reckoned it would be a good opener to ask if she liked to ride – horses, not herself, but that was what she was after. She wasn't often so blatant about it – in her job she couldn't be. If the Metropolitan Police knew that one of their mounted officers was gay . . . she could only imagine the snide cracks. She'd had enough of them already, without them knowing she was a lesbian as well.

Norma decided to go for it and walked towards the bar.

199

LYNDA LA PLANTE

Suddenly her confidence slipped a fraction as Julia turned towards her. She had not expected such dark, angry eyes. 'Hi, I'm Norma Hastings.' She put out her hand to shake and got a steely put-down.

'Are you?' said Julia sarcastically, not caring if Norma had said she was the Duchess of York.

'Can I buy you a drink?'

'Why not? Double Scotch.'

An hour later, Julia's cheeks were as flushed as Norma's, not from fresh air but from alcohol. She was very tipsy as the two climbed over a gate to head across a field to a couple of grazing horses.

'She's called Helen of Troy and if you can stable her, I'll provide the feed. It's just I've got Caper and he's a bit of a handful.' Norma pointed to a three-year-old stallion and then smiled at the quietly grazing Helen of Troy.

Julia pressed her face against Helen's nose. 'She's beautiful,' she whispered.

'Well, I even put an advert in the local papers but I've had no offers yet. I was going to let the local riding school have her – she's still got a lot of life in her. But she's a big horse, over seventeen hands.'

Julia nuzzled the soft brown nose and was already in love with her. 'Okay, I'll take her.' She beamed drunkenly at Norma. She was still plastered as she led the big horse along the manor's drive. Dolly looked out from the drawing-room window, watching as Julia wove along the path.

'What on earth is she doing with that?'

'What?' asked Kathleen, who was trying to remove a packed bag from the hoover.

'Julia's got a horse.'

*

200

Gloria peered up into Helen's face. 'Cor blimey, it's enormous this, isn't it?'

Connie reached out to stroke the horse and then stepped back. They all turned as Norma drove up in a clapped-out Land-Rover. She hopped down. 'I've brought her tack and feed. Is that the stable?'

The women looked at one another, not sure what was going on, as now Dolly and Kathleen came to the kitchen door.

'Hi, Dolly. This is Norma and this is Helen of Troy.' Julia grinned like a schoolgirl. 'She's been given to us, for free.'

'Oh, yeah . . .' Dolly looked on as Angela squeezed out, running to the horse.

Norma smiled at Dolly, and walked towards her, hand outstretched. She gave a hard handshake that almost floored Dolly. 'She'll be marvellous with kids. She's thirteen years old, retired, but if you're opening this as a children's home she'll be ideal. You can drop a bomb in front of her and she won't even flinch. She can walk through a band or a riot and she's as cool as a cucumber.' Dolly felt a bit confused as to what was going on. Norma continued, 'I've got a new hunter and I needed a home for Helen.'

Julia looked almost pleadingly at Dolly. 'She's a police horse, Dolly.'

Kathleen flinched as if the horse was about to arrest her. Dolly looked at Connie. Her voice was hardly audible, when she said, 'Did she say what I think she just said?'

'Yeah, it's a police horse.'

'Not the horse, Connie, the woman.'

Norma handed out bags of feed to Angela as Julia opened up the stables.

'A minute, love,' Dolly said, and went back into the kitchen, followed by a flushed Julia.

201

'She's beautiful, isn't she? And free! We don't have to even pay for her feed.'

Dolly folded her arms. 'Really? And Norma's a police-woman, is she?'

Julia nodded. She was still plastered and reeked of booze.

Dolly sighed. 'You should have asked me. I don't like the filth, mounted or otherwise, poking their nose around and that one looks like she's ready to move in.'

'Oh, well, I can take it back. I just thought . . .'

'You thought what? I don't ride, I've not got any kids here yet and you're leaving so what the hell am I gonna do with a horse?'

Julia gripped the back of the chair. 'I want to stay on, Dolly. I'll groom her, feed her . . . You wouldn't have to do a single thing, and I'll make sure Norma keeps her distance.'

'You better. We got an arsenal of guns on the property and none of us are what you might call environmentally friendly.'

Julia was about to return to the yard when Dolly told her that Ester had gone. She was stunned. 'Gone?'

'About fifteen minutes ago. And if you don't mind me saying it's good riddance.'

Julia hadn't believed that Ester could walk out without even saying goodbye. She checked that her belongings had gone from their bedroom before finally accepting it. She slipped downstairs for a bottle of vodka, which she took back to her room. She drank it neat from her tooth-mug, slugging it back, then decided not to bother with the tooth-mug and drank it straight from the bottle. Ester had gone, left her without so much as a note. Julia rested back against the pillow that still smelt of her perfume and started to cry, awful, silent tears, the way she had learnt to cry in prison. Ester had taken such care of her, she was afraid of nothing, and she had chosen Julia, walked straight up to her. The other girls sitting with their dinner trays had moved away from the table, but Julia had said nothing, just continued to eat, her eyes down, afraid of what Ester wanted.

'You shooting up?' Ester had said.

Julia had swallowed, still unable to look at her.

'Bad stuff in here. You'd better go cold turkey. I'll take care of you.'

Julia reached for the bottle, wanting to pass out. She didn't want to hear that deep, wonderful gravel voice in her head, smell that thick sweet-scented perfume. Ester had walked out on her without saying goodbye. Ester was the love of Julia's life and without her the fear returned, her confidence dwindled and her deep-seated guilt and shame resurfaced.

Hours later, so drunk she was hardly able to lift her head, she heard the phone ringing, cutting through her dulled senses, but she was incapable of standing upright.

'I'm at the station,' Audrey said.

'I'll be there, just wait in the car park.' Dolly replaced the phone and went out to find Gloria. She was with Kathleen, hanging over the stable door. Dolly held up the keys to Gloria's Mini. 'I won't be long, just get some groceries.'

Gloria rushed to her. 'We got to talk, Dolly. Eddie's guns – I really need them. I got to get some cash.'

Dolly opened the Mini and got inside. 'We'll talk about them later.'

'They're worth quite a bit, you know. Nearly thirty grand, Eddie said.'

Dolly wound down the window. 'And they could have got us arrested. When I come back we'll talk.'

'Okay. I'll cut you in, Dolly, that's only fair.' Dolly started the engine and backed the Mini down the drive, Gloria still following her. 'Say twenty per cent?'

Dolly drove off and Gloria watched the car disappear down the drive before she turned back to Kathleen. 'They're my ruddy guns. She's got to give them back to me, hasn't she?' Kathleen shaded her eyes to look towards the gates.

'What you think she did with them?' Gloria asked moodily.

'Hid them, thank Christ,' said Kathleen.

Audrey clutched her handbag, standing in the centre of the car park. Dolly pulled up and Audrey climbed into the Mini. The level-crossing gates were closed. 'What's up?' Audrey asked, staring at the railway crossing.

'Must be a train due.'

Raymond Dewey saw Dolly and waved. She lowered the window. 'Hello, Raymond, you on duty, are you?' He came to the car and shook her hand, then introduced himself to Audrey. She pressed herself back in her seat as his square head poked through the window. 'How long will we be kept waiting?' Dolly asked.

'Oh, might be a few minutes. Not like the mail train, always a long delay every Thursday, always a delay. This is the three twenty, local.' He returned to his stool to jot down notes in his precious book as Audrey and Dolly sat in silence. They watched the train pass in front of them before the gates slowly lifted.

'Bloody nutter,' said Audrey as they passed him, now gesturing them on like a traffic controller.

They went into the local pub and Audrey took a corner seat at the bay window as Dolly got the drinks. She clutched her bag, not sure how Dolly would take it, and when the gin and tonic was put down she knocked it back fast to try to calm her nerves. 'Right, I've got you all I could. Twenty grand.'

Dolly sipped her drink. 'I hope you're joking.'

'No, I'm not. It's all I could get. I brought bank statements, everything, you can see for yourself that's all I could get. The rest, like I told you, went into the villa. I'll sell it, split the profits, but it'll take a while.' Audrey opened her bag and took out a thick envelope. She was about to pass it to Dolly when Norma walked up.

'Hello, Mrs Rawlins.'

Dolly gave a tight, brittle smile. 'Hello, Norma. I'd offer to buy you a drink but we're just leaving. Audrey, this is Norma. She's a mounted police officer.'

Audrey gaped. 'Oh, nice to meet you.'

Dolly waved at Raymond as they passed him again and drove into the station car park. Audrey still clutched her bag. She was sweating with nerves, wishing Dolly would say something, but she drove in silence.

'I'll need my passport, Dolly, and me ticket for Spain.'

Dolly engaged the handbrake and leaned over to open the glove compartment. 'Here, take them, and give me the money.' Audrey passed her the envelope. She snatched it. She didn't count the money, just shoved it into her pocket. 'I don't want to see you or hear from you again, Audrey. Just get out of my sight.'

Audrey fumbled with the door handle, couldn't wait to

get away. She ran into the station, afraid Dolly might get out and attack her – she'd turned those chipped-ice eyes on her with such hatred. But Dolly had no intention of running after Audrey. It was, as she had said, the last time she ever wanted to see her.

Twenty thousand pounds! And she had believed she would have millions. Well, she would make do. Somehow she'd make the house work. She wouldn't let this set her back.

Gloria and Connie were sitting at the kitchen table playing noughts and crosses when Dolly got back. 'Did you get milk?' Connie asked.

'No. Shops were closed, wasted journey.'

Gloria screwed up the paper. 'About Eddie's guns, Dolly.'

Dolly took off her coat. 'We'll go and get them when it's dark but right now I'd like a cup of tea, if that's all right with you – even if we haven't got any milk.'

Julia was lying face down on the bed. She didn't look up when Dolly tapped on the door and walked in. 'I need a hand, Julia. We're going to get the guns and—' Julia tried to sit up but fell face forward. Dolly saw the empty bottle on the floor. 'You'd better sleep it off, we'll manage without you.'

'We'll need spades and a wheelbarrow,' Dolly said to Gloria and then, as Connie, all dressed up, walked into the kitchen, 'You going too, are you?'

Connie shook her head. 'No, I'm going out with that builder bloke.'

Gloria nudged Connie and said to Dolly, 'I told her earlier to get the old leg over and he'd maybe work for nothin'.'

Dolly shook her head at Gloria, as if she was a naughty kid, and then asked Connie to come into the room she now used as an office. She gave her an envelope with ten thousand pounds cash inside. 'Give this to him, will you? Tell him he'll get the rest next week and if he could get the men back to work over the weekend, I'd be grateful.'

'Okay.' Connie slipped the envelope into her pocket.

Dolly hesitated, then patted Connie's arm. 'Be nice to him. Be a help to me, know what I mean?'

Connie bit her lip. 'Sure, pay my way, so to speak.'

'Good. So you have a nice evening, then, and we'll see you later.'

Connie met John outside the manor gates. He'd changed into a suit and Connie was touched by the effort he'd made. He was all fingers and thumbs, easing her inside, apologizing for the van, before they drove off.

'I thought we'd eat out. Do you like Chinese?'

'Chinese is fine.'

'God, I'm hungry,' complained Gloria, as she pushed the wheelbarrow through the woods.

Kathleen trudged along with two spades. 'Got to hand it to you, Dolly, if you hadn't stashed them, we'd be in a right old mess.'

ent: LA PLANTE

Gloria scowled, all the time wondering just how much Dolly would tap her for Eddie's guns, but the further they walked, the more she realized how together Dolly was to have hidden them so far from the house and to have done it on her own. As if she was reading her mind, Dolly looked at her. 'I did it in three trips, Gloria, took half the night.'

Julia listened, her dulled senses making out the sound of the telephone ringing and ringing. She stumbled out of her room and almost fell down the stairs.

'Anyone here? Hello?'

No one answered and the phone still rang. She lurched towards it, snatching it up. 'Ester? Is that you?'

'Is Connie there?' said a man's voice.

Julia swung round and stared into the kitchen. 'Connie? *Connie?*'

Lennie sat back in the car, gazing out of the window.

'She's not here,' Julia slurred.

'Okay. I'm coming to meet her but I seem to be in a dead-end road. How do I get to the Grange?'

Julia began to give him directions. As they were all leaving the manor, she supposed Connie must have arranged for Lennie to collect her. She was too drunk to think of the implications or to remember that Connie was terrified of him.

Lennie slipped the portable back into the glove compartment of his shining Porsche and started to reverse. He swore when the car sank into a pot-hole, the mud splashing the gleaming paintwork. Then he drove cautiously down the lane.

*

Connie giggled as the waiter presented John with the bill and his eyes popped at the amount, due to the champagne she had ordered. But he paid up, digging into the envelope Connie had given him from Dolly. She felt a bit bad about ordering champagne and became over-friendly, rubbing his arm and, beneath the table, pressing her legs hard against his. He flushed as she kicked off her shoe and let her toes stroke his crotch. He had never come across a woman like Connie and he felt inadequate, to say the least.

'Do you think she'll be able to pay the rest?' he asked, trying to appear nonchalant as Connie's toes stroked the fly of his trousers.

'Oh, so you asked me out to find out about Mrs Rawlins?'

'No, no! It's just that I'm a one-man firm and I could go broke over this. I've ordered a lot of equipment.'

'If Mrs Rawlins says she'll pay you, then she will,' Connie purred, leaning further towards him over the top of the table as her toes did all the walking below.

'I'd better get you home.'

She looked up at him and giggled again. He was red in the face with embarrassment.

Gloria had taken over the digging as Kathleen heaved the first bag on to the wheelbarrow. 'You're stronger than you look, Dolly Rawlins. These weigh a ton.'

Angela pulled the brambles and sticks away from the third hiding place as Gloria stuck in the spade. They were on the brow of a small hill just outside the wooded perimeter of the manor's land, and could see clearly the signal box below.

'Who's at the gates?' Kathleen pointed.

Dolly looked up. She could see the flashing signal lights, the barred gates, and the builder's van.

Gloria prodded her in the ribs. 'Oi, he's got a lot of hand movement down there. You think he's givin' her one or is it just light relief?'

Dolly grimaced. Sometimes Gloria's crudeness really irritated her but she couldn't help taking another look and it did seem as if John was having a heavy grope and petting session.

He was. He had Connie's top undone and was kissing her neck and her breasts as she kept one eye on the signal lights.

'Train's coming,' she whispered into his hot, flushed face.

He moaned, and for a moment she thought he was coming too but then he sat back. 'I'm sorry.'

She buttoned her blouse and snuggled up to him. 'Are you married?'

'No, but I live with someone.'

'And where does she think you are tonight?'

'At the gym.'

'Can I work out with you one day? I love doing weights.'

The train thundered past and the gates slowly opened. 'Any time you like.' John put the van into gear and they headed down the narrow lane back towards the manor.

Lennie reversed into a field gateway. He'd already driven past the manor, stopped, had a look at it and decided that the element of surprise would be more beneficial. He was just about to get out when the van passed him. Connie didn't see him as she was talking to the bloke who was driving. Lennie saw the van drive into the manor and

210

followed on foot, well hidden by the overhanging hedgerow.

They'd loaded the wheelbarrow and were pushing it back towards the manor. Dolly walked ahead, her arm slung around Angela's shoulder. 'You know you can join special government courses, get further education, Angela, proper training in something. You should think about it, love, but you're welcome to stay on here for as long as you like, you know that. Do you like kids?'

'Oh, yeah, and I'm used to them. I've got younger brothers still at school.'

Gloria muttered as she staggered along behind the wheelbarrow with all the guns as Kathleen carried the spades. They were still about a quarter of a mile from the manor.

Connie leaned in to John and gave him a long, lingering kiss. They broke away and then she kissed him again. 'You'd better check your face before you go in. Lipstick!' She giggled as he wiped his mouth. 'I'll see you tomorrow?'

He watched her wiggle and sashay her way to the front door, turn and do her Marilyn Monroe pout. He blew her a kiss, felt stupid and quickly put the van into reverse. As he drove out, he didn't notice Lennie.

'Connie!'

She knew his voice immediately, but in the darkness she couldn't see him. 'Lennie?'

He stepped forward and bowed. 'Surprise, surprise!'

She began to pant with terror. 'You stay away from me, Lennie. Don't hurt me!'

He walked towards her, his arms out wide, smiling. 'I'm not going to hurt you. Why would I do that? I've just come to take you home, Connie.'

'I'm not coming with you, Lennie. You got to leave me alone.'

He came closer and now he wasn't playing games. 'You owe me, Connie, and you're gonna pay it off or work it off. Suit yourself.'

'I won't go anywhere with you.'

She screamed and he dived for her but she kicked out, catching him in the groin. He lost his footing, tripping over a plank left by the builders. He swore, cradling his balls and gritting his teeth in fury as he screamed, '*Connieeeeeeeee!* Don't fuck with me!'

She was running, anywhere, any place to get away from him. He started after her, yelling with rage, and she sobbed and shouted at him to stay away as she ran on, heading up towards the woods.

Dolly was rigid. She hissed at Gloria to keep her mouth shut as they all heard the sobbing and screaming.

Gloria let go of the handles of the wheelbarrow. 'It's Connie.' She ran towards the sound of the crying.

Dolly started to follow and then turned to Kathleen and Angela. 'You stay put, the pair of you, until I come back and get you.' She tore after Gloria through the woods, hearing another high-pitched scream.

Gloria had to slap Connie's face. 'It's me, Connie, it's me, Gloria.'

Connie clung to her. 'He's here. Oh, God, Gloria, he's here and he's gonna kill me. He was chasing me, he's going to kill—'

'Connie, listen to me.' Gloria whacked her hard again.

'Nobody is going to touch you, all right? We're all here.'

Dolly was breathless when she reached them. 'What's going on?'

'It's that bloke, her pimp. He's come after her.'

Dolly gripped Connie's arm. 'He won't lay a finger on you. Gloria, go and get the other two. I'll take Connie back to the house with me.'

A frightened Connie clung to Dolly as they made their way to the house. The grounds were ominously dark and silent. Wherever he was, they felt as if he was watching their every move and they ran the last few yards past the stables and into the safety of the house. Dolly latched the door behind them and Connie sobbed, 'What if he's here, in the house?'

Gloria, Kathleen and Angela wheeled the rest of the guns into the stable-yard and then carried them inside. Connie was sitting with a large brandy, her eyes red-rimmed from crying, as Julia sat with her head in her hands, so hung-over she could hardly speak.

Gloria held up a shotgun. 'Right, we got enough of these. If that prick shows his face, I'll blow it off.'

'We'll search the house,' Dolly said. 'Some of the windows are out so if he's here, we'd better find him. We'll have a good look round, then you, Connie, lock yourself in a room with Angela.'

Connie began to sob again and Dolly was almost irritated with her. 'Shut up, for God's sake! And you, Julia, get some coffee down you and sober up.'

Connie wiped her face with the back of her hand. 'He said he'd take me back.'

Dolly shook her by the shoulders. 'Nobody will make you do anything you don't want to do, okay? We'll sort it, Annie-Get-Your-Gun-Gloria and me.'

Gloria went over the grounds with the shotgun at the ready. She checked the stables, the outhouses and the yard, and even went up to the woods, but an owl hooted which gave her the willies so she scuttled back to the front door of the manor. It was ajar and she pushed it slowly. 'Anyone here?'

Dolly stood there with her hands on her hips. 'Yes. Me, you fool. Did you see anything out there?'

'Nope. Maybe he saw us and pissed off.'

'Yeah, I think you're right, but we'll keep her upstairs with Angela. Then we can sort out the weapons.'

Ester drove into the underground car park of the Club Cabar. She'd been to three and this was her last hope. She hadn't many options: it was Steve Rooney or back to the Grange. She locked up the Range Rover, checked her hair and make-up, pulled her black dress down a bit further to show off her shoulders and tits and changed her driving shoes for spike heels. 'Right, gel, do the business.'

She walked casually, full of confidence, towards the private lifts to the club. The car park was used by a number of offices in the day but taken over by the club at night so they had their own small lift leading directly into their reception. As the grille slid back, a thick-set muscle-bound bouncer in an ill-fitting evening suit and crushed carnation looked over any customers entering from the car park, as it was very much a members-only club. He nodded at Ester.

She gave him a cursory waft of her hand. 'Is Steve in?'

'Yeah, he's wiv someone now. I'll tell 'im you're 'ere.'

'Thank you,' she said crisply, and headed towards the main room of the club. Its small sunken dance floor was empty but you could hardly see your hand in front of your face for the blinking neon strips. At least the ornate, over-brassy bar was well lit and the row of red velvet-topped high stools had only one occupant: a swarthy, fat little man, drinking from a long glass with a profusion of fruit and paper umbrellas sticking out of it. He was surrounded by sexy blondes with tight envelope-sized mini-skirts and tied blouse tops showing a lot of cleavage. Even their high-heeled shoes were higher than Ester's. They were giggling and whispering to each other as the poor sucker with the paper umbrella almost up his nose slurped a drink that had probably set him back a tenner. The girls would make sure he was parted from a lot more before the night was out.

Ester perched on a stool as far away from the fat man as possible. The slant-eyed barman was doing a lot of gesticu-lating with his martini shaker to the deafening, thudding rock music that made it impossible for anyone to have a conversation.

'Hi, Ester, how ya doin?' the barman lisped.

'I'm doing fine. Gimme a Southern Comfort, lemonade, slice of lemon and crushed ice, easy on the lemonade.' She lit a cigarette as she spoke, but he knew what she liked and was already searching through the array of bottles. He skimmed up and down the bar and then whisked out a paper napkin and a bowl of peanuts before placing her drink down with a smile.

'On the house.'

'Cheers.' She sipped. He'd OD'd on the lemonade. Through the mirror and brass fittings she saw Steve Rooney talking to the crushed carnation, who gestured at the bar. Ester acknowledged Rooney, who put up his hand to indicate five minutes.

A few more punters arrived and wandered around. Ester signalled for a refill but stipulated no more lemonade, then took a handful of peanuts. It was strange. She'd been out of the business a long time, and didn't know any of the girls

215

now. She shook her head and smiled. What a life! She wanted out. She hated the whole scene, which was why she'd moved to the Grange, and for a while she had been coining it. She didn't have time for any further reminiscence as Rooney tapped her shoulder and pointed at his office. She slid off the stool, drained her glass and followed, flicking a look at the little fat man. 'I'd get out while you're still on top, man.'

Rooney eased himself round his fake antique desk and then perched on it. 'So, how's tricks, darlin'? I just hope you're not touching me for a few quid. As you can see, we're not exactly filling the joint and it's Friday.'

'It'll pick up, always used to.'

His polished Gucci loafer tapped the side of the desk. 'What do you want, Ester? I know you've schlepped round a few places tonight.'

'Warned off me, were you?'

He smiled. His eyes were pale blue covered by tinted glasses. 'You're not still wheeling around in that Range Rover, are you?'

She lit a cigarette, clicking off her lighter.

'You really are stupid, you know that, don't you? You tried it on with the wrong kind, Ester. They got a lot of dough and they'll use it to find you.'

'No kidding. Doesn't scare me.'

'It should. That was a stupid move. They paid out a lot of cash for you, and what do you do?'

'I did three years and I kept my mouth shut. They ripped me off.'

'No, they didn't. How were they to know you had a string of offences as long as both arms? They paid your taxes and your lawyer, and you come out, try to nail them for more cash, then nick the kid's motor.'

216

She stubbed out the cigarette. 'They got enough of them. What's one little Range Rover?'

'It wasn't what it was, it was you doin' it. It was stupid.'

'Yeah, maybe, but you seem to know a lot about my business.'

Rooney sighed and picked a bit of fluff off his Armani jacket. 'Because I supply them now, okay? I'm not gonna hide anything from you. It's not as if I nicked your clients. You were inside.'

'Yes, I was, and now I need a job, Rooney.'

'Don't look in my direction. I can't help you and I'm not going to put myself out for you, Ester. You never gave me a leg up when I needed it.'

'But I sent a lot of clients your way, you cheap shit.'

His face tightened and Ester would have liked to smack him. Rooney had once been a barman she had hired for special parties, back in the old days when she ran a house for two major club owners. They'd have the clients drinking and eating at their respectable joints and when they wanted a girl Ester supplied them. She kept ten good-looking tarts, and they were always busy. There were private parties for movie stars, MPs, titled perverts; in fact anyone the club owners gave membership to would at some time or other end up at the Notting Hill Gate house ... until it was busted. Ester had served a few years way back then, and when she came out of prison, she had been determined that the next place would be her own, so she turned tricks solo for four years, working the main hotels until she had enough to put down on Grange Manor House. Rooney, a barman at Notting Hill Gate, had learned fast, and soon after her bust, which he was never questioned about, he had gone to work for the club owners.

It had been Rooney who had sent her the Arab clients

for the manor, and he'd taken a cut. But, just like her bust at Notting Hill Gate, when it went down at the Grange Rooney's name was never mentioned. Rooney had even suggested to her that if she played her cards right, she might even earn extra by making a couple of videos of certain clients at the manor. He had sold a few for her, just light porn stuff, but when she told him about the tape she'd made of his Arab clients' kids, he had walked away. He told her that if she had any sense, she would as well. A couple of movie stars caught with their pants down was one thing but not the so-called flowing-robed royalty: that was asking for trouble.

'You don't know how to say thank you, do you?' she said curtly.

Rooney leaned close. 'Sweetheart, I owe you fuck all. You done nothing for me. Whatever I done, I done all by meself.'

She laughed. 'You're still an illiterate shit.'

'Maybe I am, but I'm a fucking sight richer than you are and I don't want any aggro. That's why I'm in business and you're nowhere.'

She was about to remind him of who gave him his first job, but there was a rap at the office door and Brian, the crushed carnation, appeared.

'There's a party of six kids, they said to ask for you. None of them are members but they look as if they got a few readies.'

Ester stood up, smoothed down her dress and saw the car keys on the desk. She whipped them up fast and then picked up her handbag. 'Well, I'll be going.'

Rooney asked her to go out of the back entrance. 'I don't want any aggro, Ester. I'm sorry.'

She pushed past him and he looked at Brian. 'If she's in that fucking Range Rover get it.'

Brian moved away as Rooney closed his office door and headed into the club's reception.

Ester walked out through the kitchens, down the fire escape and into the car park. She was searching in her bag for the Range Rover keys when she saw Brian stepping out of the lift, accompanied by another equally thuggish bouncer. They walked nonchalantly towards the Range Rover and leaned against it. 'This isn't yours, is it, Ester? Give me the keys, darlin'.'

'Piss off.'

Brian made a grab for her and she twisted the keys into her fist, jabbing hard at his face. She caught his right eye, a beaut, and he backed away. Ester felt her hair being torn out by the roots by his friend and she screamed, hurling the keys at him. But by that time Brian was back and taking a swing. Ester fell on to the dirty garage floor and tried to crawl away. She was kicked in the head, the ribs and the groin, curled up in a tight ball to protect herself, but they kept on kicking until she half rolled beneath a car.

She stayed there, wedged under it, as they threw her belongings on to the ground before they drove the Range Rover out of the car park. She moaned, feeling her ribs, her face. She then searched for her handbag and dragged her body upright. It was agony.

When she pressed the alarm on the keys she'd taken from Rooney they lit up a brand-new Saab convertible and, as sick as she felt, she couldn't help but smile. It was beautiful. She was just about to drag her belongings together when she heard the lift opening. Rooney slid back the gate. 'I'm sorry about that, Ester, but I've got to take the car back and if you've got any sense you take that tape back to them.'

She picked up her case. 'Thanks for the advice.'

Rooney peeled off two fifty-pound notes and tossed them towards her. 'Take a cab.'

She wouldn't let him see her grovel and pick up the notes, so she stood there until the lift had disappeared, then picked up the money, wincing in pain, and opened the boot of the Saab, tossing in her case.

'Fuck you, Rooney.' She got in and drove out fast, smiling.

Gloria had all the guns laid out on the kitchen table, a formidable collection, and she was in her element as she fingered them, showing them off as if they were fashion accessories. Kathleen wouldn't go near them but hung back, eyes popping. Julia touched the Hechler and Koch machine-gun. 'My God! You had these stashed in the house?'

Dolly was uneasy with them but at the same time knew she was looking at hard cash. 'What are they worth, did you say?'

'Thirty grand at least,' Gloria said proudly.

Dolly nodded. 'Well, the sooner they're out of here the better. You tell that husband of yours I want a cut, fifty per cent. If he doesn't like it . . .'

Gloria sniggered. 'He can't really do a lot about it. He's doing eighteen, Dolly.'

'Yes, I know. Just don't want him sending any goons round so get a contact and get rid of them – fast.'

Gloria began to roll up the shotguns in their padded cloths. She was almost tender, taking great care in replacing each one in its case. Gloria quite obviously knew what she was doing and Julia couldn't help but be a little impressed. 'Can you use these?'

'Course I can. I belong to one of the top gun clubs in the country. You got to know what you're sellin' or buyin'.' She picked up a .45, showing Julia the cartridges.

Dolly turned on her angrily. 'Just put them away, Gloria!'

'Right, right.' As Dolly walked out, Gloria grinned at Julia. 'You know, they say Hitler's mistress never died in the bunker with him. That one, dead ringer for Eva Braun.'

Julia smiled, and put on the kettle to brew some coffee.

Angela was sitting holding Connie's hand. She was still scared, jumping at every creak in the house, and sprang up when Dolly walked in.

'I'm going to bed. Julia will stay downstairs just in case he comes back but I think he's gone.'

Connie stammered, 'He'll be back, Dolly. He'll never leave me alone.'

Dolly didn't want to hear it all over again. 'How did he know where you were?'

Connie paused. 'I might have mentioned it, I don't remember.'

'Well, then, you got nobody else to blame, have you? Goodnight, Angela love.'

Angela shut the door and went back to sit with Connie. 'Why don't you call the police about him?'

Connie sniffed. 'Don't be stupid.'

'Well, he can't knock you around and get away with it.'

'No? Who're you kidding?' Connie wiped her nose with a sodden piece of tissue. 'All my life I've been on the end of a fist. First my dad, only he did a lot more than knock me around. My poor mum was so scared of him she used to lock herself in a cupboard. Even when she knew what he was doing, she didn't stop him. It meant that it wasn't *her* getting a beating and . . . Every man I've been with. I dunno why but I always thought Lennie was different, I really thought he loved me.'

Angela slipped her arm around Connie. 'We'll all look after you here.'

'Can't hide out here for ever though, can I? Because he'll come back, you know, he thinks I'm his property.' Angela was getting bored. Connie was going over and over the same ground. 'If I could get an agent, a decent one, I know I could make my living doing proper modelling, I know I could. I can't do anything else.'

'How old are you?' asked Angela innocently, and was taken aback when Connie turned on her.

'Mind your own fucking business.'

Ester kept her foot pressed to the floor. She hit a hundred and twenty, passing everything on the road, and then suddenly felt sick and veered over on to the hard shoulder. She only just got out before she vomited and sat with head bent, the driver's door open, as she waited for the dizziness to pass.

Julia saw the headlights and went to the window, wishing she had one of Gloria's guns. But then she heard the clip-clip of high heels heading towards the back door.

Angela woke and sat up. Connie was by the window. 'I just saw a car drive up.'

Angela listened. She heard a door open and close below. The next moment there was a light tap and Gloria appeared with a loaded shotgun. 'Did you hear someone?' Angela nodded. 'Right, you lock the door and stay put. I'll see to him.'

Gloria crept down the landing and almost blasted Dolly. 'Cor, you give me a fright!' she exclaimed.'

'What you think you're playing at? Put the gun away,' snapped Dolly.

'Somebody come in the house, we all heard it. Shush, listen.' They could hear a chair scraping and then Julia talking. They inched down the stairs together, Gloria in front with the shotgun.

Julia examined Ester's ribs. They were cracked, she reckoned, the deep, awful bruises looking like massive purple balls.

'I just pranged the car – steering wheel hit me,' Ester said, gasping with pain.

Julia produced a bandage and had just begun to wind it around Ester's midriff when the door burst open. Ester jumped out of her chair, flinching, as Dolly and Gloria marched in.

'Oh, it's you,' Gloria snarled.

'Yes. Sorry about this, Dolly. I was driving along and had a bit of an accident. Is it okay if I just stay for a night or two?'

Dolly folded her arms. 'You had a prang? In a car? Who you kidding?'

Ester turned away her bruised face, changing the subject fast. 'Whose is that flash Porsche parked down the lane?'

Julia looked at Dolly, then back at Ester. 'Our lane?'

'Whose do you think? I passed it on my way in.'

Gloria ran upstairs to ask Connie what car Lennie drove. She was back a moment later. 'It's his.'

Julia helped Ester to bed and then joined Gloria and Dolly to search the grounds. This time Dolly carried the shotgun, making Gloria hold up the flashlight. They toured the stables, the outhouses, and saw Ester's Saab.

'Where did she get this?'

Julia explained that Ester had told her she'd traded the Range Rover in.

'Did she?' Dolly said, already suspicious. But the search was uppermost in their minds. They walked together round to the front of the manor, getting more and more anxious as they began to wonder if Lennie was hiding in the house. The beam of the flashlight moved slowly over the grounds, the overgrown bushes and hedgerows, and then swept across the swimming pool.

'Wait! Move it back, down the deep end of the pool.' Dolly was squinting in the darkness, trying to work out what she had seen. They walked slowly towards what looked like a bundle of rags but as they moved closer, it was obviously the body of a man.

Lennie was lying face down, his hands floating in the stagnant water in front of him, one leg caught round some old rope.

Dolly hesitated only a moment. Already there were guns in the house, and her application for the social services ran through her mind. A body was all they needed. 'Get him out and move him.'

Julia stared at her. 'Are you crazy?'

'No. We get him out and bury him as fast as we can. It's almost dawn.'

'Don't you think we should call the police?' Julia asked.

'No, I don't. Get Connie and Angela – we'll all have to help drag him out. We'll put him in the back of Gloria's car.'

'I don't think that's a good idea,' Julia said, and Dolly turned on her, her face like parchment in the cold night.

'Okay. You take care of it, then.' She stalked away in fury.

Connie was brought out, and Gloria waded into the filthy water with a hook, to move the body closer. 'Is it him?'

Connie broke down sobbing, gasping that she didn't do it, she never even touched him. Dolly rejoined them, standing slightly apart.

'Well, look at the bang on his head. He must have cracked it on the side of the pool. Nobody's accusing you of doin' anything. Just stop howling.' Gloria waded in deeper, drawing the body closer to the steps.

It took three of them to drag him out of the pool. Julia pulled a big sheet of polythene from the roof of the house and they dragged the body towards it. They turned out his pockets as Gloria drove the Mini round, and rolled the body in the polythene, then lifted it into the back of the car. 'Now what?' Gloria asked, bending down to check the big end of the car. 'You know this has only just been repaired.' Dolly checked the time: it was almost five o'clock and the builders would be starting at seven. It didn't give them enough time: they couldn't dump it in broad daylight.

'Drive it back to the lean-to and we'll leave it there until tomorrow night.'

'What? In my car?'

'Yes, Gloria, unless you can think of somewhere better,' Dolly retorted.

By the time they returned to the house, Dolly had a pot of coffee on the stove and some toast made. They all trooped in and started to wash their hands, all suddenly quiet.

Ester walked in. 'Everything okay?'

'What do you think? We got her bleedin' boyfriend stashed in the back of me car and a kitchen full of guns,' Gloria said angrily.

Connie broke down into heaving sobs again and this time Dolly turned on her. '*Shut up*, all of you. Now sit down and listen.' They sat like kids, almost grateful that she was taking charge. 'You, Connie, go out to his car. Here are his keys and wallet. Any money we take but burn his cards. You then drive the car back to London, go to his flat, get the log book.' She proceeded to give Connie directions to a garage she knew in North London. She was to sell the car, leave notes cancelling the milkman and newspapers, and make it look as if Lennie had gone away. She was to clean the car of any fingerprints, likewise the flat, and she was then to return to the manor.

Connie nodded dumbly, not really comprehending, still so shaken that her whole body wouldn't stop trembling. 'Go on then, get started. Get rid of that car as soon as possible.'

Dolly spooned sugar into her coffee. 'Right, Julia, and you, Kathleen, go through the local papers, find out the most recent funeral, then check out the grave in the cemetery.'

'*What?*' Julia was about to laugh, and again she was thrown off balance by the coldness in Dolly's eyes.

'Best way to get rid of a body. Dig up the grave, dump him and cover it. Now Ester, that car out back. Is it hot? How did you get it?'

'I bought it. Well, it's on the never-never in part-exchange for the Range Rover. It's not nicked, if that's what you're thinking.'

'Gloria, you go and see Eddie. The sooner those guns are out of this place the better.'

Angela had remained silent throughout. Dolly patted her shoulder. 'I'm sorry to get you involved in this, love, but I think we're doing the best for all of us and with you driving the car that took out Jimmy Donaldson, I just think the less we see of the filth the better.'

Suddenly, hearing the name of the man she had run over made Angela's knees knock together. 'I won't say anything,' she said.

Dolly frowned. 'Well, I hope not, and that goes for everyone here.'

'It's nothing to do with me. I can't help anyone in my condition and you're the boss,' Ester said, lisping through her bruised mouth.

Dolly turned on her. 'Yes, I am, as long as you're in my house – and don't you forget it, any of you. Now I'm going to have a couple of hours' kip.'

She walked out. They were impressed by her – and a little afraid of her coldness.

Kathleen swallowed and nudged Gloria. 'I'm glad she's not found out about that business down the sauna. I think she'd bloody kill us.'

CHAPTER 10

THE MINI remained in the lean-to, dripping pools of water beneath its wheels. Julia and Kathleen checked the newspapers and then went to the cemetery. Connie was already driving to London to sell the Porsche and clean Lennie's flat. She parked it a good distance from his block, as Dolly had instructed, and set about finding the log book. Having so much to do calmed her.

Ester stayed in bed with some aspirin. Her ribs hurt and she felt dizzy if she so much as sat up. Dolly slept, the only one of them able to do so. Gloria caught the train to London and went to Brixton to visit Eddie.

Angela cleaned the kitchen; she was worrying herself into a panic about Jimmy Donaldson. As she tidied and cleared the dirty crockery, she saw the big bags of guns left by the kitchen cabinet.

Mike listened impatiently to his mother fretting because she'd missed her flight so she was now rearranging her trip to Spain.

'You got to get out soon, Mum, I mean it.'

'I will, Mike, but I got to pack the whole place up, you know. At least it's over, love. She accepted the cash, said she didn't ever want to see me again.'

He hung up and the phone rang again immediately. Mike swore when he heard Angela's voice and would have slammed it down again immediately until she whispered, 'Guns.' He had to calm her down, as she seemed so hysterical, and eventually he pieced together what she was saying: Dolly Rawlins had bags full of weapons that belonged to Eddie Radford in the manor. She had moved them on the night they had come with the warrant.

Ester walked slowly down the stairs and stopped. Angela was hunched over the telephone in the hall, acting furtively.

'I'm positive, I got to see you.'

'Who you calling?' Ester asked.

Angela whipped round, dropping the phone back on the hook. 'Just my mum. I'll get you some breakfast.'

Ester continued her slow progress down the stairs; she felt terrible. She felt even worse when Norma drove into the yard, tooting the horn to herald her arrival. 'Get rid of her, Angela, go on, get out there.'

Angela was scared stiff. 'But there's a body in the car.'

'All the more reason to get rid of her, isn't it?'

Norma was lugging down some bags of feed for the horse and smiled as Angela approached. 'Hi, I was just passing so I thought I'd drop this lot off.'

'Everybody's out,' Angela said lamely.

'Oh, can you just give me a hand?'

Angela began to help her take a sack out of her truck and into the stables. She could see Gloria's dripping Mini out of the corner of her eye.

'Did you have visitors last night? I noticed a flash Porsche parked in the lane on my way home from work but it's not there this morning.'

'No, we didn't have anyone call in.'

'Give Julia my regards. Tell her I'll maybe drop by later, see if she wants a ride.'

'Okay.'

'That's a nice car.' Norma pointed to the Saab.

'Oh yes, it's a friend of . . . er . . .' Angela almost wet herself she was so scared.

Norma wasn't really listening. She was disappointed that Julia wasn't around and returned to her truck, patting it. 'This is all I can afford. Ah, well, it gets me from A to B.'

She climbed in, and drove off past the builders, who were having a tea-break, and waved. The sun had come out, they'd been paid, so they were in a good mood, and waved back.

Dolly felt the blood rush to her cheeks as she read the letter. Her application to open Grange Manor House as a children's home had been turned down. She walked stiffly into the drawing room as Ester appeared.

'Just a word of advice. That little Angela's making QT phone calls.'

Dolly nodded, not listening, so Ester went back to bed.

Angela came in a few moments later with a cup of tea. 'That Norma brought feed for the horse. She even looked right at the Mini – I was scared stiff.'

Dolly roused herself and sighed. 'I've been turned down.'

She proffered the letter to Angela, who read it and then looked at her. 'But they don't even say why. You should at least ask them. Why don't you call them on Monday?'

Dolly considered. 'Yeah, I got a right to know why they rejected me.'

Connie drove Lennie's Porsche across the river and to the small garage Dolly had told her would buy it without asking too many questions. She was calmer now and waited as two mechanics looked it over. She'd told them it was her boyfriend's and he had just got a job abroad. They continued checking the engine and left the cash negotiation to Ron Delaney, the garage owner, a young, flashy, over-confident man wearing a bright track-suit and heavy gold chains. He didn't waste much time: if he had any suspicions about the car he didn't press them but gave a cash deal price below the 'book'. Connie accepted twelve thousand pounds in fifties and twenties, eager to get back to the manor.

Gloria waited to be searched before entering the visitors' section at Brixton. When her name was called, she hurried over to Eddie, who was already sitting at the table. He looked her up and down. 'You look different,' he said nonchalantly.

'Yeah, it's all the fresh air.'

'What you brought me?'

'Nothin'. I didn't have any time and I've not got any cash.'

'Every time you come you got a line of bullshit, Gloria. Last time you said—'

'I know what I said. It all went wrong, there's no pay-off.'

'No? What about the diamonds?'

'Fakes. So now I got to sell the gear, Eddie. I'm flat

broke and I got to pay her rent. There's no need to flog the lot but if you got a contact then . . .'

'No way.'

Gloria leaned closer. 'Eddie, I got them at the manor. We've already had one bleedin' search done – they come back and . . .' Eddie started to peel off his papers to roll a cigarette. Gloria bent closer. 'Eddie, she'll have to have a bit of a cut.'

'Who?'

'You know who. Dolly Rawlins. If it wasn't for her they could have arrested the lot of us. It's only fair.'

'Is it?'

'Oh, come on, Eddie, just gimme a name, I'll do the business. You know me, you can trust me.'

'Can I?'

Gloria pursed her lips. 'What's the matter with you?'

Eddie opened his baccy tin. 'That stash is mine, my insurance for when I get out. Now, if it was just you, maybe I'd be prepared to—'

'What you mean, if it was just me? Of course it is.'

'No, it isn't. Now you want to give her a cut, next she'll want more, so if she wants to make a deal you tell her to come and see me. Maybe I'll do a deal with her, maybe I won't.'

'She won't come in here, Eddie.'

He fingered his tobacco carefully, laying it out on the paper. 'Tell her she got no option.'

Dolly listened as Julia described the cemetery and the recent burials also that graves already dug and waiting for funerals were at the far side. Connie returned with the money and passed it over to Dolly. She had seen no one at Lennie's flat and she had done exactly as Dolly had told her. She was rewarded with a frosty smile of gratitude. Gloria arrived back later that afternoon and told Dolly what Eddie had said.

'He wants me to go and see him in the nick?' Dolly was livid. 'No way, I'll sort something. He won't be out, Gloria, for a very long time. In the meantime they're here, in the house, and I don't like it. The sooner we're rid of them the better.'

Tommy Malin wanted a fifty per cent cut. He agreed to arrange a buyer, one he could trust, and they would exchange that night. Gloria was furious – Eddie would go out of his mind. Why pay some bloke fifty per cent? It was madness.

'We pay because I want cash and I want to get rid of them.'

'Then go and talk to Eddie.'

'No. I can trust Tommy.'

'You sayin' you can't trust Eddie?'

'Can you?'

Gloria was gobsmacked.

'He's in the nick. Who knows who he'll put you in touch with? We do as I say. We sell the guns to Tommy Malin's contact.'

'We could bleedin' sell them to the Queen Mother for a fifty per cent cut,' stormed Gloria, but Dolly walked out. Conversation over.

Mike ran along the stone corridor and up the stairs to Audrey's flat. He banged hard on the door and she opened it with the chain still on. 'It's me – come on – let me in.'

She looked at him fearfully. 'What's happened?'

'I want you to put in a call for me. I just got a tip-off

about something and I can't do anything about it but maybe we'll get her after all.'

'Who?'

'Who the hell do you think?'

'Dolly? What do you want me to do?'

'Call my governor. I know he's at the station so we'll go to a pub and you put in a call.'

'Why me?'

'You won't say your name, for chrissakes. I just want you to tip him off about something.'

'What?'

'Guns. Dolly Rawlins has got bags full of guns stashed at the manor.'

DCI Craigh replaced the phone. He was working overtime and was in a foul mood, but he had come in because Traffic reckoned they had now traced the vehicle used in the hit-and-run that killed James Donaldson. The car was registered to a hire garage called Rodway Motors, but what interested Craigh was that the garage was in the Aylesbury area – close enough to Grange Manor House.

Craigh was about to leave his office when his desk phone rang. He reached out for it just as DI Palmer walked in.

'We might have got a trace on the vehicle,' Craigh said as he answered the phone.

Audrey had to cover one ear because of the racket in the pub. She turned to Mike, just able to see him sitting up at the bar, watching her. He gestured for her to hurry up and make the call, then checked his watch. When he looked at her again, she had already dialled. Audrey asked if she was speaking to Detective Chief Inspector Craigh. When he confirmed that she was, she said her carefully rehearsed speech. 'Dolly Rawlins is holding a stash of weapons owned by Eddie Radford. The guns are at Grange Manor House at Aylesbury, and worth at least thirty thousand pounds.' Then she replaced the receiver and went to join Mike at the bar.

'What did he say?' Mike asked.

'Well, nothin'. You told me to just say what I had to then put the phone down.'

Mike downed his pint. 'I'd better get back home in case he calls me there.'

'What do you want me to do?'

'Leave, as you were planning to.'

Audrey sipped her gin and tonic. 'I got to wait, Mike. I've missed my flight again, so I'll have to go back to the travel agent. You know, you could come with me, all of you, Susan and the kids.'

Mike shook his head. 'No way. You don't seem to understand. I like my job, and I don't want to lose it.'

Mike had only just walked into his own home when the phone rang. It was DCI Craigh, and he wanted him back at the station.

'What's up?' Mike asked innocently.

'Just get in here fast as you can,' Craigh said.

'Okay, I'm on my way.' Mike hung up as Susan and the kids came into the hall.

'Are we going to the swimming pool, Dad?' his youngest boy said excitedly.

'No, I'm sorry. I just got a call – they want me in.'

'But it's Saturday,' Susan said petulantly.

'I know, but . . . I got to go.'

Susan didn't believe him. She stared at him, her face

tight. 'Oh, yes? Well, I hope they're paying you overtime – you seem to be on duty all hours lately. You sure you're not just going off with that girl?'

Mike sighed. 'Sue, don't keep on about that, all right? You want to call the station and check? Go ahead, but this is getting me down. You question every bloody move I make.'

She pushed the kids to the front door. 'Maybe you give me reason to.'

DCI Craigh told Mike about the car and that it was traced to a garage near Aylesbury. 'We're going over there to check it out. And there's something else. I got a call, a woman – she may have been your contact but she asked for me. Guns. Come on, I'll tell you in the car.'

The builders were not around as it was a weekend. The coast was clear. Dolly ordered a disgruntled Gloria to start loading up the guns. They would use Ester's Saab to deliver them to Tommy Malin.

Ester became uneasy as she knew just how hot the car was. 'I can't let anyone drive it, Dolly. I'm the only one listed on the insurance.'

Dolly fixed her with a look. 'So you can drive. Gloria will go with you – unless you're planning on leaving?'

Ester said nothing and Dolly took her silence as confirmation that she agreed to help them out. 'Pack them up, go on, get started. Julia, Kathleen and I will do the graveyard shift.'

'What about Connie? She got us all into this mess with her ruddy boyfriend, why can't she help bury him?' Kathleen moaned.

'Because Connie will be doing something else.' Dolly left them before they could argue.

Connie was lying on her bed reading a magazine when Dolly entered. She didn't bother to knock. 'That builder bloke, one that took you out?'

'What about him?'

'Well, you go out with him again, make him happy, understand me? Only I don't want to fork out all the cash we got and I owe him, so you see him, give him a few more grand, tell him the rest will be coming in.'

Connie hesitated. 'What about all that cash from Lennie's car?'

'I need to pay off electricity, phone connection and keep a bit back for emergencies and groceries. Besides, I think you should earn your keep after all we're doing for you.' Dolly stared coldly at her.

'Okay. He said I could go to his gym with him so I'll call him.'

'Good. Oh – this gym. Do they have lockers, ones you can retain the key for?'

'I dunno.'

'Check it out when you call him, ask about membership and if you can leave your gear there.'

'Why?'

'Don't ask questions, just do what I tell you to.'

Connie turned away. Sometimes Dolly scared the pants off her. She had a nasty way of lowering her voice when she was angry. It unnerved her.

DCI Craigh drove into Rodway Motors' car-hire section and he and Mike went into the reception as DI Palmer walked over to the main garage. As he walked through the open doors, he saw a red Volvo up on a ramp. He called

Craigh, but he had already stepped inside the reception area. Palmer moved closer to the ramp and looked underneath it. A mechanic was checking the exhaust. 'Can you come up and have a word?' Palmer said casually. The man glared and returned to his work. Palmer sat on his heels and showed his ID.

Craigh showed the receptionist his ID and waited as she thumbed through the log book. She then looked up. 'It was hired by a Mrs Gloria Radford.'

Craigh flicked a glance at Mike, then turned back to the receptionist. She pushed the log book towards him and he read that the Volvo had been hired for one day only, the same day James Donaldson was killed. Mrs Radford had listed her private address as a flat in Clapham.

Craigh moved aside with Mike. 'She was at the manor, wasn't she? The night we busted it?'

Gordon Rodway, the owner of the garage, walked in, followed by Palmer. The car had been returned, no damage recorded, and it had subsequently been hired out four times. It had also been through a car-wash three times, polished and hoovered.

'I want no one near it. I'll have my people check it over,' Craigh said, none too happy as they all followed Rodway back to the garage. The Volvo was still on the ramp, the greasy mechanic whispering to his mate and pointing at the car. Rodway studied it and then looked back at Craigh. 'What's the interest in this car, then? We recorded the mileage, if that's any help.'

Mike walked round to the front bumpers: no dents, no paintwork scratched, it looked immaculate. If this was the car that ran over James Donaldson surely there would be some evidence, but as far as he could see there was none. The Forensic boys would comb over it; they would find something, if anyone could. Craigh decided that was enough for the weekend, until they had further information. He'd just check out Gloria Radford's address and take Sunday off.

Dolly looked at Connie in her skintight leotard. 'Well, do they have lockers?'

'Yes, and it's a hundred and fifty quid for membership.'

'Good. Join, and when you get there tonight, put this in the locker and bring me the key.' Dolly handed her a bag, which weighed a ton.

'What's this?'

'Just some personal things of mine – call them a safeguard. But not a word to any of the others. Just get John nice and happy. You don't have to screw him, I wouldn't ask you to do that, just string him along and lock this bag up for me.'

Connie went out to the front pathway to wait for John to collect her. It was just growing dark but not enough yet to move the body.

Angela was cleaning the kitchen when Dolly came in. 'Julia's looking for you, she's out in the yard,' she said.

Dolly opened the back door. 'Julia?'

She came out of the stables and joined Dolly on the kitchen doorstep. 'Yeah. Look, I don't think it's a good idea for Kathleen to come along tonight. She's getting all twitchy, says she won't be a part of it.'

Dolly sighed. She touched Julia's arm lightly; she liked her, she was straightforward, you knew where you were with her. 'Right, you and me will do the graveyard shift, Kathleen can stay here with Angela.'

'What about Connie?'

'She's doing something else. Are the guns all loaded up?' Julia nodded. Dolly glanced at her watch. 'They should get moving, Tommy said his contact will be there about ten. Ester's all right to drive, isn't she?'

'I think so.'

'Is she staying on?' Dolly asked.

'I don't know.'

'If she isn't, does that mean you won't?'

Julia flushed. 'I guess so, but I don't think she's got anywhere to go, you know, Dolly. She's got a big mouth but . . . Well, maybe you should talk to her yourself.'

DCI Craigh got back into the car. Palmer was at the wheel. 'Gloria Radford hasn't lived there for a few weeks. Flat was taken over by the council but she returned to collect something from out in the back shed. I had a look round and it's mostly filled with junk. Maybe she took the guns and stashed them at the manor.'

Mike leaned on the front seat. 'What are we waiting for? If your tip-off was right and there are guns at the manor, why don't we just bust the place?'

Craigh looked directly ahead. 'We already made ourselves look like a bunch of arseholes, Mike. This time we do it by the book. We cover ourselves and check out the fucking information, if that's all right with you – apart from that I'd like a day off. That all right with you, is it?'

Mike sat back, knowing not to push it. He stared out of the window as they drove down the road. Palmer gave a hooded look at Craigh. 'So far they've found nothing on the vehicle, Gov.'

Craigh lit a cigarette. 'Let's see if we can have a chat to Eddie Radford Monday. He might have some information. That suit you, Mike?' he said sarcastically.

'Whatever you say, Gov. Just, why wait twenty-four hours? They could shift her guns.'

Craigh checked his watch. 'Okay – we go see Eddie Radford. Then we call it quits.'

Ester eased herself up and winced. The last thing she felt like doing was driving back to London. She wondered if she could get out of it when Dolly walked in, closing the door behind her.

'How did you get the beating, Ester?' She sat on the dressing-table stool and waited.

Ester was about to lie, but gave up; she didn't have the energy. 'Okay, last time I got sent down I also got a raw deal. When I was busted, a couple of my clients got scared – you know, that I'd plead not guilty and they'd have to prove it and name my clients. They got my little black book – well, it wasn't little, it was a whopper, and I got K for kings, P for princes, no kiddin'. I was coining it, specials laid on for this Arab royal family. I was told that if I pleaded guilty, my fine would be paid, my back taxes paid and I'd get a few quid on top. I was assured I'd not be sent down. Well, I was. I got five years. They paid my legal costs, a percentage of my taxes and then walked away. Not one name was mentioned. So, I got pissed off.'

Dolly fingered a perfume bottle, then looked up. 'Go on.'

'I used to make private videos which clients would take after the show. I never made copies but on the night I got turned over, I stashed one and it was never found. When I got out, I went to them straight, said I felt I was owed some dough. They threw me out, told me that if I showed my face I'd be sorry. I then called them and said they would now be very sorry, that I had a video and I was gonna expose them.' Dolly tutted. Ester looked at her. 'It's not even that bad, just a few slags rolling around with them, but you know how Arabs are. I asked for five hundred grand.'

'And?'

'Next thing they got some punk after me with a fucking price on my head. I mean, they're all crazy! So I kind of hid out here. They won't leave me alone and the result is what you can see. They beat me up and I ran like hell.'

'Back here?'

Ester nodded. 'Yeah, but I won't be staying long, just enough time to get my face healed.'

Dolly stood up. 'Okay, at least you told me the truth. So, go do the business with Gloria and you can stay on here until you're recovered, then you do whatever you want . . .'

Ester smiled, and regretted it because of her cut lip. 'Thanks.'

Eddie Radford was really edgy. He knew word would be out he'd been lifted and that the filth were having a talk. Especially coming in to see him at a weekend. Every prisoner there would know within an hour or so – word travels fast in the nick – and he didn't like it, didn't like anyone even thinking he could be grassing.

'What's all this about?' he snapped.

DCI Craigh drew up a chair. Mike stood leaning against the wall as Craigh proffered cigarettes. Eddie refused to take one.

'I want to know what this is about,' he repeated.

'You know someone called James Donaldson?'

'No.'

'Dolly Rawlins?'

'No.'

'Gloria Radford?'

Eddie looked at Craigh, shrugged. 'Yeah, she's my wife.'

'She holding something that belongs to you, is she?'

'I dunno.'

'You're in for dealing in guns, armed robbery.'

'Yeah, that's right.'

'Eighteen years.'

'Great, you can count.'

'Can you? That's a long time, a very long time, Eddie. Be better spending time in an open prison – lot cushier than this dump,' Craigh said softly.

'Thinking of taking me out to Butlins, are you?'

Mike changed his position, staring hard at Radford. Craigh flicked his cigarette box over. 'We think your wife was driving the car that killed Jimmy Donaldson, Eddie.'

'Oh, yeah? Well, she was never a blinder behind the wheel.'

'You know about it, do you?'

'Look, I dunno this Donaldson, I don't know what you got me up here for, I want to go back to my cell.'

'But she could be charged with murder, Eddie.'

'Tough luck. I want to go.'

'If she's picked up, who's gonna flog your guns, Eddie?' Eddie frowned. 'They're being held for you at Grange Manor House, aren't they?' Eddie chewed his lower lip. 'We know they're at the manor so if we arrest Gloria you're gonna lose your pension fund. All I need from you is confirmation that they're there and in return, well, we can talk to people, recommend you get moved. We can't make promises but we can certainly talk to the right people.'

Eddie shifted his weight on the chair and reached out for Craigh's cigarettes. 'I dunno anythin' about this Jimmy Donaldson bloke or whatever Gloria's done. I dunno anythin' about that.'

'But you know about the guns, don't you, Eddie?'

Eddie removed a cigarette, lit it, and let the smoke trail

from his nostrils as he decided what he should say. He knew they were worth thirty grand, but what good was that if they were sold by that cow Dolly Rawlins? What good were they to him if he couldn't get his hands on them? What if they were gonna arrest Gloria?

'I want to be moved,' Eddie said quietly.

Craigh looked at Mike. They'd already said to him they couldn't give him a deal on that and that they didn't have any powers of persuasion to get a prisoner moved – but they would make him think that they could anyway. 'Open prison, swimming pool, tennis courts and, like you said, Eddie, some nicks are better than Butlins . . .'

Eddie flicked ash from his cigarette and rested both elbows on the table. 'She's staying with her, with Dolly Rawlins.'

They knew they'd got him, and were surprised at how fast, but he didn't seem to give a damn about his wife or her possible arrest. All he seemed to care about was that he would lose out.

'They're worth thirty grand,' Eddie said, hardly audible.

The same figure the anonymous caller had given to Craigh. He now reckoned the call was on the level, the tip-off legitimate. His weekend was now well and truly blown. He knew they would have to act on the tip-off now.

Dolly and Julia drove to the cemetery, which was in pitch darkness. Julia drove without headlamps, guided by the white tomb-stones as they moved slowly down the dirt-track road towards the recent graves. Flowers and wreaths were still strewn across the ground. They parked when they got as close as possible and took out the spades, zig-zagging their way towards the freshly covered grave. They were obscured from sight by a tall, thick hedge. One grave was ready for its occupant, the trench dug, boards place across the deep, gaping hole.

Julia carefully moved aside the wooden planks, and said, 'Let's get on with it.'

They began to dig. It was not too difficult because the earth was so fresh and they worked in silence. Only the swishing of the spades could be heard in the silent cemetery. They were digging deeper to place Lennie's body in the grave and cover him up. The coffin would then be place on top of him at the funeral. Goodbye, Lennie!

While Dolly and Julia were at the cemetery, Ester and Gloria headed for London's West End to fence the guns. Gloria squinted at the *A to Z*. Ester had insisted they cut across London by various back-streets and they were now somewhere in Elephant and Castle but neither had any idea exactly where.

'Wait a minute, go left, first left,' Gloria muttered.

Ester drove on and turned left, then swore. No entry. She sighed and snatched the book from Gloria. 'Let me see.'

'It's not my fault. Why you had to come your route I dunno, I mean, we been up and down for over an hour now.'

Ester squinted at the small squares on the map. 'I just think that what we've got stashed in the boot is not necessarily a good thing to have if we should be stopped, okay?'

'Gettin' lost with them's not a brilliant move neither,' snarled Gloria.

'Okay, I got it, we're not too far.' She began to do a U-turn, when, caught in the headlamps, they saw a police officer examining a locked gate. He turned and watched the car bang up on to the pavement.

'Oh, bloody hell. Do you see what I see?' said Gloria.

Ester looked in the mirror. He was walking towards them. She turned off the lights, careered up the road and screeched round the corner.

'Well, that was fucking subtle,' screamed Gloria.

Julia was waist deep and still digging.

Dolly peered down. 'Okay, just drop him in and cover him. It's deep enough not to smell too much, isn't it?'

Julia started to climb out. 'Yeah, the maggots'll have a field day, and it'll be deep enough, but we'll have a lot of soil to spread around and over him.'

'Let's get him out of the car,' Dolly said as she moved off, chucking aside her spade. Julia stuck hers into the ground and followed Dolly. The body was wrapped in an old carpet and polythene sheeting. They dragged it towards them and, between them, eased it from the rear of the Mini. It was very heavy and they had to resort to dragging it across the uneven ground towards the grave.

'One shoe's missing,' Julia whispered.

'Shit! Go and see if it's in the car, and hurry up.'

Julia searched the car but found nothing. 'Maybe it's still in the pool,' she said, as she helped roll the body down into the grave. They began to shovel the earth back into the hole, both working flat out, as slowly, bit by bit, Lennie was buried. Dolly stamped the earth down on top of him as Julia dragged the planks back to lay across the grave.

*

Gloria was blazing. She found it hard to believe Ester could be so stupid but at least she now understood why they'd kept to the back-streets.

'Hot? This bleedin' car's hot and you been driving it around London, almost ran over a bloody copper. I'm tellin' you, Ester, you need your head seeing to. If Dolly was to find out . . .'

'Oh, shut up. We're here now. Go on.'

Gloria got out of the car and knocked on a small door built into the big yard gates. It was opened by Tommy, who had a whispered conversation with her, and the main gates eased back. Ester drove, and Tommy and his contact began to unload the guns, carrying them into the warehouse.

Gloria had never met the buyer before, a small, softly spoken man wearing a camel coat, good suit and pinkish-toned glasses. His expert began to check over each weapon as Gloria placed them on the desk. A large space had been cleared, the blinds had been drawn, and they quietly got on with the business in hand.

Ester was surprised by Gloria, who was controlled and proved adept at handling the guns, making a good, strong sales pitch with each piece. The weapons consisted of two 9mm Browning pistols, semi automatic, four .38 Smith and Wessons, three .35 Magnum colts, two .44s, two .455 Webley's specials, collector's items, and boxes of ammunition, Westley and Richard rifles, 26-inch barrels, bead foresight and stands, two Hechler and Koch machine guns and four Kalashnikovs.

While Gloria was doing her business, Ester was selling Tommy the Saab for cash. She would take in exchange an old covered van he had parked in the yard. She admitted it was a bit 'iffy' but not too hot. Tommy raised an eyebrow.

'Come on, man, you know it's a great deal. You can switch the plates on it, get it out of the country within twenty-four hours.'

Tommy hesitated and glanced over at the gun dealers, then at Gloria who was searching one of the big bags. 'Ester, a minute,' she said, and Ester went to join her. 'Three shotguns missing. You know anything about that?'

Ester shook her head and hissed that Tommy was interested in buying the Saab.

'Good, I'm not wheeling around in it.' Gloria returned to the dealers.

'No shotguns, sorry, miscalculation, but I got a desert Eagle that's right now the gun to have. You want to see it?'

The officers in the patrol car received the information that the Saab was stolen; the owner had reported the theft two nights ago. The beat officer had succeeded in taking the Saab's registration number and had flagged down the patrol car, whose window he was now leaning against. 'I thought it might be, they drove off fast soon as they saw me, headed back towards Tower Bridge, but they could have turned off on any of the roads. Lot of old warehouses round that area.'

The patrol car moved off. As the officer watched them disappear, he turned to continue his street patrol. An old, green-painted van passed him and he didn't give it a second glance. Gloria was counting the money, licking her fingers to flick through the notes. 'Bleedin' ripped us off. Ten grand! It's disgusting. I couldn't believe the cheap bastards.'

'Well, we made up for it with the Saab.'

'Yeah, but that's not the point. I hate being skinned. They got a lot for their dough, you know. They were worth at least thirty grand. I mean, two of the rifles would cost you seven big ones alone.'

Ester headed over Tower Bridge. 'Well, I'll split the money from the car with you. Dolly needn't know.'

Gloria smirked. 'You mean about it being nicked?'

'Yeah, we just divide the cash between us.'

'No way. She gets the lot because she'll be on the blower to Tommy checking it out, you know her. And besides . . .'

'Besides what?'

Gloria stuffed the money up her skirt, wriggling it into her panties. 'Somebody kept those shotguns – and you never know . . .'

'Never know what?'

'Maybe she's got something in mind? I mean, she's pulled a couple of blinders, hasn't she? Way I see it, let's keep her happy, see what's going on in that old brain of hers.'

Ester laughed. 'Why not? In the meantime, you keep that cash warm.'

'Better to be safe than sorry,' Gloria said, as the wad of notes eased round her panties. 'They got bastards holding up motors to nick handbags now, you know, in a traffic jam, and they push a gun into your face and nick your wallet. Shocking world nowadays.'

DCI Craigh, DI Palmer and Mike headed towards Grange Manor House. They were accompanied by twelve local officers from Thames Valley and they had now secured a search warrant, this time not for diamonds but weapons. Some weekend!

*

Julia and Dolly had carried the spare earth to the hedges and scattered it around. They were filthy dirty but the job had been done. They were just stacking the spades back into the car when they heard the wail of a siren. They froze and looked towards the lane as a police car drove past, followed by two more vehicles.

'What was that about?'

'I don't know and I don't care, just so long as they're not coming into the cemetery,' Dolly muttered.

Julia walked round to the driving seat. She got in and turned to Dolly.

'Connie really owes us a big favour.'

'She'll pay it,' Dolly replied as they headed out of the dark cemetery on to the lane, virtually following the convoy of police and having no idea they were on their way to search the manor.

CHAPTER 11

D CI CRAIGH gave the signal and all vehicle lights went out; no sirens as the convoy moved slowly down the drive to the manor. There were lights on. The cars stopped and six men moved quickly to the rear of the house, six more positioned themselves around the front. Craigh, accompanied by Palmer and Mike, walked up the front steps. He tapped lightly and called quietly that it was the police. Receiving no reply, he stepped back, and Palmer hit the lock on the front door. At the same time, the men at the rear of the house got a radio message to enter via the kitchen.

The sound of the forced entry echoed like thunder inside the manor. Down came the front door as the back door splintered. They let rip with the information they were police officers.

Kathleen was putting coal into a scuttle when she heard the crash and the loud voices: *'Police! Police!'* She chucked the scuttle aside, drew open the cellar window and climbed out.

Angela almost had heart failure. She was caught midway up the stairs and started screaming in terror.

Connie was the first to return. Big John had dropped her at the manor gates. She was picked up as she walked down the drive, two uniformed officers holding her between them as they pushed her towards the front door. By now every light was turned on, the place seemed to be swarming with police and she was as terrified as Angela.

She thought they were arresting her because of Lennie; Angela thought they had come for her because of James Donaldson. They were questioned, asked for their names, dates of birth, and shown the search warrant: neither said anything.

Kathleen was equally terrified and, once out of the cellar, made a run for it, heading towards the woods. Two officers gave chase. By the time she was brought back, held between the two men, she was sobbing hysterically.

Ester and Gloria drove in just as Kathleen was being escorted from the woods. Both women were asked to step out of their vehicle, place their hands on the top of the car and stand with their legs apart. Gloria was yelling her head off, demanding that a female officer search her, as Ester shouted that she wanted to know what was going on. No one answered. They were shown the warrant as DCI Craigh walked out of the house. He instructed his men to run checks on all the women.

'What you talking about?' Gloria demanded.

Kathleen stood by the patrol car, head bowed, still crying.

'What you think we are? Bleedin' IRA? I'm from East Ham, she's from Liverpool, you got this all wrong.' Gloria was yelling and Ester nudged her to shut up. 'I want to go to the toilet,' Gloria shouted.

Ester warned her again to shut up but Gloria hissed back, 'Have you forgot I got the dough in me knickers?'

The police received information that Kathleen O'Reilly was wanted for absconding from a magistrates' court; there was an outstanding charge of fraud against her. She was ushered into the patrol car.

As Dolly and Julia drove up to the manor, they gaped at the scene: Ester and Gloria, spreadeagled over the van,

Kathleen sobbing inside the patrol car, and everywhere uniformed officers carrying big-beamed torches.

'Shit, now what?' Dolly exploded.

'Will you get out of the car?' DCI Craigh gestured for more officers to assist in searching the new arrivals.

The women were herded into the house and taken into the drawing room where Connie sat with Angela as the room was searched by a uniformed officer. Dolly looked over the search warrant and then handed it back to Craigh. 'You mind if I brew a pot of tea?'

He shook his head. If that woman had a stash of guns inside the house she was acting very cool about it but he wasn't about to call the men off, far from it. They would comb every inch of the house and grounds.

The dawn light came and with it better visibility. The search continued, both inside and out. The women sat drinking tea, eating sandwiches, but did not offer either to the police.

At half past eight on Sunday morning, Craigh gave up. He returned to London with Palmer and Mike. They had found nothing and all they had to show for eight hours' work was a missing felon, Kathleen O'Reilly. At least that was something.

Dolly examined the damaged doors and banister rails. She began making up a list of damages for which she would apply to be reimbursed and she would make damned sure they paid for it through the nose. She was angry, not just because of the warrant and the search but because it was obvious they had to have had a tip-off from someone. The question was, which one of them was it? She knew they had been very lucky: a few hours earlier and they would

253

have been caught not only with the guns but with a dead body. The women were all on edge, waiting for the police to leave. They couldn't talk, too scared they might be overheard. By one o'clock Sunday morning the remaining police called it quits and left. As soon as the women saw them moving out, they all began to talk at once.

'Eh! Dolly, what about Kathleen?'

'I don't know what to think.'

'I would never put her in the frame for being a grass,' Gloria said, as she hitched up her skirt.

'Somebody is, though,' Dolly said.

Gloria tossed the money out of her panties. 'There you go. I had it stashed in me drawers – about the only thing I've had in them for a few years.'

Dolly arched an eyebrow. 'Don't be crude.'

They counted the money, discussed the sale of the car and then Dolly looked at her watch. 'Right, I'm going to have a sleep, then I'm going to church.'

They were astonished. She yawned, asking if the boiler was on as she needed a bath.

'Church?' Gloria asked.

'Yes, church. I intend making the locals trust me – I've got to if I'm going to open up this place.' Dolly paused. 'Even though they turned me down, I'm not finished yet. I knew it wasn't going to be easy but unless I give it a chance—'

'Why don't you be realistic, Dolly? You don't stand a chance in hell. As if they would let kids come here.' Ester yawned.

'Why not?'

'Because you're an ex-con, darlin'. Now maybe you'd stand more of a chance if you applied for teenagers – better still, ex-cons, young ones coming out. They all need a home and—' Suddenly Ester laughed and clapped her hands. 'I tell you something, with my contacts, if you got a houseful of young girls we could open this place again. Coin it! What a perfect cover.'

'Run this as a brothel?' Dolly asked with a half-smile.

'Why not? It ran before and, like I said, I have contacts. Put in the cash we got from the guns, from my car – we've at least got a kick-start.'

Julia turned on her. 'Use poor kids coming out of the nick? Is that what you'd do, Ester?'

'Why not? It's not as if we've not got a couple of tarts here for starters.'

'Who you bleedin' callin' a tart?' Gloria snapped.

'Oh, come off it. You and Connie have been turning tricks and Angela's done a couple. All I'm saying is be realistic.'

Julia was furious. 'Well, before I'd get kids on the game, I'd pull a robbery. You sicken me, Ester.'

'Do I? Well, maybe we should think about the latter then. What do you say, Dolly? You got anything in mind? You know this will never get opened as a foster home so I'm asking you. You got any ideas?'

Dolly said nothing as she moved slowly to the door. 'No. The only thing I've got on my mind right now is trying to find out which one of you shopped me. Somebody here did – one of *you* did – and when I sort that out I intend, as I've said right from the word go, to open this place up. That's what I bought it for. You lot may have changed your minds but I haven't.'

They waited until the door closed behind her before they talked in whispers, wondering if she had been turned down because of the sauna episode, but they dismissed it. They started looking from one to another: was one of them a grass?

Gloria sighed. 'What about Kathleen? She was the only

one of us the filth had anything on. Maybe she was scared and wanted to make a deal.'

'No way. Kathleen's a lot of things but she's not a grass,' Julia said.

'That leaves one of us in here, doesn't it?' Gloria said, looking at Ester.

'It's not fucking me,' Ester snapped.

Julia opened the door. 'This is ridiculous. We're all knackered. Why don't we do what Dolly's doing and have some kip? We've been up all night.'

Dolly could hear toilets flushing, baths running. She was wide awake, couldn't sleep. Ester tapped lightly on the door and peeked in. 'Dolly, can I have a word?'

Dolly lay back on the pillow. 'Sure, sit down.'

'Look, I'm sorry if I spoke out of turn down there but I was just tired and right now I need a roof over my head. But at the same time, you know, that cash won't go far.'

Dolly nodded. 'No, it won't.'

'That said, you could make this work, I'm sure of it.'

'I need that cash, Ester, I'm sorry. I know what you're after and the answer is no. I need that money to pay builders, to keep the place afloat. If you want to stay on and give me a hand then you can.'

'Okay, thanks.' It wasn't what she wanted to hear. She needed money, she wanted to get out of the bloody place. 'Maybe check out Angela. She's been making phone calls.' Ester backed out and closed the door.

Dolly sat up and thumped her pillow. Next to turn up was Connie. She wanted Dolly to know that she believed in the project and was sure it would work, she loved the old house. 'It wasn't me, Dolly, I wouldn't have told anyone about the guns, I mean, I wouldn't, not with Lennie here, now would I?'

Dolly smiled ruefully. 'No, love, but Lennie could have got us all in hot water.'

Connie was near to tears. 'I know, I know. But I also want you to know that it wasn't me.'

A while after she left, Gloria tapped at the door. One by one they came, just to make sure Dolly knew it wasn't them.

The only one who did not appear was Angela.

She was lying wide awake in her bed, and jumped when Dolly walked in and closed the door. 'I want to talk to you, Angela, and I want you to be honest with me. Who are you calling?' Angela burst into tears and Dolly sat on the edge of her bed. 'Now don't cry, just tell me, we all know you're always making phone calls.'

'My mum and—'

Angela began to sob. Dolly waited as Angela blurted out how frightened she was about being arrested for running over Jimmy Donaldson. Between sobs and gasps she told Dolly about her boyfriend, who was married with kids, and now didn't want anything to do with her.

Dolly patted her hand. 'Well, maybe it's best that you're here.'

'I'm pregnant.'

She cradled Angela in her arms, comforting her, asking if she wanted to keep the baby. When Angela sobbed out that she didn't know, Dolly assured her that as long as she was at the manor, both Angela and the baby would have a home.

When Dolly came out Connie was passing Angela's room.

'She's pregnant.'

257

Connie looked at the closed door, then back at Dolly. 'So that's why she's been on the phone, is it?'

'Don't tell the others. She doesn't want anyone to know.'

Connie scooted down the stairs and into the kitchen. Gloria was sitting with Ester as Julia washed up.

'Okay, this is what we've decided, Connie,' Ester said.

Connie's eye was caught by a stack of bits and pieces of jewellery.

'We're all giving up what we can, you know, just to make it look like we're really behind this foster home crap. We don't think Dolly stands a chance in hell but . . .'

Connie pulled out a chair and sank into it. 'I got a few pieces I can give.'

'Good. It's just that she's got to trust us, Connie, we think she may be coming up with something. We don't know but Gloria said three shotguns are missing.'

'Yeah, I took them into the gym, they're in a locker there.'

Ester turned to Julia. 'See, what did I tell you? I knew she was planning something. This proves it.'

Julia was putting away the dishes. 'So we all make out we love this place, is that right?'

Connie pouted. 'But I do.'

'So do I,' said Julia.

'Yeah, well, that's 'cos of that bleedin' horse. You're never off the friggin' thing.'

Julia glared at Gloria. 'Okay, so I love Helen of Troy, but I also like this place.'

Ester slapped the table. 'For chrissakes, can we get done with *The Sound of Bleedin' Music*? All I am saying is she doesn't trust us.'

'Well, *I'm* not the fuckin' grass,' Gloria said angrily.

'I think it's Angela,' Ester said.

'No, she's not, she's pregnant,' Connie said, and they all

turned on her. She shrugged her shoulders. 'She is, Dolly just told me, that's why she's been making all these calls.'

Gloria stood up. 'Well, she's a bloody little liar. She's not pregnant.'

'How do you know?' Ester demanded.

'Because she borrowed my Tampax yesterday.' Dolly walked in and Gloria whipped round. 'We think it's Angela. She's not pregnant, Dolly, she's a liar.'

Dolly clasped her hands in front of her. 'Is she? Well, one of you get her down here. Get her in here right now.'

Angela was hauled out of her bed by Gloria and pushed down the stairs. She came into the kitchen like a frightened rabbit.

'How many weeks gone are you?' demanded Dolly.

'Two months,' Angela said.

Gloria pushed her. 'No, you're not. Why did you borrow my Tampax if you was up the spout?'

'Because I had some blood, I did, I swear on my life.'

Connie went over to her and slipped her arms around her. 'Don't cry, we believe you.'

'I fucking don't,' yelled Gloria.

Dolly scratched her head, and then said to Julia, 'Take her upstairs and examine her.'

'Oh, for God's sake, Dolly, this is ridiculous,' Julia said.

'Is it? Well, I want to know, because if she isn't then she lied to me and she could have been lying from day one. Somebody is tipping off the police, so examine her. Go on, do it.'

Julia led Angela out of the room, then Ester tapped Dolly's shoulder. 'This is for you. It's from us, all of us. We want to help out in any way we can, Dolly. Some of it's gold and—'

Gloria pointed. 'That tie-pin belonged to Jack Dempsey and that Rolex Eddie gave me. It could be a fake, though.'

Dolly picked up pieces of the jewellery, strangely moved even as she noted that they still wore their best bits. But it was, as the old saying goes, the thought that counted.

About ten minutes later Julia returned. 'I think she's more like three months than two. She was telling the truth and you can often have a few spots, even a period during the early months.'

Dolly felt awful but she had needed to know.

'So you think it's Kathleen?' Gloria asked.

'I don't know – I just don't know,' Dolly said, and drummed her fingers on the table. 'I mean maybe, just maybe, it's no one. Have any of you had dealings with DCI Craigh before?'

No one could recall having been arrested by him on a previous occasion. Connie said that she quite liked him, he'd been very nice to her; it was the younger bloke she didn't like.

Angela was suddenly standing like a child in the doorway.

Dolly reached for her and took her hand. 'I'm sorry about that, love, but I needed to know.'

Angela backed away, pressing her body against the wall.

'We're just talking about the coppers,' Dolly said.

'Well, I don't like them, any of them,' Julia said.

'Me neither,' Gloria muttered.

'Funnily enough, I'm sure I've met that younger one, the dark-haired guy, the good-looking one.'

Ester looked at Angela. She was going to ask her if she recognized him and, for some reason, they all turned towards Angela.

'I don't know him. I wasn't arrested, Ester, I wasn't charged, it's not him.' Angela was trembling and no one knew what had got into Ester as she sprang forward.

'Yes, you do! You know him!'

Angela ran out, and Ester took off after her. The women didn't know what was going on but they could hear Angela screaming so they all followed.

Angela was running up the stairs, Ester giving chase. She caught hold of Angela's foot and dragged it. As the girl fell forwards, she bumped and slithered down two stairs and Ester climbed over her, hauling her by her hair.

'Ester! Don't! *Ester, she's pregnant!*' screamed Julia.

Angela tried to fight off her attacker, pushing and screaming, but Ester smacked her face and then pursued her along the landing.

'You little liar! You're a bloody liar, Angela!' Ester was terrifying as she punched and slapped Angela, who tried to defend herself, but Ester was like a whirlwind, kicking, flicking her hands at Angela's face. 'Tell me the truth! You'd better tell me the truth or I'll fucking kill you.'

Angela dived beneath Ester's arm and ran into her own room, but she didn't have time to lock the door before Ester kicked it open and slammed it behind her. All that the others could hear was Angela screeching and Ester slapping and punching her. Dolly was first in after them, then Julia. She dragged Ester off Angela, who was sprawled over the bed. Ester was red-faced with fury.

'Ester! *Ester! Calm down!*' Dolly slapped her face.

'You just slapped the wrong face, sweetheart. Ask that dirty piece of shit who her boyfriend is. He's that bloke that was here, isn't he? *Isn't he?*'

Angela clung to the pillow, as if shielding her body from any further onslaught.

'Is this true?' Dolly asked calmly.

Angela was weeping but nodded. The others howled like dogs, all ready to have a go at her now.

'You don't understand,' wailed Angela.

'I think I do, love,' Dolly spat out, prepared to walk out

on Angela, leave her to the women, just like a cell-fight in the nick.

'He's Shirley Miller's brother,' Angela shrieked.

Dolly froze, her hands clenched at her sides. 'Get out and leave her with me. All of you, get out.'

'What you think she's doing up there?' Gloria asked. Dolly had been with Angela for about fifteen minutes.

'Suffocating her, I hope,' Ester muttered.

'So it was her all the time,' Connie sighed.

'Yeah, the two-faced little bitch,' Gloria snarled.

'One thing worse than a snitch, a child molester.'

'Thank you, Gloria, as ever subtle but . . .'

'No buts, mate, she could have had the lot of us sent down. Ester was right. I just wish I'd got a few punches in.'

Gloria looked up. 'You don't think she'd bump her off, do you?'

Angela was red-eyed from weeping but calmer now. She had explained how she had first met Mike after Ester was raided, how he had been very kind as she was under-age. He had been helpful in getting her social workers and it was thanks to him that she was never reported. They had then become more than friendly after Ester was sent for trial, they had seen one another since, but recently Mike had refused to see her as his wife had found out. When Ester had called, she had contacted him and been asked to report anything she found out about Dolly Rawlins.

'What did he tell you about Shirley?'

Angela snivelled. 'Only that you were responsible and his mother . . .'

Dolly smiled inwardly. Audrey had such a big mouth but she'd kept her son's part in it very quiet.

'What are you going to do with me?' Angela was crying again.

Dolly opened the door and held up the key. 'You can stay here until tomorrow, then you pack up and leave. I never want to see you again. You betrayed me – the only one of them I trusted. Seems I was wrong. I'll never forgive you, love, so get packed.'

The door closed silently but the key turning was loud. It made Angela sob even more.

Dolly shuffled along a pew and bent to pray. She sat back and opened the hymn book as the service began. No one paid much attention to her; she blended into the congregation. When the service was over, she shook hands with the vicar and made her way towards the gates. To her right was the big cemetery where only the night before she had buried Lennie. She hardly gave it a second thought because up ahead she had seen Mrs Tilly opening her car door. She hurried towards her.

'Mrs Tilly!' Dolly called, and was taken aback by the cold, aloof stare. 'I got a letter,' Dolly said, a little out of breath.

Mrs Tilly was in two minds whether even to speak to Dolly but her own anger got the better of her. 'You lied to me, Mrs Rawlins. When I think how much work I did to persuade the board not only to see you but make an on-site visit.'

Dolly interrupted, 'I'm sorry. Are you saying you've been to the manor?'

'Oh, yes, we came, Mrs Rawlins. Didn't Ester Freeman tell you?'

*

Gloria was looking out of the window as a stern-faced Dolly marched up the path. 'Well, the church has certainly done wonders for her! She looks ready for two rounds with Mike Tyson.'

The door banged shut and promptly banged open again because of the damaged lock. The drawing-room door was thrown wide and the women faced Dolly. She hurled her handbag on to the sofa and threw off her coat.

'Something wrong?' Ester asked innocently.

'Oh, yes, you can say that again. Now I know why they turned me down. They only came here and found the lot of you bollock-naked in the sauna.'

'Oh, come on, we weren't all naked, Dolly.'

'You, Julia, shut your mouth because you and that bitch over there were, and I quote, "in an obvious sexual embrace". I presume before you turned the hose-pipe on the governor of the board.'

They couldn't make any excuses, not that she gave them a chance to as she paced up and down. 'All of you knew you'd blown my chances and not one of you had the guts to tell me what you'd done. Eight years I planned this, eight years I waited and now you've done it. You've destroyed any hope I had of reversing the rejection. Well, the lot of you can pack up and piss off with Angela.'

She slammed the door so hard when she walked out that the chandelier shook dangerously.

'Oh, bloody hell,' muttered Gloria. 'I knew it'd come out. How do we get round this one?'

Ester was up and heading for the door. She turned and winked. 'Leave it to me.'

Dolly crashed the kettle on to the Aga as Ester walked in with her hands up as if held at gun-point. 'Just let me tell you something, okay? Don't shoot.'

Dolly was not amused. She threw tea-bags into the pot.

264

'Listen, Dolly. There may, just may, be a way round this.'

'Like what? You've blown it, all of you.'

'No, no, just listen. That bloke who came with them, beaky-nosed, bald fella with a few hairs over the top of his head.'

'Mr Crow. He's chairman of the board.'

'Ah, crow by name, crow by nature. Well, Dolly, I recognized him and maybe one of the reasons why the board turned you down, or he did, was because—'

'You were all naked in the sauna!'

'No. He used to be a regular. What you can do is pay him a private visit. Maybe *he* can do something for you. I'm sure he wouldn't want that known, would he?'

Dolly put her head in her hands. 'He was one of your clients?'

'Yeah. Work him over, Dolly. You can do it – or at least try it.'

Mike was watching TV when the phone rang. He watched Susan jump up to answer it, making no effort to take it himself. He was sick and tired of being monitored.

Susan called from the hall. 'She wants to speak to you.'

He didn't know if she was referring to Angela or his mother. 'Who is it?'

'She said her name was Dolly Rawlins.'

Mike was half out of his seat when he fell back, his face drained of colour.

'Mike? She said it's important.'

Audrey was booked on the first flight to Spain on Monday morning, her third attempt to leave. She opened the door to Mike, all smiles, thinking he had called to say goodbye, but one look at his face made her step back, afraid.

'What's happened?'

She shut the door. He walked into the living room and flopped on to the sofa.

'Dolly Rawlins just called my house.'

'Oh God.'

'She just wanted me to know that she knows about my involvement with the diamonds, with everything.'

'What will she do?'

'I don't know but I'm in deep shit because if she goes to my governor, I'll be arrested. So will you.'

'She wouldn't do that. It'd implicate her.'

'I know. That's what I'm banking on.'

'What do we do?'

Mike sank lower into the sofa cushions. 'Well, maybe you should leave anyway.'

She went to him and put her arms around him. 'Come with me, love, you and the kids and Susan. We just up and run for it.'

He pushed her away. 'I can't do that.'

'Why not?'

'I can't do anything that'll throw any suspicion on me. Can't you see? Don't you understand? I'll just have to wait, see what she wants.'

'Maybe she won't want anything.'

Mike looked at his mother contemptuously. 'Bullshit. She'll want something, question is what?'

Audrey broke down and sobbed. 'It's not fair, is it? Some people get away with murder. You know she killed that poor Jimmy Donaldson, just as she as good as killed our Shirley.'

Mike swung round and grabbed his mother's arm. 'I don't want to hear her name again. If it wasn't for Shirley

I'd never have got into this mess. I mean it, Mum! And I don't want to see or hear from you either. You got me involved in this, Mum, and I got to get myself out of it so leave, go away, get the hell out of my sight.'

He was almost at the car when he stopped and leaned against a brick wall. He started to cry – he couldn't stop the tears. He hadn't meant to say all that about Shirley. He sniffed, wiped his face with the back of his hand, then forced himself to get angry.

She was to blame, whatever way he looked at it, whatever guilt he felt. She'd married that cheap villain Terry Miller, she . . . Shirley was dead and buried, he had to get his life sorted, he had to straighten out. He was losing it, he was blowing everything that was important to him and if he didn't get hold of himself there was no one else to prop him up.

By the time he got into his car he was calmer and in control. He didn't look back to the lit-up window of his mother's flat. He truthfully never wanted to see her again.

Audrey was all packed. She'd earmarked a few items for shipping out but now she was taking down the little personal items, the photographs from the gilt mirror above the mantel. She read her younger son Gregg's last postcard, looked at the stupid kittens, and sighed. Well, he'd just have to ask around for where she was, they would tell him down the market. She tossed the card into the trash can. She didn't have the energy to worry about Gregg, or anyone but herself. Now she could even blame Dolly Rawlins for her son walking out on her. Everything was Dolly Rawlins's fault and Audrey, in a fit of rage, cursed. But then she straightened herself out: she'd be in Spain this time tomorrow, with a villa and a few quid in the bank. At least she'd beaten that bitch over the money. At least she had something to show for poor Shirley. She turned towards the sideboard as if to confirm everything was all right but she'd packed Shirley's photograph, there was nothing there, no sweet, smiling, beautiful Shirley. Audrey felt the tears, not of anger or fury or revenge: the tears were tinged with guilt because she knew she had thought about and cared more for Shirley after she was dead than when she was alive.

CHAPTER 12

D OLLY WAS directed to sit on a row of chairs in the
draughty town hall corridor. Mr Crow's secretary
walked out of his office. She didn't even glance in
Dolly's direction. Dolly stood up, watched the squat-legged
woman disappear, carrying a thick file. She reckoned she'd
at least have a few moments so she tapped and entered Mr
Crow's office. She was through with waiting.

Mr Crow looked up, frowning when he saw her close
his door. 'Mrs Rawlins, did my secretary tell you—' He was
interrupted.

'Yes, she said I could have a few moments. It won't take
any longer.'

He pursed his lips and folded his hands together, priest-
like. 'I am a very busy man.'

'I'm busy too but, like I said, this won't take a moment.
I've come about the letter.'

'Mrs Rawlins, the decision was unanimous. Obviously
you can take private action if you wish, that is entirely up
to you, but as far as I am concerned I do not at this stage
feel you would be advised to proceed.'

'All I want is to make a home for kids without one.'

'I am aware of that, but it is my job to make sure any
child placed into care will have not only the right super-
vision but the right environment.'

'Is it my criminal record that went against me?'

'Obviously that was taken into consideration, and we are

also aware that you have been questioned by a DCI Craigh regarding—' Again he was interrupted.

'You referring to the warrants? The house was searched, the police found nothing incriminating and—'

Mr Crow sucked in his breath. 'Mrs Rawlins, under the circumstances, and with reference to an on-site visit to your property, it was decided that—' Another interruption.

'You didn't really need one, though, did you?'

'I'm sorry?'

She leaned forward. 'Well, you know the manor house well, don't you? According to Miss Freeman you were a regular visitor when it was run as a brothel. I am correct, aren't I?'

Pink dots appeared on his cheeks. 'Just what are you inferring, Mrs Rawlins?'

'That perhaps you had an ulterior motive for rejecting my application, that had nothing to do with me or my criminal background.'

'Be careful what you are insinuating, Mrs Rawlins. You are, I am sure, fully aware you remain on licence for the rest of your life and—'

'I'm just stating a fact,' she said quietly.

'Then please, Mrs Rawlins, be careful. I have told you this was a unanimous decision by all members of the board. We do not feel that you would be the right person to be given access to young children. We do not feel that the manor house would be suitable accommodation. It is my only intention to make sure any foster carer recommended by the social services department is both mentally and physically—'

She stood up, yet again interrupting him, this time leaning right over his desk. 'You know, my husband said he could never go straight because people like you, like the police, would never allow him to. Well, I know about you.'

Mr Crow stood up, the pink blobs spreading. His whole face seemed redder, although this time not with embarrassment but with anger. 'I'd like you to leave my office now.'

'I'm going, and I won't come back. I waited a long time to make a home for kids a reality but it was stupid, wasn't it? I never stood a chance. Don't worry, I won't let on that you're a two-faced bastard.'

She left, closing the door quietly behind her, and he could hear her footsteps on the marble corridor outside. He was shaking with anger but he was now confident that he had made the right decision. He would make sure there were no repercussions and would add to her report that she had lied to the board. Contrary to Mrs Rawlins's denial, Ester Freeman was still resident at Grange Manor House.

Dolly drove back to the manor. She had to wait at the level crossing for ten minutes. This time she couldn't be bothered to talk to Raymond Dewey who sat, as usual, on his little train-spotter's stool, jotting down his times and numbers. He waved at her but she turned towards the lake and the small narrow bridge the train moved across. She got out of the car and walked a few paces, still focusing on the bridge. Then she turned round, towards the station and the signal box. She sauntered over to Raymond and gave him a forced smile.

'Hello, Raymond, how are you today?'

'I'm very well. This is the twelve fifteen from Marylebone.'

'Is it? You know every train, do you? All the right times and the delays?'

'That's my job.'

'I bet there's one train you don't know the times of.'

'No, there isn't one. I know every train that passes through this station, how long they take to cross the bridge and—'

'So you write them all down, then?'

'Yes,' he said, proudly proffering his thick wedge of school exercise books. 'Each train has its own book.'

Dolly took one of the books with his thick scrawled writing across the front. 'Mail train.' She flipped over the pages. He had listed every delivery, time of arrival at and departure from the station, plus delays at the crossing.

'You're very thorough, Raymond,' Dolly said, as her eyes took in his dates and times. She then shut the book and passed it back to him as the lights changed and the train went by. As the gates opened, she returned to the Mini.

'Thank you very much, Raymond.' She smiled and waved as she drove past him. She felt strangely calm, almost as if it was fate. Had she been subconsciously thinking about it? It seemed so natural. It certainly wouldn't be easy but, then, she had always liked a challenge. This would be one – but it would also be a terrifyingly dangerous one.

A few minutes later, Dolly parked the car and walked up into the woods. From there she had a direct view of the station, the bridge, the lake and the level crossing. She spent over half an hour carefully checking the layout of the land. She could tell by one look why the police had chosen this specific station to unload the money from the road on to the train. There were only two access roads, both very narrow, and room for only one vehicle at a time. Anyone attempting to hold up the security wagon as it delivered the money to the train would be cut off. The station could easily be manned by as few as four or six police officers and no one could hide out there. If they did, if they hit the train standing in the platform, they wouldn't have a hope in hell of transporting the money by road as there was no access for the getaway vehicles. The tracks were lined with hedge-rows and wide open fields, not a road in sight, and the train would head across the bridge, travelling at up to eighty miles an hour.

Dolly studied the bridge. Fifty-five feet high, the lake beneath, no access either side of the tracks, just a narrow walkway. She knew it would be impossible. How could you hold up the train on the bridge and get away with heavy mail bags on foot? It couldn't be done. Then she looked down at the lake, back to the bridge. If you got a boat, you'd still have to reach the shore, and no vehicles could get down there. Again, there were no roads, just fields, hedges and streams.

Dolly was so immersed in her thoughts that she spun round in shock when she heard twigs cracking, her heart pounding. Julia appeared, riding Helen of Troy.

'Sorry if I made you jump. I did call out!'

Dolly covered her fright, smiling. 'I didn't hear you – I didn't even see you, come to think about it. You been here long?'

'No, I just rode up, cut across the fields.' Julia dismounted and tied up the horse. 'How did it go at the social services?' she asked.

'It didn't. It's finished.'

'I'm sorry.'

'So am I. Are they easy to ride?'

'Yeah. Why, you thinking of taking lessons?'

Dolly moved tentatively towards Helen, putting out her hand to stroke her nose.

'She won't bite you. Be confident, they know when you're nervous.' Julia moved to stand behind Dolly, resting her arm round her shoulders.

Dolly slowly petted Helen's nose again. 'That Norma . . . she said this was police-trained?'

'Yep. She's very solid, nothing scares her. As Norma said, she's bomb-proof. Be good for kids to learn on.'

Dolly withdrew her hand, her face drawn. 'Yes, well, there won't be any kids to teach. I'll see you back at the house.'

She trudged off as Julia unhitched the reins and got back into the saddle. She rode away, not even aware that Dolly had turned back to watch her as she cantered into the fields.

There *was* a way to get to that train. Julia was now galloping, disappearing from sight as she jumped the hedges.

DCI Craigh and DI Palmer looked over the forensic reports taken from the red Volvo. There was no indication that the car had been involved in any accident, no traces of blood, no body tissues. They didn't have enough to bring charges against Gloria Radford and, even if she had hired the car, they had no evidence that she had run over James Donaldson. In other words, they had fuck all.

'Now what?'

Craigh looked at Palmer and shrugged. 'Well, we're up for a hard rap around the knuckles, that's for starters. The Super's getting his knickers in a twist, and we're gonna have to iron this out somehow.'

Palmer looked over their reports and noted the vast amount it had cost Thames Valley and the Met to mount the searches of the manor, together with the surveillance. All would have to be costed and all they had to date was one arrest. Kathleen O'Reilly.

Craigh tugged at his hair. 'I'm going to interview O'Reilly again. So far she's not said a bloody word, but you never know.'

'Bring her in, shall I?'

Kathleen had been taken to Holloway. She would stand trial again for the previous charges of fraud and kiting but, as Craigh had said, she was unforthcoming and had only admitted to her name and the previous charges. She insisted she was just staying at the manor and that Dolly Rawlins had no knowledge of her previous record or that she was on a wanted list. All she did was pay Rawlins rent.

Mike appeared, sidled round and tried to make himself invisible when Craigh nabbed him. 'I'm going to talk to O'Reilly again but the word from the Gov is to stay well clear of Rawlins. We got to get ourselves out of this mess so you make sure your reports are tight as a nut.'

Mike hesitated. 'What about my sister?'

'Less said about her the better. We're in enough trouble as it is so just get on with the back-log of work on your desk.' Craigh glared at him. 'This isn't over yet, son. We could all be in trouble. We never found any diamonds so that's been sorted, understand?'

'Yes, sir.'

Craigh walked away, and Mike wandered to his desk and sat down. His heart was thudding in his chest. Had he got away with it? Or was that call from Rawlins going to be some kind of threat? He felt sick to his stomach and when he reached for his files his hand was shaking as if it didn't belong to him. He was scared that Rawlins would put him in the frame. If she did, he was finished.

Kathleen was as non-committal with Craigh as she had been the night she was arrested. She didn't know anything about any diamonds or guns; all she did was rent a room from Dolly Rawlins.

'What you think she is? Some kind of female Al Capone? Why don't you leave her alone? All she's doin' is tryin' to open a home for kids and you're harassing her, that's what you're doing.'

Craigh thanked her for her observations and left. Kathleen seemed to know she would go down for at least five years this time. She appeared resigned to it. Maybe she didn't know anything about Rawlins and maybe, he began to mull it over, they had been pressured into the searches and warrants by Mike Withey because he had personal motives. The more Craigh thought about it the more he made up his mind that if the Super tapped on his shoulder, then he'd point the finger at Mike. He wasn't going to take all the blame. Mike Withey had a lot to answer for and if it came down to it he would have to.

Dolly sat with a mug of tea. She was deep in thought when Ester walked in. 'Angela's still in her room. Gloria took up a coffee at breakfast time, told her to get packed, but she's still in there.'

Dolly got up and poured the dregs of the tea into the sink. 'I don't care, just get rid of her. I got to go up to London, have a word with Kathleen.'

Connie walked in with three sheets of paper. 'Dolly, you wanted John to give estimates for the damage when the police raided the house.'

Dolly inspected the figures and gave a wonderful smile. 'These are good. Oh, Connie, can I have a word?' She said to Ester, 'Can you leave us for a minute?'

Ester sloped off, and Dolly dried the mug carefully, placing it back on its hook. 'There's a signal box at the station, young bloke on duty – I think there's two of them. Will you get to know them? Find out what time they come on duty, when they're off and who does nights, that kind of thing.'

'Why?'

'Because I want you to.' Connie pulled a face and Dolly moved closer. 'This time, Connie, if needs be you fuck them because I want that information. I want you to know that signal box layout better than your own body, understand me?'

Connie stepped back. 'Yes, . . . all right.'

'Good – and don't tell any of the others, just get on with it.'

Dolly went out of the back door and called Julia, who was leading Helen of Troy back into the stables. 'A minute, love.'

Ester caught Connie as she went up the stairs. 'What was that about?'

Connie looked back down the stairs. 'She said not to tell you.'

'So, what did she want?'

Connie repeated what Dolly had told her then carried on up the stairs. Ester was about to go into the kitchen when she overheard Dolly talking to Julia. 'You see Norma, try and find out about the security at the station.'

'Why?' Julia asked, as she pulled off her boots.

'Don't ask questions, just do it. I want to know about the local police and the security around the station. She'll know. If she doesn't then fine, but test her out.'

Julia felt uneasy but there was a toughness to Dolly that unnerved her so she kept quiet.

Dolly walked into the hall. She saw the drawing-room door closing: Ester had made a quick move in there so she wouldn't be discovered. 'Ester.'

Ester popped her head out, acting surprised. 'Oh! What you want?'

'That kid, the train-spotter. He's got books, train times and—'

'We can get you a timetable you know, Dolly.'

Dolly's mouth was set in a thin tight line. 'Yes, I know, but I want the times and details of one specific train. The mail train. Get his book off him but do it without him knowing.'

'That shouldn't be too hard — he's mental anyway.'

Dolly picked up the phone and began to dial. Ester hovered a moment before she went into the kitchen.

Julia was still there, drinking a cup of tea. 'She's planning something, isn't she?' she said.

Ester nodded. 'Yeah. I knew it. I always knew that if she had her back to the wall she'd come up with something.'

'Yeah, but what is it?'

Ester leaned close, one eye on the door. 'I think it's the security wagon that delivers the money to the mail train.'

Julia let out her breath. 'Jesus Christ.'

Ester kept her eye on the door, afraid Dolly would walk in. 'She held back three shotguns from Gloria's stash. She reckoned she was going to do something. Well, she was right.'

Julia rubbed her arms. 'Do we really want to be involved in it, though?'

Ester nudged her, grinning. 'What do you think? Let's just play her along, see what pans out. In the meantime, we got this place, we got board and food, so why not?'

Dolly drove into George Fuller's car park. He was the lawyer who had represented her at her trial. A clever, iron-faced man employed by many top-level crooks, he was expensive but he was as tough as his face and even when he smiled a greeting, he seemed to be sneering.

'Hello, Dolly, good to see you. Sit down.'

She perched on a chair in his immaculate office and passed over the estimates from the builders. 'I'm being harassed. I want them off my back, George.'

He nodded, then lifted his briefcase on to the desk. 'Right. We can go there now and you can fill me in on the way. I'm in court at two so we've not much time.'

Dolly stood up. She liked George, he got straight to the point. He held the door open, beckoning her to follow him.

They drove to the police station in Fuller's immaculate green Jaguar and Dolly told him exactly what had occurred since she was released from Holloway. She also asked if he would take on Kathleen O'Reilly's case as a favour to her. He inclined his head a little, and then gave that icy smile. 'If she can meet the fees, then yes.'

'She can't but I will.'

Ester and Julia had already left to begin their assignments. Julia was calling at Norma's cottage and Ester went to talk to Raymond Dewey. Connie was already at the station, watching the man in the signal box. He had a pot belly and she felt he would have heavy BO. She shuddered but then, crossing to the signal box, she saw the pleasant-faced young man who had given her a lift the day she arrived. She saw him walk up the steps, as the pot-bellied man banged out.

'You're late again, Jim.'

'Sorry, Mac, got held up.'

'Oh yeah? Who was it last night, then?'

Jim guffawed as he entered the signal box. Connie waited a moment and then ran out, colliding with the fat man. She was right. He was a walking BO advert. 'Oh, I'm sorry,' she gasped as she fell forward and then yelped. 'My ankle, oh . . .'

It didn't take long for Jim to come down the steps with a glass of water as Connie sat at the bottom. She sipped the water and then tried to stand but had to sit down again.

'I'm sorry, love, I just didn't see you. Do you need a doctor?' Pot-bellied Mac looked down into her face, concerned.

'I'm all right, just a bit dizzy.'

Jim helped her up and looked at his mate. 'You go off, Mac, I'll take care of her. Maybe she should just sit here for a while.'

Mac muttered that he just bet his mate would take care of her, and trundled off towards his beat-up Ford Granada. 'See you tomorrow, Jim.'

But Jim wasn't listening. He was supporting Connie, his arm around her.

'Lucky sod,' mused Mac, as he drove out. He wouldn't have minded taking care of her – she was a cracker.

DCI Craigh stared at the estimates then at George Fuller and at the impassive face of Dolly Rawlins. He didn't really look at them properly – he was too edgy. Fuller had detailed the police warrant issues, times and dates, and that on her release Rawlins had, in his estimation, been harassed. If it was to be made public, not only the waste of public money but that a woman who had served her sentence and been released with every good intention of building a home for ex-prisoners, had been picked on, there would be trouble. Craigh tried to interrupt but Fuller stopped him, not letting him get a word in.

'We obviously know that a Mrs Kathleen O'Reilly was arrested at Mrs Rawlins's establishment but she was unaware of any of the outstanding charges levelled at Mrs O'Reilly and all the women resident at the manor are, as you must be aware, ex-prisoners. But as Mrs Rawlins was attempting to open a home to give these unfortunate women a chance to straighten out their lives, then it is only to be expected that residents would be, like herself, ex-prisoners. To my mind there has been a flagrant misuse of policing and the harassment could be levelled at your department. If it were to be made public in one or other of the papers, I'm sure it would make for popular reading, if a touch unpopular for the Metropolitan Police?'

Fuller hardly drew breath. His steely, quiet, authoritative voice hammered home his points and lastly he dropped in his ace, not as a threat but as a fact. 'Also, it is possible that one of the men in your team, Detective Chief Inspector, has a private vendetta against Mrs Rawlins, totally without proof. And this also brings up the added insult that you have accused Mrs Rawlins of being associated with a James Donaldson who, I understand, recently died while in your custody.'

Craigh felt the rug being pulled from under him but he remained calm. His hands clenched into fists on the desk, and he said nothing, but gazed ahead at a small dot on the wallpaper.

'So if you would please give the estimates your due care and attention, I would be most grateful if Mrs Rawlins could receive payment for the damage to her property as soon as possible.'

Fuller rose, gestured to Dolly to accompany him to the door. She shook Craigh's hand but did not smile as Fuller waited for her to leave in front of him.

'Thank you for your time, Detective Chief Inspector.' Fuller closed the door after him. Craigh ground his teeth; it had been tough keeping his mouth shut. He would have liked to punch the bastard. His eyes glanced down at the detailed list of damage done to the manor during the two raids. He turned over the pages that listed deep freezers being turned off, banisters and rails damaged, the front door, the rear door. Then his jaw dropped as he read the total figure.

'Ten thousand quid? *Ten grand?*'

Dolly was rigid as she waited for Kathleen to be brought into the visiting section. Coming back inside made her feel ill, the hair on the nape of her neck standing up as she kept her eyes down, refusing to look in the direction of any of the prison officers. All she wanted to do was to say what she had to say to Kathleen and get out.

Kathleen was led through the door from the prisoners' section. She was wearing a green overall, her own shoes, and an Alice band that someone must have given her to keep her thick red hair back from her wide white face. She looked tired, defeated and bloated.

Dolly reached over and held her big raw hand. 'Hello, Kathleen love.'

'Well, I'm back. I knew it'd happen one day but you know I just hoped we'd make some cash so I could get me and the kids to Ireland. It was just a dream, really. I should have known I'd be picked up one day. I'm just sorry it was at your place.'

'So am I, but I've got you books and there's money between the pages. Give a few quid out to some of the girls, ones that knew me. Rest you use for whatever. I got George Fuller taking on your case, I'll find the money to pay him.'

'I never said nothing, you know, Dolly.'

'I didn't think you would, Kathleen.'

'I'm no snitch.'

'It was Angela. We found out she'd been knocked up by that young copper.'

'The bastard.'

'She's no better. We've chucked her out on her ear.'

Kathleen flicked through the pages of the paperback novel, looking at the neatly folded fifty-quid notes. She suddenly looked at Dolly; her eyes seemed dead. 'I could have said something, though. I could have said about the diamonds, even the guns, but I didn't.'

Dolly waited, knowing she was going to be hit. It just surprised her that Kathleen would try it on, even after she'd hired her a bloody lawyer.

'I'll get at least five this time,' Kathleen said without expression. Dolly made no reply, waiting as Kathleen fingered the paperback. 'I want my kids taken care of, Dolly. Sheena, Kate and Mary. They're in a convent but they'll be split up soon, I know it. Not many places can take three kids, three sisters, they'll split them up, so . . .'

Dolly looked at her, hard. 'So what, Kathleen?'

'You take them, Dolly. I've written to the convent, made you their legal guardian. You just got to sign the papers. I want you to look after them until I get out.'

'I can't do that,' hissed Dolly.

'Yes, you can. You wanted kids in that place – well, now I'm giving you mine. You take them, Dolly, please. Please don't make me talk to the coppers about you, take my kids.' Kathleen bowed her head, as big tears slid down her flat cheeks. 'I was a lousy mother but I'd turn grass for them. I would, Dolly. They're all I've got that's decent. Please, take them, keep them together for me.'

Dolly gripped Kathleen's hand tight.

*

Just after Dolly had left the manor, Gloria marched up the stairs and banged on Angela's bedroom door. 'Oi, what you doin' in there? We want you out. Come on. Angela?' She tried the door. It was locked but the key was not on the outside.

'Angela?' She banged on the door, turned the handle and pressed it hard, but it was securely locked from the inside.

Gloria darted out to the stables and picked up a hammer. Connie appeared.

'That Angela has locked herself in so I'm gonna break down the door and drag her out by the scruff of her neck.'

She went back upstairs and hit the door hard, then the door handle, and Connie pushed. It eventually gave way and they stumbled into the little box room. Angela was lying on the floor by the bed, face down. Beside her was a bottle of bleach. When the two panic-stricken women turned her over her face was blue, her mouth burned, but she was alive.

Julia was walking up the driveway and looked up to the top window as she heard Gloria scream at her out of the window to hurry. She jumped up the stairs three at a time and burst into the bedroom. Connie had Angela on the bed but stood helplessly to one side.

Gloria hovered. 'She's drunk bleach, Julia. I dunno how much but look at her mouth!'

Julia barked orders, to call an ambulance, get jugs of water, and drew Angela into a sitting position, feeling inside her mouth as Gloria and Connie hurried out, glad to be told what to do.

'Angela, can you hear me? Angela? It's Julia.'

The girl lolled forward. Julia tested her pulse, which was

very weak, and began to pour water down her throat from a jug Connie had brought in.

Dolly was shown into the Governor's office. She was freaking out: being in the visitors' section was bad enough, but now, in the office, she hated it. All she wanted to do was leave.

Mrs Ellis had tea brought in. She was friendly and seemed to want to discuss Kathleen's wish that Dolly become her children's legal guardian.

Dolly sipped the tea, refusing to meet Mrs Ellis's eyes, looking anywhere but into her face.

'Do you have a job?'

'Not easy at my age but I've got a few things I'm working on.'

'I know about your application to the social services. Dolly, to run an institution requires training and people with qualifications.'

'It was just a home, Mrs Ellis. This place is an institution. But it doesn't matter now, I was rejected, they didn't think me suitable, and if you don't mind I don't want to discuss it further.'

'If you need any help in the future . . .'

'I won't, thank you.'

'You know, Dolly, it isn't wise to keep up some friendships you make inside. It is much better to make a clean break.'

Dolly slipped the cup and saucer back on to the desk. 'Thank you, and thank you for the tea, but I've got to leave now.'

Mrs Ellis stood up, put out her hand to shake Dolly's but she was already at the door.

'Will we be seeing you again?' she asked, still forcing herself to be pleasant.

'No, I won't come back. Goodbye.'

Mrs Ellis sat back in her chair. Dolly had looked well, almost affluent, stylish, but she was hard, a brittle quality to her every move, and she had not smiled once. An unpleasant woman, Mrs Ellis mused, but then her attention was drawn to other matters and Dolly Rawlins was forgotten.

The ambulance rushed Angela to hospital. Julia had gone with her but left when Angela was taken into the emergency section. Gloria had been upset but by the time Julia returned she was arguing with Connie, saying it wasn't anyone's fault but Angela's and she wasn't going to waste any pity on her. She could have got them all arrested.

'She's only eighteen,' Julia snapped, irritated.

'Yeah, so was I when I first went down but I still never grassed anyone. She's got no morals, coming here, playing us for idiots.'

'The way we all tried to play Dolly?'

'No, we fucking didn't,' screeched Gloria.

'Yes, we did,' Connie said stubbornly.

'Well, it's all going to change soon, isn't it?' Julia said quietly.

'What you mean?'

Julia sat down. 'We think she's planning a robbery.'

Gloria gaped. 'I knew it – I fucking knew it. Soon as those shotguns was missing I said to Ester, I said to her, "She's got something going down," and I was right.'

Connie shifted her weight to the other foot. 'I wish to God in some ways I'd never come here. I never done anything illegal in my entire life.' Gloria snorted and she glared. 'I haven't. I'm not like you, Gloria. We all know what you are.'

'Oh, yeah, what am I? You tell me that.'

Ester had come in, unnoticed, and answered, 'A loud, brassy tart. So what's all the aggro?'

'Where've you been?' Gloria asked.

Ester took off her coat and chucked it over a chair. 'Talking to that half-wit Raymond Dewey. Dolly wants to know the times of the mail train.'

Gloria's jaw dropped and she drew a chair close. 'Is she gonna hit the security wagon, then? One that does the drop for the mail train?'

Julia crossed to the back door. 'If she does, it's madness. According to Norma they have the place sewn up. The local police come out in force, cut off the lanes. There's no main access, we'd never get a vehicle near, never mind one that'd carry anything away.' She pushed at the broken door and sighed. 'This is crazy, you know, even discussing it.'

Ester looked at her. 'No harm in it, though, is there? Unless you'd prefer to talk about Norma. Do you want to talk about Norma?' Ester repeated the name with a posh, nasal twang. Julia pursed her lips. 'Oh, have I hit a sore point? Don't want to talk about Noooorma, do we?'

'No, I don't. And stop being childish.'

'I'm not being childish. It's you that's got all uptight and your little mouth is all pinched up. All I'm doing is making conversation about Norma.'

Julia glared, then half smiled. 'Jealous?'

'Who me? Jealous? Of what? Norma? Oh, please, do me a favour. I couldn't touch anyone with that arse anyway.'

Julia opened the door. 'You don't have to, but I do, and it's quite tight, actually.' Ester's face twisted in fury. 'She has a very good seat, as they say in riding circles.'

Julia was out of the door, shutting it behind her, before

Ester could reply. She was pleased: Ester's jealousy was proof that she cared.

Dolly drew up and parked outside Ashley Brent's electrical shop. She squinted at the meter and shook her head with disgust: twenty pence for ten minutes – it was a disgrace! She walked to the boarded-up door of the shop, rang the bell and waited. Eventually a voice asked who it was.

'Dolly Rawlins.'

There was a cackle of laughter and the sound of electronic bolts being drawn back before the door opened. Ashley Brent stood in the centre of his shop floor, arms wide, his glasses stuck on top of his bald head. 'As I live and die. So you're out then, gel. Give us a hug. You're looking good, sweetheart. How long you been out, then?'

'Oh, just a few months. Takes a bit of getting used to, especially those ruddy parking meters.'

'Don't tell me. I mean, in the old days you could find a broken one, use it for the day. Now they tow you away if it's busted, tow you if you're a minute over, tow you for any possible excuse. What they don't do is tow the fuckers that block off the traffic. I'm telling you, everything nowadays is geared to get the punter, Doll. You're screwed in this country if you got a legit business, taxed, VAT . . . It's like we got the Gestapo after us for ten quid rates due but then you hear of blokes coining it and they're on social. Makes you sick.'

Ashley was a man who had verbal diarrhoea and it was always the same: he hated the Conservatives, hated the Liberals, the Labour Party, the blacks, the Jews. In fact, Ashley was a man who existed through his own venom and it was rumoured that when he went down for a short spell, his cell-mate had asked to be moved because Ashley even talked in his sleep. He offered tea, more verbals about the council estate across the road and, lastly, his kids. He went into a tirade about his thankless bastard kids and Dolly waited, looking around the equipment in the small, secure shop. Ashley was an electronic genius and ran a business loosely labelled as security devices and trade equipment. In fact, he sold bugs, receivers, transmitters, microphones. You name it, Ashley had it in his well-stocked shop and workroom. He ran a strictly cash deal for those wanting certain items and kept no record of them being purchased. Dolly spent three hours with him and left with a briefcase and a small carrier bag. He had filled and checked her parking meter as she sat and learned how to handle the equipment. It was mostly simple but a few items were more complicated. He was patient and gave good advice, yet never pressed for details as to exactly what the items would be used for. Whatever else Ashley was, he was totally trustworthy. You paid for that. Dolly gave him ten thousand pounds cash.

She was now very short of readies to pay the builder. Even with the money from Audrey and the guns, it was running out fast.

Susan Withey opened the door.

Dolly smiled sweetly. 'Hello, I'm Mrs Rawlins.'

Susan hesitated. 'Mike's not here.'

'Ah, pity. Well, could I come in? I want to talk to you.'

'I don't think so.'

'I do. It's about Angela, your husband's little girlfriend.' Susan stepped back and Dolly pushed past her. 'Oh, this is very nice. You do the decorating yourself, do you?'

Susan shut the door and followed Dolly into the sitting room.

It was after seven and they were all waiting for Dolly, not sure whether to start supper without her, wondering what she'd been doing all afternoon.

'There's a car coming up the drive now,' Gloria said, 'but it's not Dolly. Looks like a flash Mercedes or somethin'.'

Ester ran into the hall and looked through the broken stained glass in the front door. She tore back.

'Get rid of them. They'll want me. You tell them I don't live here any more. Get rid of them, Gloria.'

'Why me?'

'Because you're so good at it.' Ester shot into the kitchen, pushing Julia back just as the doorbell rang.

Gloria opened the front door. 'Yeah?'

'Ester here?'

'Ester who?'

'Freeman.'

'No. Sorry.'

Gloria tried to shut the door but it was kicked open. The man was swarthy, handsome-ish, with dark heavy-lidded eyes, a slightly hooked nose and thick oiled-back hair.

'Eh, what you doing?' Gloria shrieked.

'I want to speak to Ester.'

'She don't live here, well, not any more. She sold this house.'

Gloria was lifted off her feet and hurled against the wall. She screamed but he gripped her face between his hands and pushed her head hard into the wall three times until she was too terrified to scream. She just stared wide-eyed.

'You tell Ester we need to speak to her, understand?'

Gloria nodded as he slowly released her and then as if to

290

make sure the message was understood he swiped her with the back of his hand and she fell to the floor. She didn't get up, not until the front door closed behind him. Then she slowly staggered to her feet as Ester peered out of the kitchen.

'Well, thanks a fuckin' bundle for that,' said Gloria, touching her nose. 'He whacked me into the wall, whacked me in the face and you friggin' let him do it.'

'Was it Hector?' Ester asked as she peered out of the broken window.

'I dunno who it was – he was too busy whacking me to give me his fuckin' name. Look what he done to me face.'

Julia held Gloria's face between her hands and pressed her nose. 'It's not broken.'

'Oh, great, I should be grateful for that, should I?'

They all jumped as a car tooted and Ester shrank into a corner. 'Shit, are they back?'

Connie went over to the door.

'*Don't open it*,' Ester hissed.

'It's Dolly,' Connie said. 'She's driven on round to the back-yard.'

'Don't say anythin' about this, Gloria,' Ester pleaded.

'Well, she might just notice me nose is red and bleedin' and me blouse torn,' Gloria retorted in fury.

'Look, they want money. I've not got it so just cover for me – you know how she can get.'

Dolly called out, and they all turned towards the door. They couldn't believe their eyes.

Kate and Mary were twins aged nine and Sheena was five. They all had bright curly red hair like their mother, round white faces with blue eyes, and were dressed in an odd assortment of charity clothes. They were sullen-faced as if they had been crying and they clung tightly to each other in fear.

'These are Kathleen's kids and they're moving in.' Dolly held up her hands. 'Don't anyone say anything. There was nothing I could do about it, they're here, so let's make the best of it. Can someone get a room ready or two? Do you want to sleep together?'

The three little girls nodded in unison and clung even tighter together. 'Right, let's get your coats off. Connie, bring their cases in from the car and someone put some supper on and get a room aired . . .'

Gloria turned away. 'I'll do it. I just fell down the stairs and hit me nose so I need to go and wash me face.'

Mike charged in. Susan was sitting on the sofa, clutching a handkerchief.

'Has she left?'

'Yes. I went into the hall to call you and when I went back she just said she had to leave.'

Mike marched up and down. 'What did she want?'

Susan stood up and hit him. 'She told me about you and that Angela. She's pregnant, did you know that? That bloody tart you've been screwing is pregnant.'

Mike closed his eyes and sank down on to the sofa.

'Well? What are you going to say? Don't you have anything to say to me?'

'What else did she want?'

'Isn't that bloody enough?'

Mike leaned back. At first it was just treacle he'd felt round his shoes, then ankles, then it felt like cement. Now it felt like someone had fitted him with a straitjacket. Susan waited but he didn't say a word. She stormed out, slamming the door behind her, and he stayed there, eyes closed, head back, trying to assimilate everything, sort it out in his head.

What did Dolly Rawlins want? He never even gave Angela a thought – he was too concerned with himself.

Beneath the coffee table, which was placed against the wall, was a 13-amp adaptor. A table-light plug was fixed into one but in the other socket was a plug, not connected to any electrical appliance. The switch was turned on. The plug was a neat transmitter, that Mike was even paying for. Not that he knew or even contemplated that anyone would be bugging him. But Dolly was. She had inserted the plug the moment Susan had left the room.

'Neat, isn't it?' Dolly said, as she showed the women the second 13-amp adaptor she'd bought. She then showed them two pens that were also transmitters, pens you could even use to write with. They stared like a group of kids at the equipment: the small receivers, the black box and, lastly, the briefcase that would enable Dolly to open up three electronic channels and record anyone she had bugged.

'What's all this for?' Ester asked.

'What do you think?' Dolly said, as she studied the leaflets.

'You planning on bugging us?'

'Don't be stupid, Connie. These are to be put to good use.'

Dolly glanced up at the ceiling as she heard a soft cry. She said to Gloria, 'I thought you told me they were asleep.'

'They were last time I looked in but it's a strange house, Dolly, and, well, they're scared.'

Dolly hurried upstairs and crossed to the room set aside for the kids. She eased open the door and could see them lying huddled together. The twins were sleeping but little Sheena was mewing like a kitten. 'What is it, darlin'?'

'Dark,' came the whimpered reply.

Dolly fetched her own bedside lamp, and covered it with a headscarf. 'There, how's that, then?' Sheena's eyes were wide with fright. 'Would you like me to read you a story?'

The little girl nodded and Dolly opened one of the cheap plastic suitcases and took out some dog-eared books.

'Which one is your favourite?'

'*Three Little Piggies*,' Sheena whispered.

'Okay, *Three Little Piggies* it is. Oh, you're all awake now, are you? Well, cuddle up and I'll read you a story.'

Dolly read until one by one they fell asleep. She went on until she'd finished the book and whispered, 'No one will blow my house down, no big bad wolf. This is my house.'

Downstairs, Gloria picked up a transmitter. 'She's obviously serious about it. This gear must have set her back a few quid.'

They heard Dolly coming down and started to make conversation.

'What time did Angela leave?' Dolly asked as she walked in.

'She went out in style,' Gloria said, then repeated what had happened, only a little shame-faced that she hadn't told Dolly immediately.

'She tried to top herself,' Ester said, but then Julia interjected that she had called the hospital and she was off the danger list. They were unsure, however, if the baby would be all right.

Dolly sighed. No matter what she felt about Angela she was sad. Dolly yawned. 'You go and see her tomorrow, Julia, take her a few things. Just check on her.'

'She'd not get me whippin' in grapes, she deserves all she gets, the nasty little snitch,' Gloria said.

Dolly yawned again.

'So, you gonna tell us, Dolly, what all this gear is for?' Ester sat next to her.

'Yes, but not tonight, I'm too tired. We'll discuss it in the morning.'

'Is it the security wagon?' Ester asked.

'Nope. Like I said, we'll talk about it tomorrow, I'm run ragged now.'

'It's the train, isn't it?' Connie said.

Dolly slowly got up. 'Yes, it is.'

'The mail train?' Ester asked, springing to her feet.

'That's right.'

Julia was resting one foot on the fire-guard. 'You'll never do it, Dolly. I spoke to Norma. She said the security for the drops is really tight and there's no access by road. You'd never get a truck or a car up there without the cops knowing. That's why they chose this station, for its inaccessibility.'

'We wouldn't be doing it by car.' Dolly was on her way to the door.

'On foot? How the hell could we carry big fat mail-bags?'

Dolly cocked her head to one side. 'We wouldn't carry them and we wouldn't be going by car, or on foot.'

Ester smirked. 'Helicopter, is it?'

Dolly opened the door. 'We hit the train on horseback.' They fell about laughing. Gloria snorted like a braying donkey. Then they saw that Dolly wasn't smiling. She looked from one to the other, her voice quiet, calm, without any emotion. 'Julia gave me the idea, so as from tomorrow we start to learn to ride. Every one of us. If we can't do it, then we look for something else. There's a local stable within half a mile of here. They've got eight horses. We're all booked for the early-morning ride so I don't know about you lot but I need to get some sleep. Goodnight.'

She shut the door behind them and not one of them could speak.

'I've never been on a horse,' Connie said lamely.

'Me neither – well, nearest I got was a donkey ride on Brighton beach,' Gloria said.

'It's bullshit, isn't it, Julia?' Ester said flatly. 'She's joking.'

Julia prodded the fire with the poker. 'I don't think she's joking. One, she's laid out for all that equipment, two, she was up by the woods, checking out the station. I think she's serious. That's why she's made Connie, me, even you, Ester, start checking it out.'

Overhead, the chandelier creaked as Dolly walked along the floor above them. Her footsteps sounded ominous and the long shadows cast from the fire were scary as they loomed large across the big dilapidated room. One after another they opened their mouths as if to say something but nothing came out. They were all thinking the same things. Was Dolly serious? Was the robbery for real? But it was Julia who broke the atmosphere, laughing softly. 'She's pulling our legs. Let's have a drink.'

CHAPTER 13

ANGELA WAS sitting hunched on her side, a sodden piece of tissue in her hand. She had cried herself into exhaustion. She didn't look up or turn when the door opened as she thought it would be a nurse. She knew it couldn't be her mother – she hadn't called her, hadn't wanted to speak to anyone. She felt so sick and sad; she had never meant to hurt the baby but now it was too late. She was no longer pregnant; she had miscarried early that morning.

'There's grapes and some clothes to change into.'

Angela recognized Dolly's voice but was afraid to look at her so she just curled up tighter.

'I know you lost the baby, Angela, and I'm sorry, sorry for what you've done to yourself.' Dolly laid out the things she had brought. She stood near to the bed, not close enough to touch Angela. 'Maybe it's for the best, but it won't seem like that now.'

'You'd know, would you?' came the muffled reply.

'No, I don't really know at all. I ached for a baby, Angela, all my married life, so no, I wouldn't know what it feels like to lose one, be it my own fault or not.'

Angela sobbed. Dolly was so cold and hard and she so badly needed someone to put their arms around her. 'Please be nice to me, Dolly, *please*.' Angela turned and held out her hand to Dolly.

'Come to the house and . . .'

'Can I stay? I'll cook and clean for you.'

'Pack the rest of your things. That's all I came to tell you. You have to leave but we'll keep your things safe until they release you from here. And you should eat those grapes, almost eighty pence a pound.'

The door closed behind her and Angela flopped back on to her pillow. She felt totally dejected. She wished she'd killed herself properly, wished she had never woken up because she had nothing to live for, and no place to go.

Dolly walked into the kitchen through the back door, the smell of burning bacon making her wrinkle her nose.

'Oh, sorry, Dolly, it's me. I can never get the hang of this Aga. I dunno whether to put stuff in the oven or stick it on the top there.' Connie shovelled charred bits of bacon on to a piece of paper towel, dabbing the fat off it. It broke up into little pieces.

'I been in to see Angela. She lost the baby.'

'Julia told me. She's just bathing the girls – they've had their breakfast.'

Ester appeared. 'Serves the little cow right. Any breakfast going?'

They came in in dribs and drabs but no one seemed inclined to start up the conversation about the proposed robbery. 'You all got boots, jeans to ride in?' Dolly suddenly asked.

Gloria looked down at her wellingtons. Julia arrived with the three children, who hung back shyly at the door. Seeing her, Gloria asked, 'Will these do?'

Julia shook her head. 'No, but there's no point in wasting good money if you're only going to go once. Might as well wait and see, right, Dolly?'

Dolly was eating scrambled eggs and burnt toast. 'I'll

need to borrow a pair of trousers. You girls are going to be left alone just for a while, I got some things for you to do.' They were sitting at the big kitchen table as Dolly laid out drawing pads, crayons and picture books. 'Now you be good, stay put in here and wait until we get back. Don't leave the house, and I'll know if you do because I'm gonna ask the builders to check on you.'

'They not comin' today,' piped up little Sheena.

Dolly patted her head. 'Ah, you don't know, they come and they go. Just be good girls and watch the clock. When the big hand gets to—'

'I can tell the time,' said Kathy, one of the twins.

'Good, then you stay put for two hours in here and I don't want to have to tell you again!' Dolly was trying her best but she wasn't used to handling little kids, as well as a houseful of adult ones.

Julia fitted her out in an old pair of her jeans which were too tight and the flies gaped but, as Julia said, why waste money? They piled into Gloria's Mini, all five of them, and headed for the local stables.

'I see they bleedin' downed tools again,' Gloria said as they drove out of the manor.

'They'll pick them up again as soon as they get paid,' Dolly snapped.

'I thought our Connie was supposed to be keeping him happy,' Gloria sniggered.

'I'm already workin' on him and the bloke in the signal box. I don't intend to get through all the ruddy workmen. *You* do it.'

'My darlin', I'd do it any time and place, it's a question of willingness, right enough; but not on my part.' Gloria hooted.

Dolly closed her eyes. Sometimes Gloria's constant sexual innuendos really got under her skin. She never missed an opportunity for snide digs and asides about getting her leg over. 'I wish you'd watch what you say, Gloria, now we got the girls living in. And that goes for us all. Cut down on the swearing.'

'Well, excuuuuuse me for livin'. I can't help bein' the way I am, it's called frustration. I see her getting her leg over at every opportunity and—'

'*Shut up!*' roared Dolly.

'It's the truth! I've not had a good seeing-to in years and it's not for want of trying, lemme tell you.' Dolly knew it was pointless attempting to change Gloria. 'Mind you, this horse ridin', they say it gives you a climax, did you know that, Dolly? I'm lookin' forward to it.'

When they got to the riding school Sandy, a young stable girl with a high-pitched Sloane Ranger voice, began to bring out the horses, all shapes and sizes, as her assistant saddled them up. Julia began sorting through hard hats, which were compulsory, and they switched them around and tried them all on. Sandy kept on taking sly looks at the group of women and couldn't help tittering as they appeared to be first-timers, apart from Julia who had obviously ridden before and was there to offer as much assistance as was needed, which turned out to be a lot. Just getting them mounted took considerable time, and when Julia left they all looked petrified, including Dolly. When her horse suddenly bent his head to eat some grass, she almost came off with a high-pitched 'Help!'

They had a two-hour lesson and at the end of it they could all mount and dismount, knew how to use the reins, and had been led up and down the field. Gloria wandered into the stables, cocksure, as if she had just won the Grand National.

'It's quite easy, isn't it?'

Sandy smiled. 'Yes, if you're a natural.'

'You think I am, then?'

'We'll see. You haven't really been riding yet.'

'Course I have. We been round the field ten times.'

'There's more to it than that, Gloria.'

By lunch-time none of them could walk. Their legs were stiff, thighs in particular, and everyone moaned. Dolly had booked them in for another lesson in a second stable twenty miles away. They cranked themselves into the Mini again.

'I don't think this is a good idea you know, Dolly,' Gloria gasped. 'I mean, I'm knackered after just two hours – and my legs! I think I've done serious damage to them.'

Julia waved them off and decided to take the little girls out for a walk, but before she could set off, Big John arrived and said he needed to speak to Mrs Rawlins. Julia told him she was not at home but asked if she could help. 'Well, it's just that she's supposed to pay me the second instalment. We're behind now, and she did say today. I've got the lads on another job until she pays, but this scaffolding needs finishing and we got all that cement ordered and the sand.'

'I'll tell her to give you a ring.'

'I hope so. This was a cash deal and she's put me in a very difficult position.'

'She'll call you.'

He hung about a moment, then asked, 'Connie here, is she?'

'She's out.'

He returned to his truck; he was determined that until he saw the colour of Mrs Rawlins's money he was not going to finish anything off or order another bag of cement, nothing. The reality was that he had been so desperate to get his firm off the ground that he'd stretched himself to the limit. He had a nasty feeling that his inexperience was going to teach him a hard lesson.

The afternoon riding session brought grave doubts that

any one of them would be capable of ever being let off a leading-rein. Out of the four Connie was the best and the most confident, Gloria the worst. She yelled and shouted abuse to the embarrassment of the others and the very county stable-girls. When they returned to the manor, Dolly was certain they could never do it and she would have to think about something else.

She sat with the children, made them their tea and read them a story. *The Three Little Piggies* was requested yet again by Sheena and for half an hour Dolly lost herself in the story and in the warmth of the three little girls. They were gradually becoming less dependent on each other, more open. Dolly constantly repeated that the manor was their home, no one would take it away from them; it was theirs, their mummy knew where to write to them and when she was back she would know where to find them. That was why she had brought them to the new place.

Early next day Dolly drove into the village, toured the second-hand shops, and returned laden with hacking-jackets, jodhpurs, second-hand riding boots plus two men's riding coats. Some of the clothes were in good condition, some not so good, but she laid them all out, choosing the best for herself. That morning the lesson was booked for ten and, creaking in agony, the women argued and fought over each item like ten-year-olds. Gloria stuffed two pairs of thick woollen socks inside a pair of men's riding boots as they were far too large; Connie squeezed into a pair that were too small but highly polished which she'd grabbed before Gloria. They didn't look any more professional – on the contrary, they were like something out of a Thelwell cartoon and their riding was no better.

Sandy, the stable-girl, led them all into the field connected to the stables and they proceeded to learn how to trot with gritted teeth and loud moans.

Julia remained at the house with the children, cooking breakfast and taking them on a ramble around the grounds. They were shrieking with excitement when she brought out Helen of Troy and they each had a turn at being led round the yard. None of them had been in the country before or ridden a horse, and their excitement touched Julia. As a child she had wanted for nothing, she even had her own pony, and it made her realize just how wonderful a place the manor could be for kids like Kathleen's.

There was a lot more they needed to sort out but no one seemed inclined to open up the subject. It was obvious to everyone that the riding was a fiasco, the reality of the robbery far removed. Yet it hung in the air, unspoken, and as Dolly seemed disinclined to discuss it, no one else did.

It was early afternoon by the time everyone had cleaned themselves up, and the washing machine creaked under the weight of all their dirty clothes. The boots were lined up and the little girls given the task of cleaning them for fifty pence a pair. Dirtier than ever, polishing away, Sheena seemed to have a considerable amount of boot polish round her mouth but, seeing they were happy, Dolly said nothing and called all the women into the office.

They stood around, waiting, as Dolly closed the door and crossed to her desk. She picked up a small black notebook and sat down. 'Right, it's obvious we're gonna need two lessons a day.' She jotted down the costs and they all exchanged glances. 'In the meantime, we'll just carry on as if we're progressing, even if we don't seem to be.'

Gloria leaned on the desk. 'I got to be honest, Doll, I'm not cut out for this riding business. It's me size, you see. Being small I can't get me legs round the horse.'

Ester snorted. 'Get them round that Eddie, though.'

'Chance'd be a fine thing. I've not had 'em round a male for a lot longer than you!'

Dolly was irritated. 'Shut up. Now we ride twice a day, two hours a session, and that's final. You get a small horse.'

Gloria pulled a face and sat in a winged chair. 'You're payin'.'

'Yeah, I am paying for everything, so shut up and listen, all of you.'

Dolly had that edge to her, flicking through the book, jotting down expenses. Julia stood by the window. 'The builder was here, Dolly. You know he's got a delivery of bathroom equipment arriving and he's a bit sore. He could start causing trouble.'

Dolly moistened her lips. 'Yes, I know. We'll start with him.'

Dolly pointed at Connie and told her to keep Big John happy, to see him as much as possible and give him five grand that evening.

Gloria swung her legs. 'All right for some. I wouldn't mind keeping him happy – got a nice arse.'

No one paid her any attention; they were listening to Dolly as she described the old cess-pit half a mile from the house. 'I need to get it cleared, see how deep it is, so this afternoon, Gloria and Julia, that's your job.'

'Oh, great! I just got meself cleaned up,' moaned Gloria, but again she was ignored.

'Connie, when you see the builder, I want you to order via his firm, without him knowing, about twenty kilo-bags of lime.'

'Why? What do we need them for?' Connie asked.

'To fill the pit,' Dolly said patiently.

She jabbed a finger at Ester. 'You have an assignment. I want you to find out just how tough it is to unhitch a train carriage.'

'Oh, sure,' Ester said, smiling as if it was as simple as buying groceries.

'I'm serious. The mail carriage is in the centre of the train, it's an ordinary carriage. I want to know how you can unhitch it.'

'How the fuck do I find that out?'

'You've got a big mouth, Ester. Use it. Off the top of my head you can go to the railway museums, chat up a guard, *not* at the local station – any way you think – but I need to know how hard it is to unhitch, if it's done manually or—'

'Fine, I'll do it,' Ester interrupted.

Dolly ticked her memo in the notebook, turning a page. 'Tonight, Connie, you go and see your boyfriend in the signal box. This time you find out the layout, how many alarms there are, how long it takes to get the law to the station.'

'You must be joking,' stuttered Connie.

'No, love, I'm not. We have to know exactly what goes down when that mail train arrives, what he does, what—'

Connie broke in, 'How do I do that?'

'Find a way, love.'

'Well, one minute you're telling me to be with the builder, then the signal-box guy. I can't do both of them.'

'Yes, you can,' Dolly snapped, and then looked at them all. 'You have to do just what I tell you or this is finished before it's started. I don't want any arguments.'

'Can we ask what you're doing?' Ester leaned forward.

Dolly closed her book and stood up. 'I'm going to London so I'll need the car. I don't want the kids left alone so one of you bath them, feed them and put them to bed. I might be late.'

She walked out and they watched her go, no one saying

a word until the door latched. 'She's nuts, you do know that, don't you?' Ester said angrily.

'But you're still here,' remarked Julia tartly.

'Yeah, but not for long if she carries on like this. We got a right to know what she's doing.'

Gloria cranked herself out of the chair. 'Well, like she's always saying, she's paying out so let's get on with it. I mean, I'll do your job if you wanna do the cess-pit.'

Ester was no way going to dig shit. She was still in agony from the ride. 'I can't. I'm still injured.'

'Well, then, we just do what Hitler says,' Gloria mused.

Connie said, 'Okay, but I'll never get that information, you know. I'm not supposed to even be in the signal box.'

'Take him a bottle of wine,' Julia said, and stroked Connie's shoulder. 'One for the builder as well.' Connie shrugged her away.

'Right, let's get on with it,' Julia said, and one by one they went to do their allocated jobs.

Angela left the hospital, caught a bus and then made her way down the lane to the manor. No one was in sight so she pushed open the front door.

'Hello? Anyone home?'

Ester appeared on the stairs and glared at her. 'Just stay put, no need to come in.'

'I've come for my gear.'

Ester disappeared along the landing. The three girls peeped out from the kitchen. Angela looked at them, then up the stairs.

'They're Kathleen O'Reilly's kids,' Ester called down.

Angela smiled. 'Hello.'

'Hello,' said Sheena.

'How ya all doing?'

Before they could reply, Ester returned with a suitcase which she hurled down the stairs. 'There's your gear. Piss off and don't come back.'

Angela was near to tears as she picked up her case. 'I got no money.'

'My heart bleeds. Go on, get out.'

Angela walked back down the drive, dragging the suitcase, sniffing back the tears. She didn't see Gloria and Julia way in the distance, digging and clearing the cess-pit. Both wore thick scarves round their faces as the stench was disgusting. They heaved bucket-load after bucket-load, chucking it into a wheelbarrow.

'This is making me sick,' said Gloria and retched.

Julia heaved up the wheelbarrow. 'Keep at it. We've only cleared a quarter of it.'

'It's not on, you know. This could give us a disease, it's disgusting. I mean, this is – this is old shit, you know that, don't you?'

Julia paid no attention as she wheeled the stinking, thick, gooey mud over to a pile of rubbish, smouldering with old bits of furniture and junk. She tipped out the barrow and stood back from the thick black smoke. She turned back as Gloria peered down into the pit.

'Now what? I can't reach in any further with the bucket,' she yelled.

'We'll have to get into it,' Julia said.

'I'm not gettin' in there,' shrieked Gloria.

'Well, one of us has to. We'll toss for it.' Julia picked up a rake and asked whether Gloria wanted the rake or flat side. Gloria bellowed she wanted the rake side. Julia tossed the rake into the air and it came down flat side.

'You bloody did that on purpose,' Gloria yelled. She looked down into the pit again and back to Julia. 'I got an idea. Why don't we get the kids to do it?'

LYNDA LA PLANTE

Julia gave her a hard push. 'No way. Just get on with it, Gloria. Sooner it's done the better.'

Connie breezed into Big John's yard. He was sitting on the steps of his small hut and looked up and waved.

'Hi, how are you?' She beamed as she crossed to him.

He lowered his eyes. 'Look, Connie, this has got nothing to do with you but that Mrs Rawlins is making me bankrupt.'

Connie sat next to him and passed over the envelope. 'Here you go, and there's more coming in a day or two.'

John opened the envelope and then stood up. 'I'd better go and split this between the men.'

'Oh, right now?'

He looked down into her upturned face. 'I got to. When they finish the job they're on, they'll be on their way. If you want that roof done at the manor, I got to pay them.'

'How long will you be?'

'Ten minutes.'

She got up and slipped her arms around him. 'Then I'll wait, but only ten minutes, and we can have a . . .' She kissed him and he gasped for breath when he broke away from her. 'Don't be long,' she whispered, biting his ear.

He blushed, glancing towards the gates then back to the small wooden makeshift hut. 'You know, anyone can walk in here, Connie.'

She giggled. 'Exciting, isn't it? Besides, you can lock the main gates, can't you? But I think it's better if they're open and we screw knowing somebody'll walk in any minute. And look, I brought us a bottle of wine.'

He was all over the place, kissing her, groping her beautiful breasts, and then he ran like hell to his truck. He shouted back that he would be no more than ten minutes.

308

Connie started to undo her buttons and he could hardly put the key into the ignition. She was still standing there on the steps of his hut, blouse open, as he clipped the gatepost in his haste to get out. She didn't even wait for the tail end of the van to disappear before she shot into the hut and began to sift through all his papers and order forms. She found a trade supplier and ordered the bags of lime to be delivered directly to the manor for a cash payment. She gave John's firm's reference and as soon as she replaced the receiver she hurried out, picking up her bag with the bottle of wine. Next stop, the signal box.

Mike had just finished his lunch and was about to go back to the station when the call came. He was eager not to let Susan answer it in case it was Angela again. They almost collided in the hall, they were both so desperate to reach the telephone.

Mike snatched it up. Susan stood with her hands on her hips.

'Hello, is that Mike?'

'Yes, it's me.' He knew who it was – he recognized the voice.

'Who is it?' Susan said petulantly.

'It's my governor.' He glared at her so hard that she turned away and stomped into the kitchen.

'What do you want?' he said quietly, afraid Susan would be listening.

'Need to see you, love, it's urgent. I'll be at the Pen and Whistle pub in the saloon bar, six thirty.'

'I can't – I can't see you.'

'I think you can, Mike. Six thirty, you be there. It's the pub on the corner by your mother's flat.'

Mike was about to speak when the line went dead. He

stood there, holding the receiver, and then dialled his station. He was put through to the incident room and told them he was not feeling too well so he would be in a bit late. Then he looked towards the kitchen. He was sure that Susan was listening. All his anger and frustration surged against her as he dropped the phone back down.

Ester, being lazy, called a number of railway museums but was not getting the information she needed. She then tried another tactic by saying she was making a documentary film for the BBC and could she speak to anyone working at the museum who could assist her. She was given various numbers to call for permission to interview railway technicians. However, permission was not granted by British Rail, so she was now contacting the private railways, saying the BBC documentary had full backing of the transport ministry, who were co-financing the film.

She looked at the list of essential items listed by Dolly: size and weight of the train compartments, couplings and sidings. Underlined was how long it would take to unhitch one carriage from another. No way was it going to be easy.

Big John had only been gone twelve and a half minutes, during which he had flung the money at his labourers and driven straight back to his yard. He ran a comb through his hair, wished he'd got a spot of cologne and locked the big double gates before he ran to his hut. The door was closed and he threw it open, beaming.

Connie had left, no note, nothing. She'd even, he noticed, taken the bottle of wine with her.

*

Still carrying her suitcase, Angela walked along the road towards Mike's house. It was growing dark and it had taken her hours to hitch a ride from the manor. She saw Mike's car parked outside his house and was in two minds whether or not to go and ring his front doorbell. She wanted to confront him, tell him about the baby, but the nearer she got the more her confidence dwindled. She sat on a wall, wondering if he would come out. She didn't want to see his wife.

Mike and Susan were having one hell of a row. She was demanding to know about Angela, about the phone calls, and he was refusing to answer. 'You stay out all night, you come and go and don't speak to me. How do you expect me to feel?'

Mike clenched his fists. 'Susan, I've told you, there is nothing – *nothing* between me and this girl.'

'Then why does she keep calling you? Why was that Mrs Rawlins round here? Is it true that she's pregnant?'

'Leave it alone, Susan. I mean it. Just shut up about it. You're driving me nuts.'

'And *you're* driving *me* nuts,' she said in a fury, watching as he grabbed his coat. 'Where are you going?'

'Out. I can't stand it here.'

'One of these days you're gonna come back here and the locks will have been changed.'

He sighed. 'Sue, listen, give me a break. I've got a lot on my plate right now and I just can't tell you about it.'

'Try me, go on, try me!' she shouted.

He ran his hands through his hair. He didn't even know where to begin. How could he tell her about his mother, the diamonds, the trouble he was in at work? He knew she couldn't deal with it. Right now, Angela was the least of his problems. He was afraid of what Dolly Rawlins wanted, scared he was heading even deeper into trouble, but he couldn't tell anyone, especially not his wife. Susan broke down in tears as he walked out. She ran up the stairs and was about to open the window, call out to him that they had to talk, when she saw him. And what was worse, she saw Angela.

Mike yanked open the car door when she confronted him. 'We got to talk, Mike.'

He got in and slammed it. 'No, we haven't. I got nothing to say to you, Angela, just go away from me. I don't want to see you. Stay away from me and my house.'

'I lost the baby, Mike.'

'I don't care, Angela, you hear me? I *don't care*.'

She was sobbing, looked like an orphan with her suitcase. 'I got no one to help me, Mike,' she wept.

He dug into his pocket and pulled out his wallet. He took all the money he had and held it out. 'Here, take this, *take it*, it's all I got on me.'

'I didn't come for money,' she wailed.

He pushed the money at her. 'Take it, Angela. I can't see you, please stay away from me. *Go away, Angela*.' He threw the money on to the pavement, and started the car. She sobbed even louder and he hesitated, but then he saw the time: it was six fifteen. Although he was afraid to meet Dolly Rawlins he was also afraid not to, so he drove off.

Angela picked up the four twenty-pound notes, unaware that Susan was watching from the bedroom window. The two of them were crying. Susan knew it had to be the girl and she'd seen her husband giving her money, which made it even worse. She wished she had enough money to get the locks changed there and then.

*

Gloria and Julia were both in the cess-pit, still clearing away the filth. It was deep, and their heads appeared at the lip as Ester carried out two mugs.

'All right for some,' moaned Gloria, accepting the tea.

'It's deep, isn't it?' Ester remarked.

'I'd say this is for the mail-bags,' Julia replied. 'What do you think?'

'I dunno – who knows what the old bat's doing? But as long as it's not for us, who cares?' Ester set off towards the house.

Gloria looked at Julia. 'What if she's got us diggin' a bleedin' grave? Just so long as Dolly Rawlins doesn't intend finishing us all off. She shot her old man, you know. I wouldn't put nothing past her.'

Later that night, Connie was perched on the counter in the signal box, a chipped glass of red wine in her hand, which she clinked against Jim's mug. 'Cheers.'

He moved closer. 'You could get me the sack you know, Connie.'

'Who's gonna know I'm here?'

'Well, anyone passing can see us.'

She slithered off the counter to sit on the floor. 'Now they can't.' She began to run her hand up his trouser leg.

'Hang on a second – lemme just sort this out. It's the six o'clock, then we got fifteen minutes.'

Connie watched as he pulled levers and answered the phone. She began to ease down her panties. She held them up, waving them. 'Can I have another drink down here?'

Jim saw her panties, began heaving the rail levers faster than he ever had before while Connie crawled across the floor and started undoing his flies. By now she had a good sense of where the phone connection wires ran but she

didn't have any knowledge of the alarms. All she knew was
that it might be a very long night.

Dolly sipped the lemonade, flicking through her little black
notebook. Mike stood over her as she looked up then
smiled.

'Nothing for me but get yourself a drink, love, if you
need one.'

'I don't.' He sat down, having a good look around the
bar. 'What do you want?'

Dolly shut the book, had another sip. 'Some information
– sort of like a trade.'

'What information?' he asked, his heart pounding. He
knew something bad was coming but when it came it left
him shattered. 'I can't find that out! That's classified!'

She leaned forward and tapped his arm. 'Yes, you can
and you will, otherwise I will have to inform your superiors
about those diamonds, about your mother. It's up to you,
Mike. Tell me now if you don't want to do it. You must
have some old friends from the army days – they might be
helpful, but if you don't want to do it . . .'

'I've just said so.'

'Oh, I know you did, but you see, Mike, I don't think
you really believe that I'd be prepared to sell myself down
the tubes. But I would, I'd go back inside and I wouldn't
be on my own. You'd be sent down as well, and they might
even get your mother back from Spain. You tell me now –
can you get the information I need?'

He shuffled his feet, took another look round. 'How
long have I got?'

'Two days, no more.' She drained her glass, placing it
carefully back on the beer-mat. 'I'll call you, don't you call
me. Two days.'

He sat, head in his hands, as she walked out. The cement was drying, up to his chest now. He didn't know whether to throw the table through the pub window or do as she had asked: find out how much money the mail train was carrying, and if they were to continue the same route. He looked at the slip of paper she had passed him with the name of the security firm she had taken from the vans she'd seen outside her local station. It was a well-known firm: he didn't know if he could get any information from them. He needed a drink, a large one, to stop himself shaking. No way would he be able to go in to work. He really did feel ill.

Dolly drove back to the manor and, as she turned into the drive the headlamps picked out the large rubbish tip still burning. She got out, leaving the lights on, and walked towards it. She examined it, satisfied it was big enough and, most certainly, deep enough.

When she got in she found the kitchen in a mess: dirty soup plates, tinned mince on a pan left to one side, dried-out baked beans in another, stacks of used cups and mugs. Every surface was food-stained and filthy. She pursed her lips and dumped her handbag, throwing aside her coat. She found Ester lying stretched out on the sofa with a glass of wine, reading the *TV Times*. Julia was asleep in an easy chair, the television blaring. Neither heard Dolly. She walked up the big staircase, looked into Connie's room but it was empty. Then she went up to the second landing to the children's room.

The last person Dolly expected to see was Gloria, wrapped in an old dressing gown, sitting with Sheena on her knee. The other two were fast asleep in the big old-fashioned double bed. 'Oh, said the little pig. What will the big bad wolf do?' Gloria rocked the child, stroking her hair. 'Well, he'll huff and he'll puff and he'll blow the house down.'

Sheena lifted her tiny hand to Gloria's cheek. 'You're not our mummy, are you?'

Gloria shook her head. The little girl's question touched her heart – so many different homes, so many different foster carers, the little girl was completely confused.

Gloria kissed her. 'No, I'm not your mummy.'

'Doesn't she love us any more?'

'Yes, of course she does. But you know, Sheena, a long, long time ago I had a little girl, just like you, and I had to go away, just like your mummy has had to go away. My little girl never had a nice house to live in and I couldn't ever see her again but you will. Your mummy being away doesn't mean she doesn't love you. She does. And she's arranged for us all to look after you until she comes back. Do you understand?'

'No.' Sheena yawned.

'My little girl never understood but then it was too late, you see, I couldn't see her. But you'll be able to see your mummy. One of us will always take you to see her so you won't forget who she is, and in the meantime we'll all be like double mothers. How's that?'

Sheena was asleep, and Dolly stayed where she was, looking at a Gloria she hadn't known existed, a sad, lonely Gloria who was being so gentle and caring, so unlike the hard, uncouth exterior she showed to them all. They all had secrets, all had hidden pain. Somehow she had not expected Gloria to have so much.

CHAPTER 14

CONNIE WAS doing up her blouse and Jim his trousers at the same time as he closed the gates for the nine-thirty express to pass through. John stood at the level crossing, waiting, impatient that he'd just missed the orange light. As it turned to red, he looked at the signal box, as if to blame it for his being held up, and saw her, laughing, her arms wrapped around the attendant. He was stunned. He kept blinking, sure he must have been mistaken. It wasn't his Connie up there, was it?

Connie skipped down the steps, looked up and blew a kiss, then hurried towards the taxi-rank. She was in the cab heading for the manor when the gates opened and didn't see John charge up the steps of the signal box or witness his embarrassment when Jim opened the door.

'Connie here, is she?' John blurted out.

Jim covered well. If she had been caught in there with him, he'd have been in trouble. Not that he knew who the big broad-shouldered bloke was. He just acted dumb.

'No, nobody here but me, why?'

John looked past him into the hut. 'No reason. Sorry, mate. Sorry to bother you.'

He walked down the steps, then stopped. Jim was still at the door. He wanted to say she was his, but decided against it. Better to make sure that she was before he threw his weight about.

Jim knew he'd have to ask Connie about the bloke but

only when the time was right. They'd not even been out on a proper date yet. Half of him still couldn't believe what had taken place – he'd never experienced anything like it. Blown in his own signal box! But there was no one he could tell, especially not anyone from the company as he'd be fired on the spot. It had happened though, and as if to assure himself that it really had he drew Connie's lacy panties from his pocket.

'Shit, I forgot me knickers,' Connie said as she walked into the house, slamming the front door. They weren't worth going back for. She called out she was home, then hurried into the kitchen and began to draw on the back of an envelope everything she could remember. She was just finishing when she heard the front doorbell ring.

Ester came in, looking perplexed. 'I didn't hear a car, did you, Connie?'

'No. Who do you think it is?'

Dolly appeared on the landing. 'Answer it, Ester.'

Ester pushed Connie forward. 'You answer, just in case.'

Dolly thumped down the stairs as the bell rang again. She went for the door and swung it open. Angela stood on the doorstep. 'I'm sorry, I got no other place to go – thumbed a lift back.'

'Well, love, you can thumb one right out again,' Dolly replied.

Connie felt sorry for Angela. 'Ah, let her stay for just one night.'

Ester scowled. 'You joking? No way, chuck her out, Dolly.'

'Oh, please don't! I'll cook and clean, I promise.'

Dolly opened the door wider. 'Right, one night. Go up

on to the top floor. Your old room's gone so use another, then come down and clean up the kitchen and make us some dinner.'

Angela almost kissed her hand but Dolly stepped away, letting the door bang shut.

'You must be mad,' Ester said, going back into the drawing room.

Connie smiled at Angela but got pushed into the room by Dolly. 'Give us a call when it's ready, will you, love?' Dolly said as she went into the drawing room.

Gloria clattered in. 'I don't fucking believe that girl's cheek. I just seen her making up her bed.'

'Just for tonight,' Dolly said.

'What? Are you crazy?'

Julia yawned. 'Well, the kitchen's a mess, the kids' room's a mess, we need somebody to cook, do all the ironing and washing, plus she's going to cook dinner so that should keep her occupied for one night, anyway.'

Dolly sat down, took out her notebook, and flicked through it.

'Bit bleedin' risky, isn't it?' Gloria said, warming herself by the fire. 'That boyfriend of hers – what if he's sent her?'

Dolly looked up. 'You want to hear him? He's got problems, his wife . . . But so far he's not made any calls to his station about us. I think we got the bloke by the balls.'

They focused on Dolly as she took out the tape and slipped it into the small cassette player.

'You got him taped?' Ester said.

'Didn't I tell you? Have a listen.'

'You got him taped at his house? What about at his nick? It's not who's he's calling at his home that'd worry me but what he and his mates are doing.'

Dolly said nothing because she knew Ester was right.

They sat round listening to Susan and Mike arguing. They all laughed, apart from Ester, as if it was a joke. They even heard his kids yelling. Dolly left them to it, went to the kitchen to have a private confab with Angela. She could feel Ester's eyes on her and it unnerved her slightly, only because she knew Ester was right: Mike had also to be monitored at his station.

Angela was working herself into a sweat, washing dishes, scrubbing the floor, cleaning all the surfaces, as if to prove she was worth her keep.

'You want to stay on, do you?' Dolly asked, as she drew out a chair to sit at the kitchen table.

'Yes. I'll do anything to make up for what I done, anything. I know you won't ever forgive me but . . .' Angela sat opposite Dolly, trying to explain about the baby and Mike, but Dolly took her hand.

'Shut up. Now, are you still seeing him?' Angela shook her head.

'I see. Well, you might have to prove yourself, Angela – not just to me but to the others. Does he know you were driving that car that killed Jimmy Donaldson?'

'No! I hate him, Dolly, really, I wouldn't help him. I swear on my life I wouldn't.'

Dolly propped an elbow on the table. 'Well, you remember this, Angela, because if you betray me again, if I find out that you're grassin' back to him, then you'll go down for murder and I'll make sure of it. You understand, don't you?'

Angela felt scared but she nodded. In truth, she didn't have anywhere to go – even her mum had refused to let her stay. The manor was the only place she had been able to come to, and she clung to Dolly's hand. 'I'll make it up to you, I swear I will. I'll do whatever you want.'

'Good girl. I want you to keep house, feed us and take

care of Kathleen's girls. And I will need you to do a few things for me.'

The women had obviously been talking about Dolly because when she returned they fell silent. She picked up her notebook.

'Dinner's not ready yet so let's get this sorted before we eat.' She asked each of them about their day, making copious notes, frowning at Ester who, she felt, had not done enough. She was told to go out the next day and get more information on the carriage links.

'Good work on the cess-pit, Gloria and Julia.'

They felt a little like schoolgirls and didn't enjoy it.

Dolly then turned her attention to Connie. She was more than pleased with her sketches and that the lime was on order and on its way. The hastily drawn diagrams were not yet good enough, they needed far better ones and descriptions of the security measures, the alarms and codes used to contact the local police. Connie agreed she would have another evening with Jim – even spend the afternoon with him because he wasn't on duty until four thirty.

'That's not written down here, Connie,' Dolly said sternly.

'Well, I just told you.'

'That's not good enough. Put everything down so I can check it all out. Is that understood?'

Dolly began to allocate them the next day's jobs, to be fitted in as well as the two rides already booked. She ticked off each item. She wanted Julia to get hold of Norma's police cape and, if possible, her hat.

'We could hire some,' offered Julia.

'Yes, we could, and be seen doing it. Don't keep

321

questioning me – just get on with what I tell you to do and don't argue.'

'It might not be that easy.'

'Why not? I've seen it in the back of her truck. Go and keep her friendly, just like Connie's doing with the signal-box attendant. Plus, Connie, keep your eye on those shotguns at the gym. Go there tomorrow – just keep checking them.'

Dolly continued down the list and then told Julia to accompany them on the rides the following day. 'Who's looking after the kids?' she asked.

'Angela, and don't argue. Until I say different she stays. We need her, and somebody's got to keep them happy and well looked after.'

'I think that's a mistake,' said Ester.

Dolly snapped her book shut. 'Do you? Well, Ester, driving around in a stolen car is not just a mistake but bloody stupid. You could have been picked up in it. You think that Tommy wouldn't have told me, that I wouldn't check up on the two of you? And that's something you all got to start thinking about, I will check up on everything I ask you to do and I'll keep on checking until I'm satisfied.'

'Fine, who's checking up on you?' said Ester.

Dolly's voice was icy quiet. 'You want to question me, Ester, then you can pack your gear and leave right now. Either we do this my way or we don't do it at all.'

Angela tapped on the door and peeped round. 'Dinner's on the table,' she said meekly, and scuttled out.

They all started to head for the door, but Dolly caught Ester by the arm. 'Just a second, love, I want a word.' The others left the room.

Ester stood, hands on her hips. 'Don't get me wrong, Dolly, I'm not questioning who's the boss. I just have a few more brains than some of the others.'

'Do you?' Dolly sighed. 'I already said I don't call wheelin' around in a hot car very clever, and I don't call having blokes arrive and knock the hell out of Gloria very clever either.'

'What you want me to do?' Ester said angrily.

'I want you to sort out this blackmail business. We can't afford to have loose ends. What have you got on them?'

'I told you, it's a video-tape.'

'Take it back. Clear it all up, Ester, or the whole thing is off. I mean it. Something like this could bring us all down.'

'Oh, yeah? And what about you and this copper? I know you've done something with him. That's why you got his home bugged.'

Dolly rubbed her eyes. 'Sort out the tape, Ester. Tomorrow. By then I'll have some information from this copper, and I'll know more. But you're right, I *am* using him but I just don't know how far we can trust him.'

'What are you doing, then?'

Dolly gave a strange half-smile. 'Taking a leaf out of your book. Just playing it, see how it pans out!'

She left Ester disgruntled and uneasy: she didn't trust Dolly or like her handing out the orders. She wasn't used to being the underdog.

They ate in silence. They were all tired out and Angela crept round like a wounded dog. She'd noticed all the riding boots and, trying to make conversation, asked if she could maybe have a ride on Helen of Troy.

'Not right now, Angela. You're not that welcome back yet,' Dolly said sweetly.

'We're all trying to get into the local hunt.' Ester said it as a joke but she was taken aback when Dolly agreed.

'Yes, we're getting into the country way of life. It's doing us a lot of good.'

323

Hooded looks flitted across the table and conversation flagged again.

Dolly walked with Julia in the darkness up through the woods and down to the railway line. 'Bring her up to the line, Julia. See if she really is as bomb-proof as that Norma said.'

Julia agreed, uncertain why Dolly had asked her to walk with her. She was tired out but right now felt it was better simply to agree with whatever Dolly said.

They looked down the railway line to the small bridge, the wide lake, and back to the level crossing. They said nothing but their minds were racing. Dolly was trying to assimilate in quick flashing pictures exactly how she intended holding up the train. Julia could see only disaster. She reckoned that with or without the horse it was going to be impossible.

'I think we'll need a boat – that's another expense,' Dolly said, almost to herself.

Julia looked back at the lake, trying to read Dolly's mind, but she was already heading back to the manor. Surely . . . Julia mused, *surely* she wasn't going to hold up the train on the bridge. If so, why did she need them to ride?

The following morning Julia couldn't stop sniggering. They were worse than she had anticipated – even with more than eight hours of lessons they were incapable of cantering and all still seemed very ill at ease. They were still on the leading-rein, none good enough to ride alone.

Julia rode towards Dolly and said quietly, 'I hope you've got a plan that now excludes the horses, Dolly, because none of you could make it across the fields. There's five sets of hedges to jump and—'

Dolly pushed her horse past Julia. 'I'll tell you when I've changed my mind and instead of smiling at us like we were stupid kids, start helping. Better still, ask if you can take over teaching without that spotty stable-girl, she's as bad as you with her smirking.'

Dolly might have sounded positive but she wobbled dangerously. Julia didn't laugh – she didn't dare. Dolly had that look of angry determination on her face, the one she wore when you knew it wasn't worth arguing with her.

That afternoon Julia took over the lesson and she was a much better teacher than the stable-girl. For one, she was a lot tougher and shouted when they made a mistake, but she soon had them cantering. Gloria came off but she got back on after Julia screamed at her and Julia had to hand it to her – she kept on with a look of grim fury on her face, which was good. It was the first time she hadn't looked scared to death.

Angela had hot soup ready and waiting. The children had been given their tea and were playing outside, brushing and clearing the yard for yet more fifty pences. When they were half-way through eating the soup, the telephone rang and Ester, as always, dived out to see who it was, wanting to be ahead of anyone else. She called that it was for Julia, and went upstairs for a bath. She leaned over the banister as Julia went to the phone. 'I presume it was your mother, she asked if you were in surgery! Haw, haw, haw.'

Julia picked up the receiver. It wasn't her mother but the housekeeper, who was upset. Julia's mother had had a stroke, and was very ill.

'My mother's ill,' Julia said unemotionally. The women all looked at her. 'A stroke. I'll have to go and sort it out. Can I use your car, Gloria?'

'No, you can't,' Dolly said, clearing the plates.

'Well, I'll take the truck.'

Dolly turned and smiled. 'Why not ask that friend of yours, Norma? Maybe she'll drive you over – be a good chance to talk to her.'

Julia shrugged. 'Okay, but I don't know if she's around, she may be on duty.'

Dolly ran the water in the sink. 'Don't forget we need the riding cape and her hat.'

'I hadn't forgotten, Dolly. I'll give her a call, see if she's at home.'

Norma opened the front door, smilingly. 'Hi there.' Julia explained what had happened to her mother. 'You're in luck, I'm off for two days so it's no problem.'

'I appreciate this,' Julia said, stepping into the neat cottage hallway.

Norma picked up her coat and car keys. Julia noticed that her police cape and hat were stashed in the back of the vehicle. She had no idea how she would go about removing it but that was the least of her problems: first came her elderly mother. 'Just one thing, Norma, about my old lady. She doesn't know I was in prison, she still thinks I run a practice.'

'You mean she didn't ever know you were in prison?'

'Why upset her? It was better this way.'

Norma turned into the road and they drove off. 'I hear you had another visit from the locals?'

Julia gave her a sidelong look. 'Yeah, that's right. First

they thought we were hiding some diamonds, then guns. It was a waste of time and money all round.'

Norma nodded. 'Mrs Rawlins has quite a reputation.'

'Oh, have you been checking up on us?'

Norma swore as they drew up by the station level crossing. 'Oh, bugger it. Let's hope it's not the mail train.'

They sat silent, watching the gates clang shut, and then Julia leaned back in her seat, slipping her arm behind Norma. 'They have a lot of security on for the mail train?'

Norma pointed along the road. 'Yes, but as you can see, it's quite simple. That's why they pick on this station, no easy access for any car coming up either side of it and they'd never get as far as the motorway, the place is alarmed all along the track, special link to the police station. They can be here in under four minutes.'

'Really?' Julia said, feigning disinterest.

'You know why they use the security vans?'

'No?'

'Because of the vulnerability of the big stations. Last big robbery was at King's Cross so now they have armoured trucks, police escort to an out-of-the-way station like ours, then they put the bags on board and it's a clear run through all the stations. Train goes at around eighty miles an hour.'

Julia began to caress Norma's neck. 'Well, thankfully it's not the mail train today, no coppers, just you!' She leaned over and kissed Norma, embracing her as the passenger train moved on down the line until the gates opened and they continued on, passing Raymond Dewey on his little stool. He waved to Julia and she waved back.

'Poor sod, what a life,' she said.

'Oh, he's happy enough,' Norma said, and then touched Julia's hand lightly. 'I'm glad you called.'

'So am I,' Julia replied, then stared out of the window.

It was going to be a long drive and Norma irritated the hell out of her.

Dolly asked Connie to come in for a chat. She closed the bedroom door. 'You're seeing that signal-box bloke tonight, aren't you?'

'Yes, I told you.'

'Where's he taking you?'

'Dinner at his place.'

'Good. Slip him a couple of these sleeping tablets. You can have a good search around his place. Maybe he's got papers or something that'll give us the alarm codes.'

Connie took the two tablets wrapped in a bit of tissue and slipped them into her pocket. 'I'll be down the gym first, check on the shotguns.'

'Good girl.'

'Thank you, Dolly,' she said, without a smile.

As she was walking out, Dolly caught her hand. 'Something bothering you, is there?'

'What do you think? But, like you said, I owe you for Lennie so I'll do whatever you say.'

'You make sure you do.'

Connie wouldn't meet her eyes. Instead, she continued out, closing the door behind her. Dolly rubbed her eyes, and pinched the bridge of her nose. God, they infuriated her. She was always having to check up on one or the other – it was like having a house full of kids. Well, she had kids for real and she wouldn't let Kathleen down, but she knew it was going to be tough to keep the girls at the manor. She would have to start thinking about what she would do with them after the robbery. She felt tired out.

*

Angela was in the kitchen when Dolly came in. 'Want to go into London, love? Only I got to drop Gloria off, got her usual visit with her husband so you might as well keep us company.'

It was not until they had left Gloria at a tube station that Dolly told Angela what she wanted her to do. She said it so quietly that Angela didn't get nervous or even ask too many questions, she simply agreed. She was scared about going into the police station but Dolly stood outside waiting, encouraging her.

Angela asked at the desk to speak to Mike Withey. The duty sergeant asked her name and then called the incident room. 'What did you say your name was, love?'

'Angela Dunn.'

When Mike was told she was waiting in reception he marched straight out to her, grabbed her by the arm and pulled her out on to the street.

'I told you I didn't want to see you again.'

'Please, Mike, I just want to talk to you, just for a minute. Look, I bought you a present, I don't want to make you angry.'

'I don't want anything from you, Angela. I just don't want to see you ever again.'

Angela held out the pen box but he turned away so she took it out and showed it to him. 'It's a pen.'

'Great, Angela, just what I needed.' She slid it into his top pocket, and he turned away from her. 'I don't want it.'

'Please, just give me a few minutes, please, Mike. I got to tell you something – it's important.' He rubbed his jaw. 'Mrs Rawlins said she'll call you tomorrow morning, she wants to know what would be a good time.'

Mike faced the wall, feeling as if someone was about to ram his head into it. 'What else did she tell you?'

'Nothing, just that she would be in touch but for you to tell her what time.'

He licked his lips. 'Tell her I've nothing for her, not yet, but I'll be at home – say in the morning about ten.'

Dolly sat in the car, the briefcase open on her lap. She adjusted the channel and could hear Mike as clearly as if he was sitting next to her. She reckoned it was going to be quite a long night but she had to know if she could trust him – or Angela, for that matter. So far she had said exactly what she had been told to say, and the added plus was that they were even in Dolly's sight. She hadn't reckoned on them coming outside to talk.

Angela watched him hurry back into the station before she headed towards Dolly. She could see the aerial stuck on the side of the car. 'Was that okay?'

Dolly beamed. 'Yes, love. Get in, I've a few things I want you to do for me. Can you stay at your mother's?'

'Why? Can't I stay on at the manor?'

'Yes, but I want you to do a few things for me first thing in the morning. Have you got a passport?'

'No.'

'Well, first thing tomorrow I want you to get one and I want you to take mine, with this letter. I'm the girls' legal guardian and I want them put on my passport, just for a holiday. Then you come straight home. And, Angela, you don't say a word about this to any of the others or they'll go ape-shit – you know the way they feel about you.' Dolly gestured for her to leave there and then.

'What are you going to do?'

'Oh, drive around a bit. Go on, off you go.'

'My mum won't let me stay, Dolly.'

Dolly counted off some twenty-pound notes. 'Well,

here's money for a hotel – just the one night, love, then you get home first thing.'

She watched her walk off down the street. Angela turned and waved. Dolly acknowledged her, then saw the channel light blinking in the briefcase and put in her earplug. Mike was making a phone call. The pen worked perfectly, and she could hear him clearly; marvellous little invention. She smiled to herself as she listened to Mike talking, arranging to meet someone, and the more Dolly listened the more she smiled. She was sure she was right. She'd got the smart little bastard right by the balls. But better to be safe than sorry.

Gloria saw that Eddie was all wired up the moment he was let through the gate to the visits room. She'd brought a few odds and sods for him, not much, and fifteen quid. He took them without so much as a thank-you.

'So, how you keeping?'

'Oh, I'm havin' a really good time in here, Gloria.'

She had known it would start.

'You look different,' he muttered.

'Yeah, well, it's all the fresh air.'

'So you're still at the farmhouse then?'

'It's a *manor* house, Eddie, and yeah, I'm still there.'

He began to roll a cigarette. She waited for him to ask about the guns but he continued with the cigarette.

'Anythin' gone down there?' he asked nonchalantly, keeping his eyes on his roll-up. She sat back, watching him, and then he looked up, and she knew, but she never gave so much as a flicker. In that moment she also knew she was stronger than him, and maybe she always had been.

*

Mike had no notion that he was wired up and Dolly Rawlins was taping every word he said. She was even right behind him when he went to visit an old mate from his days in the army, leading her directly to the security firm that handled the money for the mail train.

He had brought a bottle of Scotch and was shown into the security firm's office. His friend Colin had been a bit surprised to hear from Mike as he hadn't for quite a few years and he wondered what he was after. But Mike soon got over that, saying he was putting out feelers for work if he was to leave the police force and a friend of a friend had told him that Colin had a cushy job.

Dolly had to hand it to Mike, he was quite a smooth operator. She listened as he chatted on about his army days, about how badly he was paid and how, with a wife and two kids to keep plus a mortgage to pay, he was getting sick and tired of the Met. She was parked fifty yards from the security firm's main depot and would have remained there if she hadn't seen a police patrol car cruise by. She did one slow tour round the block and then she was out of range of the transmitter. She decided to call it quits for the evening. Most important was that she felt secure that if anything was to go down from Mike's home, she'd be ready for it. She headed for home, everything she was planning playing over and over in her mind. She became more disheartened as the miles clocked up. Was she in over her head? Did she really believe she could go through with it? Just thinking about it exhausted her. Had it been like this with the widows? What the hell was she playing at?

Then he began to talk to her. It didn't take her by surprise – Harry's voice often came to her, not like some whispered menace, nothing like that. In fact, it was the normality of the sound of his voice in her head that had often soothed her. She used to talk to him, silent conversations as if he was in the room with her, his deep, warm tones as clear as if he was sitting in their old drawing room in their house in Totteridge. He used to sit up late many nights. Sometimes she'd take him in a warm glass of malt whisky with just a sprinkling of sugar. 'You all right, darlin'?'

'I am, sweetheart, but there's nobody else I can depend on as much as myself so I just make sure I'm covered back, front and sideways, because there'll be nobody else looking out for me.'

Harry never discussed what he was working on so diligently. It was a game they had played, and she would sit close and ask him if he wanted to talk about it . . . how she loved those times. Harry would sip his drink and often be sitting close enough to have a hand resting on her shoulder.

'Well, darlin', I got this tricky little situation. Not sure who to trust with an important delivery and it's only tricky because it could have repercussions.'

She never asked names but in a roundabout way, he would tell her about who he mistrusted and why, and the best way to ensure they became very trusting.

Still driving, one part of her mind concentrating on the road, the other listening to Harry, it wasn't until Dolly stopped at a garage to fill up with petrol that she lost his voice and listened to her own. 'Cover your backside, Dolly, your sides and your front, before you make the next move.'

Mike remained with his pal Colin as they drank their way through the entire bottle. He had not discussed the type of work Colin did, taking his time so as not to create any suspicion. Colin was a little ill-at-ease in case he was caught drinking: as he was the foreman he could get into trouble. But Mike laughed – he was, after all, a copper if anyone should interrupt them. Just in case, Colin slipped out to check no one was likely to disturb them.

As soon as he left the office, Mike looked over the time sheets on the desk, the lists of officers' names, but found nothing pertaining to any mail-train pick-up or delivery. It was a big firm and Mike was about to try one of the drawers when Colin returned.

'You're gonna have to go, the night staff'll be on duty any minute and we're not allowed to have anyone in here.'

'Okay. When can we do this again? Only – if I leave the cop shop, I don't want to walk out to nothing. Is the pay worthwhile?'

They discussed the money and Mike brought the conversation gradually round to what kind of work he would be looking at, if it was boring and involved just driving around the country. Colin grinned. 'No way, this is one of the top companies, we don't deal in small stuff – this is big. That's why they like us army boys, you know, men that can handle themselves. We're shifting big loads of money.'

'Oh, yeah? What you call big, then?'

Colin gave a shifty look around and leaned in close. 'Come and have a look out in the yard, see the new vans. They're all armour-plated, blow your mind, all work on timers, high-tech stuff. We do the Royal Mail deliveries.'

Mike looked suitably impressed and followed his friend into the yard. Not until half an hour later did he discover just how much the security firm carried. He was told in an awestruck whisper but had no time to react as Colin hustled him outside. They arranged to meet for a drink the following night. By then Colin would have made enquiries to see if there were any openings for someone with Mike's experience.

Dolly switched off the lights and got out of the car. She was exhausted; it had been a long night. She couldn't wait to get to bed but as usual she toured the house, checking who was in and who wasn't. Julia was still out, so was Connie, and Ester was watching some late-night movie.

'Julia called, said her mother was really bad and that Norma's staying over with her.'

Dolly smiled. 'Well, that's good, give them a lot of time to talk.'

Ester made no reply, concentrating on the film. 'You've still got to sort out those carriage links, you know, Ester.'

'I'll do it tomorrow, after the morning ride.'

'Okay – and at the same time sort that business out with the tape.'

'Yeah, I hear you, Dolly. Where's Angela?'

Dolly was about to go up to bed when Ester asked, 'Where've you been?'

She swung the door back and forth. 'Checking out that copper. I think we can trust him.'

Ester turned from the TV set. 'Well, I hope you're right.'

'So do I.' The door closed silently behind her.

Ester went back to watching the film, angry that Julia was with Norma, angry that she could never get a hold on Dolly. She didn't trust her and the more she thought about it, the more angry she became. She reckoned it was all a waste of time.

'She's back, then,' Gloria said as she walked in.

'Born in a field, were you, Gloria? Shut the door.'

Gloria kicked it closed and leaned against it. 'Where's she been?'

'You think she'd tell me?'

Gloria wandered to the sofa and perched on the arm. 'You think she's a bit wacko?'

Ester shrugged, and Gloria slid slowly down from the arm of the sofa to sprawl beside her. 'How long you gonna give all this riding business? I mean, she's not serious, is she?'

Ester switched off the TV. 'You ask her. I keep trying but she just fobs me off, keeps telling me to do this and that, wants to find out how to unhitch a train carriage.'

'Well, that's easy.' Gloria yawned. 'Get some Semtex and blast them apart, that's what I'd do. No way could you or me or all five of us lift one of them heavy links. I'm telling you she's got a screw loose, I thought that when I heard her telling you. All you need to do to get a carriage loose is blow it apart, never mind farting around trying to unhitch it. We'd be there all night.'

Ester fixed her eyes on Gloria and said, 'You still interested?'

Gloria bit her nail, spat it out. 'Depends, don't it? Like how much is in it. Right now this is all fantasy, she got us riding up like *Annie Get Your Gun* – I dunno what's in her head. Does she expect us to start blasting the train from the horses? Well, lemme tell you, until I know just exactly how she got it planned, I am not saying whether I'm in or out. And if you got any sense you do the same.'

Dolly listend to them, could hear every word, and she wondered if Gloria was right, if they should use Semtex. She wondered where they could get some and then she sat on the bed looking over the eiderdown. Laid out, just like Harry used to do it, were her notes and plans for the robbery. She took out the small earpiece and tossed it on to the briefcase, no longer interested in the conversation below. Maybe it was becoming crazy, maybe she was crazy, because she had now decided that the best place to hold up the train was dead centre of the bridge. She was about to switch off the channel connected to the drawing room, but stopped herself.

'So how did it go with Eddie?' Ester was asking.

'Oh, usual, pain in the arse. I'm gonna crash out, see you in the morning.'

Dolly flicked off the microphone and heard Gloria's bedroom door bang shut. She concentrated, pulling her own door slightly ajar, certain she could hear muffled weeping.

Gloria had her face buried in the pillow, trying to cry without being heard. She hadn't expected it to hurt so much. She physically jumped when Dolly touched her, whipping round. 'You go creepin' around like this an' you'll gimme a heart attack,' she said, shrugging Dolly's hand away.

'What you crying about?'

Gloria shook her head. 'Sad movie on downstairs.'

'What happened with Eddie, Gloria?' Dolly sat down on the side of the bed.

Gloria sniffed, wiping her face with the back of her hand, and then decided there was no point in lying. 'He knew the guns was here and he said the filth paid him a visit, said they was gonna book me on murder, like they knew I was drivin' that fuckin' car. They told him about Jimmy Donaldson.'

Gloria pushed her head into the pillow. 'Well, it wasn't me, an' if they come after me for that then I'll tell them it was that cow Angela. I'm not taking the rap for that – I wasn't even fuckin' driving.'

Dolly straightened the candlewick bedspread. 'They got

nothin'. If they had, love, they'd have sorted us out – and fast. They got nothin' on that car.'

'And you'd know, would you?' snapped Gloria.

'Yes, I'd know. So, go on about Eddie.'

Gloria suddenly deflated and out fell the tears. 'He grassed us, Dolly, he told them about the guns. He admitted it, said I should get out, like he don't know what went down here, just that he told the coppers his stash was at the house.'

'I see,' Dolly said softly.

'No, you don't see, Dolly, you don't see at all. He was my husband and he would have got me put away if they'd found them, got us all done, I suppose. But he's my husband and he stitched me up. All the years I stood by him, probably would have waited you know – I mean, he's not much but he is my husband.' Gloria sniffed again, and then shrugged her shoulders. 'Well, now you know, so you want me to pack me bags? I'll understand, I don't wanna walk but I reckon you got a right to kick me out.'

Gloria didn't expect the gentle embrace, and it made her want to sob. Dolly held her a moment, stroked her fuzzy, bleached, dry hair and Gloria could hardly make out what she said she spoke so softly. 'S'all right, love, I understand. You stay on here because I understand.' Dolly took out a crumpled tissue and handed it to her. 'Yes, I understand. You're hurting now, probably always will, but it gets easier, believe me, it gets easier.'

'You're all right, gel, you know that?' Gloria said and started to cry again as Dolly left the room.

Dolly creamed her hands and then her face, wiping the tissue across her cheeks. There were no tears, she didn't think she had any left, but she'd felt that hurt, that pain inside like a jagged bread knife. She saw his face again, saw him standing waiting for her in the darkness, the lake behind him as dark as the night. And yet his face was so clear, as if lit by a pale flickering light.

'Hello, Doll.' He had lifted his arms to embrace her and she had moved that much closer. She didn't want to miss. She wanted to shoot him in his heart. She had succeeded.

CHAPTER 15

JIM HUGGED Connie tightly. He was feeling very drunk but not yet as drunk as Connie had hoped. He'd had three pints in the pub and one and a half bottles of wine at his home, plus two of Dolly's sleeping tablets and he was still rapping, his face flushed, his eyes unfocused, but no way was he about to pass out.

'I love you,' he said, hanging his head.

'I love you too,' she lied.

'You do? Is that the truth?'

'Yeah, I love you, Jim.'

He stepped back, arms wide. 'I don't believe it. You love me?' She was getting really pissed off with him. Then he got down on his knees at her feet. 'Listen, I know we haven't known each other very long but I own this house, I mean, on a mortgage right? But I own it and my car and . . . you really love me?' He kissed her hand, getting a bit tearful. She passed him another drink and he gulped it down. 'I need a drink to do this, I never thought I would, give me another . . .' She poured the remains of the bottle into his glass and he swallowed that too, still on his knees. 'Will you marry me?' He looked up into her face as he slowly fell forward, his arms clasped around her legs, unable to keep himself upright.

'Jim. Jim?' She squatted down beside him but he couldn't open his eyes. He was out for the count. She slipped his duvet around him and put a pillow under his head before

searching his pockets, his wallet. Connie searched every
drawer and closet but still found nothing as he snored
away, now curled up on his side. She was about to give up
when she saw a small diary at his bedside. She flicked
through it: just the odd memo about dental appointments
and mortgage payments but listed at the back was a neat
row of numbers. She jotted them down, didn't know if they
meant anything or not, and then replaced the diary, turning
off the lights and letting herself out. Jim remained fast
asleep on his bedroom floor.

Connie waited for the late-night bus and had a long walk
home at the other end. It was raining and she got soaked,
so by the time she let herself into her bedroom she was in a
foul mood. She couldn't sleep straight away because she
still felt angry; she was being used, she told herself, almost
as much as when she was with Lennie. Well, she wasn't
going to take much more of it. Let one of the others get
pawed all over, she was well and truly sick of it. She cuddled
her pillow tightly. She even felt a bit sorry for Jim, who'd
obviously fallen hard. He'd even asked her to marry him,
though whether or not he'd still remember doing so in the
morning was another matter.

Connie tossed and turned, and then felt terribly sad. Jim
was the only man in her entire life who had asked her to
marry him. She bashed her pillow to get more comfortable,
before deciding to make herself a nightcap.

Connie was surprised to see Ester sitting in the kitchen
in a dressing gown, like herself, her hands cupped round a
mug of hot chocolate.

'Can't sleep, huh?'

Ester shook her head. She hated to admit it but she was
jealous: she couldn't sleep for thinking of Julia being with
Norma. 'You have a good night?' she asked.

'Depends what you mean by good,' Connie answered,

resting herself against the Aga. 'I found some numbers listed in his diary. They may be the codes, they may not be, I dunno. He asked me to marry him.'

Ester looked up. 'What?'

'Yeah, funny, isn't it? He's a nice guy, and so's the builder bloke, but all their niceness does is make me miss Lennie.'

'What?'

'I can't stop thinking about him.' She fetched a mug and spooned in some Horlicks.

'Well, you'd better stop bloody thinking of him. You'd better forget he ever existed, even more so after what we all did to get rid of his body.'

Connie poured hot milk into the mug and stirred it, then joined Ester at the kitchen table. 'Why is it the bastards of this world mean more than a nice bloke?'

'Because, sweetheart, you're a sucker.'

'I am not.'

'Course you are. Lennie beat the living daylights out of you.'

'He loved me in his way.'

'What way? Who you kidding? He had you on the game and you call it love? He's not worth even thinking about – no pimp is.'

'He wasn't my pimp.'

'Pull the other one and grow up. He pimped for you, wanted you back on the game. That's why you ran off and left him so don't start fantasizing that it was all lovey-dovey and he'd have you in a cottage with kids and roses round the garden gate. He was a piece of shit.'

'You didn't even know him,' Connie retorted.

'I didn't have to. Know one, know them all. And you got so used to being his punch-bag you—'

'I wasn't!'

'*Yes, you were!*' Ester pushed back her chair and took her dirty mug to the sink, crashing it down on the draining board. 'You got loving all confused with being smacked, sweetheart. Wallop, I love you. Hit me and it means that you do. Beat me up and it means you love me even more – but then, when he's got you on all fours, crawling like a dog, he'll give you one last kick and you're out, used, abused and your head fucked up.'

'You'd know, would you?'

'Yes,' Ester hissed.

'That why you go with women?'

Ester slapped Connie's face hard. Connie sprang to her feet, ready to go back at her, but Ester was too fast, already walking out of the kitchen. 'You got no right to do that.'

'And you've got no right to think you know anything about me. But lemme tell you, I know men, know them better than you, anyone else in this house ever will. Right now you make me sick, moaning about that two-bit punk. We all went out on a limb for you – we fucking buried him! Instead of bleatin' on about how much he loved you, you should thank Christ he's out of your life.'

'Oh, yeah, my life's so much better now, is it?'

'It just might be.'

Connie followed her to the door. 'Is it really going ahead, the robbery? I mean, for real?'

Ester had doubts but right now she was not about to voice them. 'Go and get back to bed. We'll all know soon enough.'

She went upstairs and Connie took her half-finished drink to the sink. She noticed that, as usual, Ester had not washed her mug, or even bothered to rinse it under the tap.

For want of something to do, she began to clean around the sink.

Norma washed up their supper dishes, taking her time as she felt awkward in the strange, rather old-fashioned house, and Julia had been very distant, almost aggressive. Julia's mother was very ill; the stroke had robbed her of speech and movement, and she lay in her bed, her eyes open wide as if staring directly at the ceiling.

Julia had been shocked to see her so immobilized and, as a doctor, she had quickly assessed her condition and known instantly she would need round-the-clock nursing. It would be impossible for her to remain alone at the house, even with a housekeeper. She had sat beside her mother for most of the afternoon. She had a lot to say to her, always had, but they had never really talked. Now they never would. Her mother would never speak again. Julia even had to change her as she was incontinent, had washed her as if she were a baby, cleaned the bed and tidied her thinning white hair. She had not said a word but her gentleness was touching. Now she sat staring at the silent figure, knowing a home was the only option left to her as the elderly housekeeper could not be asked to take care of her, and a nurse was out of the question financially.

Julia held the frail, bony hand. 'Oh, Mama, we should have talked. I'd have liked you to know who I am but, well, it's too late now.'

Norma peeked in. 'I've cleared the dishes and washed around the kitchen. It was a bit grimy.'

'Thank you.' Julia didn't want to talk to Norma, almost resented her presence.

Norma crept to the bed and looked at the old woman.

She made not a sound, never moved a muscle. There was just the vacant stare at the ceiling.

'You can share the bedroom with me,' Julia said quietly.

Norma whispered that she would go downstairs and watch television, and crept out again. Even her creeping around annoyed Julia – maybe because she herself wanted to scream.

She began to pack her mother's nightwear, hairbrushes and toiletries in a small bag, ready for the move. She would arrange a private ambulance in the morning and check all the homes that would take her. She opened and shut drawer after drawer as quietly as possible so as not to disturb the invalid, carrying the garments back and forth to the open case on a low bedside chair. She thought she should perhaps put in some bedjackets or cardigans and started to search through the dressing-table drawers. She saw the newspaper clippings, hidden beneath a fine wool shawl. At first she didn't think anything of them but then, as she removed the shawl, she couldn't help but read the headline: 'Local Doctor in Drug Scandal'.

Julia's heart pounded. She sat down on the dressing-table stool and got out the neat stack of clippings. They detailed her arrest for possession of heroin, her charges for selling prescriptions and her trial and sentence. The secret she had so painstakingly kept from her mother, all the years of lying and frantic subterfuge had been a waste of time because all the time she had known.

She screwed up the clippings into a tight ball and hurled them into the waste-bin but it was a while before the anger rose, humiliation uppermost at first, before she raged at what her mother had forced her to do, and she turned to the silent figure in the bed.

'You knew! You knew, all those years, and you never told me, you never *talked to me!*'

In the drawing room below, Norma heard the banging and scraping from above and she ran up the narrow staircase. When she got to the bedroom, she stood at the doorway, frightened, as Julia shook her mother's bed until it rattled, until the old woman seemed about to roll out of it.

'No, Julia! No, stop it! For God's sake, *stop this*!'

Julia then turned her fury on Norma, ready to lash out at her, at anyone who came near her, but Norma was quite able to take care of herself and gripped Julia tightly. 'Julia, it's me, it's Norma, stop this . . .'

'She knew, Norma. All the years I've broken my fucking back keeping it away from her, and she knew.'

Julia slammed out of the room. Norma didn't understand what she was talking about but she quickly settled Mrs Lawson back on her pillows and tucked in the bedclothes. She leaned over the bed, touching the frail, wrinkled hand. 'It's all right, she'll be fine.'

Norma felt such sadness as the mute figure's helpless fingers tried to hold on to her and tears rolled down her cheeks. 'Don't worry, you'll be taken care of, Mrs Lawson, and I will look after Julia.'

Only the tears indicated that the old lady understood.

When Norma went into Julia's room, she found her lying on her bed, the bed she had used as a girl, and with fists clenched cursing her own stupidity.

She said, 'You shouldn't have done that, upset her like that.'

'What do you know?' Julia spat out angrily.

'Well, maybe she can't talk but she can hear, Julia.'

'I don't give a shit.'

Norma began to massage Julia's back. 'I understand.'

'No, you don't,' Julia said, her face buried in the pillow.

'Try me,' Norma said softly.

Julia rolled over and looked up into her face. 'This was my bedroom, and you know something? I knew I was gay when I was about twelve or thirteen. She was a stable-girl at the local riding school and we came back and we did it in here, then Mother served us tea. We laughed about that.' Julia sat up and leaned against Norma. 'I have wanted to make her understand, to know who I was since then, Norma, but she wouldn't even let me discuss my life. All she wanted was for me to be married and have kids. She still asks . . .' Julia mimicked her mother asking if she had a boyfriend and then she bowed her head. 'You know, maybe she even knows about me being lesbian but she just could never talk about it.'

'So what are you going to do?'

Julia sounded resigned as she said, 'Get her into a home tomorrow, sell this place and that's it. There's nothing for me here. Maybe there never was.'

Later that night Norma washed Mrs Lawson. She kissed her and switched off the light before going up to bed with Julia. They made love and then Norma fell asleep. Later, Julia crept out from under the covers and slipped from the room. She removed Norma's police riding cape and hat from the truck, closing the back as quietly as she could. She packed them into a case and left it in the hallway before returning upstairs. But she did not go back to bed immediately. Instead she inched open the door to her mother's room: she had not moved from the centre of the bed, seeming somehow trapped inside the tight sheet across her chest. She appeared to be asleep.

Julia stood, staring at her, for about five minutes, and then silently left the room. She no longer felt anger, just a total lack of energy, as if she had been drained, and it was then she remembered. Her pace quickened as she went into the bathroom. She had to lie flat on the tiled bathroom

floor as she unscrewed the cheap formica surrounds of
the bath, pulling them away and reaching in, searching
until she found the tin medical box. Not until she had
re-screwed the panel into place did she open the old
battered white box with the scratched red cross in the
centre. Slowly she opened the lid and sighed: there were
the rubber tube, the hypodermic needles, the tiny packets
of white cocaine and one small, screwed-up, tin-foil square
of heroin.

The following morning Julia had made some lists of
what items she wanted from the house. She had arranged
for a local estate agent to come in and also for a home to
take her mother. It was expensive and Norma suggested
they ring round a few others. 'Nope. With the money from
the house I can pay for it.'

'Are you okay?'

'Yes, I'm fine. Just got a lot to get sorted.'

Norma couldn't quite understand Julia's attitude. She
had been talkative at breakfast and had been on the go since
then. She simply put it down to her way of dealing with
the situation and never thought for a moment Julia was
high.

She didn't see her mother again. Norma got her ready
for the ambulance. Julia refused to help when the ambulance arrived, remaining in the drawing room when they
took her away. She was still making phone calls, cancelling
milk, papers, and the housekeeper.

'She's gone,' Norma said sadly.

'Okay, we can leave in about half an hour.' Julia continued writing, calculating how much the house would be
worth. As it had been remortgaged three times, there would
be little or nothing left from the sale. She was going to
need money more than ever before, and if it wasn't from

the robbery, she would have to find some other means to finance her mother's stay at the home.

Norma did not notice her hat and cloak were missing until they left. She didn't seem unduly worried, blaming herself for forgetting to lock the truck. 'Probably be some kids. It's a wretched nuisance because I'll have to fork out for the replacements but at least they didn't nick the truck.'

'Yeah, that's good,' Julia said, and indicated the small case she was carrying out to the car. 'Just a couple of things I thought I'd take back with me.'

Norma started the engine. 'Well, if you need storage space, I've got a huge barn, and your mother has some nice pieces of furniture, antiques.'

As they drove off, Julia didn't look back. The house and her mother were in the past now. She was as good as dead and at least there would be no more lies. She stared out of the window. 'Stupid woman, why? Why did she never tell me she knew?'

Norma said nothing, knowing that Julia wasn't expecting an answer. They headed back to the manor and Norma wondered if Julia would thank her for being with her, for caring, for loving her. 'I love you, Julia,' she said softly.

Julia continued to gaze out of the window, wondering if Ester was missing her. Then she began to think about the train hijack and started to smile: maybe it was the drugs, maybe it was just the thought of doing something so audacious, so, crazy that lifted her spirits.

'Feeling a bit better?' Norma asked.

'Yeah, I'm feeling good, really good!'

*

Dolly was in a ratty mood. She had slept badly and the riding lesson had not been successful. The women bickered and argued, and without Julia they had been subjected to the scorn of the stable-girl as they attempted to canter. By the time they returned to the manor, Dolly had to face the added frustration of finding John waiting to talk to her. She was running low on cash and he stood in her office, refusing to budge.

'I just want to know what's going on. If I lay the men off, I won't get them back. You got half a roof, scaffolding up, I got cement and sand out there. I've laid out for the equipment, Mrs Rawlins. I've kept my end of the bargain.'

'Look, I'm sorry about this but there have been a few problems. If you give me another day or so—'

'But you say that every time I come here.'

'I know, but I can't help it if people don't pay me. It's not that I like doing this to you.'

'The place is unsafe, Mrs Rawlins, and you got kids running around.'

Dolly opened a drawer and took out the last of the cash from the sale of the guns. Five thousand pounds. Now she was almost cleaned out. 'Look, do what you can. If you have to lay a few of the men off then you have to do it but this is all I've got right now.'

John gritted his teeth as he counted out the money, then stashed it in his pocket. 'Okay. At least I'll finish the roof.' He walked out and she could hear him banging down the hallway. She scratched her chin. The idea of the robbery was fading fast. There was no way they could do it, not for a few months, anyway. They couldn't manage the horses, never mind hold up the train.

*

Gloria yelled from the yard for someone to get Dolly as the truck had arrived with the bags of lime. More money had to be paid over to the driver before he would even lift one of the twenty-kilo bags down from the back of the truck. Dolly then had to pay out for the skip that she had ordered. Money was always going out and nothing was coming in.

'What we gonna do with all this lime, then?' Gloria asked, prodding the bag.

'Tip it into the old cess-pit.'

'Oh, yeah? Well, who's gonna do that?'

'All of you. Get them out there.'

'Bloody hell,' moaned Gloria.

Dolly clenched her hands. 'Just get on with it!'

Connie, Ester and Gloria changed into old clothes, big thick gloves and scarves to cover their faces, and began to slit open the bags and tip them into the pit. The lime clouded and burnt their eyes and made their skin itch so there were further moans and groans. Julia returned, bright and breezy as she stood looking at the three figures resembling snowmen.

'It's not funny! You get changed and give us a hand and stop grinnin',' Ester snapped.

As Julia walked off, Connie called after her, the only one to ask about her mother, and Julia shouted back that it was all taken care of. Ester then hurled a sack aside and followed Julia. 'Did that Norma stay with you?'

'Yep, and I got her hat and cape.' Julia held up the case cheerfully.

'Well, you keep her away from here,' Ester said angrily, and Julia smiled happily because Ester was obviously jealous, and went towards the house.

In the kitchen, she found Angela giving the three girls some lunch, and Dolly sitting moodily at the end of the table with her notebook open. She looked up as Julia walked in. 'How was your mother?'

'Mute,' Julia said, and then leaned close to Dolly. 'Got the hat and cape.'

Dolly nodded, then looked to the three girls. 'I don't want any of you going near the big pit out at the back. If you do, you'll get a very hard smack and you won't be allowed to ride Helen of Troy, do you all understand? I see one of you even close to the pit and I will make you very, very sorry.'

Their expressions were glum, and Angela poured another cup of tea for Dolly.

'What's in the pit?'

'Mind your own business, Angela. Take the girls for a nice long walk up to the woods.'

Dolly didn't touch the tea but went out to see how the others were doing. She stopped off at the stables to fetch an old thick canvas bag and walked over to the 'snowmen'. 'When it's finished put this in, see how long it takes to disintegrate. Then fetch some corrugated iron. Take it off the stables roof at the back, and put it over the pit.'

Gloria saluted as if to a sergeant-major but Dolly was not amused and walked off round to the front of the house.

'Well, she doesn't get her hands dirty, does she?' Connie said.

Julia raked at the canvas bag. She showed it to Ester – it was disintegrating fast. 'It works.'

'Yeah, my gloves are rotting, my eyes are red and weeping, my skin feels like I got lice crawling all over it and you and Dolly have done bugger all to help us.'

Julia laughed, as Connie and Gloria dragged two big sheets of rusted corrugated iron towards the pit. 'You can laugh, Julia, but we're all knackered – we've even been riding this morning.'

'How you all doing?' Julia asked.

Ester threw her gloves into the pit. 'We're bloody useless. Gloria almost fell off.'

'I didn't,' Connie said proudly.

Julia slipped her arm round Connie's shoulder. 'That's because you, my darling, have a good seat!'

Ester stared hard at Julia. She was in a very expansive mood – it wasn't like her to be so tactile or amusing. 'You been drinking with that Norma?'

'Nope.' Julia then single-handedly lifted one sheet of the corrugated iron to bang it down over the pit. 'Just feeling good, Ester.'

Mike knew something was going down when he saw Craigh and Palmer having a confab in the corridor. As soon as they saw him, they turned away.

'What's going on?' Mike asked pleasantly.

DCI Craigh sighed. 'A lot, mate. Seems the ruddy estimates that bitch Rawlins sent in are now with the Super and he's gone ape-shit.'

'Shit,' Mike said ruefully.

'You said it, and it's all over us. We got to get it sorted and, Mike, don't expect to get off with a slapped wrist because I'm not covering for you and nor is he.' He jerked his thumb at Palmer. Palmer gave an apologetic shrug.

Mike hesitated. 'What if I'd got a tip-off about—'

'We don't want any more of your fuckin' tip-offs, we got enough problems.' Craigh prodded Mike with his index finger. 'You sit at your desk. This Rawlins business has left us with a lot of aggro and there are back cases that now take precedence. But if there's to be an internal investigation, I'm warning you, I'm not taking the rap.'

Craigh stormed off down the corridor and Palmer looked after him, then back at Mike. 'Super's in with the Chief now so we just have to wait. Maybe it'll all blow over.'

Mike could feel the pit of his stomach churning. He felt trapped and he couldn't see any way out of it. When he got to his desk there was a message to call Colin. Mike held the slip in his hands, half of him wanting to come clean, to tell Craigh everything. He wanted to tell them about Angela and about his mother, but the more he thought about just how much there was to confess, the more he freaked. He was trapped, all right, and there seemed no way out.

Mike took the pen Angela had given him out of his pocket and sucked at the end of it. Then he looked at the clock. He had another couple of hours' work before he could skive off. Maybe the best plan of action was to play it all out, go and see his mate again, go and talk to Rawlins, and then make the decision as to whether or not he should spill the beans.

While Angela was putting the children to bed, Dolly sat behind her desk and the women came in to see her 'Shut the door,' Dolly said quietly.

They lined up, sensing something was going down. Dolly tapped the desk with her pencil, flicking through the little black book. She pointed at Connie. 'You. We have to find out if the numbers you got from the bloke at the signal box are the coded alarms.'

Connie chewed her lip and sighed. 'How do I do that?'

'Get in the signal box and, I dunno, switch on the alarm, see what happens.'

Gloria sat down. 'Well, we are professional, aren't we?'

Dolly glared at her. 'I want you to scout around under the signal box, see where their main electrical and phone cables are, see if we can cut them off.'

'We still going to do it, Dolly?' Ester asked.

'I'm thinking about it,' she replied, as she looked through her book.

'Well, I'm telling you we'll never uncouple the carriage, no way. It's too heavy.'

'Get some bleedin' Semtex and blow the fuckin' thing,' Gloria snarled.

Dolly directed the pencil at Gloria. 'Eh! Shut it, I'm giving out the instructions, not you. And where do you get Semtex from, just as a matter of interest?'

'I dunno. It was just a suggestion,' Gloria said.

'Thank you for that,' Dolly said sarcastically.

'We're never gonna do it,' Ester said.

'Have you sorted out that tape business?'

'When have I had the time?' Ester said.

'You do that tomorrow.'

Dolly ran her fingers through her hair, then leaned on the desk. 'We got to start riding better.'

They all groaned. Dolly took out the pen and opened it, slipping in the small batteries. 'Connie, give this to the bloke in the signal box. This transmitter you place somewhere inside the box. The tail wire, make sure it hangs loose so we get a clear reception. Shove it on a shelf or somethin'. Shouldn't be too hard, it's only just bigger than a matchbox. I've got one under the signal box already but the batteries need changing.'

'We got anything from the signal box?'

Julia snorted. 'Yeah, we know when they eat, fart and go home.'

Dolly was surprised at Julia – she wasn't usually so crude. 'What's the matter with you?'

Julia wiped her nose on her sleeve. 'Got a bit of a cold coming on. Apart from that I'm fine. How are you?'

Dolly raised an eyebrow. 'I'm fine, Julia, but we don't want you in bed sick if we got to ride with you.'

Ester propped herself on the desk. 'Dolly, when are we gonna be told just how we go about the whole thing? I mean, you're a great one for giving orders but we don't really know what we're doing all this for.'

'I'll tell you when I'm ready or when I think you're ready.'

'Oh, fine, yes, ma'am, two bags full, ma'am.'

Dolly's face was frightening, but she didn't blast off, she just said calmly, 'Yes, it will be fine, Ester, but I'm paying out and I don't want any stupid mistakes, like driving round in a stolen car. Like blokes coming here to slap you or any one of us around.'

'Okay, okay, we've been over that.'

'And we'll go over and over it until I'm satisfied. Now get on with what you have to do, all of you.'

Julia sniffed and looked at Ester. 'What do you want us to do?'

Dolly jerked a thumb towards the receiver and the headphones. 'You take it in shifts to listen in at the signal box.'

'Who's listening in to the copper?' Gloria asked.

'I am,' Dolly said as she picked up her briefcase and walked out.

Ester nudged Julia. 'You think she's listening in on us?'
'Put money on it,' Gloria said.

It was a long night, Julia and Ester taking it in shifts, boring hours of listening in at the signal box. It only became interesting when Connie entered and started talking to Jim. She hitched up her skirt as she perched on the table and crooked her finger at him. 'I got a present for you.'

Jim was a bit sheepish and hung-over. 'Look, Connie, about the other night.'

'Forget it, you said a lot of things that maybe you didn't mean.'

'No, I meant every word, I just didn't mean to pass out.'

She wound her legs round his waist. 'Here, this is for you.' She unwrapped the pen and slipped it into his top pocket. 'Keep it close to your heart.'

Ester looked over at Dolly as she walked in. 'He's got the pen. It was a bit distorted to begin with but now we can hear them snogging clear as a bell.'

Dolly glanced at Julia, who had the earpiece in. 'I'm off, be back late. I'm taking Gloria's car.'

Julia beckoned to her and she moved closer. 'I think they're having it away, lot of heavy breathing, you want to hear?'

'All I want to hear is the code for those alarms.'

Julia pressed the earpiece further into her ear. 'That's what he's just talking about. Must have been a quickie in-and-out job.'

*

Connie pulled down her skirt and stepped out of her panties as Jim closed the gates for a passenger train. He did not mess around when it came to working, he was very serious, and Connie edged behind him to wrap her arms round his chest.

'No, just stay off me a second, I got work to do, darlin'.'

Connie sighed, moving close to the alarm box and special telephone. 'If something went wrong on the rail, Jim, what would you do?'

'Get the sack if they found you here.' He looked towards the station as the train headed up the tracks.

'I mean if there was an accident,' she asked, sliding down so as not to be seen from the station.

'Well, with the alarms I got a direct line to the local cop shop, fire brigade and ambulance. They can all be here within four minutes.'

'What about the live wire cable?'

She watched him as he went about his business, pulling the levers down, moving backwards and forwards across the hut.

Julia switched on the main speaker and she, Ester and Dolly could hear the train thundering past the signal box. Then they heard something else, a third voice.

John had been playing detective, waiting, and now he knew he was right – he could see her curly blonde hair. He was standing at the gates, his car engine ticking over, when he looked up at the hut. He knew it was her. As the gates opened and the train passed, he saw her more clearly. She was laughing and chatting away. He drove into the yard beneath the box and ran up the wooden steps. He banged on the door.

'Connie, I know you're in there. *Connie!*'

He burst into the signal box, and Jim whipped round.

'What you think you're doing?' John yelled at Connie.

'Seeing an old friend,' she shouted back.

'She's my girlfriend.' John moved towards Jim.

Jim looked at Connie in confusion 'What's going on?'

'Nothing!' she shrieked, pushing at John.

'You liar! This is the second time I've seen you up here! I'll get him the sack, that's for starters. You shouldn't be up here.'

'I can go wherever I like, it's no business of yours.'

'Yes, it fucking is!'

John threw a punch at Jim who ducked, looking down at the station, terrified someone would be watching. He then went back at John.

'Look, mate, I dunno who you are but you'd better get out of here.'

John grabbed Connie. 'She's coming with me.'

'I am not! You don't own me,' Connie yelled, kicking out at him. She was close to the alarm switch, within inches.

Dolly put her hand over her face. 'One of you had better get up there, get her out.'

The alarm went off. Julia winced, the sound was so loud it screamed through the room. 'Jesus Christ, it's the fucking alarm!' Ester yelled.

Jim's face drained of colour. He shouted for Connie and John to get out as he dialled the station to report a false alarm. Connie saw him punch in each number and closed her eyes, desperate to remember each one in order as John tried to haul her out. They could hear somebody shouting from the platform below. 'Get out of here!' Jim roared. If Connie or John was discovered in his signal box, he'd lose his job for sure.

By now a passing patrol car had heard the alarm and was already heading towards the station, siren blaring.

John dragged Connie down the steps and had only just shoved her into his van when the patrol car hurtled into the yard. The two uniformed officers got out as Jim appeared at the top of the steps. 'It's okay, no problem. It was just a routine test.'

The officers hesitated, one continuing up the steps to discuss it further as the other crossed to John.

'What you doing here?'

John grinned. 'Sorry, mate, just having a quickie with the girlfriend when it went off, talk about being caught short.'

The officer nodded, looking into the van. Connie tittered nervously.

'Well, you shouldn't be in this area, so go on, on your way.'

John drove out, Connie sitting as far away from him as possible. 'You had no right to do that, you know,' she said. 'I don't belong to you. I can have as many boyfriends as I like. You even live with a girl and I don't get uptight about that.'

'I don't live with anyone any more.'

'Well, don't blame it on me.'

John slammed on the brakes. 'It's over between us because I thought you were serious about me.'

'Oh, do me a favour.'

'I just did. You could have been arrested for being up there with him, you know, and he'll probably lose his job.'

'Only if you rat on him.'

John clenched the steering wheel till his knuckles turned white. 'I don't understand you, I thought—'

'You thought what?' she said, her face red with anger.

'That maybe you . . . that I was seeing you, Connie. I made a mistake.'

'Yes, you did, John. I don't like being told who I can go out with by you or anybody else. If I want to screw—'

'Stop talking like that.'

'Talking like what?'

He turned on her. 'A cheap tart.'

She slapped his face and pushed at him with her hands, almost wanting him to slap her back, but he shook his head and turned away. 'I'll take you home.'

He started the engine, feeling sick. He didn't know how to handle her or what to say. He really thought she cared for him but, then, she'd ditched him the other day. 'Why have you led me on?' he asked softly.

She slipped her arm around his big, wide shoulders, massaging the nape of his neck. 'I'm just not ready to get serious about anyone, not yet.'

He shrugged her hand away. 'Not as if you were any spring chicken. How old are you, anyway? You carry on like this and no decent man'll want you.'

Connie felt as if he had punched her, harder than anything Lennie had ever given her. 'I'm twenty-nine.'

'Well, you got a good figure but I don't think you can count, sweetheart. You're not twenty-nine, I am.'

She didn't know what to say. She just felt the tears welling up, trickling down her cheeks. She was thirty-five but he made her feel as if she was old and worn out. He had hurt her deeply and she was incapable of even trying to come on to him. She snuffled as the van turned into the lane by the manor.

'Just drop me here,' she said quietly.

He stopped the van sharply, then leaned across her to open the door for her.

'Jim asked me to marry him,' she said as she climbed out.

'Well, he's a sucker. He can have you and I won't rat on him. With you he's gonna need every penny he can make unless you do more of those films you told me about.'

She slammed the door shut hard and teetered off along the uneven road in her stilettos. John watched her perfect arse as she sashayed along, her perfect figure and her curly blonde hair. Then he drove on, wondering whether or not he could make it up with his girlfriend. Maybe he should even ask her to marry him, she was a decent girl. Connie was trash, he'd sort of always known it, and sometimes it takes a Connie to make you come to your senses.

Julia passed him as she returned to the manor, not realizing he had given Connie a lift back. She turned into the drive and pulled up alongside Connie, winding down the window. 'I was sent out to see if you needed any assistance.'

'I obviously didn't,' snapped Connie, and continued towards the front door. She watched Julia head round to the stables before she let herself in, and ran up the stairs. She couldn't face any of them but Dolly caught her halfway. 'Eh! You get the alarm codes? You set them off, didn't you?'

Connie sniffed, refusing to turn back to her. 'Yes, I got them, but right now I want to be alone.'

'Right now, Connie love, we discuss it. Come down here.'

'Just stop telling me what to do, I done what you

wanted, now leave me alone.' She went on up the stairs. Dolly looked at her watch and then back to the drawing room. She was tired herself but she had to make sure Mike wasn't setting them up. She felt it was all falling apart and it seemed, at times, that she was the only adult amongst them. She didn't feel like their mother in any way but she was beginning to think she should call it all off, get rid of the lot of them. She smiled then: she'd got the perfect place, she could push each one of them into the lime pit.

Connie sat in front of her dressing table mirror, studying her face. Why had John said she looked old? 'Maybe because you are old,' she whispered, and then twisted her neck, pouting her heroine's smile. 'Gonna be rich, though, and then you'll be young and beautiful, and . . .' She stared at herself and for the first time knew she would go through with any robbery Dolly Rawlins had in mind. Rising out of her beloved Marilyn was a Connie that rarely appeared, the other side that she hid away, the angry, bitter, tough little Liverpool tart that'd give any lad a back-hander, just like her dad gave her, like every man seemed to think he could dole out to her. She'd taken the punches, taken the shit, seemed like all her life she'd taken the easy way out, and she wasn't going to take any more. She pouted and then let her wide sexy lips close into a tight line. 'Fuck you, Marilyn Monroe . . .'

Connie breathed on the mirror and, with the tip of her finger, traced the numbers Jim had called to contact the police station. All he'd said was that it was a false alarm. This was valuable information; now Dolly had the code for the alarm. Connie beamed: she wasn't as dumb as they all made out, but, as the numbers faded in the mirror, she began to panic, searching for something to write them down. She found her black eyebrow pencil and a piece of tissue, then closed her eyes, replaying in her mind the moment Jim, in his panic, punched in the numbers. She might be no good with words, for reading and the like, but she'd always been able to count. No punter ever short-changed tough little Connie Stephens by a penny.

When Dolly appeared, she asked her twice if she was sure she had the right code, staring at the tissue with the childish figures.

'Yeah, those are the numbers. If the alarm goes off, we call that number.'

Dolly gave that odd smile. 'You did good, darlin', very good.'

Connie preened but there was no further praise as Dolly left the room, folding the tissue into her pocket.

She was pleased; it meant that the signal-box telephone wires had to be beneath the hut and if all Jim had used was a telephone, all she had to do was cut the wires because the alarm would also be connected to the central box.

Dolly went out alone later that night. She used a map-reading torch, inching her way beneath the signal box, to check for herself. And, sure enough, in the area marked 'No Admittance', was a large, secure, BT fixture, similar to those in residential areas, the ones an engineer sits by with hundreds of tiny wires, and you pass him by wondering what the hell he is doing. Dolly could just make out that she would need some kind of sledge-hammer to prise it open. It didn't matter which wire belonged to which telephone; she'd simply hatchet her way through the lot of them.

Dolly enjoyed the walk back to the house in the darkness. The air smelt good and clean, a light rain had fallen, the ground sparkled in the moonlight, and her expression wasn't the usual taut grimace but a sweet soft smile as he talked to her in that low soft voice.

'Check everything out for yourself. Never leave anything

to chance or to anyone else. Remember, Doll, look out for yourself.' Dolly stopped and his voice died. It was strange, as if she knew she would never hear it again, because a new thought began to dawn. What if it had been her voice that Harry had listened to. It had been Dolly who had quietly put him in the right direction. She had never been given the credit by him and had never acknowledged how much he had listened to her. Perhaps not until it was too late. But by then she had been betrayed and he had forgotten his own warnings. He could never have anticipated that she would kill him.

CHAPTER 16

MIKE HAD a few beers with Colin. He'd called him to say that the prearranged dinner would have to be on another night as there were problems at work; some of his mates had got flu so he was doing extra night shifts.

They talked for a while about the army but then Colin switched the subject to Mike possibly being taken on at his company.

'Yeah, well, you know, Colin, I've been thinking about it, but it sounds like it'd bore the pants off me. I'm not into schleppin' around in a security wagon all day with a few drops here and there.'

Colin downed his pint. 'You got it wrong, Mike, this isn't that kind of company. Like I told you, we handle the big stuff.' He leaned in and lowered his voice. 'We deliver the sacks to the mail-trains. Ever since they had the big robberies at the main stations, we were brought in. You know about them?'

Mike drank some beer. 'Nah, they'd be handled by the Robbery Squad, special division, well, if it's a big one.'

Colin stood up, buttoning his jacket. 'Well, if anyone hit what we're carrying it'd be the biggest in history.'

'Oh, yeah?' Mike could feel his bladder giving way.

Colin leaned ever closer and whispered something as Mike looked on in stunned amazement. 'You kidding me? That much?'

Colin winked, tapped his nose. 'That's classified information but that's how much.'

'Shit. That's mind-blowing.'

'Yeah, and so's the security. Routes change every few months, just to safeguard it ever being leaked.' Colin patted Mike's head, grinning. 'Think about it and we'll have that curry next week.'

'Okay, how about next Thursday?'

Colin agreed. 'Fine by me. We'll take the wives, shall we? Make a night of it.'

Ester slipped her arm around Julia, drawing her close. 'What are you taking, Julia?' She tried to move away but Ester held on tightly. 'I know, Julia, I can tell by your eyes and your mouth. You get very chatty. So what are you taking?'

Julia shoved at her. 'For chrissakes, nothing. What's got into you?'

Ester pushed her away. They kept their voices low, afraid to be heard. 'Lemme see your arm.'

'No, I won't. Why are you doing this? Don't you trust me?'

Ester pinched her face. 'No, I don't. You've been acting up since you got back from your mother's.'

Julia shook her off but Ester grabbed her again. 'Tell me, Julia, or I'll tell Dolly.'

Julia rolled her eyes. 'Okay, look, I took one hit, some gear I'd left at Mother's, just the one, I swear before God. I was feeling so bad, and that Norma was hanging on to me.'

Ester got out of bed and looked around the room. 'I'll find it, if you got a stash here. I'll find it, Julia.'

Julia reached out for her. 'Darling, there's nothing, on my mother's life. There was just a teeny-weeny bit. I wouldn't get back on it, you know that.'

Ester slowly allowed Julia to draw her back to bed. 'I hope not, Julia, because if you *have* started, you're fucked. And if Dolly found out she'd kick you out of here so fast.'

Julia wrapped her arms around Ester, kissing her neck. 'I wouldn't do it, Ester.'

They kissed and then curled up together as Julia tried to think of a good hiding place for her stash and Ester wondered if she should warn Dolly. To use Julia in the robbery if she was back on junk would be dangerous. Then she started to think about returning the video and the more she thought about it, the more she began to think she should piss off and leave. The robbery was becoming a farce anyway.

Gloria felt restless. Her back ached constantly from all the horse-riding and she kept thinking about Eddie, wondering how he was. Not that she missed him; if she calculated the years they had been married, the time spent together was minimal because he had been in and out of prison so much and she had been inside herself on and off. It hadn't really been a marriage at all. He was just somebody that was connected to her, bad or good, and there was nobody else. Her kids didn't even know who she was by now. She wouldn't know them if she came face to face with them. Maybe it was having the little girls around her that brought back the memories. She'd had her kids taken away when she first got arrested. Like Kathleen's girls, they had been shuttled from one foster home to another before she signed the adoption papers. She did it to give them a better life. She wondered if they had, and then started to cry. She cried for the long, wasted years and eventually fell asleep.

It felt as if she'd only just dropped off when her door was banged loudly.

'Come on, get up! Time to ride.' It was Julia. She was usually the first up and about as she took Helen of Troy out in the early mornings.

That morning they had a breakthrough. It happened almost all at once: the fear left them and they went from a canter into a gallop and at the end of the two-hour lesson, they all began talking at once, well pleased with their prowess. The general up feeling continued as they ate the eggs and bacon Angela had prepared. Coffee and toast went down as they listened to Julia giving each one separate hints as to where they had gone wrong that morning.

Dolly had a private discussion with Julia. She was getting worried that the stable-girls might get suspicious and she wanted Julia to book in at the other place so they could switch for a while. This also meant they would have to get used to different animals, which Julia was a little pessimistic about, but Dolly was insistent. She also mentioned to Julia about finding out exactly where they kept the keys to their local stable-yard and then asked her to find out how they could clad the horses hoofs.

'What do you want to do that for?' Julia asked.

Dolly kept her voice low. 'We'll make a hell of a lot of noise coming out of that stable. We got to ride down the lane, past two cottages, so look into it. We got to be silent.' She went back to her coffee and was left at the table with her precious notebook as Angela washed up. Ester and Gloria checked the tapes to see if there had been any developments at the signal box. They were now armed with Connie's information and the number she had seen Jim dial to cancel out the police. They also knew they had four minutes before the police could get to them unless a panda car happened to be cruising nearby.

Gloria had also been under the signal box. She had called out for Buster, a make-believe dog, but nobody had stopped her as she clocked the electric cables, the main electricity-power sector and the telephone wires. Gloria had also seen the large Danger signs with the red zig-zag and hadn't dared get any closer as they unnerved her. Shivers went up her aching spine because the voltage was so high: Connie had told them at supper one night that a dog got on to the line and was thrown up into a tree!

When Gloria got back to the manor, she had severe doubts. 'How do we get on the line? We'd get blown into a friggin' tree if any of us hit that cable.' She was drawing a map of the signal box and the railway junction. 'If the gates open and that train moves, it's gonna go over the bridge, right? Well, after that it'll pick up speed and no way is it gonna stop.' Gloria prodded her diagram with a chipped fingernail.

Ester frowned, turning the map round. 'Maybe she's gonna think to stop it just at the crossings, then we ride up to it.'

'No way. She stops it there and we're screwed. There are lanes either side of it – we couldn't stop a cop car with a bleedin' horse!' Gloria sniffed.

Julia leaned over them, arms around each of their shoulders. 'Maybe she's gonna blow it up.'

'Oh, shut up,' Ester rapped.

'We still got three shotguns,' Gloria said flatly, 'but it's a bloody big train.'

Ester shook her head. 'No way, they'd be like ping-pong balls off the side of the train.'

They all remained staring at Gloria's drawing as she took a thick red pen and drew in the Danger zig-zags. 'These will blow us off the track without any shotgun, loves.'

Ester said to Julia, 'You know, I think it's time we had a

serious chat. We're all here being ordered around to do this and that and she's keeping her mouth shut, scribbling in that ruddy black book of hers. I reckon we've got to face her out, ask her just what she intends doing and, more important, how she's gonna do it.'

Gloria crossed to the window and drew back the curtain. 'We got a visitor. Shit! It's that ruddy cop, Angela's bloke. I told you we couldn't trust that two-faced bitch.'

They huddled at the window, watching, as Dolly walked towards Mike, who was getting out of the car. 'Stay put, love, let's just go for a drive, shall we?'

Mike waited for Dolly to get in beside him and then reversed, turned the car round and drove out.

'What do you make of that, then?'

Ester sucked in her breath, 'Well, I dunno about you two but I think it stinks. What's she doing driving around with him? What's he doing here anyway?'

Dolly and Mike parked in a small turning which led into a field. He said what he'd come to say and then waited.

'Ex-army bloke, is he?' Mike nodded. 'You sure it's the truth?'

'All I'm saying is what he told me. Now, I done what I said I would and that's it.'

Dolly pursed her lips. 'Yes, but I'm worried. I mean, how do I know I can trust you?'

Mike leaned back in his seat. 'I have to trust you. Don't stitch me up, Mrs Rawlins.'

'Oh, I know, love, but I've got more to lose than you.'

'I got my job, my kids, my wife. I don't want to know anything else. Like I said, I've done what you asked me and that's it.'

Dolly examined her fingernails. 'Sorry, love, it isn't. I need some Semtex.'

'*What?*'

'You heard.'

'I can't get that kind of thing!'

'What about your friend?'

'You must be joking! He works for the ruddy security firm, I can't go asking him for bloody Semtex. As it is I've got myself in trouble – he thinks I want a job with his firm. No way.'

Dolly shifted her weight in the seat. 'What about some of your other old army friends? Could they help at all?'

'Look, I got to go, I can't do any more.' He hung on tightly to the steering wheel. 'Let me off the hook, Mrs Rawlins, and if you want some advice, whatever you're planning, and I've got a bloody good idea what it is, you'll never hit that security wagon. It's armour-plated, they got a convoy, cops at the front, cops at the back, they keep right on its tail. You do yourself a favour and scrap whatever you're thinking of doing.'

'Why? Because you know about it?'

'Because it's a no-hoper right from the start and—'

'And?' Dolly waited, watching him, seeing him sweating.

'Look, I grass on you and I'm in the frame so hard I'd get time just for what I done to date – I won't grass on you. All I'm doing is telling you to pull out, forget it. I don't care how many blokes you're using, you'll never do it.'

Dolly opened the car door and looked down at him. 'Thanks for the advice, maybe you're right.'

She straightened up and could see Angela heading towards her with the three little girls. 'Here's Angela and, Mike, she doesn't know anything. You tell her and she'll freak out.'

'Well, at least that's something.'

Angela was almost at the car when she saw Mike. 'Hello, my darlin's.' Dolly held out her arms for the girls and they ran to her. One had been collecting some pussy-willow twigs and presented them to her.

'Thank you.' She turned to Angela. 'Have a word with Mike, just a few minutes, I'll wait here.'

Dolly took the girls towards a hedge and began looking for a bird's nest, but she could hear what they said and she'd noticed that Mike still had the pen stuck in his jacket pocket.

Angela sat on the edge of the passenger seat, the door open. 'Hello, Mike.'

'Hello, sweetheart.' He reached out and took her hand. 'Look, I know what I said to you the other day was crass, I wasn't thinking. I'm sorry about the baby, I really am.'

She clung to his hand. 'I love you.'

He sighed. 'I know, but, Angela, it can't work. I got a wife and two kids and I've no intention of leaving them. I never had. If I led you to believe I would, then it was a shit thing to do but you have to know, it's over, sweetheart. It should never have started.'

'But it did, Mike.'

'Yes, I know, and it's all my fault but you're better off without me.'

She started to cry, and he cupped her face between his hands. 'I'm sorry, really sorry.'

Dolly coughed and called over, 'We should go, Angela love. Say goodbye to the nice man, girls.'

The three little girls waved at Mike, even though they had no idea who he was. Angela got out of the car, weeping. He pulled the door shut, feeling like a heel. He wound down his window. 'Mrs Rawlins, can I have a quick word?'

Dolly went to the window. 'You hurt her, get her involved, and I'll see you get busted.'

'Will you now?'

He knew the threat sounded empty. 'Why? Why are you even thinking about it? You got those kids.'

'And you got their mother banged up,' she spat out fast and he turned to face her.

'You got that house – why? Tell me why.'

She seemed bored by the conversation. 'Because I won't have it for long, I'm broke.'

'So are a lot of people but they don't do what you're doing.'

She cocked her head to one side. 'I'll look after Angela, don't you worry about her. You just worry about me, Mike love, and remember, I know everything.'

Mike felt worn to a frazzle but he knew she wasn't finished with him yet. It wasn't anywhere near over; now, somehow, he had to get hold of some Semtex and it made him sick just thinking about it.

They watched him drive down the lane, Dolly with a small child's hand in hers. 'Don't cry over him, Angela, he's not worth it. You're gonna lead your own life now.'

Angela picked up little Sheena as they all walked down the lane.

'You ever been to Switzerland?' Dolly asked suddenly.

'No, I never been nowhere abroad,' Angela said.

'Well, as soon as you get that passport, you're gonna get us secret travel tickets, all five us, with not a word to the others, because that's where we'll all go, Switzerland.'

Dolly breezed into the drawing room and was confronted by a stony-faced Gloria, Ester, Julia and Connie.

'We want to know what the hell is going on,' Ester said angrily.

Dolly put her hands on her hips. 'You sorted out that business with the video, have you?'

'You know I haven't,' Ester snapped.

'Then when it's done, when I'm ready, we'll talk. That goes for all of you, all right? *Is that all right?*' She crooked her finger at Connie. 'You go and get the shotguns today. You, Gloria, give them all a lesson in how to use them. Go up into the woods and don't come down again until you can all handle them.'

'You know how to use them, do you, Dolly?' Gloria asked sarcastically.

'My husband made sure I could always take care of myself. And you, Ester, sort that video business. You, Julia, get the cladding for the horses, and, Connie, you go to that builder, and tell him to order a leaf-suction machine. I dunno what you call them but they suck up garden leaves.'

'I can't see him,' Connie said petulantly.

'Why not?'

'Because I hate his guts.'

Dolly turned on her and pushed her backwards. 'Then unhate him, just do it. That goes for all of you. We get through today and then maybe tonight we'll talk.'

They watched her walking out, calling for Angela and the girls to get ready.

'What did that cop want?'

Dolly stopped as she reached the door. 'You'll know later. *Angela!* Dress them up in warm clothes.' She turned back to the angry women. 'We're going on a boat. See you later for the ride.' The door closed behind her.

'I think she's bats,' Gloria said.

Ester shrugged. 'Well, she's got until tonight and then

we force her to come out with whatever she's got inside that twisted head of hers.'

'She is twisted, isn't she?' Connie said.

Julia sprang up, 'Well, let's get cracking. We'll know by tonight so why waste time talking about it? Let's just do what she wants and keep her happy.'

Dolly began to row. She had one oar, Angela the other, and they began to propel the boat slowly to the centre of the small lake, the three girls sitting on the seat at the bow.

'Look, look, it's a bridge,' Sheena said, pointing.

Dolly nodded. 'Yes, love, it's a bridge. Maybe we'll see a train crossing it today.'

The boat made its way, rocking – neither Angela nor Dolly was adept at rowing. It took them a while to get to the centre of the lake and then they sat and rested as Dolly caught her breath. She leaned on the oar and carefully monitored the bridge: there was at least a good twenty-foot drop down to the lake beneath at the lowest point of the bridge. She then glanced at the boat-house on the other side.

'Is this your boat, Dolly?' Kate asked.

'No, love, it belongs to an old man, lives not far from the manor, in one of those cottages. He lent it to me.'

'Can we come out again?' Sheena piped up.

'Yes, we can borrow his boat any time we want.'

They shouted with excitement and Dolly spotted the floating dock. 'Let's go over to that boat-house, Angela, maybe we can go ashore for a little walk.'

The innocent-looking boating party headed towards a small wooden jetty. Two speed-boats were tied up, well covered with green tarpaulins. Dolly made each girl remain in their seat until she herself had stepped ashore to guide each one out with Angela's help.

'Can we go in a speed-boat?' Sheena asked.

'Not today, darlin', another time maybe.'

Angela was told to take the girls for a ramble, while Dolly remained sitting at the side of the jetty. She began to make notes in her little black book, her eyes flicking from the jetty to the bridge, from the lake to the undergrowth, and then she focused on the bridge for a long, long time.

The women lined up to practise with the shotguns. It was not as much of a fiasco as Gloria thought it was going to be. She showed them over and over how to load and unload the cartridges before she would allow them to fire. She told them sternly that they must pay close attention. She'd not listened when her dad was first showing her – it had been at the fairground – but she'd been over-confident. She held up her left hand. 'See that? Did it when I was twelve. It wasn't a shotgun, it was an automatic but it snapped back and bang, me thumb hung off at a very dodgy angle, so listen to what I tell you. We can't afford no accidents. Take the weight into your shoulder, left hand to steady and support the barrel, right index finger on the trigger, but no need to give it much strength, they're oiled and you need just a light squeeze, don't jerk it. They got a big kick these shotguns, so be prepared for it. If you don't hold it right, like what I'm showing you, you'll get a bruise on yer collar-bone an' it could whack into yer cheekbone, bring tears to your eyes, I'm tellin' you.'

Dolly stopped rowing as they heard the shotgun blasts. She turned towards the woods and then waved to Angela to stop rowing as she took out her notebook and quickly jotted something down. *Bang!* the shotgun went again.

LYNDA LA PLANTE

'Somebody's firing a gun,' Angela said.
'Yeah, be up in the woods. Duck-shooting around here.'
Angela said, 'I haven't seen any ducks.'
'Well, you wouldn't, would you? Soon as they hear a blast they take off.' Dolly suddenly roared with laughter. Another bang. This time Dolly frowned. It was very loud and the last thing they needed was some nosy-parker wondering what they were doing. *Bang. Bang*. She started to row as further gun blasts went off. She couldn't blame them, she'd told them to do it, but she hadn't reckoned it would be quite so loud. *Bang. Bang. Bang*.

Julia lowered the shotgun. The tree they were aiming at was splintered. 'Maybe we've done enough for today. The last thing we want is some bastards coming up here to find out what's going on.'

They all agreed, and under Gloria's beady eye unloaded and collected all the spent cartridges before they started back to the manor. Mid-way they stopped. The shotguns were now wrapped in their waterproof covers, and the women stashed them in the trunk of a dead tree.

Ester had already left for London and Connie for the builder's yard. Julia was sitting at the kitchen table, cutting old sacks with a knife. 'I can use these with a drawstring, pad it out with some sawdust, that should be enough.'
'Fine. Do it in the stables, not in the kitchen. And when Gloria comes back get her to help you.'
Julia snatched up the sacks. 'Right, and we got a ride booked for five o'clock. I found out the stables' key is always left under a plant pot and . . .' But Dolly was ushering the girls ahead for an afternoon kids' programme

378

on TV, so Julia went out to the stables, closing the gate behind her. Opening one of the packets of cocaine, she took out a pocket mirror, and laid a small amount of the powder on the mirror. She chopped it deftly and fast. Then she took an already tightly rolled five-pound note and snorted, sniffing hard, licking the residue off the mirror. She felt better, carefully replaced the mirror and the fiver in her pocket, and then started hacking at the sacks. Stacking the squares in a neat pile at her feet, she had cut up about eight when Gloria burst in.

'Bleedin' walked to the local shop. What a load of half-wits! I dunno, they look at me like I got two fuckin' heads.'

Julia studied Gloria. She was wearing a pair of jeans that were too tight, a strange purple silk shirt, knotted at the waist with her tits half hanging out from some wire contraption brassière that went out in the fifties. Her blonde hair was in need of bleach, the black roots over an inch long. She was also wearing a baggy man's riding jacket. 'It's the wellington boots, Gloria, they're very sexy.'

She laughed, a loud barking sound. 'Piss off. I need them, having to wade through that bloody mud lane. Them pot-holes get you every time.' She squatted down, picking up one of the cut squares. 'What're these for, then?'

'The horses' hooves.'

'Oh, of course! Any fool would have known that. What you talkin' about?'

'Dolly's orders, Gloria, so don't ask, just start sewing.'

Connie leaned against the hut door and peeked in. 'Hi, how you doing?'

John looked across and went back to opening his bills. She strolled in and leaned closer. 'You were very rude to me last night – you know that, don't you?'

He sighed. 'Yeah, but I'm not sorry, and don't sit on the desk, it's got a wonky leg. What do you want?'

'Well, you're supposed to be fixing our roof and, like, nobody is there so Mrs Rawlins sent me to ask when you're going to do it.'

He scratched his head. 'Tomorrow. I got a few things lined up for today and the men are all out.'

Connie slipped on to his knee. 'Well, that's convenient, then, isn't it?'

He wouldn't put his arm around her but leaned back in the old swivel chair. 'What do you want?'

'What you didn't give me the other afternoon.'

She circled his face with her hands and kissed him, prising open his mouth with her tongue. He didn't resist for long and his arms were soon wrapped around her. She could feel his erection and wriggled on his knee. 'Oh, you're very easy to please, aren't you?' she whispered, licking his ear. He started to unbutton her shirt and she kept on licking and kissing, hoping someone would come in and he'd have to leave. When they remained uninterrupted she knew he would screw her. Well, she'd been screwed in some worse places – but never for a machine that sucked up bloody leaves.

Ester leaned forward to the taxi driver. 'Okay, love, I'm going in this house here. I want you to wait. If I'm not out within five minutes, will you ring on the doorbell? And keep this for me.' She passed over the envelope with the tape. He looked at it, then at Ester. 'Five minutes.'

'Yep, that's all, no more.'

They were parked outside a big elegant house in the Boltons. She stepped out, adjusted her dark glasses and walked slowly up the covered canopied entrance. She stood for a moment on the steps, noticed the two security cameras before ringing the bell. Part of her was saying what a stupid bitch she was to come here and do what Dolly had told her, but if it kept the old bitch quiet, why not?

Hector opened the door and looked at her. 'Surprise, surprise! Ester Freeman herself!'

She stepped in and he shut the door behind her. She raised her arms as he frisked her for a weapon, spending more time than necessary patting her entire body. 'Poor way to get your rocks off, isn't it, Hector? Here, look in my handbag. I've not got the cash for a gun, darlin'.'

Hector searched it. 'What do you want?'

'To get off the hook.'

He smirked at her. 'You got a lot of bottle, Ester. Either that or you're fucking stupid.'

'Look, prick, right now I'd go down on you for fifty quid, I'm that broke, so let's stop the crap and talk.'

Hector ushered her along the thick-piled cream carpet into a double-doored drawing room filled with china cabinets and more Capo di Monte than they have at Asprey's. 'Sit down.'

'Look, I got five minutes. If I don't walk out that cab driver out there will come in.'

'That really scares me. Sit down.'

She sat on a peach-silk-covered chair and crossed her legs. 'I've got the video, the only copy. You can have it but I just want to know that you'll stop pestering me.'

Hector perched on an identical chair, swinging a set of gold worry beads round his finger. 'What you done with the Saab? You nicked it, didn't you? Rooney was screaming about it.'

'You must be joking. I wouldn't touch any motor of his, more than likely hot as shit. He's just a liar and he got his heavies to give me a real going-over. You get your bloody

Range Rover back, did you? He gave me the money for a taxi. That was the last I saw of Rooney.'

'So what you after? If it's money, you're even more stupid than I give you credit for.'

'To give you the video of your boss's kids screwing two of my girls. You can have it back and for nothing. I just want to know that it's over.'

Hector chortled. 'Don't be so fucking stupid. You've been a naughty girl, and you know he won't let you off the hook. You shouldn't have been so greedy – you got paid a lot of dough.'

'I also did three years and I'm telling you, you beat me up, knock me around, and I'll go straight to the cops. This time I'll give them names, all right, and he won't get off with his diplomatic immunity this time.'

Hector was about to hit her when the door opened. Even though Ester couldn't see who was behind it, she knew, from Hector's face, it was the boss.

She saw the cameras at the corners of the embossed ceiling – the whole place was monitored so every word they said must have been overheard. She waited as the two men whispered outside the half-closed door, and began to get a little uneasy, afraid Hector might turn back and beat the hell out of her. She was putting a lot of trust in the cab driver.

Hector gestured for her to join him. 'Your lucky day. The tape.'

'I'll go and get it but it's over, Hector.'

'Yeah. Like I said, it's your lucky day. Come on.'

They went out just as the driver was getting out of the taxi. Ester got into the back. 'Give him that envelope, love.' The cabbie looked at Ester, then at Hector, and reached in for the envelope.

Hector snatched it out of his hand and pulled down the

passenger window. 'Ester, this had better be the only copy. If it isn't, you won't just get a rap round the head, you'll get taken out, understand?'

Ester rapped on the glass between her and the driver. 'Marylebone station.' They drove off, Hector watching from the pavement, as the cabbie eased back the partition.

'I won't ask what that was about, darlin'.'

'Good,' she said, slamming it shut. She sat back in the seat. Maybe it was for the best. It just pissed her off that if she'd had the right back-up, been able to afford a few heavies, she'd have made a lot of dough on that video. As it was, she didn't have more than a few quid to her name. She hated being broke. She hadn't been dependent on anyone since she first went to prison aged seventeen. She'd learned then not to trust anyone, especially a man, had spent the majority of her life sussing men out, what they wanted, and she'd given it, until she'd made enough money and got girls to do it for her.

She was still in debt up to her eyeballs with the bank but that didn't concern her — that kind of debt never did. She'd just move on. What did concern her was where she would move to. She gazed unseeingly from the cab window. If Dolly really was serious about the robbery, she would live abroad, maybe Miami. All she needed was a break and a lot of cash — she'd always needed both. When she'd had the cash she never got a break because she'd been busted so many times. Ester had spent much of her life in prison, all over the country, busted if not for prostitution, for kiting and dealing in stolen goods. At one time her only ambition was to be top dog in prison and she had become it, taking more punishment or solitary than any other con. She climbed up walls with hysteria, kicked and bit prison officers with a blind fury that used to overtake her. Sitting in the cab, remembering, she reckoned that Dolly Rawlins would be at the end of one of her furies very soon. She'd taken enough of her orders, enough of her bullshit. There had better be a talk when she got home, and if there wasn't she'd let Dolly have it. It was about time one of the women did. They were being taken for suckers.

Ester paid off the taxi but didn't give him a tip – she couldn't, it had cleaned her out of all the cash she had. The journey back to the manor didn't calm her down, quite the reverse. She was about to challenge Dolly: if she wasn't serious about robbing that security wagon then Ester would do it.

CHAPTER 17

MIKE WAS late getting back on duty after the meeting with Dolly and Angela. When he passed the main desk, the duty sergeant looked up at him, wagging his finger. 'You're in it, mate. DCI Craigh's been in and out looking for you.'

Mike pulled a face and went into the incident room. 'Hear DCI Craigh's looking for me, anyone know where he is?'

Palmer looked in at the door, overhearing. 'Where the fuck have you been?'

'I was at home, then I got sick and—'

Palmer moved closer. 'Super and the Chief are in with the Gov, they want me and you. I think it's coming down.'

Mike slumped into his seat. 'What they want?'

Palmer looked over to the door and back to Mike. 'Well, that bloody ten grand claim from Mrs Rawlins started it all. Now, well, they're digging into everything.'

'Shit.'

'Yeah, all over us, so get your act together.'

Mike began to get out his files as Palmer was tannoyed to go to the main conference room immediately.

'Is it gonna stay internal?' Mike called after Palmer.

'I bloody hope so,' he said as he disappeared.

*

Craigh's hands hung loosely in front of him. He had been explaining why they had begun the investigation into the diamond robbery. The Chief had gone over everything. Tight-lipped, he read about the two warrants and listened to the reason behind the investigation into Dorothy Rawlins.

'I'm not interested in a robbery that went down eight, nine years ago. Right now we have to straighten out this entire fiasco because that's what it is, from the death of James Donaldson down. One minute you got her with a supposed stash of diamonds, the next with weapons . . .'

Craigh went over the reliable tip-off syndrome and was interrupted by the Chief. 'You call Eddie Radford reliable?'

Craigh coughed and pulled at his collar. 'Well, we got a phone call with the information that a certain amount of weapons belonging to Radford were being held at the Grange Manor House.'

The Chief slapped the reports. 'I can read, Detective Chief Inspector, but what I am reading into all this has a slightly different slant from what you're trying to bullshit me with.'

Craigh sat back in his chair. He didn't look up, he could hear the flick, flick of the pages as the Chief went through one file after another, and then slapped the top one.

'You want to tell me about DS Mike Withey?'

Craigh loosened his tie. He had tried to cover for Mike, but it was pointless now.

'I am referring to the fact that his sister, a Shirley Ann Miller, was shot in the armed raid that you and your team have been trying to . . .'

'Sir, I have to say that at the outset of my investigation I was unaware that Withey had any personal grievances against Mrs Rawlins. But that said—'

386

'That said, Detective Chief Inspector, Rawlins was never accused of having any part in that robbery. She was never accused because there was never any evidence to connect her with it. She was charged with the manslaughter of her husband, not the diamond robbery.'

'Yes, I know, sir, but—'

'But I am suggesting that your DS, because of his personal motivation—'

'He believed that Rawlins did, in fact, have something to do with it, sir.'

'Her husband might have, before she shot him, but dead men can't talk.'

'Nor can dead girls,' interjected Craigh.

The flick, flick of the stack of files and reports continued for at least three minutes before the Chief spoke again. 'There is still not one shred of evidence to link Dorothy Rawlins to that robbery, and it's clearly written here and verified by not one but six members of the social services that she was actually being interviewed by them at the time of this man Donaldson's unfortunate accident.'

Craigh looked at his Super, who remained stony-faced with his head bent low, refusing to look at Craigh.

'When questioned about Donaldson, Mrs Rawlins agreed that she had made contact with him. She also agreed that he was holding certain items for her to collect on her release from Holloway prison, and I quote, "Mr Donaldson was keeping two Victorian garden gnomes for me. They had been in the garden at my house in Totteridge."'

'That really is bullshit, sir.'

The Chief looked hard at Craigh. 'So is most of this, but we take very seriously Mrs Rawlins's allegations of police harassment, and we also have to take seriously her claim for ten thousand pounds' worth of damages done to her property.'

Craigh knew that had been at the bottom of it all, the bloody claim for damages.

'I would now like to interview DI John Palmer. Thank you for your time, Detective Chief Inspector. That, along with a lot of money, has been wasted. I have also been discussing a back-log of work in your division that should by rights have taken priority over this entire Rawlins situation.'

Craigh stood up and shoved the knot of his tie up to throttling position. 'Yes, sir.'

Palmer took one look at Craigh's face as he walked out and hissed out his breath. 'Bad, huh?'

Craigh nodded. 'Look, it's no good trying to cover for that prat Withey. I'm not carrying the can for this, so don't you. They know all about his sister so just tell the truth.'

Palmer would have liked to talk further but he was asked to enter the boardroom by a WPC who had been taking notes throughout.

Craigh looked around. 'Where is he? Has he come in yet?'

Palmer paused at the door for a moment. 'He walked in about ten minutes ago, said he'd been sick.'

Craigh knew that Mike would be sick all right when they finished with him and he knew what the outcome of the internal enquiry would be: that one or other of them would be just that. Finished. He just hoped to Christ it wasn't going to be him.

Half an hour later, Palmer left the boardroom. He looked even worse than Craigh had when he walked out, and he just hoped he'd not screwed himself. Mike was sitting with a plastic beaker of coffee in his hand. 'How did it go?'

Palmer gave a wry look. He went closer before saying

quietly, 'They don't know about the diamonds, seems the
big gripe is about Donaldson and that ruddy ten-grand
claim Rawlins's lawyer put in.'

Mike exhaled and then swallowed. 'What did they ask
you?'

'A lot. But, Mike, they know about your sister, I mean,
I never said anything, they knew before I went in. I know
the Gov wouldn't have told them so you—'

Palmer was interrupted as the female officer stepped into
the room and asked for Mike. Palmer watched him follow
her like a doomed man. He took off to find Craigh and
compare notes.

Mike knew it was going to be heavy but he had not
anticipated the icy anger of the Chief. He knew he could be
up for suspension but he hadn't bargained for the fine and
return to uniform for a year. That had taken the wind right
out of him. No way would he be back with the hard hat –
not after all he'd been through. Even the job at the security
company was better than that, and probably better paid
too.

'You have abused your position as a police officer. You
have used personal grievances to instigate a full-scale investigation of Mrs Dorothy Rawlins without disclosing to
your superior officer your personal motives.'

Mike remained with his head bowed as the cold voice
continued that he had not disclosed on his original papers
that his sister had been married to a known criminal and
had taken part in and been shot during an armed robbery.
He interrupted, 'She was dead, sir. I didn't think there was
any reason to put that—'

He was silenced by a wave of the Chief's hand. 'There
was every reason and you know it, so don't try and be

cheeky. If we had been privy to this information, it would obviously have been taken into consideration by DCI Craigh and it would have been his decision either to go ahead with the investigation without you or decide not to, whatever the case may be.'

Mike licked his lips. 'I'm sorry, sir, but I feel I should mention that both DCI Craigh and DI Palmer acted with the utmost professionalism throughout, and I apologize for misinforming them and for not filling in the required data on my application to join the force.'

The Chief nodded. 'You were accepted because of your exemplary army record, noted in the letters from your commanding officers. You are a highly intelligent and dedicated officer. I do not wish to lose you but at the same time action must be taken.'

Mike looked at his hands and then straightened his shoulders. He resigned there and then, and felt as though a great weight had been lifted off his shoulders. What his wife would think about it, what he would do, he couldn't give much thought to. He just wanted to get out, have a drink and go home. They had not discovered his part in the switching of the stones or the part his mother had played, and right then he didn't even want to get her by the throat and throttle her. He might later. All he wanted was to get out of the room and have a few drinks. He needed to get drunk.

Both Palmer and Craigh were waiting and they seemed really twitchy. It was Mike who smiled, lifting his arms wide in a big open-handed shrug. 'Well, one of us had to go and it was my decision. I've resigned, so how about a drink?'

Craigh banged him on the shoulder, unable to hide his relief. 'Maybe you should think about it. I mean, they didn't ask you to leave, did they? It wasn't the big heave-ho?'

'No, but the "back in uniform" did it. I'm out. Just get me to the pub.'

Palmer gave Craigh a small wink. He was just as relieved and suddenly Mike seemed like a good friend. He had, after all, let them both off the hook.

Ester took off her best suit and hung it in the wardrobe. She only had a little time before they were due out for the riding class so she pulled on her old jeans and a thick sweater and was just stamping into her right boot when Dolly came in. It irritated Ester that she was expected to knock if she entered Dolly's bedroom, even her tin-pot office, but she just barged in.

'Is it sorted?'

Ester stamped into the left boot and stood straight. 'Yep, it's sorted and the tape's back in their hot sweaty hands.'

'You've not got any more tapes or business like that, have you?'

'No, I haven't. That was all I had.'

Dolly walked out half-way through Ester's reply, and she could have slapped her. She picked up her riding crop and followed her into the hall.

Gloria and Connie were in the kitchen getting into their riding boots. Gloria was complaining about sewing the sacks; she'd cut her fingers and was pissed off that no one else seemed to be doing any work but her. Connie overheard and came charging out of the kitchen. 'What you think I've been doing half the afternoon – enjoying myself? Well, if you want to take over and screw for—'

'That's enough,' warned Dolly, pointing to the kids, and Connie glared at Dolly with hatred.

'The leaf machine will be delivered tomorrow morning. It costs fifty-four pounds, cash on delivery, all right?' She flounced back into the kitchen as Dolly drew on a pair of leather gloves.

'Right, we all set?' she said calmly, and walked out of the front door.

'I swear before God I'll punch her straight in that smarmy arrogant face,' Ester said quietly.

'I'll get one in before you,' Gloria said as they left.

They rode different horses from usual and were unsteady to begin with but soon got their confidence. They did not ride alone: their instructor was an older woman who spoke in a deep, theatrical, upper-crust voice, which they all kept mimicking. Not that she appeared to notice as she was too busy giving them instructions. 'Ever-ee-body, please pay h-attention, knees grip, oh so tightly, reins held loosely, and walk h'on.'

They walked sedately down the country lane and paused as Mrs Fruity opened the gate to the field and gestured for each one to enter with a loud booming, 'Walk on, walk on and form a circle, please.'

Gloria was still imitating her when they returned to the manor two hours later. They cranked themselves out of the car to Gloria's 'Walk on, come along now, walk on . . .'

Julia galloped down from the wood and called out. They turned and watched the way she neatly skirted the building, plants and wheelbarrows.

'How did it go?'

'Oh, frightfully well,' shouted Gloria.

Connie smiled. 'We're h'all being pat down far the local hunt, lovey, she simply thinks we're soooooooo good.'

Julia laughed and then turned Helen of Troy towards the stables. The women followed and grouped outside the loosebox as Julia took off her saddle and carried it inside.

'You've each got to learn how to clad the horses' hooves this evening so we might as well do it now. Practise on Helen,' Dolly said, raking the mud off her boot.

'Oh, what hever you say, Mrs Rawlins,' Gloria said, still being Mrs Fruity, and Dolly actually managed a small tight smile.

Gloria had her hand under the cold-water tap; it was already swelling up. 'The fuckin' thing trod on me hand.' She showed it to Angela.

'I wish you wouldn't swear so much, not in front of the kids,' Angela said, peeling potatoes.

'Oh, fuck off,' Gloria said as the water soothed her hand. 'Where's the Queen Mother?'

Dolly walked in, already bathed and changed. 'She's here, Gloria, and Angela is right. Please don't swear in front of the girls.'

Gloria screwed up her eyes, sure Dolly couldn't have heard her. 'Listening at keyholes now, are we, Dolly?'

'With your voice it's not necessary, you can be heard all over the house.'

With the bickering, Dolly reckoned it was time they talked but she didn't say a word throughout dinner, and the edginess grew worse, mostly from Ester, until Dolly tapped her hand. 'Ester, we will talk later. I don't think we should discuss it now. Why don't we all eat in peace and then have a drink together when Angela is clearing up?'

'Just so long as we do,' Ester said.

'We will.' Dolly passed the bowl of potatoes.

'Well, this makes a change from pasta,' Gloria said, shovelling more on her plate. They were all eating big platefuls because of the exercise they'd taken and each one of them seemed to have changed considerably. Their skins were fresher, hardly any trace of make-up on any of them; even Gloria's usual thick eye shadow and mascara were no longer evident and Connie hadn't a false nail in sight. Ester retained a glimmer of her old sophistication, more so that evening because she had been to London. Only Julia seemed to have changed physically. She was not as thin as she had been but, unlike the others, she was more used to country life and appeared to fit into the surroundings better.

Mike could have done with some food inside him. He hadn't eaten all day and he got drunker than both Craigh and Palmer put together. By the time they had driven him home, he was feeling well pissed and stumbled out of the car as they parked outside his house. He leaned against the bonnet, banging it with the flat of his hand. 'Thanks, see you.'

'We'll talk tomorrow,' Craigh said, opening the window.

Mike stepped back. 'Yeah, but I'll be having a lie-in for a change. Goodnight.'

They watched him reel up his path, heard the milk bottle crashing down the step but Mike ignored it as he tried to aim his key into the hole. He lurched into the house, banging the front door. He got as far as the stairs before he slumped down and sat there, his head in his hands, feeling sick as a dog. It all came down then and he moaned, resting his head against the banister.

'Are you all right?'

'Yeah, I'm fine.'

Susan stared at him from the top of the stairs. She had just bathed and washed her hair. 'Your dinner is in the oven, probably dried to a bone, but if I knew what time you would be coming in then—'

'Shut up, Sue, leave it out – just for one night.'

Mike stumbled into the kitchen and she returned to the bedroom. She knew he was drunk, not only by the way he was reeling around but she could also smell it. Well, he could just stay down there, she wasn't going to speak to him. She locked the bedroom door, picked up the hair dryer, turned it on full blast, and opened last week's issue of *Hello!* magazine. She hadn't intended having an early night but she would now.

In the kitchen, Mike burnt his fingers on the plate, almost dropping it, and then sat at the table, staring at the atrophied stew. He got a bottle of HP sauce and shook it, his chair scraping as he got up and sat down again. He picked up his fork and then couldn't face eating. Instead he sat in a stupor, wondering what the hell he was going to do with his life. He had screwed it up badly and he wondered how he would pay for the mortgage, the kids' schooling. He flopped forward, knocking the plate of stew on to the floor.

'My bloody mother, she got me into this, the stupid cow.' He laid on his arm on the formica table and looked with drooping eyes at the stew and HP sauce over the floor. 'Sod it.'

Ester looked at the dregs in the bottle. 'Well, this is the last of the wine.'

Dolly held her glass by the stem and sipped. She put it down, got up and opened a drawer in the desk. She took out one of the girls' big blank-paged drawing books and slowly undid the cap of a thick black felt-tipped pen. 'Right, this is what I intend to do. I don't know if we can do it, not yet, but this is what I've been working on.'

They sat in front of her, squashed on to the sofa as if they were at some kind of lecture.

'I don't want any interruptions, not until I've finished, then you can ask whatever you need to know.'

They nodded, waiting, staring at the blank sheet of paper. Dolly spoke quietly, without any kind of emotion whatsoever. She took her time, clearly drawing each section as she spoke, starting from the manor which she marked with a big cross, the stables, and detailing how they would pick up their rides and move silently down the lane.

She drew the railway tracks, the bridge and the lake. She then marked in red the danger cables, the areas of vulnerability, and no one said a word as, slowly, her plan began to shape up. It was ridiculous, it was insane. She was not even thinking about hitting the security wagon itself. She was aiming to remove the money from the train. And not, as they had supposed, at the level crossing or just before it or after, but *on* the bridge. She wasn't waiting for a reaction but her eyes narrowed as she looked over the rough drawings, her face set in concentration.

'Er, you gonna do it ... Did I hear right? We're not going for the cash on the security wagon but when it's on the train?' Gloria's mouth was dry as she spoke, not really believing what she'd heard.

'Yes, that's right, we go for the train.'

Gloria swallowed. 'And we go for it, not at the station or at the level crossing, but, er ...'

'On the bridge,' Dolly said softly.

'Bloody hell,' Gloria muttered, and looked at the others, but they remained silent, staring in turn at the drawings and Dolly, who still seemed intent on them.

Ester was just about to find her voice when Dolly stabbed at the thin lines depicting the rail-tracks. 'These are live wires, very high voltage. There's a narrow parapet right along the entire edge of the bridge, two good positions to

396

cover us, and a big notice here.' She smiled. 'One that says "high voltage, danger", but it's big enough for one of us to hide behind. There's another boarding here and one on the opposite side of the lake. The railings are lower so we position two of us there.' She made neat crosses and then turned the sketch round. 'We've got to stop the train half-way across the bridge. We mark out the position with fluorescent paint. I've paced it and I reckon we can stop it almost dead centre of the bridge.' She continued in a quiet, almost monotone voice, taking them through each stage of the raid. What she never said was exactly which of them was to do what, and no one was inclined to interrupt. She drew the signal box, the electric cables, the telephone wires and as her drawings began to take up one page after another, she became more animated.

The women realized just how much thought Dolly had given to the overall plan; how they would drop the money from the bridge, where the horses would be tethered. They were still silent, hardly daring to breathe, let alone question her. They noticed that on some pages there were neat lists of items required, further pages had more odd drawings, and Dolly flipped through them, tapping her pencil on the table. 'Well, I think that's nearly all of it. I'll need to know if we can get one of the speed-boats, and if not, we have to find one. We also need a big powerful flashlight positioned here on this jetty. It'll blind the guards but, most important, we'll be able to see the live cables, especially Julia as she is in the most dangerous positon of all, right here, up ahead of the train.' Dolly snapped the book closed and looked at the row of stunned faces. 'So that's it.'

Ester let out a long, drawn-out sigh. 'It's even more crazy than I thought possible. It's not crazy, it's bloody insane, and no way will Julia ride her horse up on to the tracks.'

Julia got up and stuffed her hands into her pockets. 'I'll speak for myself, Ester.'

Ester sprang to her feet. 'But you can't take this seriously, none of us can, we couldn't do it.'

Julia sniffed and put her head to one side. 'You know how much is on the train?'

Dolly ripped up the drawings and threw them on the fire. 'Yes.'

Gloria's eyes were on Ester. 'How much?'

'That copper was useful, he found out for me.'

Ester said sarcastically, 'You telling me he knows everything?'

'No, not everything, but I got him, I can trust him.'

'You mean like you did Angela?' Connie said.

'How bloody much is on the fucking train?' shouted Gloria.

'And I've warned you about swearing,' Dolly said crossly.

Gloria fell back in disbelief. 'Oh, fine. I say a few four-letter words and you get pissed off. At the same time you're standing there planning how to rob a fucking train.'

'Stop swearing,' Dolly snapped.

Gloria hugged her knees, about to get up and slap Dolly as she had warned Ester she would. Ester was standing with her hands clenched so tightly, also trying to stop herself from walloping Dolly.

'How much is on the train?' Connie asked softly.

'Could be up to forty million, usually between thirty and forty million.'

You could have heard a pin drop. Dolly looked at their gaping mouths and that smile came again as she said softly, 'Penny for them?' None of them could speak so Dolly said she fancied a cup of tea and went to put the kettle on.

Julia was the first into the kitchen after Dolly. She lolled at the door. 'Well, that gobsmacked the lot of them. You even stunned Ester into silence.'

Dolly set down the mugs on a tray and gave a sidelong look at Julia. 'They sent you in, did they? See if the crazy old cow's stripping naked and dancing in the full moon?'

'Nope, they're sort of discussing it.' Julia drew out a chair. She began to roll up a cigarette. 'They're also scared, you know – scared to dismiss it as a no-hope situation and scared to face the fact that it might just work.'

Dolly rested her hands on the edge of the table, her body inclined towards Julia. She almost whispered, 'It's crazy but it's also brilliant and I know it could work, I know it, Julia.'

Julia licked the paper, her eyes on Dolly. 'Yeah, I guess you do know it but it's also very dangerous. We could all get ourselves killed, just like little Shirley Miller.'

Dolly froze. Julia watched her eyes narrow, her hands form into tight fists. 'So what I want to ask you, Dolly, is why? I mean, you could maybe manage this place, get some kind of job, we all could for that matter.'

She ground out, 'Money.'

'No other reason?'

'What do you want, a moral one? Well, I don't have it. With money you can do what you like. Without it in this world you're nothing, you don't count.'

Julia patted her pockets for her matches, the cigarette dangling from her lips. 'Does it scare you?'

Dolly turned to the teapot. Behind her Julia struck the match, still keeping her eyes on Dolly's rigid back.

'Look, Dolly, all I know is you got a lot of contacts for semi-crooked deals, maybe you could do some kiting, bit of this and that, unless you're trying to emulate your old man. Harry, wasn't it?'

Dolly took out the milk from the fridge, crossed back to

the tray of mugs. She carefully placed the bottle down on the tray.

'You know, somebody once told me he always worked with ledgers or books, I dunno, but he used to write everything down, like you've been doing, and I was just wondering what's going on in your head, Dolly. You trying to be him, go one better than him? Only I don't fancy risking my life for some screwed-up reason.' Dolly lifted the tray and stood poised. 'I killed him, Julia, I looked straight into his face, into his eyes, and I saw the expression on his face the second before I pulled the trigger. It was a combination of shock, disbelief and, best of all, fear. After doing that, nothing scares me. I'm not like my husband, I'm better, I always was. I was just very clever at always making sure he never knew it. Now, will you open the door and I'll take the tea in. I'm sure they've all got a lot to ask me.' Julia laughed softly, opening the kitchen door to the hall, standing back for Dolly to pass her.

She stayed in the kitchen, smoking until the thin reed of a cigarette was down to nothing but a tiny scrap of sodden paper. She then chucked it into the sink and walked out. She needed a line; she was feeling so high and she wanted to get even higher. In the dark old stable, with Helen's heavy snorting breath, Julia laid out her lines and snorted each one, and then she licked the tiny mirror and started to laugh.

'Oh, man, if my mother could see me now!'

CHAPTER 18

JULIA URGED Helen of Troy forward. She scouted the area at length but there was no one in sight. They had arranged to have a ride before the stables opened for business, on the condition that Julia led them. It was not the first time that Sandy had allowed the women to ride solo with Julia, and none of them wanted her to see how accomplished they were becoming. They had their ride at six in the morning and after every lesson they returned the horses to the stableyard.

Julia and Helen of Troy continued checking the area. Their breath hung in the cold air, and not until Julia was truly satisfied that it was all clear did she lift her hand with the stopwatch as a signal to the waiting Ester, who then relayed it to the others.

The women pushed their horses forward until they formed a line over the brow of a hill, waiting for Julia to join them. Not until she was alongside, stopwatch at the ready, did she give the 'go' signal, and they all set off at a gallop. It was not a race against each other but against the stopwatch. Each rider had her own specific job to rehearse and accomplish. They jumped the hedges, split up, paced their positions, re-formed and started again. Eight times they timed the ride until exhaustion took over, especially with Dolly. She was gasping and heaving for breath as Julia monitored each one, shouting instructions and orders until it was too dangerous to continue in case they were seen.

The horses were stabled and the women drove back to the manor. Julia was waiting with the stopwatch. They were still out of breath, faces flushed, shirts dripping with sweat. Julia ticked off Connie for not being in her position on time and angrily told Gloria and Ester she had seen both of them almost come off and if they fell and injured themselves it would finish the whole caper. She didn't leave Dolly out, admonishing her for holding back too long and delaying by reining in her horse.

'Sorry, I knew I was behind.' She had to bend over as she had a stitch in her side.

Not until they had discussed in detail the entire morning's exercise did they sit down for breakfast, laid out and made ready for them by Angela. Later, Dolly took a boat out with the little girls, rowing across the lake, eating crisps and drinking lemonade on the small jetty. The girls had a wonderful time and when they went off to play hide and seek with Angela, Dolly stashed the can of petrol behind the small boat-house. She shaded her eyes to look towards the bridge and saw Julia and Ester sitting on the wall at the end. She then called the girls to get back into the boat as it was time to leave.

Gloria was out of sight at the far end of the bridge. She had an artist's drawing book and was sitting up on the wall, seemingly intent on sketching, when the train passed in front of her. However, she wasn't looking at the blank page but counting slowly, pressing the earpiece into her ear, heard by Julia and Ester at the opposite end of the bridge. Connie was the only one left at the house. She was on 'listening' duty, recording everything from inside the signal box.

None of the women discussed the robbery in actual terms, it had become 'The Job', and as the days went by, the rehearsals and time-keeping preoccupied them all and relieved any tension; they had plenty of time to co-ordinate everything that needed to be done.

There was still one area Dolly had not tackled openly: the stopping of the train itself. It would be done by Julia, on the tracks, with a flashlight, and as she would be wearing Norma's police cape and hat she would look official. She would hold her position for some time as the train moved over the tracks, giving the driver fair warning that something was amiss. Because the train would be moving slowly, there was no chance of it running into her. The real danger was whether she could hold Helen of Troy steady, standing between the rails side on, with a massive and dangerous high voltage cable beneath her belly.

Julia had rehearsed the side-stepping move many times. On two occasions Helen had bucked and almost thrown her off. She had not rehearsed on the tracks themselves but on mock-ups she had made from logs, and Helen was getting better all the time. What worried Julia was that when she stopped the train and it paused on the bridge, what would make it stay there? If the driver felt any danger, he might start up the engine and move the train forward. 'It's all very well, Dolly, marking out where it's got to stop, but how do we make sure it stays there while we get the bags out?'

'Semtex.'

'Pardon?'

Dolly was listening to the tapes she had collected from Mike's house. She was now sure he hadn't grassed on her. But could he get the explosives? She still didn't know.

'Semtex,' Julia repeated.

'Yeah, we'll blow it on the bridge.'

'Oh, brilliant. And if it's not a rude question, where the hell are you going to get Semtex from?'

Dolly continued checking the tapes. 'I'll tell you when I've got it.'

Julia shook her head, almost wanting to laugh. 'Oh, fine. Which one of us is going to be mad enough to use it?'

Dolly packed the tapes away, annoyed. 'I'll let you know that an' all, but one thing I will tell you is that I'm not prepared to do anything, not one thing, until I'm sure it'll work.'

Julia stuck her hands into her pockets. There seemed to be nothing left to say. In any case, Dolly was in one of her moods and it wasn't worth attempting to have a conversation with her. If anything, she had grown more distant than ever; her mind seemed elsewhere.

Dolly felt at times as if she was a juggler trying to keep all the plates spinning on the ends of sticks, trying to keep the women calm, trying to eliminate the risk factors. Nothing must be left to chance, and if she needed a few more weeks, months, even, she'd take them. She spent hours with her little black notebook, jotting down things she must remember, crossing out others she had accomplished. Sometimes she sat in the dilapidated conservatory, wrapped in a coat, staring into space as she pictured each section of the heist. Could it work? Would it work? Was she insane? As yet the women weren't restless and she put that down to fear. Even Ester, of late, had simply got on with the job in hand and was no longer pushing for supremacy. Dolly surmised that would probably come. Ester was sharper than the others, more dangerous, and Dolly suspected she was just biding her time. She monitored each one, watching closely as to how their nerves were holding out. So far so good, but it was still like a game. When it became a reality, they would begin to show their real state of mind.

A piece was missing from the jigsaw. Dolly knew it, and kept on returning to the bridge, the train and the damned explosives they still had not acquired. This was the most dangerous and most daring section of the entire 'game', and without that, it could not commence.

The missing piece came from an unexpected person. A call came from Mike: he wanted a meeting but not at the manor. Dolly was unnerved by this. Would this be the moment he grassed? Was he wired up? If so, she would have to be too, but she made no mention of the meeting to the women. She travelled by train to London and met Mike in a small café by King's Cross station.

Mike was not obviously nervous but a little tense, as he put down two cups of tepid tea. It took him a while before he came to the point, looking around then back to Dolly.

'What do you want, Mike?'

'I'm out. I've given in my formal resignation today. It goes without saying they've accepted it and that's thanks to you.'

Dolly sipped the tepid milky tea with distaste. 'So what do you want?'

'Obvious, isn't it?'

'Not really. Why don't you tell me?'

Mike again glanced around and Dolly leaned closer. At no time did he mention the train, the robbery or anything illegal, simply that he would be interested in helping her out on the business she had inferred she was going into, that he had a contact that might help him get the order she had mentioned.

Dolly nodded, tapping the edge of the saucer with her spoon. 'You ever driven a speed-boat?'

Mike tugged at his tie. He waited as she took out her

notebook and jotted down three things. 'That's what I need.'

Mike breezed into the house where Susan was vacuuming the hall.

She looked at him in surprise. 'What you doing home?'

He switched off the hoover. 'Come in. I got something to tell you.'

Susan followed him into the living room, where he sat on the sofa. 'I just got fired.'

'What?'

'I just got fired. Well, not quite, I handed in my resignation. So that's it, I'm out of a job.'

'What do you mean, that's it?'

'I'm out of the Met. They found out about my sister and—'

Susan sank into a chair. 'Your sister? What are you talking about? What sister?'

Mike sighed. 'You've seen her face often enough, the blonde girl in the photo frame at Mum's.'

Susan had seen the photo, it was hard not to, and a long time ago she had asked who it was. She'd never been interested enough or, for that matter, spent enough time at Audrey's, for the photo to make any impression.

'She was my sister.'

'Oh, come on, Mike! What's this all about?'

'I'm trying to bloody tell you, if you'd just shut up.'

Susan leaped up. 'You tell me one second you're out of the Met, next you're talking about some sister I've hardly ever heard of. How the hell do you expect me to react? What's she got to do with your job?'

'She's dead.'

'I know – I know she is, Mike.'

Susan flopped back in the chair and closed her eyes. She was just about to say something when he continued.

'Shirley was younger than me. I'd already signed up when she was still a teenager. I had a brother in Borstal so I wasn't going to lay it on the line about the antics of my family when I joined the Met. A lot of blokes have some member of their family that's a bit dodgy and Gregg's just an idiot. I never had much to do with him, even less than Shirley because he was younger than her.'

Susan leaned forward. 'Will you get to the point, Mike? I'm trying to follow all this, honestly I am, but I don't understand why you've brought her up in connection with your job. She's dead, isn't she?'

Mike put his head in his hands. 'She was married to a right villain, bloke called Terry Miller. He'd done time for armed robbery, then he was on some job, a big raid on a security van and he . . . he got burned to death.'

'What? I don't believe I'm hearing this. If this is some kind of a joke . . . You said she was killed in a car accident.'

Mike snapped, *Just fucking listen!* I don't know all the ins and outs but after Terry died, Shirley got in with some people and . . .' The more he tried to explain, the more insane it all sounded. He was almost in tears. 'Shirley was shot in an armed raid nine years ago.'

Susan was stunned into silence. Mike's face was white as a sheet as he stumbled through the rest of the story: how he hadn't even returned for her funeral, how he had cut her out of his life and tried for years to cut out his mother too.

Susan's mouth went dry. She couldn't go to him to put her arms around him because she was so confused and close to tears. 'Is this . . . this little tart you've been seeing all part of it, then? Is that why you're suddenly telling me all this?'

'No, it isn't. She's got nothing to do with it. If you must know it's Audrey, it's all down to that stupid bitch my mother. She screwed me up but I'm going to get out of it.'

'Does that mean you're leaving me and the kids? Is that what this is all about?'

Mike moved to her side and gripped her arm. 'Sue, listen to me. I have no intention of leaving you or the kids. I've told you that it's all over between me and Angela, it should never have even started. That was me being fucking stupid and I'm sorry I put you through it. But, Sue, you got to trust me now, really trust me, because I need you. I need you to back me up, not go against me. I want you to do just what I tell you to. It's very important I have just a few weeks on my own to sort my head out, okay?'

She pushed him away. 'You *are* leaving me, aren't you?'

'No, I'm not, but I want you and the kids to go and stay with Mum in Spain.'

'What?'

'Don't start with the "what" again, you heard me. Get the kids out of school. I've arranged for you and them to go and stay with Mum.'

Again Mike put his arms round her and she fought against him but he wouldn't let her go. She broke down and started to cry.

'Don't, please don't. You got to trust me, Sue, you have to. It's for all of us. I'm going to get a job, I mean it, but I'll just need a bit of time before I can join you in Spain. I swear on my life, I'm not lying. I love you and I love my kids.'

Dolly stood ten yards down the road from Mike's house. She could hear every word they said and when she heard

Susan agree to go to Spain, sobbing her heart out, she removed the small earpiece and slipped it into her pocket. She reckoned she could trust Mike but he had still not got her the Semtex. The conversation he'd had with his wife and his having left the police were good, and he had already implied that he would be willing to be more than just blackmailed into helping her. Now she had him exactly where she wanted him – and she needed him. Dolly had calculated that without him there weren't enough of them to do it, but until he brought the explosives, she would not be a hundred per cent sure. Cautious as ever, she was not allowing herself to move ahead until she had had a further discussion with Mike as to exactly what part he would be prepared to play.

Dolly was in a very good mood at dinner that evening. She opened a bottle of cheap wine and they all accepted a glass. She made no mention of Mike or her visit to London. It was obvious something had gone down because of Dolly's good mood, but it didn't spread to them. Instead it bothered them.

Angela served the dinner, the children having eaten earlier, and after the meal Dolly went up to read them a story. The little girls had become much more open and smiled freely now. In fact their presence made the entire house more relaxed. No one ever spoke about their plans in front of them and, apart from Ester, the women had become genuinely fond of them, especially Angela, whom little Sheena doted on. They had new frocks and shoes and socks, a big room full of toys and they began to use the word 'home' for the manor. Having so many rooms to run free and play in, and so many adults caring and making sure they were happy, had had the desired effect: the little girls were happy and loved.

Angela peeped in to see Dolly tucking them up. Sheena had so many teddy bears lined up there was hardly room in the bed for her. 'I got everything you told me to get so I'll be in my room if you want me,' Angela whispered.

Dolly turned off the night-light – the girls were no longer afraid to sleep in the dark – and went into Angela's room. She sat on the neatly made bed and checked all the passports. It touched her to know she really was their legal guardian.

Angela pointed to hers. 'Me photo's terrible. I look like I'm scared stiff.'

Dolly put them back into the envelope. 'I'll keep these safe, love, and not a word to anyone or they'll all want to come on holiday with us.'

'If anything happens to me, Angela, I want you to promise me you'll take care of the girls. There'll be money provided for you, I'll see to that.'

Angela slipped her arms around Dolly. 'Have you forgiven me?'

Dolly seemed to cringe from her embrace and Angela quickly released her. 'Just go about your business here, love. Don't ask me to say things I don't mean. You'll know when I've forgiven you. I need you to make up for a lot of trust you destroyed. That's hard to forgive.' She opened the bedroom door. 'Put your TV on, there's a good film. Don't come downstairs. I'll see to the dishes. Goodnight, love.'

Angela had never known anyone like Dolly before: she seemed so lonely and yet there was something about her that made you frightened of trying to get through that barrier, as if it would break a dam of feelings that she covered so well. And Angela began to understand how she had hurt Dolly, hurt her more than she could have imagined, because she had shown Angela a genuine affection not shown to any of the other women. She was glad they would be going away together and she would in no way jeopardize that by telling any of the others about the proposed holiday and the passports.

In turn, Dolly had kept the robbery plans secret from Angela. Forever looking ahead and pre-planning, she was already preparing for the time when she had the money and would leave England with Kathleen's kids. It would be a long holiday, maybe Geneva or some other place in luxury, and the less Angela knew about what was going on the better. Dolly might be unforgiving but Angela was useful, and she could not help liking her, as she had from the beginning. But as well as being useful for taking care of the kids and keeping them out of the way, Angela was a good cover, and a useful weapon against Mike, should she need it.

Ester was waiting at the bottom of the stairs. 'You'd better come in and listen to this. It's got us all anxious.'

Dolly switched on the speaker so that they could all hear the tapes from the signal box. There was a series of phone calls from the station master to Jim. The mail-train was never mentioned but something referred to as the 'special', due the following Thursday, was being rescheduled due to a fault with the engine. The 'special' would not be arriving as prearranged but at a later time and, as Jim's second already had a previous arrangement, the station master wanted to know if Jim could do the late shift. Jim was heard to moan about his hours on and off duty, and then came the big worrying line.

'Well, we won't have this bloody problem for much

longer. After Thursday it'll be re-routed to another station, thank Christ.'

'So what time is it due?'

'Be late, Jim. Around midnight.'

Dolly replayed the last line a few times and then switched off the machine. 'Shit. I hope that's not what I think it is.'

Ester's hands were on her hips. 'You hope? Jesus Christ, what do you think we all feel? If next Thursday is the last mail-train through here we're fucked.'

Dolly was waiting for Mike at the end of the lane, sitting in the Mini estate, smoking. She saw his headlights flash once, twice, as he drew up and parked a few yards ahead of her.

The women were tired of discussing the taped phone call from the signal box. They sat wondering why Dolly had suddenly upped and left them at eleven o'clock without a word to a single one of them.

'I'm getting sick of this,' Ester said.

Julia yawned and stretched her arms above her head. 'Well, she's a secretive cow, and we all know it, but maybe it's a good thing. We'll never be ready by Thursday, so my guess is it's all off and the question is what do we do next?'

'Oh, shut up.' Ester turned on Julia, who laughed. 'It's not funny, we've been working our butts off and for what?'

Gloria looked at her chipped nails, felt the rough skin on her hands from the horse's reins. 'I don't believe it, after all we done.'

Connie pursed her lips. 'I never believed it anyway. I mean, I've gone along with it, like everyone, but in my heart I never really believed we'd do it. Did you? Honestly?'

Ester glared at her. 'For forty million quid, sweetheart, I was more than fucking thinking of it.'

'I'm just repeating what Colin said, Mrs Rawlins. That next Thursday he's got to be on duty so he couldn't make dinner with me, something about having problems with the engine, so instead of being back in London he was having to do a late-night drop. He never said the time.'

'Midnight,' Dolly said softly and Mike stared. Dolly rolled down the window. 'Did he say it would be the last train coming this way? Anything about rerouting it?'

Mike bit his lip, shaking his head. He then leaned over to the back seat. 'You won't need this, then, will you?' He unzipped the bag. 'Mate from Aldershot, owed me a favour.'

Dolly looked into the bag and then into his face. 'You fancy a walk, do you? Maybe a nice quiet row across the lake? Show you where I plan to blow up the train.'

Mike thought she must be joking, but she wasn't. He felt his bladder about to explode but he nodded and she sat back.

'Drive to the end of the lane, we'll walk via the woods.'

Mike explained in detail how dangerous Semtex was and gave her a diagram as to how it should be used. Dolly listened attentively, making Mike repeat himself a few times, then quietly talked herself through the procedures. He stressed over and over again that only a small amount was needed.

They walked on in silence until they came to the lakeside and gazed into the black water.

'You'll need money now you got no job. I might be able to get a few grand to you.'

Dolly stood still as he slowly turned to face her. 'Can I

413

ask you, and I want the truth, Mrs Rawlins, did you have anything to do with that diamond robbery? Did you set it up?'

She looked into his eyes and lied. 'No, love, it was nothing to do with me. I admit I was after the diamonds but, then, who wouldn't have been? Even your mother was after them. It was nothing to do with me.' Mike kept staring into her face and she held his gaze. 'I never would have put Shirley at risk. I know I've said things to you in the past and said things about her I shouldn't have but, believe me, I never knew she was on that raid. It was all down to my husband. It was Harry's doing. You think I'd have let her take the risks?'

Mike shrugged. 'Just from what you said before, it sounded like you set it up.'

'No, love, it was my husband. All I ever done was kill him. But that was a personal matter.' She could feel him hesitating, and she gestured to the bridge. 'You know how much is on that train, love, don't you? Now do you want just a few grand in your pocket or a couple of million? Take those kids and that pretty wife of yours to live in Spain. Sunshine, sea and sand, good for kids.'

He was half in shadow, his face caught in the moonlight. 'What would I have to do?'

It was after two o'clock in the morning when Dolly eventually got home. She opened the front door quietly and didn't switch on the lights, but they were not asleep and, slowly, in their dressing gowns, they all appeared on the stairs and landing.

Dolly took off her coat and hung it up, picked up the kit-bag Mike had given her and walked over to the bottom stair. She leaned on the newel post.

'We do it Thursday. In some ways it's probably better for all of us so late at night. If they change the route then it'll be our only chance.'

Not one of them said a word, but Dolly could feel their fear rising. She spoke softly and yet they were so silent they could hear every word clearly. 'We've got two days.' She looked at the frightened faces, one by one. 'Now we'll see who's got the bottle. Are you up for it?'

Ester was the first to say yes, the others took their time but one by one they hesitantly agreed.

'Good.' Dolly said it like a school-teacher and then smiled. 'Goodnight, then.'

No one could sleep that night as it dawned on them that The Job was for real and they had only two days to go. Toilets could be heard flushing throughout the night as their nerves hit their bladders. Only Dolly's room remained silent and dark as she slept a deep, dreamless sleep, knowing the last piece of the jigsaw was in place. Her only worry was that it might have come too late.

Angela dished up breakfast, aware of the uneasy silence round the table. She put it down to them having argued or something, but none of them felt like talking or finished their eggs and bacon apart from Dolly. She had cut up soldiers for the little girls to dip in their eggs and reprimanded Sheena for using her sleeve instead of the napkin to wipe her mouth. The others could hardly wait for the children and Angela to go on their morning ramble, eager to be left alone to discuss the robbery, but Dolly seemed more intent on making sure they had on their wellington boots, thick scarves round their necks and hats before she waved them out of the back door.

As it closed, they all started talking at once, asking one question after another, but Dolly moved past them and into the hall. 'I need Gloria and Connie this morning.'

Ester threw down a half-eaten piece of toast. 'That's it? Don't you think we should fucking talk about this?'

Dolly returned and stood, granite-faced, in the doorway. 'We've talked, Ester, and we've been talking for months. If I still have to talk any one of you round then it's off. You know what is to be done, each of you. Now we have to finalize the last stages.'

'That's what I want to frigging talk about,' shouted Ester.

'No, love. You've got your jobs. The last part is to do with Connie and Gloria, nothing to do with you. When that's done, we'll have a meet later this afternoon after the ride.' Dolly left the room.

Ester glowered at Julia. 'Christ, I'd like to throttle her.'

'Feeling's mutual,' came the reply from Dolly in the hall.

Gloria looked at the sports bag as Dolly unzipped it. 'Now, I've got the instructions written down. You need very little and the most important thing is to know the exact place where it's got to go. You'll have to have it in place on the bridge and . . .'

Connie felt her knees go and she slumped on the sofa. Her mouth was dry. 'I think it's just the time of the month. I come over a bit faint.'

Gloria paid her no attention. She was studying the diagrams and then the sports bag. 'I never handled nothin' like this you know, Dolly.'

'Well, you'll have to practise, so start doing it.'

Gloria goggled. 'Where do I do it, for chrissakes?'

Dolly wafted her hands. 'We got enough acres, Gloria. Just go outside and start practising. But remember you need only a small amount. It's all written down there.'

'Who give you this?' Gloria asked.

'Mind your own business.'

'Well, it is my fucking business because we're dependent on him or her knowing what they're doing for starters. I'm not playing with Lego here, you know. This is high explosives.'

Connie had tried to stand up but then fell back again. If she'd felt faint before, now she virtually passed out.

Dolly felt her head. 'You're not runnin' a temperature, are you?'

Gloria picked up the bag and looked at Connie. 'I know what it is. It's called shittin' yourself with nerves. You watch her, Doll, she's a liability.'

Connie struggled up. 'I'm not, you leave me alone, it's my period, I always feel like this.'

Dolly gestured for Connie to join her. She had a small, high-voltage generator on the floor. 'Right, love. You get this over to the little landing-stage on the lake. I'll get one of the others to carry it with you and then we got to get the light fixed up and hidden.'

Connie's legs went again and her face was ashen. 'But do you think it's a good i-i-idea for us to be lit up? Anyone will be able to see it for miles around and—'

'We're not gonna be doing a cabaret act, Connie, we want it on for no more than three minutes at the most. Then we're out of there. It won't last much longer — batteries'll run down.'

Ester moved closer to Julia as they stacked the cladding bags for the horses' hooves. She pulled away bales of straw to reveal big leather saddle-bags to be strung across the animals' flanks. She tested one. 'I hope these'll hold the weight.'

There was a loud *boom!* and the sound of breaking glass.

Both women froze and Ester peered out of the stable door. 'What the fuck was that?'

A second boom shook the stables and Ester rushed out. Julia strode after her in a fury, almost knocking her aside. 'I told her not to do it close to the bloody stables.'

Ester looked back at Helen of Troy. She hadn't flinched – unlike the pair of them.

Gloria picked herself up. An old greenhouse was devastated, a gaping hole in the ground. She was covered in soil and debris and shakily holding the dustbin lid she had used as a shield.

'Are you out of your mind?' Julia screamed.

'I got to fucking practise, haven't I?'

'Not inside a greenhouse, you idiot. Look at the glass it's showered everywhere. You stupid bitch! You could have made the horse bolt – and you could have killed yourself.'

Gloria dusted herself down and smirked. 'I know what I'm doing.'

'You could have fooled me,' Ester shouted, keeping her distance. 'Just go further away from the house.'

Gloria yelled back that she was only doing what Dolly had told her and began to check the instructions. 'I used too much, that's all. It's not like dynamite, you know.'

Dolly steamed towards them, passing them without a word. She stood with Gloria, inspecting the damage. 'How much did you use?'

'Not a lot,' said Gloria. She looked ruefully at Dolly. 'Sorry.'

Dolly opened her notebook. 'Julia reckons we'll need it at this point of the bridge, here and here.'

Gloria looked at Dolly's tight, neat writing. 'Yeah. We been over it day in day out. That's the best spot, train still moving very slowly so it'll get the impact.'

'Just don't blow the carriage up, Gloria. You do that, the

money will be blown to smithereens. More important, there are three guards inside that carriage, and I don't want anyone getting hurt.'

Gloria nodded. 'I'll have another go.'

Connie and Julia rowed across the lake, the boat low in the water with the weight of the lamp, the cables and the battery-operated generator. Julia did most of the rowing as Connie felt faint and couldn't stop shaking. They dragged the boat alongside the jetty and then began to move the equipment, constantly keeping an eye open for anyone either side of the shore who might spot them. Julia wore leather gloves and told Connie off because she hadn't put hers on. They then dusted the lamp down just in case she had left her fingerprints on it. The gear was stashed in bushes, alongside the petrol, and they headed back to the shore, Julia rowing again as Connie trained the binoculars towards the bridge.

Susan and the kids left London the next day, after Mike received the formal acceptance of his resignation. It was Wednesday, and he began to wonder if he really was going to do it. Alone in the house, he started to get nervous but it was too late to back out now . . . He opened a bottle of vodka and had three or four mouthfuls before he calmed down. He had to rent a car, sell his own – there was a lot to get organized and it began to take his mind off just what he had got himself into. There was no getting out of it now unless he made a run for it and joined the kids and Susan in Spain. But, then, if he did that, what was he going to do with the rest of his life? The phone made him jump, his heart beating rapidly.

'Hello, love, it's me,' Dolly said softly.

Mike answered, and she could tell he was having kittens just by the sound of his voice.

'The wife and kids gone, have they?'

'Yes, this morning.'

'Good. Angela will be at your place Thursday with the girls.'

'*What?*' He sounded like his wife.

'Two reasons, love. One, you got a nice alibi, just in case you're ever questioned. She'll be there all night and will say you was with her. And you will be – well, for part of it. She doesn't know about the robbery, love. All I'm using her for is to give you a safe alibi if – pray God you won't – you need one. Might cause a bit of aggro with your wife but if nothing untoward happens, she won't know, will she?'

'Angela's to stay here, in my house?'

'Yes, love, because I don't want her and the kids around when it goes down. Like I said, she's not involved in this, she's caring for the girls. Friday she'll get the first train out and back here. You just go straight to the airport. All right, love?'

His voice was even hoarser. 'Yes.'

There was a long pause. 'Well, you get on with your business and keep steady and out of sight. Goodbye.'

When they drove back after their riding lesson, it became obvious that tension was building because they found it impossible to make any small talk. Only Dolly chattered on.

'Norma home, is she?' Dolly asked casually.

'You know she isn't,' she said flatly.

'Just checking. You got her keys still?'

Julia sighed. 'You *know* I have. We've been over and over it, Dolly, and it's the only place.'

Ester leaned forward from the back seat. She looked at Dolly and then Julia. 'I don't trust that Norma.'

Dolly paused at the level crossing as the train signals blinked. She pulled on the handbrake as the gates closed. 'We don't have to trust her, Ester, just use her. She's another one. You think her friends at the nick would approve if they found out not only that she was a big dyke but fraternizing with—'

'Shut up,' Julia said softly.

'It's true, though, isn't it? Somewhere in Norma's head she's getting a kick out of slobbering over you, and you know it, but you're going to have to watch her like a hawk because when this goes down, she'll be the first to point the finger our way. Maybe give her even more of a sexual kick.'

'Leave it out, Dolly.' It was Ester now, as she saw Julia's back go rigid.

'No, you leave it out,' Dolly said, her mouth a tight thin line. 'We need Norma, we've had Julia play her along for enough time. We got to use her place to stash the money, like we used her to get the cop's hat and cape. Now we use her picturesque little cottage. It's the only place close enough to us and the only place the cops are unlikely to search. She's one of them.'

Ester gave Julia's shoulder a squeeze. It was funny, really, Julia being such a decent woman that she did not want to involve Norma, and yet prepared to play a major part in the robbery. It really didn't add up. She felt more love towards her in that moment than she had for a long time, and she liked it when Julia pressed herself closer, their bodies touching in an unspoken embrace.

Dolly's beady eyes missed nothing. It was good, she thought, the pair of them backing each other up because, come the night, she reckoned Julia would need a lot of confidence, maybe even need to snort that stuff she used.

Dolly knew about it – not much escaped her – but she was clever enough not to mention it.

Julia fed Helen of Troy, checked on the sacking and bags for the umpteenth time that day. When she came back, Dolly was standing at the kitchen door, throwing half-eaten sandwiches out for the birds.

'You're something else, you know that, Dolly Rawlins?'

Dolly brushed the crumbs from her hands and then stared at them, palms upwards. They were steady and she smiled. 'My husband used to say that, only he always called me Doll. Funny, I hated to be called that but I used to let him, nobody else.'

'Gloria sometimes calls you Doll, doesn't she?'

Dolly looked up into Julia's face. She was a handsome woman and it was as if only now it struck her just how good-looking she really was. 'Being in prison I got called a lot of things. Got to the point I didn't really care any more, but I used to, in the old days.'

'Prison tough for you?' Julia asked casually.

Dolly hesitated a moment and then folded her arms. 'You know, I reckon there were only a few really criminal-minded women in there. Most of them were inside for petty stuff, kiting, fraud, theft, nothing big, nothing that on the outside a few quid wouldn't have put them right. Everything comes down to money. The rest were poor cows put inside by men, men they'd done something for.'

'That doesn't include me,' Julia said softly.

'You were a junkie. That's what put you inside.'

'No, Dolly, I put myself inside.'

'Because you were a junkie, your guilt put you in there. You tellin' me you really needed to flog prescriptions? You wanted to be caught for your shame. I mean, you take how many years to qualify? Doctors when I was a kid were like high society, shown into the best room when they came round on a visit. My mum was dying on her feet but she got up, made sure the house was clean before the doctor came.'

Julia took out her tobacco stash. She began to roll a cigarette, thinking that she had never, in all the weeks she had been living with Dolly, actually talked this way with her.

'Eight years is a long time inside that place, Julia. Maybe I met only four or five of what I'd describe as dangerous women that deserved to be locked up. The rest, they shouldn't have been there but when most of them were released, they'd been made criminals by the system, humiliated, degraded and defemalized. Is there such a word as that? Defemalized?'

Julia said nothing, rolling a cigarette, and Dolly continued in a low unemotional voice. 'The few that were able to take advantage of the education sessions might go out with more than what they come in with but most of them were of below average intelligence, lot of girls couldn't read or write, some of them didn't even speak English. Lot of blacks copped with drugs on 'em. They was all herded in together.'

Julia licked the paper. She found it interesting. The more Dolly talked, the more fascinated she became by her. The woman they all listened to, at times were even a little afraid of, Julia guessed was poorly educated, maybe even self-taught. This was accentuated by her poor vocabulary and her East-End accent, which became thicker as she tried to express herself.

Julia struck a match and lit her cigarette, puffing at it and then spitting out bits of tobacco. 'Out of all of us here, who would you say was a criminal?'

423

Dolly reached out and took Julia's cigarette, smoking a moment. 'You want the truth?'

'Yeah.'

'Ester was first sent down at seventeen. She's spent how many years in and out of nick – a lot, right? But as much as I don't like her, I know there's a shell around her. Dig deep and you'll just find a fucked-up kid that stopped crying because there was never anybody there to mop up her tears.'

Julia was surprised. She took back her cigarette and sat on the step 'What about Gloria?'

'Well, she's been in and out like Ester and, on the surface, you could say she's a criminal or been made one by her sick choice of men. But again there's pain inside that brassy exterior, lot of hurt. She's borne two kids and given them away – you never get over that. You, Julia, have got all this anger inside you, self-hate, hate for your mother.'

Julia leaned against the door-frame, irritated, wanting to change the subject, but Dolly continued in the same flat voice. 'Connie's the same. Few years on she'll be another Gloria but she's not as bright. Some man will still screw her up – it's printed on her forehead. But, you know, we all got one thing in common.'

Dolly gave that cold smile and Julia lifted her eyebrows in sarcasm. 'Come on, Dolly, you tell me what I've got in common with Connie.'

'Defemalized, Julia. Not one of you could settle down and lead a normal life. Prison done that, it's wrenched it from our bellies.'

Julia chuckled. 'That's a bit dramatic. Speaking for myself, and being gay, I'm not and never was—'

'You're still a woman, Julia, no matter who you screw or what you screw. We're outcasts – that's what they done to us, made us outcasts of society.'

'You think men feel the same way?'

'I dunno, but when you get to my age there's not much left a man wants from me – can't have kids, too old, and when did you ever hear of a fifty-year-old bloke going for a woman the same age?'

'That still doesn't answer my question. If every woman in our situation turned—'

'Bad?' Dolly interrupted, and her arms were stiff at her sides. Her voice was low-pitched and angry. 'They wouldn't have given me a chance. Whatever good I wanted to do, without money – like I said before – you're nothing. Not in this day and age. It's all that counts.'

Julia persisted, 'If we'd never tried it on, got you here, how do you think it might have turned out?'

Dolly's eyes were so hard and cruel, Julia stepped back, shocked. 'I reckoned there were only five criminals in the nick with me. Well, I was number six.'

'I don't believe you, Dolly. You had dreams of opening this place, of doing good, fostering kids, that's not criminal.'

Dolly turned away and Julia was sure she had hit the vulnerable target: did Dolly blame them, hate them? Would she in the end betray them because of what they had done? She watched as Dolly relaxed, as if in slow motion, turning her head to face Julia, and smiled, this time with warmth, her eyes bright.

'You telling me with my cut of forty million quid I can't have this place up and rolling? I can go down Waterloo Bridge, pick them off the street and bring them back. I won't need any social services, I won't need anyone telling me what I can and can't do because with money you can do anything. That's all it takes, Julia. Money, money, money.'

Julia grinned. 'Well, let's hope we pull it off.'

'We'll do it, Julia. It's afterwards we're going to have to worry about because we're gonna be hit, and hit hard. We foul up in one area and we will go down. Every cop will come round here, we'll be searched and the house taken apart. We'll be questioned and re-questioned, they'll rip the grounds up . . . They'll never leave us alone, for weeks maybe months.'

'If we pull it off,' Julia said quietly, and Dolly guffawed a loud single bellow.

'If we don't, we don't. But if we do, nothing will stop me. Every single one of us can go for what we want, do what we want, be what we want.'

Julia's heart began to thud in her chest. Dolly's face was radiant with unabashed excitement. 'I'm not scared, Julia, not for one second. I'm feeling alive for the first time since I killed him.' She lifted both her arms skywards, like an opera star taking the adulation of a packed house of applauding fans. With her arms raised, head tilted back, Julia could see the pulse at the side of her neck beating and felt suddenly terrified, as her heart banged in her chest, and certain Dolly Rawlins was insane. As if Dolly read her mind, she lowered her arms and tapped Julia. 'Don't think I'm mad, Julia. If we do exactly as we have planned to the letter, we'll pull it off. But holding them all steady will take the pair of us all our time, so let's go back inside.'

She didn't wait for Julia but walked into the house. Julia, the one she trusted as being steady, had to have a heavy line of coke before she could follow her. It didn't calm her down, she felt paranoid and sat in the stables, hunched up, her arms clasped round her knees, as her whole body shook with nerves. It was almost ten o'clock and the following night she knew they would be getting ready for the raid. Just thinking about it made it worse.

CHAPTER 19

T HE DAY blurred as they went about their business. A taped call from the signal box had verified that the train would be arriving at midnight. It was referred to only as the 'special' as Jim checked the alarm and police-station lines.

Angela left with the children and arrived at Mike's home at three o'clock, unaware of what was to take place that evening. Mike opened the door, handed her the keys, and said he had to leave but would be back that evening. He didn't touch her and was distant, even when she tried to reach for his hand. 'No, just settle the kids in, I'll be back later.'

She closed the front door, and went straight to the wall socket receiver as Dolly had instructed her. The girls were playing with Mike's sons' toys and Angela had a good nose around before she started to cook spaghetti for them. They had been scared of moving to yet another home but they all called Dolly and said hello to her and were told they would see her the following day. That reassured them and they went back to playing.

In a hired car, Mike headed for the manor. He had plenty of time so he drove carefully, making sure never to exceed the speed limit. The last thing he wanted was anyone to remember him so he didn't stop at any petrol station, and

427

just continued slowly, his gut churning, concentrating on the neat list of instructions which gradually calmed him.

The women checked and rechecked their lists in their minds: Julia the cladding and the bags, and the big machine for clearing up leaves. She tested the engine, the suction hose and the long trail of flex ending at the socket in the stables. The machine would be used to hoover up the money and they had already tested it to be certain that the suction was strong enough for their needs. Julia then went on to check the lime pit. It was ready for the mail bags to be hurled into; the lime would eat away at the thick canvas, which again had been tried and tested. It was also deep enough to accommodate the number of bags they would be bringing from the train. The corrugated iron slats were standing by in position, the builder's skip was in place and already attached to the truck so it could be towed across the pit opening. She was less tense than she had been the night before but she had a half-bottle of whisky with her. Connie did her jobs. Gloria and Ester headed for the bridge, with a dog's lead, looking like innocent walkers, calling out for the fictional lost dog. They returned to the house, mission completed. Each reported to Dolly and she ticked and crossed out the jobs as they were done. Gloria collected the shotguns and cleaned and polished them.

Gloves, hats and boots were laid out in the kitchen. Norma's police cape and hat were in readiness for Julia. The hours ticked by slowly, every minute seeming to take half an hour, and Connie believed the hands of the clock were not moving, she'd looked at them so many times.

Dusk came, and Dolly asked if anyone felt hungry. Nobody did. They were still quietly going about their tasks, checking and double-checking everything.

'Keys are in the same place at the stable,' Connie said, sitting down. She kept coughing as if she had a tickle in her throat and her hands felt icy cold with nerves.

Mike parked the car and, wearing a black polo-necked sweater, black ski pants and sneakers, a black woollen hat, eased the old rowing-boat silently into the water. He had a fishing rod and a bag with him, nothing else. He rowed across the lake to the opposite side. He saw no one, heard not a sound. The lake was black, the bridge in darkness, lit only by the flash of the signals as a train passed across and on into the distance. He tied up the boat alongside the small wooden jetty and crossed to the anchored speed-boat. He pulled back the canopy and climbed inside, checking the ignition and wiring. That accomplished, he went into the woods and searched for the lights. His gloves were sodden but he didn't remove them. He had to pull away the bracken and twigs hiding the gear and he carried each item to the end of the jetty, where he set up the high-powered spotlight. The silence was unnerving, nothing moved and the lake remained still and dark. He could not risk testing the spotlight, just hoped to God it would work. If it didn't, there was nothing he could do about it.

By nine thirty, the women were anxiously waiting for the time to pass. They didn't speak but the atmosphere was very tense. Connie continued to clear her throat until Gloria said she should have a drink of water as it was getting on her nerves.

'I'm sorry.'

'That's all right, love. Just a sip, mind – remember what I said about you drinking.' Dolly was reading a magazine.

'I hope we can trust him,' Ester said for the umpteenth time. Dolly ignored her but she wasn't really seeing any of the magazine pages of knit-yourself-a-bolero or the new-fashioned beachwear. She knew Mike had a hell of a lot to lose: two kids, a wife and a future, to put it plainly, but she didn't bother saying anything to Ester. She'd said it before and knew it was just Ester's nerves talking.

Gloria crossed and uncrossed her legs, just as she had for the last half-hour. They were at breaking point.

'Time to get dressed,' Julia said, and walked out. Connie sprang up and Dolly tossed aside the magazine.

'We've got a while yet, Connie, just relax.'

Julia pulled on her boots, a thick sweater over her shirt and began to do up the big rain cape. Like an omen, there was a sudden roll of thunder.

'Oh, shit,' Ester said, running to the window. 'It's gonna rain.'

'Never mind the rain,' Dolly said calmly. 'If it's raining the cops won't hang around.'

'If there's a storm the horses will freak,' Julia said as she picked up Norma's police hat. 'If the thunder makes them edgy, pull the reins in tight,' she said, putting on the hat, and walking to the kitchen door.

'Where are you going?' Ester said sharply.

'Just to take a leak,' Julia said, slipping out.

'You've already been,' Ester said, following.

'Let her go,' Dolly said quietly, and Ester turned back, drew Dolly aside.

She whispered, 'She'll be snorting coke.'

'I know, but if she needs it to straighten out, then let her do it.' Dolly ignored the other women's gasps, and looked out of the window. 'It's coming down hard, the ground will be slippery.'

'Oh, Christ,' Connie said, panting with nerves.

Dolly opened a bottle of Scotch and got down some mugs. 'For those that need a bit of bottle.'

Upstairs Julia knocked back half a tumbler of vodka and then snorted two thick lines of coke, the last of it, but, then, this might be her last night. She stared at her reflection in the dressing-table mirror. She looked huge in the big cape and boots, and she put on the hat, pulling it down low over her face, tucking in her hair. She had a black scarf round her neck, and she tested that it was loose round the front, ready to ease over her face. She looked at her reflection for a long time and then smiled. She was confident, and as she held out her hand in front of her, it was steady – even if her head wasn't.

Julia got back as the women began pulling on their boots. No one spoke. She passed through the kitchen and a roll of thunder heralded her opening the back door, which still caught a bit from the damage of the police raid, and she yanked it hard. They could see the rain coming down in a sheet outside.

'Well, take care. Hold the reins in tight, make them know who's boss, especially over the jumps.'

They nodded, and Ester went over and reached up to kiss her face. 'Take care, Julia, for chrissakes. Take care on that live rail.'

Julia smiled. 'It's Helen that's got to take care. I don't want her thrown up into a tree like that dog Connie told us about.'

Connie moaned softly. She was chalk-white but at least she'd stopped coughing. One good belt of Scotch had stopped that.

'See you later.' Julia went into the stable to saddle up Helen. She was the only one not to have her hooves clad as Julia would not use any road. She was to head to the far side of the bridge over fields and cross far along the line

431

from their level crossing to ride back to the bridge. They all had their coats on when they heard Julia moving out. The clock registered ten thirty.

Mike blew into his gloves. His hands were freezing and he was sodden from the downpour. A bolt of lightning had lit up the bridge and lake for a second and he just hoped to God it had not lit him. There was still no sign of a living soul.

The convoy was half-way to its destination. The heavy rain did not slow it down and the armoured security wagon was cushioned between two police cars as it continued towards the station.

Colin was at the wheel, maintaining radio contact between all three vehicles. The empty mail-train left Marylebone station. At first they were told to stand by and wait as the engine was still playing up, even after a complete service, but the problem ceased as soon as they gained speed. The carriage to be used for the collection of the mailbags was at the centre of the four-carriaged train. It looked like an ordinary passenger train except for the blacked-out windows. The three guards sat inside playing cards, a good hour to go before they picked up the money bags. They were relaxed and casual.

'I'll be glad when tonight's over. I hope to God they don't make this a regular thing, I hate getting home this late. Anyone know the next route they're gonna take?'

'No one does.'

'Bloody train's clapped out. You'd think carrying this much dough they'd have some kind of high-powered armour-plated one, wouldn't you?'

The rain splattered on to the carriage windows. 'Your deal, mate, and let's hope this doesn't get into a fuckin' storm, we'll be soaked.'

'I won't. I'm not moving out. Let the security blokes carry the gear in. Right, ace's wild, this one's dealer's choice.'

His two friends groaned as the train continued down the tracks, unimpeded by any other. There was an ominous distant roll of thunder.

Julia moved slowly across the field. She was worried they would all have trouble as the ground was slippery, the mud forming in some of the ditches between the fields. She opened two gates in readiness. They stuck in old tractor ruts and she had to dismount to secure the gate back, lifting it slightly over the squelching mud. She checked the time; she'd have to get a move on, the gates had already delayed her by three or four minutes. Julia pushed the horse on in the dark night. She was just a shadow, no lights, no street-lights. She began a steady canter in a wide circle. She had a long ride ahead to get back to the far end of the bridge, right round the far side of the lake and then up a dangerous high bank to take Helen on to a narrow ledge before moving down on to the line itself. It didn't worry her – she'd been doing it for weeks – but she felt uneasy about the heavy rain. The steep bank was slippery and Helen could stumble or, worse, she might inadvertently hit the dangerous high-voltage cable, but she didn't slow her pace, just kept going.

The women parked the Mini in a narrow field gateway. They kept to the grass verge as they headed towards the stables, passing two small cottages. Lights were on in both and they moved silently in single file: Dolly, Gloria, Ester and, coming up at the rear, Connie.

They saw no one, and there was only one street-light to worry them, almost directly outside the cottages. They carried the cladding and saddle-bags between them, only Gloria, Ester and Dolly with the shotguns. They found the stable key and unlocked the main doors. By torchlight they began to clad the horses' hooves in the thick sacking bags. It was eleven fifteen; they had three quarters of an hour before the train was due.

When the horses were ready, they rode out one by one, each with their orders and position, the rain still pelting down. The sacking would give more grip in the mud.

Dolly was first out. She walked her horse down the lane, then made for the woods. It was inky black and not a light could be seen until she broke from the cover of the trees and headed towards the railway line below. She had to cross a small bridge about half a mile from the signal box. She winced as the horse's hooves thudded on the wooden-planked bridge. She held the reins tightly, keeping to the narrow grass verge, and started to make her way along the side of the tracks. She slipped off the horse and tied him up firmly. She had seen no one, and in fact she began to be glad of the rain as it was really pelting down. Dolly squeezed under the protective wired fence, already cut in readiness, and moved inch by inch towards the station car park. Above was the signal box, lit up, with Jim inside. Dolly crept beneath it, taking out the wire-clippers and the razor-sharp hatchet. Now she would have to wait and hope to God nobody walked by the slip-road and saw her horse tethered. But as they had done it eight or nine times and no one had ever passed even close to it, she hoped they would not tonight. Half an hour seemed like a long time.

Connie and Gloria, using a different route, rode, like Julia, to the far side of the bridge. Unlike Julia, they did not have the long ride to get on to the tracks. The horses slithered a little in the mud but, on the whole, were steady as they galloped towards the far side of the lake. They had one riderless horse, Ester's, as she had already gone to her designated position, on the far side of the bridge. Once there, with the shotgun ready and loaded, she was to wait for the train. It would not be stopped in front of her; they were going to blow it half-way across the bridge, further down the track, the old railway sign the only protection for Ester if too much Semtex was used. She prayed that Gloria now knew the right amount.

Dolly could hear the distant rumble of the train. It was still so far down the tracks she couldn't see it but she tensed up in anticipation, hoping that the others were in their positions and ready.

Connie and Gloria tied up the three horses firmly. They were a bit frisky and didn't like the continuous heavy downpour. Connie followed Gloria as they passed the jetty and Mike appeared. He did no more than look towards them, signal, and start to move to the end of the jetty. He then crouched low, waiting. There were still about twenty minutes before the train was due at the station.

Gloria and Connie moved to the end of the bridge, along the railway line in the opposite direction from Ester. Gloria motioned to Connie to remain behind as she bent low and, keeping pressed to the small parapet at the edge of the rail, she checked that the wires and the plastic-covered packages were all intact. She worked quickly and only hesitated once as she double-checked the live and the earthed wire. She had gone over it so many times she now closed her eyes tight and swore. 'Please, dear God, have I got it right? Red into the right socket, blue into the left and the earth

435

between them?' She pictured the neat drawings Mike had made that Dolly had told her to burn, wishing she still had them.

'You can do it blindfolded. Come on, gel, don't blow your bottle now.'

Gloria inched her way back towards Connie, who was holding her shotgun. She whispered, 'Can you see him? Is he in position?'

Connie screwed up her eyes to peer over the bridge and looked twenty-five feet down. It was pitch black. 'I can see something at the end of the jetty.'

Gloria nodded. They were under strict instructions not to speak, not to say one word throughout the robbery. She could just make out the outline of the tethered horses by the trees.

Julia had a tough time riding Helen down the steep bank. The horse didn't like it one bit and kicked out with her back hooves as Julia held on like grim death. She gritted her teeth as they slid further towards the track. Helen tossed and jerked her head but they were on the narrow edge before the line itself so Julia eased Helen forward, one hoof at a time, on to the centre plank. Either side were the live cables but there was an eight-inch-high border and she began to move Helen slowly down the precarious narrow plank. She was as dainty as a ballerina, encouraged and patted, as they got closer and closer to the spot Julia had rehearsed for stopping the train. Now came the really dangerous move: she had to turn Helen to stand sideways on, blocking the entire rail. A roll of thunder made her freeze as Helen tossed her head. Not liking the narrow ledge, the horse lifted one foreleg and almost came down on the cable but Julia shouted sharply, 'Still', a police command, and the wonderful old horse froze her position. Julia waited for her to settle before turning her and moving slowly sideways.

Mike brought the boat further round. He had the spotlight switch in his hand. He could see none of the women, but knew they must be in position because the horses were tethered.

The lead police patrol car pulled into the station forecourt, and an attendant switched on the exterior lights. The platform was lit up in readiness as the train approached, the level-crossing gates clanging shut. The rear police patrol car remained just behind the security van as the guards waited for the go-ahead to begin moving the money bags on to the train. The rain was bucketing down. Two officers had not got their raincoats with them so they took shelter under the platform awning.

Jim, his hut lit up, watched the train hiss to a halt. He gave the thumbs-up to the driver who waved from the train cabin. He did not get out, simply waited in his cabin for the signal to move on.

The guards opened the central carriage, carrying clipboards and documents. Two guards from the security wagon approached and checked their documents with the other guards and as the police formed a protective line either side of them, they opened the wagon and began to carry the bags aboard the train. They moved fast, expertly, calling the identity number as each bag went aboard. It took no more than ten minutes for the train to be loaded. As the carriage gates closed, the security guards returned to their empty wagon and the police didn't hang about either. They waited only for the signal from the signal box, and the engine hissed and began to move down the tracks, across the closed level crossing and on to the bridge.

Dolly saw the security wagon move back the way it had come and then the two patrol cars draw away from the station. She was willing them to move off, out of sight, one hand on the electric power switch for the signal box, the other clenched around the hatchet for the alarm wires. She knew exactly which ones they were because this moment, like the entire raid, had been rehearsed. The mains box opened and closed four times. Even so, when that power went out in the box, the moment of panic for Jim was only going to last a second or two before he hit that separate linked alarm switch. If that went off, the two cop cars could turn back within minutes and they'd have major problems. She had to pull the main switch and slash the wires within seconds of each other.

The train passed, one carriage, second carriage, mail carriage, last carriage, and she said to herself, 'Now, now, now.'

The lights switched from red to off, perfect. The signal box went completely dark. Jim didn't panic, went towards the emergency generator but, as he was about to switch it on, he heard something from beneath him. He could not ascertain what it was, his eyes still unaccustomed to the dark.

Dolly slashed down the hatchet. The wires strained and two or three remained intact. She slashed again and then pocketed the hatchet before clipping at the cables. One sprang away, then the second. She had four more to go as Jim began to panic. His delay in getting worried gave Dolly the valuable time she needed to put the live wires against the generator sides. If Jim tried to switch on up in the box he'd get quite a shock – not enough to kill him but enough to stop him trying it again in a hurry.

Dolly ran under the fence, and was almost at her horse when she froze. Jim was hurtling down the signal-box steps, having almost been thrown across the signal box when he tried the emergency generator. He leaped down the steps, still semi-shocked, and fell to the ground. He moaned, clutching his ankle, rolling in the grit of the signal-box forecourt. He couldn't hear Dolly, let alone see her, as she mounted and headed towards the bridge, the train moving slowly up ahead. But her horse was nowhere near as well trained as Julia's so it was a much slower ride. He was nervous and skittish and no matter how much she pressed him forward, he refused to go at speed.

The guards aboard the mail carriage had no idea anything was wrong at the station. They were moving and would soon pick up speed as usual, the bridge crossing always being slow. The windows of the carriage were all blacked-out; they saw nothing, heard nothing.

The train driver didn't look back. He was used to the bridge crossing and could do it blindfolded. In fact, he looked over to the lake a moment before the flashlight swung from side to side twenty yards up ahead of him. He put his hand up to shield his eyes from the bright light as it swung, indicating for him to stop. He began to brake in plenty of time, moving almost at a snail's pace as he leaned out of his cab. All he could see was a police officer standing sideways across the track.

'You fucking crazy?' he screamed. Now he rammed on the brakes but they were still travelling so slowly, it didn't jolt or jar the rear carriages. The train just slowly trickled to a halt. He presumed something had fallen across the tracks, waiting as the interphone rang from the centre carriage. He picked it up. 'There's a problem on the line, let me get back to you.'

He still held the phone as Julia began to move closer, very slowly. He leaned even further out. 'You're taking one hell of a bloody risk – there are live cables under you.'

Still she waited. Then she switched on the flashlight again, shining it at the driver's face, as she eased the horse on to the narrow verge, moving away from the rail-tracks, backing Helen dangerously along the stone-flagged parapet. Again he yelled at her, asked what was going on, but she was edging further and further *away* from the train and to safety. If it started and tried to pass her, there wouldn't be room for the horse – it would swipe her belly.

'What the hell is going on?' the driver yelled again. The guards were now lifting up the blinds on the covered windows. The train had been stationary for one and a half minutes.

Julia was within six feet of safety when she turned the flashlight on once, twice, three times and Gloria pressed down the detonator. They were just a fraction off but the explosion ripped through the second carriage instead of directly between it and the mail carriage. She swore as the carriages rocked and shuddered and the railway line buckled under the impact. Next she crawled to the second device and thumped it down. This time it was almost right on its marker as the rear carriage broke loose. The explosion was terrifyingly loud, echoing across the water, glass and metal splintering. There was hardly a window left intact. The guards sprawled across the floor lying face down. They didn't know what was going on.

Gloria had used too much Semtex and there was a dangerous gap in the bridge itself. The tracks beneath the carriage had buckled towards the gap but in the frantic next stage they didn't realize the imminent danger as there was so much going on. Some of it was rehearsed or surmised by Dolly, and Julia didn't waste time being impressed, but it was Dolly's calm voice she could hear in her mind, 'Soon as you move from the track, you chuck this into the main front carriage, as close to the driver as possible. It'll work on a long radius and scramble any calls he tries to make from the train to the next station. It won't give us long but it'll be long enough.' It was another of Ashley Brent's toys.

Julia was clear and galloping to her next position. She now collected Dolly's horse and began to drag it towards the others down below by the lake. Dolly was on foot and running towards the centre of the bridge.

Ester rammed her shotgun through the broken window. The men inside still lay sprawled on the floor in terror as two more shotguns appeared through the broken windows from the other side. Dolly was the only one to give the order and she screamed it. 'Open the doors. Come out.'

Mike switched on the powerful beam of the positioned spotlight, twisting it a fraction to aim directly at the centre carriage. He had seen the train moving off and knew or hoped the driver's phone would be scrambled. Then he jumped into the speed-boat and with the rowing boat trailing behind, headed at top speed for the bridge. He cut the engines as he came directly in line with the spotlight. It covered the doors of the train and the path down to the rowing boat.

The dazed and terrified guards came out one by one. Dolly took up her position, screaming instructions as she pointed the shotgun towards them. 'Lie down, face down.'

Suddenly she saw, to her horror, that the mail carriage was slowly moving to the gap in the bridge. It was going to go over the side as it creaked and groaned towards the gap.

The guards lay down beside the track, as, unaware of the danger, Connie and Gloria went aboard. Ester came round to the open doors. The sacks were passed out and dropped into the rowing boat, easily seen by the spotlight. Inch by inch, the carriage kept moving closer to the hole as they worked frantically. Below, Mike stacked the bags, gesturing to the women without saying a word. They all knew the danger but Dolly stood over the men, who didn't move as they lay face down listening to the bags crashing down and the awful sound of the carriage as it ground towards the gap.

The guards were helpless to do anything and, if they moved so much as a muscle, they felt a hard dig in the centre of their back. The women all wore ski masks, not one showing her face as they worked on, lifting, passing, dropping the mail-bags, the danger obvious, the carriage *still* on the move.

Jim had limped to the nearest house and called the police. He was incoherent but kept repeating police and train and bombs. It was confused but the police were moving out and heading towards the railway station. They would be there in four minutes.

*

Ester was first to leave. She ran down to the horses and loosened the reins of hers, dragging him towards the water. Julia was already waiting, looking with desperation towards the bridge. Then the spotlight cut out, the batteries overloaded, leaving the bridge in darkness. 'Jesus, God, they're gonna go down with the bloody carriage. It'll hit the rowing boat.' She wanted to scream out to them to get off the bridge but still the bags came over until the boat sat low in the water.

'Get out, move it,' muttered Ester.

Gloria was next to leave, and the carriage suddenly shot forward by three feet, so that it hung like a see-saw over the bridge. Mike started the speed-boat. He didn't care if they lost one or two bags – he wasn't going to risk being under the bridge any longer. He opened the throttle and headed back to the jetty. Next stage was hurling the bags out of the boat and into the saddle-bags on the waiting horses. Mike began helping Ester and Julia. They turned as they saw masses of bricks and twisted metal crash from the bridge. Connie, still inside the carriage, whipped round to see Dolly waving for her to get out, but she froze as the creaking grew louder and louder.

Dolly looked at the men, and back to Connie. She reached out and grabbed her by the arm, dragging her forward.

'Jump.'

Connie pulled back, stiff with fear, but Dolly repeated, the delay taking vital minutes. They would never make the run back to the horses and she pushed at Connie again. '*Jump!*'

Dolly pulled Connie to the edge of the crumbling bridge, and half-holding, half-dragging her, they jumped the twenty-five feet to the water below. The shotgun flew from Dolly's hand as she hit the water.

Connie surfaced first, gasping and flailing in the water with her hands. 'I can't swim.'

Mike had hurled out the last bag. He had stacked two in the speed-boat and jumped aboard, heading across the lake towards the other side, unaware that both Dolly and Connie were in trouble in the water. Connie was bringing Dolly down time and time again as she clawed and scratched at her in a desperate panic to stay afloat.

Julia lifted her filled bags off Helen and climbed back into the saddle. 'Just keep moving as planned – *Ester, go on!* We'll catch you up.' She kicked the horse's ribs and set off into the lake, Helen not batting an eyelid as they waded deeper and deeper. Connie and Dolly remained dangerously close to the water underneath the rocking carriage. Bricks and concrete slabs began to plummet into the water.

Julia waded deeper, and Connie clung to Dolly, who tried her best to keep the frightened woman afloat. They had no time to clutch at Julia's hands so they just grabbed Helen's tail as Julia turned in the water and headed back to the shore. Gloria and Ester had gone, leaving the tethered horses standing loaded with mail-bags.

As they reached the shore, Connie began to scream but Dolly slapped her face hard. 'Get out of here! Get on your horse and get out! *Move it!*'

Connie, sobbing and soaked to the skin, stumbled to her horse. She could hardly mount but neither Julia nor Dolly paid her any attention as they heaved Julia's bags on to Helen. They had a long way to go before they were finished.

Mike left the boat, ran to his car. He remained calm, refusing to allow himself to put his foot flat to the car floor. If he was caught now, speeding or otherwise, he had two mail-bags crammed with money in the boot. He took the route away from the station and as far from the manor as possible. He had every road listed and directions at the ready. Dolly Rawlins hadn't left anything to chance. He hadn't seen that she and Connie had almost drowned.

The police cars, four in all, were hampered by the closed level-crossing gates and lack of information, but by now the scream was on that the mail-train had been hit and their radios blurted out instructions for blocks to be set up on all major roads within the area. They had no information as to what getaway cars were being used by the bandits. Their instructions were that all vehicles were to be stopped and searched.

No police car could get anywhere near the bridge. The guards were running down the sides of the track, their only exit from the bridge. The carriage remained balanced. Police vehicles began to attempt to make their way down to the lakeside. There was pandemonium on all sides and as they tried to question Jim he broke down. He didn't know anything, he could tell them nothing, he had seen no one, no vehicles. He was still in a state of shock.

The three guards were in a similar state as, one by one, they were helped from the bridge. One man was bleeding badly from where the glass in the carriage window had slashed his cheek. An ambulance was called.

Mike made it on to the motorway. No road block was as yet set up but he didn't look back, he just kept on driving. It was a long drive home and he wasn't safe yet. He wouldn't be until he boarded the plane. He didn't give any thought to the women. He just drove and stayed within the speed limit.

The final stages were hampered by exhaustion but not one of them flagged. They pushed themselves on. They had galloped across the fields, up through the woods, keeping to cover as much as possible. They galloped down from the woods into the manor grounds, their bags thrown from their horses and left by the side of the lime pit, which was open and ready.

Julia leapt from Helen in her haste to start ripping open the mail bags. She hurled the money into the skip and threw the bags into the lime pit. Connie rode up, hurled her bags to the ground and, still sodden from the lake, wheeled her horse round and galloped off, passing Dolly, the last to return, just as she headed down from the woods.

Julia grabbed Dolly's bag, ripping it open. The money was stacked high in the open skip but she never stopped and, as the pit gurgled and hissed, she pressed the empty canvas mail bags down with a rake. Without pausing for breath, she dragged the corrugated iron across the pit. She hooked up the skip chains to the old truck standing by in position and began to drag it across the pit, over the corrugated iron. It left deep indentations in the wet ground – the rain had not stopped all night.

Meanwhile, the rest of the women restabled the horses, gathered up the cladding used on their hooves and took them to the stableyard tip. They threw them in and set fire to them but they were so wet they took a while to ignite. The horses' tack was replaced in order. No one spoke – they could hardly draw breath from exhaustion and panic – but they were still going by their plans, even down to replacing the stable-keys in their hiding place. Then they went to the parked Mini, where Gloria was waiting patiently at the wheel. They almost had to haul Dolly inside she was so tired. But it was not over, not yet.

By the time they returned to the manor, Julia had still not finished. She was hoovering up the money from inside the skip, then emptying it into thick black rubbish bags, each one tied hard at the neck. Gloria ran from the Mini as the others moved into their jobs, lifting the bags, stashing them into the back of the car. They pushed and squashed them inside as bag after bag was tied and handed over.

Gloria and Connie began a slow studied walk, eyes to the ground to look for any single note that might have come loose. They didn't need any torches now as the sun was coming up and it was light. The Mini stashed to the roof, Julia and Ester drove out. They knew they could be stopped at any second and neither spoke as they drove on, both their mouths bone dry with nerves. They still had not seen a single police car as they drove into Norma's cottage pathway and round the back to the barn.

It was pitch dark, and Julia used a small map torch held in her mouth to force open the door of the old coal chute. It had been painted as the cottage was now centrally heated but the chute was wide enough to take a coal bag and long enough for the bags to be rammed against each other. The other end of the coal chute was blocked off, bricked over down in the cellar. All they had to do was stuff the bags down the hole and replace the covering. Julia had brought some blackened putty to replace any dislodged from the wall as the door had not been opened for years. It was painted black, with design and date picked out in white and red – a feature of the old cottage wall. Now it was more of a feature to them because it held all their money. They had to shove hard to get the door to shut when they'd finished.

Dolly had now joined Connie, who was on her hands and knees searching the ground. The shotguns had been ditched in the lake, the mail-bags were hopefully rotting, but still it was not over – not until Dolly was satisfied they were in the clear. One note and they'd be screwed. They found four or five but kept on searching as Gloria raked over the deep tracks left by the skip. She brought stones and branches and stamped them down to disguise any movement around the pit.

They did not stop until Julia and Ester returned. Then they parked the Mini and headed into the kitchen. Dolly set light to the black book in front of them and threw the ashes into the waste-disposal unit. All their equipment had already been dumped in the local tip but still they checked that there was no incriminating evidence around the house. It was almost seven o'clock before Dolly ordered them to change and get into their beds. 'They'll be coming and they'll be around for a long time. We just sit tight, stay calm, and keep on here as if nothing ever happened. This is the most difficult part. Any one of you can blow it so it's up to you all now, and I dunno about you lot but I'm totally knackered.'

She walked slowly up the stairs and they saw her going to her room. No one congratulated anyone, Connie broke down crying and Gloria gave her a squeeze, telling her to hold it together. They then went their separate ways to bed.

Julia hugged her pillow tightly, the exhaustion still held at bay by adrenalin. She watched as Ester flopped back on the pillows. 'Well, so far so good. We did it.'

Ester drew up the sheets around her chin and turned away. Julia leaned over her. Ester was crying and Julia kissed her shoulder, but didn't say anything because she felt like weeping herself.

Connie cried herself to sleep.

Gloria lay wide awake, waiting for the knock on the door. She was still waiting when she fell into a deep sleep of exhaustion like the rest of them.

Dolly, in her room, couldn't stop smiling. It felt so good – *she* felt so good. She couldn't think of sleeping and she had one eye on the clock, waiting to hear if Mike had made it home without any trouble. In the end she felt her eyes drooping and couldn't stay awake. She slept with her arms clutching her pillow like a lover.

Mike let himself into the house. He emptied the money bags, putting the cash into two big suitcases and covering them with clothes he'd already got prepared. He then sat in the dining room, watching the mail-bags burn. It took a long time and a whole packet of fire-lighters as the canvas was supposed to be fire resistant. He even poured some white spirit on top of them but it was a hard job for them to catch alight. Then he took the ashes outside and tipped them into the dustbin, went back in and emptied two rubbish bins full of junk Susan had chucked out while she had been packing. It was a while before he was satisfied the ashes could not be found.

Angela was fast asleep in his bed. He stood watching her from the doorway. She looked so young and innocent that he couldn't resist kissing her just one last time. She woke with a start.

'Will you call home and tell Dolly you and the kids are okay? Do it now, so she's not worried about you.'

She yawned and sat up as he walked to the door. 'I'll get the girls dressed and start breakfast.'

Dolly could hardly raise her head. Her whole body felt stiff all over as if she'd been in a boxing match. She blinked as the phone cut through her brain and eventually reached out for it. It was Angela, just to say they were fine and would get the first train back.

'Good.' Dolly leaned back on her pillow. 'Get a cab from the station, will you? And some fresh bread from that little corner shop.' She hung up and looked at her bedside clock. Mike was home safe. He'd made it. She closed her eyes, wondering if they all would. Any moment she knew the scream would go up and she would bet any of the cash they'd got stashed away that the manor would be one of the first places they started at. 'Well, let them come,' she whispered to herself. 'We're ready and waiting.'

CHAPTER 20

ANGELA, AS instructed by Dolly, had caught the first train back to the manor. She had not used the local station but the main-line station, again as instructed by Dolly, who didn't want Angela getting off the train into a swarm of cops. She simply used the excuse that, as it would be so early, Angela wouldn't be able to get a cab at the local station so it was better to use the main-line one.

Angela arrived back at the manor at eight o'clock. The girls were about to run upstairs but she told them to stay quiet and not to wake up the house. She set about preparing breakfast, the girls laying the table and helping her.

Angela hadn't known any of the women to sleep in so late and she asked one of the girls to check if Helen of Troy was in the stable, wondering if they had all gone out for an early ride. The girls remained outside, calling back that Helen was in the stable. Angela fried eggs and bacon, sausages and some cold potatoes. It was all keeping warm in the oven when the women came down, bleary-eyed and still wearing their dressing gowns.

'Hi! Had a late night, did you?' Angela asked, as she started getting out the plates.

'Yeah, we had a bit of a night,' Gloria muttered.

'Aren't you going riding today?' Angela asked. It was unusual for them not to be up and out by now.

451

'No. Stables have got some kids' party so we can't,' Ester said as she creaked into her chair.

'There was something going on at the station,' Angela said as she served the eggs and bacon.

'Oh, yeah, what?' Gloria asked, as she poured the tea.

'I dunno, but there were loads of police and all along the lanes were more patrol cars. They even stopped us in the taxi.'

'You don't say,' said Julia, as she buttered her toast, and then asked casually if the morning paper had arrived.

She passed it over. 'It's got nothing in it.'

Dolly walked in, her hair in pin curls. Unlike the others she was dressed. 'Angela love, go and get the girls inside. They're getting filthy out there in the yard.'

Angela went out without argument and Dolly sat down. She reached for the teapot, was just about to pour a cup when the sirens wailed. 'Well, here they come,' she said quietly.

They all watched her as she continued to pour the tea. The front door bell echoed through the house, and Angela opened the back door. 'There's police all over the place! They're up in the woods.'

Dolly looked at Ester, jerking her head. 'Go see what they want.'

Ester hesitated only a moment before she pulled her dressing gown closer and they could hear her flip-flop slippers as she went into the hall.

The police were searching every house within a five-mile radius of the station and that included every outhouse, stable and barn, every greenhouse. Every standing building was being searched from top to bottom, and the Thames Valley police pulled in every man possible to sweep the area. Scotland Yard's Robbery Squad were already at the scene of the raid as hundreds more officers were drafted in to the immediate area to assist in the search. No vehicle had been found, no witness; the raid appeared to have happened without a single person seeing it.

The police interviewed the women and they all stated they were at home together the entire evening, went to bed at around eleven fifteen. They had heard nothing and kept up a bewildered act that might have been up for an Oscar, as they asked what had happened. A murder? A rape? A kidnapping? But they were told nothing as the uniformed officers began the search outside. They searched every cupboard, every chest and wardrobe, the roof, the chimneys, under the floorboards, the sauna area. The police were polite, diligent and stayed there for almost eight hours until they had to move on. They found nothing.

By lunchtime the press had arrived and now it was headlines in the evening papers: the biggest train robbery in history had taken place and Thames Valley were using more than four hundred officers to comb the entire area. By now the police knew that a man masquerading as a police officer had daringly held up the train, and the robbery had been committed by possibly five or six men. They had been armed, and the public were warned that if they should have any evidence or suspect anyone, they were to act with caution as the men were deemed to be dangerous. The owner of the speed-boat had been arrested but released after questioning. The signal-box attendant, Jim, had also been questioned and released as the police drew up the lists of suspects. They had, as yet, found no evidence, and had no clues as to the present whereabouts of the stolen money. The amount was not disclosed.

The women did not dare believe they had got away with it as the searches and questioning never ceased throughout the first three days after the robbery. Helen of Troy had been examined but not taken in for questioning, as Julia joked with the police.

Everyone in the area who owned a horse was contacted. Even the local stables were questioned and their horses examined but the train driver could only describe the horse that had been standing on the line as shiny and black. The rain-soaked cape had made Helen of Troy appear that colour but as she was chestnut brown, it let her off the hook.

Every day they came and went away. Dolly knew she was a prime suspect but, if she was, they didn't take her down to the station for questioning. They didn't take any of them in; they just continued to comb the area. Norma's cottage became a stop-over for the locals to drop in for tea. She had arrived home on the morning of the raid and, although she had invited a search, hers was the only house that was not done over. They had a look at her three-year-old hunter, but she assured them he was in no way capable of riding across live cables. She suggested they maybe try the nearest circus.

The officers had laughed. It was the audaciousness of the crime that couldn't help but hook them all in. It was called the Wild West Hold-up by the *Sun* and from then on every paper referred to the raid in jokey cowboy terms.

In some ways Norma was disappointed that when all the excitement had gone down – a raid at her local station no less – she had been on duty outside a cinema in the West End for some big charity. The crowds had got out of hand and she had been called in with two other officers, but nothing untoward had happened apart from a soaking as it had rained all night long. By now she had replaced her cape and hat but it had been a long, boring, wet night.

The police now believed that more than one horse had

454

been involved. They had discovered the scattered hoofprints in and around the lake but, as the riding school took pony treks up that way, it became more and more difficult to ascertain how many there were, let alone from which direction they had come. The women had been using the same routes as the stables so the ground was covered in hoofprints and droppings.

There still remained the fact that not one vehicle had been traced or stopped by the road blocks, put up within ten minutes of the raid. But as the motorway was only a short distance from some of the narrow lanes, they could not exclude the possibility that the robbers could have got through.

The village was agog, the lanes filled with sight-seeing tourists who hampered the police, as did the riders from all the local stables. The ribbons to cordon off certain areas were removed at night but officers were retained on day-and-night duty, digging up wells, searching every inch of the railway lines, every tunnel and pot-hole, every drainpipe left on the surface of the ground.

On the fourth day, Dolly almost had a fit when she saw John and his workmen filling the skip over the lime pit. They were stacking it with rubble from the old greenhouse. It remained half filled and she just hoped that by the time it was moved, the lime pit would have done its job.

The women gardened, hoed the vegetable patches, cut back and pruned trees, appearing busy and unfazed by the continued search. But the paranoia was starting. They were worried about the dustbin liners filled with money and they couldn't understand why they hadn't been found. Did the police know about them? Were they waiting for them to collect them?

Julia was eventually instructed to visit Norma, just to suss out the safety of their precious money. She had severe doubts when she called on her because, as Norma opened the door, she could see three uniformed coppers sitting in her kitchen. 'Hi! Long time no see,' Julia said breezily.

'I meant to call you,' Norma said, stepping back. 'Come on in, coffee's on.'

'No, I won't. You've got company.' Julia remained on the doorstep but gave a loose wave to the men who stared at her.

'Don't be stupid, come on in.'

'Another time,' Julia said, but the officers appeared behind Norma. They had all been at the manor at one time or another and were pleasant to Julia, who was still standing on the doorstep.

'Thanks for the coffee, Norma.' They began to file out and Norma looked at Julia. 'Go in, help yourself.' Julia hesitated and then went into Norma's hall. She stood watching as Norma hurried down the path. The officers stopped and turned towards her, as she called after them, 'It's just a thought. You wanna walk round the back with me?'

They seemed a bit puzzled but realized she wanted to say something so followed her round the side of the house out of sight of the front door.

'Look, I know this might sound odd, but have you searched my barn?'

They grinned. 'Why? You telling us you got the money, Norma?'

'No, I'm serious. It's just that I don't think you have. I know you've been in the stables and backyard but has anyone checked out my big barn?'

They saw she was serious. 'Why?'

Norma kept her voice low, stuffing her hands in her pockets. 'Well, I dunno. That bunch from the manor, they're all ex-cons, you know. She's one of them.' Norma looked back along the path. 'I just remembered she asked if she could store some gear and I said she could. I just hadn't expected quite so much, so have a look for yourselves.'

Norma unlocked the barn door and opened it. The officers peered inside to see stacks and stacks of black rubbish bags tied tightly at the neck. They went in further as Norma hung back. 'Look, you have a search around. I'll go back and keep her talking, just in case.'

Julia moved fast, her heart pounding. She almost flew down Norma's cellar steps, checking to see if anything had been moved, if there was any possible way the bricked-up cellar chute had been damaged. She peered into the small, dark cellar. 'Stupid, don't be so bloody stupid,' she muttered to herself. It was bricked up and even had stacks of boxes pushed up against it. Just as her heart slowed down, it started hammering again as feet crunched on the gravel outside. She could hear them talking and her whole body broke out in a sweat. She didn't want to be obvious, didn't dare go outside, but they were standing right by the coal chute door. Would they see that it had been dislodged and replaced?

Julia tried to keep her breathing regular but she was panting. The voices continued, but she could not make out what they were saying. She went back upstairs and to the kitchen window. Norma was smiling as she headed away from the barn with the police officers. Her hand shook as she poured the coffee and she spun round when Norma breezed in through the back door. 'You want a biscuit?' she asked brightly.

'Nope, I've not got much time. I've got to get back, help out, the builders are provin' a bit expensive so we're doing a lot ourselves and you know what it's like. Moan, moan, who's doing their fair share becomes the high point of every meal.'

Norma poured more coffee. I'm not good at lying, Julia thought, it's written all over my face. 'What are you doing to me, Norma? Shopping me to your friends?'

Norma gave a big false laugh. 'No, they just asked if they could look over the barn.'

'Oh, Christ,' Julia said, and Norma looked up sharply. 'I feel awful. You've got a whole barnful of Mother's things, but I've sold the house and . . . you did say I could use the barn.'

The back door opened and one of the officers stood leaning on the door-frame. 'Thanks, Norma, we're on our way.'

Norma jumped up and hurried to the door. 'Any problems?' The officer shook his head and went down the path to where his mates were waiting.

Julia pushed back her chair noisily. 'Thanks for the coffee. Maybe we can have dinner one night?'

Norma flushed. 'Sure. I'm back in London for the next part of the week but maybe after, when I come back.'

'Scared of being seen with me in front of your pals, are you?'

Norma flushed even deeper. 'No, of course not, but right now this place is like Scotland Yard. The world and its mother is down here and they keep on dropping in.'

Julia walked down the narrow hallway. 'Yeah. They're dropping in a lot at our place, too, but they don't get quite so warm a welcome. See you, then.'

Norma wanted to say something – she did feel guilty – but Julia had already walked out, her hands stuffed into the pockets of her old hacking jacket, and she didn't turn back, smile or even wave. 'Two-faced cow,' she muttered as she turned into the lane. But then she stopped. This was dumb – they needed that bitch. She smiled at Norma as she stood at her door and walked back over to her, cupping her face in her hands. 'Stay cool, darlin', nobody really gives a fuck who you screw. If it's me, so what? I like you, Norma, don't turn away from me. Don't make me not trust you.'

Norma leaned against her a moment, and whispered that she was sorry. 'Please see me when I come back next week. Please?'

Julia was smiling as she backed down the path. 'Can't wait until then. You take care now.' She wanted to wipe her mouth with the back of her hand. She hated the touch of Norma now, and the sooner they got their cash and left the district the better. But at least the money was still safe, for a while anyway.

They were all lulled into a false sense of security as the days passed and even the newspapers no longer screamed out headlines about the robbery. It was now slipping back to pages five and six. They all remained at the manor, waiting. Dolly continued to make them work around the grounds and the house, continually on show.

Gloria took more and more interest in the children. She was wonderful at making up games and puzzles. She had unending patience with them but, like all the others, the waiting was getting to her.

Julia rode every day and sometimes encouraged one of the others to take Helen out, but Dolly was wary of letting the police see that they could all ride so even that created arguments. Julia had started drinking heavily in the evenings because she had sold her mother's house and still had a few hundred left over after paying the bills at the nursing home. She was generous and gave them all a few quid but spent most on vodka and always had a half-bottle close at hand.

Ester was the moodiest. She stayed in bed until midday, refusing to help out as she felt it was all a waste of time.

Connie began to work out for hours in their gym. She kept well away from John and even further away from Jim. She painted her nails, bleached her hair, content to spend the time daydreaming of a successful career in the movies. She was planning to go to Hollywood with her share of the money, and the dressing-table mirror became the cameras. This amused Connie but annoyed everyone else as she swanned around.

Jim had been questioned so many times his nerves were in shreds but he never at any time disclosed to the police that Connie had spent time with him in the signal box. He did this not to protect her but his job. In the end he had to take two weeks' leave as his nerves were so bad, and was given sedatives and sleeping tablets by his doctor.

Evenings were spent watching television and videos. The days and nights dragged on but Dolly would never mention the robbery. She continued to impress Julia. She was like a rock: calm and always pleasant, trying to keep their nerves from fraying.

One evening Ester freaked and started yelling that she wanted her cut, she wanted to leave, and if the others wanted to stay then they could.

'You stay here, Ester, we all stay here until the cops clear the place. If it's weeks or months, we stay on, and we divide it up when I say so and not before.' Dolly was icy calm, her eyes flicking from one woman to the other. 'Let it all out now because nothing will change my mind. You knew this was going to be the way it went down. Just wait.'

Angela loved the house. She didn't mind working in it or the gardens and she adored the little girls, who were filling out, rosy-cheeked and boisterous, the only people unaware of the growing tension and the reason for it.

*

DCI Craigh and his men had read the reports on the robbery in the papers and heard about it from mates connected to the Robbery Squad at Scotland Yard. They had early on given the tip-off regarding the women, especially their interaction with Dolly Rawlins. DI Palmer had actually roared with laughter as Craigh had read out the details of the scam and wondered if Rawlins could possibly have any connection with it.

'Oh, yeah! she's a real *Annie Get Your Gun*, Gov. I mean, can you see that frosty-faced bitch riding a horse? That's how they reckon it was done, you know. Rawlins's got to be over fifty, near sixty.'

Craigh pulled a face but he had sent in a report. He received no feedback so presumed she must have been questioned and dismissed as a suspect. Still, he wondered whether if she had not played a part in it, maybe she knew who had, but this was not his department and he had other, more pressing things to worry about. One in particular. George Fuller, Dolly Rawlins's lawyer, having received no reply to his original letter regarding the damage to Rawlins's property, now sent in a reminder, requesting an update. Craigh was confronted by his irate chief as he, too, had received a memo from his superior. The ten-thousand-pound claim was ludicrous, and Craigh insisted that no way had they created anywhere near that amount of damage. He had hoped it would simply be forgotten, though it obviously hadn't. He was told to discuss it further with Mrs Rawlins, and if necessary get an estimate of their own before any money was paid out. Craigh and Palmer reckoned that if they confronted Rawlins, she would probably back down. They could offer her a deal, perhaps a quarter of the estimated damages.

*

The women were all watching television. It was early evening, and the girls were being bathed and changed ready for bed. They were more tense than usual because the police had returned yet again and the skip covering the lime pit had been removed, leaving only the corrugated iron sheets in place. Gloria had eased a part of the sheet back and prodded inside. She had felt a thick wedge about three feet down but she was satisfied the mail bags had disintegrated. But it still made them all uneasy.

Out riding and not far from the bridge, Julia had seen the frogmen diving and searching the lake. She hoped it was too deep for them to discover the shotguns but, on her return, she asked Gloria if she was sure that if they were found there would be nothing to incriminate anyone, no fingerprints, no serial numbers.

They all were certain they had never handled the guns without gloves and Gloria recalled that she had cleaned them thoroughly before the raid. However, the pressure of the hunt getting so close made the tension, a constant undercurrent, surface again. Dolly continued to calm them, telling them everything going on was only to be expected. But they were all volatile, tempers flared easily, and when, two nights later, the lights of the patrol car flared across the window, they immediately tensed.

Dolly peered through the curtain and drew it back tight. 'It's cops and not local. It's that DCI Craigh and his sidekick.'

'What do they want?' Gloria asked; she sounded scared.

'We'll find out. All of you get in the kitchen and stay there. Let me talk to them. Just stay in the kitchen.'

*

DCI Craigh examined the front door and looked at Palmer. 'How much she claim for this? I reckon this stained glass was already broken.'

Palmer looked at the door and stepped back. 'They done the roof. Place is looking good.'

'Yeah, be looking a lot better if she gets that ten grand.'

Craigh rang the doorbell and the lights flooded on in the hall. He peered through a broken pane. Dolly was coming towards the front door. Just as she opened it, the children came running down the stairs in their slippers and dressing gowns.

'Come in,' Dolly said pleasantly, and opened the door wider for Craigh and Palmer to walk past her. They looked at Angela as she came half-way down the stairs with a bath towel in her hands. 'Go into the drawing room.' Dolly gestured, and the men nodded at Angela before entering.

'I'll just say goodnight then I'll be right with you.' Dolly was kissing Sheena and picking her up in her arms.

'Will you tell us a story?' Sheena piped up and Dolly said she couldn't just at that minute but Angela would. She stood at the bottom of the stairs as they ran along the landing to their bedroom. 'Night, night, Auntie Dolly.'

The kitchen door remained closed and Dolly glanced at herself in the hall mirror.

Craigh looked around the untidy room. A fire was burning low in the grate. 'Great old house this, isn't it?' he remarked.

Palmer looked up at the high honeycombed ceiling. 'Yeah, needs a lot done, though. These old places always cost a bundle.'

'Bloody cold.' Craigh rubbed his hands. He sniffed, taking in the torn velvet curtains and the threadbare carpet.

Obviously there was not a lot of cash floating around. 'Whose kids were they?'

'Dunno,' Palmer said, as he sat down on a lumpy old sofa. He rose to his feet immediately as Dolly walked in and closed the door.

'So, what do you want?'

Craigh looked at Palmer, cleared his throat. 'It's about that claim for the damage we're supposed to have done to your property, Mrs Rawlins.'

Dolly moved further into the room and she couldn't stop the smile. Because it was one of such relief.

Ester drummed her fingers on the kitchen table, her eyes on the closed door. 'What you reckon they want?'

Julia poured herself a big vodka. 'We'll find out soon enough. Any of you want a drink?'

'No, and you're hitting the bottle a bit too hard.' Ester pushed back her chair angrily.

'Where you going?' Gloria asked Ester.

'To the toilet, if that's all right with you.' Ester opened the kitchen door silently and peered into the hall.

'Don't go in there, Ester,' Connie said hesitantly, but she was already out, listening at the drawing-room door.

Craigh was still standing with his back to the fire, and Dolly was sitting in a big, old winged armchair. She gave a soft laugh. 'So what you here for? You want to make a deal, is that it?'

Ester froze. The kitchen door opened wider and Gloria peeped out. Ester hurried across, pushing her inside. 'She's making a fucking deal with them,' she hissed.

'What?' Julia said in disbelief.

'I just heard her. Connie, get out the back and see if they're alone – see if they got any back-up. Go on, do it.'

Connie opened the back door and slipped out. Gloria had dodged behind Ester and gone into the hall to listen for herself. Ester followed and pulled at her arm. 'Go and search her room,' she whispered. Gloria glared but Ester pushed her hard, pressing her ear against the door.

Dolly's voice could be heard clearly. 'No way! You must be joking. I'll do a deal but not for a quarter. Let's say half.'

Craigh looked at Palmer and then back to Dolly. 'You'll get it in cash.'

'Oh, it has to be cash,' Dolly said. She got up from the chair and moved closer to Craigh. 'Fifty per cent.'

'I can't do that,' Craigh said louder.

Ester dived back into the kitchen as Gloria scuttled down the stairs after her.

'Look at this lot! Fucking passports – she's got Kathleen's kids on hers and there's one for Angela.'

Julia could feel her legs turning to jelly. 'Oh, shit.'

Ester pushed at Julia. 'She's doing a deal for fifty per cent of the cash, I just heard her. She's going to shop the lot of us! How much proof do you want?'

Ester shoved the passports under Julia's nose and then looked back at the closed door. 'Right. We got to get that money. You, Julia, get Gloria's car, get over to Norma's, take Gloria with you.'

Connie came back in from the yard shaking. 'There are police in the lane with dogs and some up in the woods but they're not heading towards us, they're just sort of patrolling as usual.'

'Shit.' Ester walked to the deep freeze and opened it. She delved inside, brought out a huge twenty-pound frozen turkey and carried it to the sink, turning on the hot water. Julia was putting on her coat, heading for the back door, as

Ester removed a .45 pistol from the inside of the bird. She dug further inside and brought out the cartridges.

Julia grabbed her wrist. 'Jesus Christ, Ester, what *are* you doing?'

'She's selling us right down the river! What the hell do you think I'm doing? Go and get the money, get as much as you can, and we're getting out of here. I said we couldn't trust her! I *warned* you! Now do it.'

Again Julia hesitated but Gloria gave her a shove. 'I'll come with you, let's go.'

Dolly was chuckling at Craigh as he tried to deal, and then she patted his arm. 'All right, you win, gimme three grand and we'll call it quits. You should have been a market trader, you know. But it's got to be cash.'

On Dolly's last line, just as she placed her hand on Craigh's arm, Ester walked in, the gun held in her right hand, her arm pressed close to her body.

Dolly turned, smiling towards Ester. She was feeling so good and confident because she knew now they had nothing to worry about. Craigh and Palmer weren't there because of the robbery and she couldn't wait to have a laugh about it with them all. Then she saw the gun. It was all over within seconds. Dolly was faster to register Ester's intention than either police officer and, as she lifted the gun to fire at Craigh, Dolly moved forward, protecting him with her body as she screamed one word. '*No!*'

She felt the scorching red-hot explosion as if it came from inside her, and her blood splattered Ester's face, making DCI Craigh take an involuntary step backwards, arms up to brace himself as if he was to be hit next. Palmer side-stepped at the same time and red dots of Dolly's blood speckled his shirt. Ester's body was rigid, her teeth clenched, her arm still outstretched. She pulled the trigger again. The second bullet spun Dolly a half-step backwards and everything began to blur. She could hear a distant, distorted voice and she saw her own face.

'I have never committed a criminal act in my life.' The board of directors looked towards the straight-backed Dorothy Rawlins.

Ester fired the third bullet.

'No, I killed someone who betrayed me, there's a difference, Julia.'

Ester pulled the trigger again.

No pain now, she was urging her horse forward, loving the feel of the cold morning air on her face, enjoying the fact that she had succeeded in learning not only to ride but gallop flat out and jump hedges and ditches – at her age.

Ester fired again, her terror growing with every fragmented second.

Dolly's shirt was seeping blood and she still remained on her feet, but the impact of the fourth shot had, yet again, forced her backwards. The images and echoes of voices were fainter and she could only just make out the figure in an old brown coat standing by a garden gate. 'It's me, Dorothy, it's your auntie. Your mum won't talk about it but that young lad, he's no good. You got a good life ahead of you, grammar-school scholarship.'

At the sixth bullet, her body buckled at the knees, her hands hanging limply at her sides. 'I'll always be here for you, Doll, you know that. I'll always love you, take care of you. Come on, open your arms wide and hold me, hold me, sweetheart, that's my girl. Come on, come to me, it's all over now.'

At last she lay still. In death her face looked older: there was no expression – it was already a mask. Her mouth hung open, and her eyes were wide, staring sightlessly. The shooting had taken only the time it took for Ester to fire six shots at point-blank range, but in those seconds Dolly

Rawlins's life flashed from the present to the past. She had died a violent death like her beloved husband. She had not been expecting it; she had been confident, proud of herself and looking forward to a future, looking to make her dreams of a children's home come true. Maybe that had all been a fantasy, maybe this was how it was meant to end. Fate had drawn these women together, and it was fate that it was Ester who killed her, Ester, who she had never really trusted. She had taken such care of them all, checking her back and sides just like Harry had done. And yet, like him, she had faced death straight on, face forward.

Now her cheek lay on the old, dirty, stained carpet, blood trickling from her mouth and her body lying half curled in the foetal position. Her death had been as ugly as her husband's, the only difference being that she had never betrayed anyone.

The sound of the shots brought the officers in the woods running towards the house, shouting into their radios as the others in the lane turned back towards the manor. A patrol car had already received the call and they in turn radioed for further assistance.

Within minutes, the manor was surrounded. Gloria and Julia were hauled out of the Mini, Connie was arrested halfway up the stairs, and Ester was handcuffed to DCI Craigh. She said not one word but stared vacantly ahead, her face drained of colour.

One by one the women were led to the waiting patrol cars and taken away. They were in a state of shocked confusion. None of them spoke or looked at each other.

Dolly Rawlins lay where she had been shot, a deep, dark pool of blood spreading across the threadbare carpet. She had been covered by a sheet taken from the linen closet. It was covered in bloodstains. Angela sat huddled with the little girls. They had heard the gunfire but did not understand what had taken place. For the time being, Angela was allowed to remain with the children but downstairs the house was full of movement and police, plain-clothed and uniformed, were outside in the grounds, watching the women being led out.

Dolly Rawlins's body was removed, after a doctor had testified she was dead, and taken directly to the mortuary. Angela saw the stretcher from the little girls' bedroom window. They stared down, not understanding, and then Sheena asked Angela if she would read their favourite story, *The Three Little Piggies*.

'The big bad wolf huffed and he puffed but no matter how hard he tried, he could not blow the house down.' The tears trickled down Angela's face as she closed the book. It was the end of the story.

The old coal chute at Norma's Rose Cottage, with its door dated 1842, was never opened by the police. Cemented into the wall and bricked in from the cellar, there seemed little point. It remained a rather kitsch feature of the 'olde worlde' cottage. Therefore no one discovered the sixteen black bin liners, each tied tightly at the neck, each containing millions of pounds in untraceable notes. Sixteen heavy-duty, black bin liners, tied tightly at the neck.